Angel of Liverpool

Elizabeth Morton

Angel of Liverpool

MACMILLAN

First published 2021 by Macmillan
an imprint of Pan Macmillan
The Smithson, 6 Briset Street, London EC1M 5NR
EU representative: Macmillan Publishers Ireland Limited,
Mallard Lodge, Lansdowne Village, Dublin 4
Associated companies throughout the world
www.panmacmillan.com

ISBN 978-1-5290-6023-2

1 3 5 7 9 8 6 4 2

A CIP catalogue record for this book is available from the British Library.

Typeset in Sabon by Palimpsest Book Production, Limited, Falkirk, Stirlingshire

Printed and bound by CPI Group (UK) Ltd, Croydon, CR0 4YY

Visit **www.panmacmillan.com** to read more about all our books
and to buy them. You will also find features, author interviews and
news of any author events, and you can sign up for e-newsletters
so that you're always first to hear about our new releases.

To Peter

One

Liverpool, 1946

'Saints preserve us! Go back and sit at your desks, girls!' exclaimed Sister Boniface, standing at the front of the classroom. She was turning bright pink under her stiff white coif and habit. The row of twitching, excited schoolgirls strained and wriggled in their chairs to get a better look. Evie O'Leary, however, was unusually still, transfixed by the dress on a cream satin-covered hanger that was hooked onto the lip of the hinged blackboard. The creases had been meticulously ironed out only that morning by Sister Mary Clotilda, who was standing beside Sister Boniface, beaming proudly.

Carefully, Sister Boniface peeled off the tissue paper, which floated away like gossamer. There was a gasp from the girls. It was the most beautiful thing Evie had ever seen. A spotless white dress with a ruched bodice, falling away in delicate pleats from the waist that cascaded all the way down to the floor. It had white lace sleeves elasticated at the elbow, and small satin ruffles around the hem.

'Now, class, would one of you like to tell us why I have come here today?'

1

Eager hands shot up into the air. Of course, they all knew. They had been talking about this for weeks.

'Yes, you, Mary,' said the nun, pointing to a girl with blonde hair in a neat ponytail coiled up on the top of her head. 'Come up here and tell us.'

The air thickened with expectancy. The girl came to the front of the class. 'The Crowning of the May,' she replied.

'Perhaps you'd like to tell us about it?'

'Yes, Sister. The holiest girl in our class will be allowed to wear this dress for the Crowning of the May. It's a long dress, no one else will be allowed to wear a long dress, and so that's how everyone in the church will know she's the holiest.'

'Not just holy. Holier than holy.'

There was a hushed silence and another intake of breath. 'This is going to be a tough contest, girls. This dress is unmatched in its sheer beauty, so whoever I choose to wear it will have to show they are the very essence of goodness and purity. Actually, come to think of it, if I decide no one is deserving, it might not get worn at all.'

Sister Mary Clotilda's face fell as she thought of her red raw fingers and tired eyes and the hours she had spent in the diminishing light, stitching, hemming and embroidering the dress with tiny forget-me-nots and crucifixes.

'Rest assured, I will be watching each and every one of you.'

'What if it doesn't fit the holiest girl?' said Eunice, a chubby, wide-hipped thirteen-year-old with sturdy legs.

'Your purpose is not to turn heads, but to turn hearts towards our Heavenly Father,' Sister Boniface replied, sharply.

Eunice slumped in her chair and went back to sucking on the frayed cuff of her jumper.

'But Sister, how will you know?' asked Evie in a small voice.

The nun squinted towards the desk at the back of the room. 'Know what, Evangeline?'

'Whether someone is good *all* the time. What if someone is really holy in school and really bad at home?'

'Jesus is watching you, Evangeline O'Leary. Don't think you can outwit him. And don't think you can outwit me, either. I can safely say that unless there's a dramatic change in your behaviour, you won't get within a sniff of it.'

Evie dropped her head.

'Sister, what kind of things make us the holiest?' asked another girl, earnestly taking a red pencil out of her box of Lakeland colouring pencils.

Evie guessed that Sister Boniface was about to start quoting the little red catechism book, showing off as usual how she knew the flaming thing by rote.

'Well, of course, we can all look to our catechism for clues as to what I'll be judging you on. Let's have a go . . . I'll dive in. What is moral virtue?' asked the nun. 'Moral virtue is honesty, justice, purity and self-control. What is cardinal virtue? Cardinal virtue is prudence, justice, fortitude and temperance . . .'

A few keen girls were murmuring along with the nun.

'Of course, prayerfulness, cleanliness, godliness,

are all important. But it's the girl who can show she's made a real difference in her behaviour that I will be looking out for. Should I go on, Carol?'

The girl finished scribbling down the nun's words in an exercise book and looked up.

Another hand shot up.

'Put your hand down, Marjorie. Might I just say this to you, all the hours you spend mooning over Bing Crosby won't get you anywhere close to the long dress either. It also won't get you into heaven, so maybe now's the time to concentrate on your homework rather than that fella's dopey blue eyes.'

Marjorie blushed crimson.

Sister Boniface paced slowly between the desks, tucking her hands up her sleeves. 'This will be more than just daily Mass and saying your prayers, though you can certainly put that down on your list. I won't say any more because I know you're a girl with good intuition, Carol,' she said, widening her eyes, as if to suggest some hidden secret between herself and Carol Connelly. 'Each day I will choose a different one of you to do certain tasks, the usual: ink monitor, milk monitor, but I will also be asking you to do different things, *unexpected* things,' she said mysteriously. 'And I will be watching you all closely.'

Evie was wondering what exactly *godliness* was. It sounded vague, something more than just going to church; but she was sure she wasn't a girl with good intuition, so she didn't dare ask.

'Now make an orderly line, and you can come up and look at the dress one at a time. But no touching, no grubby fingers.'

Evie took a shy look down at her fingers. There was dirt under her nails, black smudges on the tips of them. She wiped them on her blue tunic. She could never imagine having something as beautiful as this dress. Her life was full of brutish, drab things: shoes with nails hammered into the heels to make them last, her mother's hand-me-downs, coal scuttles, tripe, rag-and-bone men, her youngest sister's croup. She had never even seen a dress like this, let alone touched one or felt such lovely fabric close to her skin. She could never be the one. It would be impossible. And yet . . . and yet . . .

The idea began to take shape in her head. Surely if you were the very worst, you would have more of a hope at standing out if you became the very best? No one else in this class could show a real difference like she would.

'Stop pushing, girls!' cried the nun. 'Really! We don't want to fall at the first fence, do we? A month, you have. A month to prove to me that you are worthy of the dress. Now, after you pack your bags, make your way to the domestic science lab, where I'll be waiting for you. Today I will be teaching you how to lay a breakfast table and how to wash and starch an apron. If you want to marry a good husband and keep him, you'll need to know the essentials. Don't dilly-dally, girls.'

Evie continued to sit staring out of the window.

'Evangeline, get a move on! Are you listening? Are you listening to me, Evangeline O'Leary?'

*   *   *

On the walk home to Coghlan Street, Evie's palms began to prickle with excitement as a wild determination took hold of her. She lived in run-down Sailortown, in the shadow of the docks, with her parents, younger brother and sisters in a small, cramped house midway along a ramshackle terrace. Since the war, these buildings had been regarded as slums designated for demolition by the Corporation.

She poked her hand through the letterbox, groped for the key hanging on the string, and opened the door with it. When she came in, she found her mother sitting at the table. Scattered over the worn oilcloth was a scrappy pile of mismatched white-ish cotton offcuts. The material was no more than a bundle of rags: some pieces frayed, some stained and some with holes in. Evie winced. Her mother raised her head wearily and gave her a brave smile.

'Hello, love,' she said.

'Mammy, put them rags away,' said Evie, hopping from foot to foot.

Her mother stopped pushing the needle through the rags and looked up at her. 'Why? I'm making a start on your Crown of the May dress . . .'

'Good news! Smashing news! Oh Mammy, I'm going to have such a beautiful dress,' said Evie, her green eyes shining.

Her mother looked at her. 'Well, I'm doing my best,' she said. 'Owen Owen's department store had a bin day.'

Evie smiled. 'No, don't worry about that. Sister Boniface showed us the long dress today. Oh Mammy, you should've seen it. I'm going to start praying so

6

hard. I'm going to be so holy. And I'm going to be the one who will be walking up the church aisle wearing that dress.'

Her mother put down the needle. 'Oh God, I thought they'd stopped all that nonsense. That went out with the ark. It's 1946!' A frown played across her face as she rearranged her sewing basket, over-flowing with needles and cotton reels, tangled ribbon and bits of elastic.

'I can do it,' her daughter said. 'I *can* do it, I can be the holiest, I'm sure I can. I just have to become good.'

'Oh, Angel. You *are* good. If those nuns knew how you look after me and your brother and sisters, how difficult it has been for us – what with my bad chest, my blasted nerves, your dad and his gammy leg . . .'

'You have to help me with the catechism,' Evie babbled on. 'It's hard and I've tried before and they always give me the medicine when I don't get it right.'

'The medicine?'

'The bitter pill. The whack across my knuckles with the ruler. I hate that awful Sister Hairy Elephant. She's the one who dishes out the punishment.'

'Angel, you're doing it again. It's Sister *Mary Oliphant*.'

'Everyone calls her Sister Hairy Elephant . . .'

'But not to her face, love . . . You'd think you'd have learned, after the trouble you got into.'

'Oh, but Mam, you should have seen the dress. It's so pretty. It's got flowers, and even a veil with a cross embroidered on it, and a beautiful floaty train. Clotty made it. She's the only kind one in that place.

7

I'll look like Olivia de Havilland,' she said, twirling around the kitchen.

'Olivia who?'

'Olivia de Havilland . . . oh, never mind . . .'

'Sweetheart, how are you going to be the one Sister Boniface chooses over all the others?'

'I'm going to change,' Evie said earnestly. 'They'll notice me more than anyone. They'll be so shocked.'

'Oh, Angel. Sometimes in life it's better not to have such high expectations, and then you won't be disappointed . . .' But Evie shook her head; she didn't want to hear. It felt so narrow, so limiting.

'You're an angel,' her mother continued gently. 'Didn't I name you Evangeline for a reason? Even if everyone else in this house and the whole of Liverpool calls you Evie.'

'The nuns at school call me Evangeline. And they *definitely* don't think I'm an angel,' Evie said, curling her lip and rolling her eyes.

'Well, they would if they could see how you've looked after me. How you've taken care of your dad, and Vic and Sylvie and our Nelly. You deserve that long dress, for sure, but I'm not certain if that's the kind of goodness they're talking about. And can you really change? You've no hope if you're still kicking around with Frankie. None of us have recovered from that stunt with the mouse.'

Evie chewed her lip, thinking back to the mayhem when Frankie had slipped his Popeye sweet cigarette box into Evie's schoolbag. He hadn't told her there was a mouse inside it, and somehow it had escaped and scampered in and out of the desks. Sister Mary

Oliphant had ended up running around the classroom and trying to whack it with a Bible.

Putting a finger under Evie's chin, her mother tilted up her face to meet her eyes. 'You are the holiest, the most beautiful, with the purest heart, poppet. I'm just not altogether sure the sisters will see it that way.'

Two

The next morning as she set off to school, instead of hopscotching in and out of the gutters and kicking up leaves and stamping in puddles as she and Frankie would normally do on such a drizzly morning, Evie tried to focus her mind on the day ahead. Cleanliness, she said to herself, the nuns insisted it was next to godliness. Normally her loose, straggly red hair would be blowing into her face or pasted to her cheeks by the wind, but today she had styled it in one long plait like everyone at school did. She held her hands under the stirrup pump in the road and, with a twig, scraped the dirt out from under her fingernails.

It was the thought of the dress that pushed her on. It was just the wretched catechism that she had always struggled with. Who made us? God made us; who is God? God is the infinitely perfect Supreme Being – she could manage that. But when it got to questions like, what is the superabundant satisfaction of the Blessed Mary Virgin and all the saints? – not a cat in hell's chance. *Impossible.* Whenever she recited the answers they came out in back-to-front sentences and vague approximations, and usually it ended with her flinging the book across the room in frustration. But this morning she was determined to master at least Part One. As she walked along, she took a small red book out of her jibber pocket and leafed through it. So many pages! Ridiculous. But if others were able to do it . . . well, she wasn't stupid. She had passed the eleven plus, and she was in the Remove class – 'removed' from the rest of the year, because they were considered clever enough to read the *Iliad* and recite *The Rime of the Ancient Mariner* – and she had a head for numbers. Sister Mary Clotilda was always telling her so. That's why she was there, and she often came top of the class in arithmetic tests.

When she arrived at school there was a small huddle at the gates. Some were already lining up in the playground, from where they would go separate ways through the doors marked Boys and Girls.

'Frankie,' she said with an earnest expression on her face, 'I'm going to have to stop playing kick the can. And knock down ginger. In fact, pretty much everything.'

'Yer what?' he said, nearly choking on a liquorice shoelace which he had wound round his finger and stuck in his mouth.

'It won't be forever,' she said. 'Just until May.'

'Why, what's happening in May?' he asked.

'Nothing,' she replied. She didn't want to tell him about the dress. She knew he would only laugh. Boys were like that. 'But I need you to stop asking me to do stupid things. Like pestering me to knock on people's doors, and the like.'

'But you're my pal,' he said.

She narrowed her green eyes at him. 'Just until May,' she said.

* * *

The first lesson consisted mostly of singing, Sister Dorothy thumping away at an out-of-tune piano and the class belting out 'O Mary We Crown Thee with Blossoms of May'. Evie enjoyed this lesson because the boys and girls were brought together for an hour and it meant she could be with Frankie. Flipping open her hymn book, she raised her chin and sang gustily. Frankie, sitting at the desk behind her, giggled behind his hand. When he leaned forward and said, 'Why are you singing in that voice like an air-raid siren?' she shrugged and decided she wasn't going to answer. He poked his ruler under his desk so that the sharp edge of it prodded the backs of her legs.

When he still didn't get a response, he took her long plait, which had by now freed itself from the top of her head, and, laughing, went to dip it into his inkwell.

When the hymn came to an end, Evie twisted round in her seat and snatched back her plait with a yelp. 'Give over, Frankie – I told you!'

'What's going on back there?' asked Sister Boniface testily, sweeping into the classroom at just the wrong moment. Evie's cheeks flamed. 'What are you two talking about?' A ripple of excitement went round the room.

'I'm waiting for an answer.'

'Nothing,' said Evie.

The nun narrowed her eyes. 'Frankie O'Hare, wipe that smile off your face. And you, Evangeline O'Leary. Stand up.' Evie pursed her lips and threw a black look at Frankie. She always knew she was in trouble when she was called by her full name. *Evangeline O'Leary.*

'If it's so interesting, so *scintillating* a conversation that you're having, perhaps you would like to share it with the rest of the class. Go on.'

Evie blushed. 'Sister, I was telling him I'm going to be good.'

'Were you now?' said the nun.

Why did Sister Boniface always have to shame her? thought Evie. The other nuns were bearable, some even quite kind – but this one! She felt embarrassment flaming up in her and burning her cheeks. The sister turned to the class. 'So, everyone. Do we think Evangeline can change her ways?'

She felt her hands sweating.

'Please, Sister, I—'

'Be quiet. Come up here. Tell me, what have you been doing to make me change my mind about you, Evangeline?'

Evie faltered. She made the long, slow walk to the front of the class from the back row.

'Pull up your socks,' said the nun, wrinkling her nose in disgust.

As Evie bent to tug the drooping socks, she thought that if only she could tell her about putting her mother to bed every night, bringing her meals every day, trying to tame her brother, giving up food so her little sisters wouldn't go hungry. But she couldn't. Not in front of the class. She stood up, pulled back her shoulders. 'Sister, I've been learning the catechism,' she said.

The nun raised an eyebrow. 'Let's hear it, then.'

Evie felt herself sweating. Why did she have to bring up the flipping red book again? The trickle of moisture pooling in the nape of her neck began to dribble down her back. And she couldn't even think what the first prayer was. She tried to visualize the words on the page, screwed up her eyes and pressed her fingers to her temples as she made an attempt to remember what they looked like, but it was as if they were swimming in front of her.

'Go on,' said the sister. 'I'll give you an easy one to start off with. What must we do to gain the happiness of heaven? We're waiting.' She was making an elaborate show of rearranging the crucifix around her neck in the valley between the two mounds that were her huge bosoms.

'To gain the happiness of heaven . . .' she mumbled.

'Go on. We haven't got all day.'

'To gain the happiness of heaven . . . we should . . .'

'Not let Frankie O'Hare put his filthy hands up your jumper . . .' Mary whispered to Carol Connelly, and giggled.

The sister sighed and took out a Parker fountain pen, unscrewed it, and idly squeezed ink from it onto a piece of blotting paper.

'Sister, I can't remember,' stuttered Evie.

'Any of you?' Sister Boniface asked, interrupting her task with the pen. The girl at the front desk, the one who was crazy about Bing Crosby, shot her hand up in the air.

Evie's eyes were swollen with tears now. She felt her lip trembling. She had barely even begun and she had proved herself to be a useless failure.

She turned to the nun. 'Sister, can I please try again?'

'No, you can't try again. Go back to your seat,'

14

snapped the sister. 'Now, whose turn is it to be milk monitor this week?'

'Milk monitor, I'll do it!' Evie said desperately. 'And ink monitor! Book monitor, I can do that as well! And the registers!'

'My, we are keen, *Evangeline*. Very well. I'll give you one more chance. Let's see if we do any better. You can start with the milk,' Sister Boniface barked.

Evie found Sister Boniface in the courtyard waiting with the milk crates, the bottles already at risk of turning sour in the morning sunshine. She lugged one into the classroom and handed the third-of-a-pint bottles round the class. How could so many greedily slug down the whole lot through straws in one go, when she found it so disgusting? The smell of milk on the turn filled the room as everyone drank it, the sound of slurping and satisfied burping making Evie's stomach churn. Sticking her straw into the silver foil top, wrinkling her nose, she saw the sister scrutinizing her from the corner of her eye. Today she would have to drink it. She went back to her desk and raised the bottle to her lips, sucked the straw, and straight away, she felt it repeat on her as she tried to swallow it down. She screwed up her eyes – it was sickly and revolting and she felt herself retch with each mouthful, but she was being watched and she was determined to do it.

'Drink it, Evangeline,' said the nun. 'Our government fought bitterly for every impoverished child like you to have the gift of this milk and you're turning your nose up at it? How ungrateful. I hope we're not going to be pouring it down the sink like I caught you doing last time?'

Evie shook her head.

After draining the bottle, she went round the class collecting the empties, put them back in the crate, and took it outside. Sister Boniface followed her into the corridor. 'Sister,' she said quietly in a low voice, bobbing in a curtsey. 'My mother is very sick. The doctor says she has emphysema. On top of her nerves. I was hoping, well . . . it would make her so proud if I . . . if, if . . .'

'The dress is an honour you have to earn. There's no place for sentiment.' The nun turned her back and began rearranging the plastic daffodils that stood in a vase on a bookshelf. It was a dismissive gesture, cold and unfeeling. 'Evangeline O'Leary, I know all about you and I know all about your family. And believe me, I'm very sorry, but we really don't want to hear the sob story. Offer it up to God, why don't you? As penance for all the headaches you give us teachers. There's plenty others who are in the same boat. Theresa O'Dowd lost her parents and her two sisters in the Durning bomb; Kathleen Walshe's brother came back from the war with half his face off. But you lot? The O'Learys? You're all still alive and breathing, aren't you?'

Rage coursed through Evie's veins. Barely, she wanted to yell. My brother and sisters are starving and stick-thin as beetles, my hapless da can't seem to hold down any kind of job, my mother isn't right in the head. And God knows when the gossip is going to stop about what she got up to with Luigi

Galinari whilst me da was away fighting in Africa. 'At it like knives' were the horrible words Evie had heard whispered behind doors, and it still hurt to think of it. Instead she blurted out, 'But that's not fair!'

'Life isn't fair, Evangeline O'Leary,' the nun replied. 'You're nothing more than a carroty nuisance. You've your head in the clouds, all right, if you think you will be the one wearing the long dress,' she added pityingly. 'Now go and tidy up the books and do the ink.'

Tears stabbed Evie's eyes. *A carroty nuisance?* What a horrible thing to call her. Her mother said her red hair made her rare and radiant, but maybe Sister Boniface was right. Treading carefully across the zig-zagging blocks of the polished oak parquet floor, she went back into the classroom. Her next task was to pick up the books on the desks and put them in alphabetical order on the shelves. As she did it, she felt the familiar surge of frustration and sadness – which grew even stronger when she glanced at the dress, still hanging on the blackboard.

She rearranged the wooden-handled dipping pens into the jars. Then she tipped the ink powder into the jug with a long metal spout, filled it with water from the sink in the corner of the room, and stirred it with a spoon. Pouring the blue-black ink into the white porcelain inkwells, which were sitting on a tray, she then took the inkwells and put one into the ink hole of each desk. Those lucky ones who had their own bottle of Quink, she didn't have to do.

There was one desk with a blue fountain pen lying in the groove across the top.

Afterwards, Evie wasn't quite sure how it happened; maybe it was the bell that surprised her. But as she turned back from placing ink into the first row of desks, the entire tray of inkwells and the jug of ink somehow tumbled off the desk where she had placed them and clattered to the floor.

She gasped. At first she could only watch as the pool of blue ink spread across the floor and started dribbling between the floorboards. As if that wasn't bad enough, when she ran and snatched paper towels from the sink, she saw to her horror that a few tiny spots of blue ink had splattered onto the pristine white gauze of the dress that hung on the blackboard. How? It was feet away!

Evie felt a deathly shiver go up her spine. Panic took over her body: her breath quickened, her heart raced. She could feel her legs shaking and wobbling underneath her, and a sickness rose to her throat; she thought, *what have I done?* In a blind frenzy, she took the dress off the hanger and rushed back over to the sink in the corner of the room, which was surrounded by pots of congealing paint in plastic cups with lids on, brushes stuck in a hole in the top. She began to run a tap, shoved the dress under it. But when the water touched them, the tiny blue ink spots transformed into a hideous, cauliflower-sized blue stain. It looked like a map of Africa.

Evie screwed up the dress, bundled it under her jumper, and hurtled out of the room and down the corridor. Where she was going, what she was going to do next, she had no idea, and there was still blue ink all over the floor. She had left the scene of the crime, but the evidence rendered the whole running away exercise entirely pointless. Guilty, said the blue footprints – guilty, said her blue fingertips – guilty, said the blue smudge across her cheek. Panting, she glanced back over her shoulder when she reached the end of the nuns' corridor that led to the chapel. Praying that no one had seen her, she pressed herself back into the alcove. But all hope died as she heard the sound of soft, rhythmic footsteps, those rubber soles squeaking across the wooden floor. Often the sisters seemed to walk in pairs, heavy feet moving together, their habits swishing, wooden crucifixes and keys hanging from their belts and bumping against their thighs beneath starched underskirts.

'Evangeline O'Leary, come out from there,' said Sister Boniface. 'I would recognize that head of hair anywhere.'

But when she stepped out from the deep alcove and they came face to face, she was surprised to see that Sister Boniface was grinning. 'God alive, you've a blue nose!' she cried. 'Why do you have a blue nose? *Bright blue*, it is! Will you look at her blue nose, Sister Mary Clotilda! That's hilarious . . . Wait 'til I tell the other sisters!'

Tears welled in Evie's eyes. Sister Boniface was still laughing, her face crinkling and creasing, but then suddenly the nun wore a very different expression. 'Wait!' she cried. Evie froze. 'What in the name of

Our Lord Jesus are you hiding under your jumper? Show me!'

How quickly could a person's expression turn from laughter to fury? As Evie unfurled the bundle of lace, gauze and chiffon with the monstrous stain on it, she thought: that's it, no long dress now. Her mother would just have to go back to sewing the shabby offcuts with her gaping stitches. Evie would have to line up with all the others at the Crowning of the May ceremony looking like she was an orphan, and shrug it off as if it didn't matter to her.

She only wondered why it took so long to feel the short, sharp crack across the top of her head and the hand gripping her under the elbow, sharp fingernails sinking into her flesh and twisting. She cried out, clutched her hand to the top of her head. The dress fell to the floor. And there were no words.

'You did that deliberately!' The nun's face was swollen with rage, her eyes bulging out of their sockets.

'No, I didn't! It was an accident . . .'

'You did that deliberately because you're a bitter, jealous, spiteful girl! You've got a devilish streak in you, all right. More fool me for trusting you!'

'Cross my heart and hope to die, it was an accident. On my mammy's life!' Evie was beseeching, desperate, entreating the nun to believe her.

'God is watching you, Evangeline O'Leary. God sees every little thing you do. And I mean *everything*,' Sister Boniface sneered. 'You've ruined the Crowning of the May for everyone. Now get out of my sight – and don't let me ever see you again.'

She gathered the dress into her arms and swept

off – but Clotty just stood there, tears brimming in her eyes. She seemed as upset as Evie. 'Oh, Evie,' she said. Her hand was trembling as she reached out to touch the young girl's arm. 'Oh, Evie, darling. What on earth have you done?'

Three

When Evie arrived home, her mother knew immediately that she had been crying. 'Oh, love,' she said. 'What's the matter?'

'I hate Sister Boniface,' cried Evie.

'What's happened? What have you done now?' said her mother.

Evie looked away, gazed into the distance, collected her thoughts and willed herself not to cry. She shrugged.

'I'm not sodding going to the Crowning of the May,' she said, turning her face to the wall and kicking at the skirting board.

'Of course you are. There's no need for that kind of language,' said her mother. 'It's a grand day. Everyone goes. You'll love it. And the party afterwards is in the nuns' garden. You wouldn't want to miss that. All the lovely jam sandwiches and cake. Strawberry meringues they had last year. Imagine. Come on. I need to pin this on you.'

Evie's eyes filled with tears as she viewed the dress her mother had attempted to make out of scraps. The stitches gaped; there was a patch over one of the seams. Her mother had tried her best, but it was still awful.

'I don't want to go,' said Evie.

Her mother stood, preparing to tell Evie to stop being so melodramatic, but then suddenly clutched at her side, wincing. Evie reached out to steady her, took her sagging arm and sat her back down in the wooden rocking chair in front of the range, rearranging the crocheted blanket over her knees. 'Should I get you a hot drink, Ma?'

'I need a hot toddy,' she said. 'There's milk in the jug, just a little splash of whiskey. That'll do the job.' Evie hesitated. 'Don't you start,' said her mother.

Evie saw that her mother's hand was shaking. She wished her father would come through the door with Victor, her brother. They had gone down to Paddy's market, where they had a stall selling the bits of coal that Victor would collect after they fell off the delivery carts. Her dad would know what to do. He had only told her the day before that if her mother asked for a drink again, she should refuse and fetch him immediately. But that would only lead to another row, which would lead to another fight, and what was the point of that?

Unscrewing the top of the whiskey bottle, she slopped in the bronze liquid and handed the glass to her mother.

'You're such a good girl, sweetheart,' said her mother, reaching out and placing her palm flat on Evie's cheek. 'I don't deserve you. And you're such a beautiful girl. The boys will go mad for you soon. You don't know it, but you are, my love.'

She raised the glass to her mouth, let out a

satisfied sigh after taking a gulp of the liquid, and waited for the fuzzy veil of drink to make the pain go away. When she finished the drink her head lolled back in the chair, and she closed her hollowed-out eyes. Evie rearranged the cushion and kissed her lightly on the top of her forehead, but just as she was about to leave her, her mother squinted and sat up. 'Angel, your nose is blue. Don't you look funny? Why d'you have a blue nose?' she murmured.

'The Corporation have sent me,' Sister Mary Clotilda said the following week, after Evie had successfully dodged school for several days.

The sister was standing on the front doorstep, talking to Evie's mother; Evie could see her through the parlour window, and she could hear their voices. 'They take a very dim view of children who truant, Mrs O'Leary. Too much school missed in the war. We have new rules now. They're doing great things for families like yours. Malt and cod liver oil. Free school dinners. Milk. Nit nurses. Big changes. All for the good . . .'

'It's food we need in this house. I have to fill my four kids from the ankles up, not just the stomach. Bales of food, we need here, Sister.'

'I'll see what I can do. Can I speak to Evie?'

'She's not here.'

'Oh, but she is, Josephine. I can see her,' said Sister Mary Clotilda.

Evie moved away from the curtain.

Her mother faltered. 'Angel!' she called.

Evie appeared, a little sheepish and embarrassed that her mother had lied to a nun.

'Hello, dear,' said Sister Mary Clotilda. 'We need you to come back to school, Evie. There's a good girl.'

'But the dress,' said Evie, falteringly.

'Tch,' Clotty said. 'It's only a dress. It was just the outer skirt that was ruined. I've sorted it out with a few stitches and a new piece of tulle. It's good as new,' she lied. 'Come on, now. You should be in school.'

It occurred to Evie how young Clotty was – maybe even pretty, under that habit.

'Sister Boniface won't want me to come back . . .'

'Nonsense. She's got other things to worry about. And like I said, Sister has to answer to the government now. She can't sit around all day listening to her Bing Crosby records anymore. *Too-ra-loo-ra-lie*-ing all the hours God sends.' She winked at Evie, whose eyes widened. 'Just between you and me, Evie. Will I tell her you'll be in tomorrow?' she said kindly.

The following day, when she returned to school, she met Frankie in the passage. He was excited to hear the story of the dress and the blue ink direct from his friend.

'Eh, Evie, everyone's jangling about it!' Evie blushed. 'Don't be shy about it. Everyone hates old Bony Face.'

In choir practice, which they were preparing for the May Crowning, Sister Mary Oliphant, who loved pointing her stick as she conducted the class, gestured

25

towards a boy at the front. 'You! Desmond Costello,' she cried. 'Stand up! You're singing out of tune! At the end of this stick is an idiot!'

'Which end?' whispered Evie to Frankie, and they giggled together behind their hands.

'And you two! Wipe those smiles off your face!' the nun snapped. As Evie fought more laughter bubbling up inside her, she realized that she was actually glad to be back.

May was fast approaching, and Evie managed to keep out of the way of Sister Boniface. The day arrived before she knew it. Morning sun burst through the smeared windowpane and into the small room she shared with seven-year-old Victor. He was lying on the bed playing with a wooden train, pushing it up the wall. When Evie opened the window, she could hear the soft and distant bell signalling morning Mass.

She went downstairs, feeling a little sick. The dress her mother had made her was lying on the floor in a crumpled heap. They would be going, ashamed and penniless, and once again her heart sank. Thank God her mother wouldn't be there; she was too ill. At least she wouldn't see the looks Evie would get when everyone saw her in a dress made from old hand-me-downs.

'Sweetheart,' said her mother. 'Close your eyes . . .'

Evie frowned. She shut her eyes tight.

'Now turn round, and open them.'

Evie shuffled round. When she opened her eyes, she gasped.

'Ta-dah!' said her mother, as she produced with a flourish a brand-new white dress, all clean lines. 'Do you like it?' she asked. There was a pair of white satin shoes held between two fingers of her other hand.

'Mammy . . . it is *beautiful*.' But as she looked, a worried frown played across Evie's face. This dress was not made from old offcuts – this dress had been bought from a shop. 'I don't understand, though. Where did you get it? *How* did you get it?' For a second, she faltered.

'Never mind that,' replied her mother. 'Go and put it on and show your father.'

Evie nodded. She went upstairs with the dress, pushed her arms into the sleeves and pulled it over her head.

'Mam?' she said, when she reappeared in the parlour.

'Oh, you look so gorgeous,' gasped her mother. 'I'm so sorry I can't go – I'm sorry I won't be there to see you.' Then she knelt, grasped Evie's wrists and said seriously, 'Always remember that I love you.'

Evie smiled bravely. Part of her was struck by the oddness of the way her mother had spoken, so solemnly and strangely; but part of her was relieved. Though she felt ashamed to admit it to herself, she wouldn't have wanted her mother hobbling in with a stick, everyone staring and feeling sorry for her. 'Da will tell me all about it,' her mother said, returning the smile.

Her father came in with Victor and Evie's little sisters, Nelly, five, and Sylvie, who was six. They hopped around her excitedly. They had on their Sunday best; Victor was even wearing a bow tie his father had lent him. Sylvie was in a simple cream smock dress and Nelly was wearing her best summer white frock, which Evie recognized as once having been her own.

'Look at our socks!' said Sylvie, plonking her foot onto the table to show off the pretty frills their mother had sewn around the tops of them.

'You look like a princess, Evie,' said Nelly.

Evie smiled. But then she saw a look pass between her mother and father.

'Don't,' said her mother. 'Don't, Bill . . .'

And as the girls crowded round Evie and they stepped out in the hallway, she heard her mother say, 'You go ahead. I don't want to them to see me crying. They will only accuse me of being drunk.'

She arrived just in time to meet Frankie on the church steps. Looking around, Evie thought how astonishing all the girls looked: beautiful in their diaphanous veils and white lace gloves, clutching their prayer books. The effect was all the more striking in the summer sunshine, with the white ribbons fluttering in the breeze – it took her breath away. Even she, with her copper hair showing up gold and red in the sun and her white stockings, looked as if she was not a real person, but a shimmering angel.

She linked arms with Frankie, and they were joined by others from St Aloysius School. All the time, Frankie and Evie talked and whispered. 'Have you seen the Queen of the May? It's that sixth-form prefect with the turned-up nose who wears all those bloody badges on her cardi. She's wearing a pointy bra, you can see the shape of it through that dress.' said Frankie. They laughed too, as they made their way into the church, at Eunice, who was wearing a dress that Evie said made her look like a blancmange. Not surprisingly, Carol Connelly had been chosen to wear the long dress and given the much-coveted job of holding the Queen of the May's train.

'What a stitch-up,' said Evie. Carol had on red lipstick and painted nails, and was looking 'right hoity-toity', as Frankie said. All the girls were dressed all in white – white shoes, white ribbons, little white crocheted cardigans, white floating gauze veils. The boys wore suits and smart polished shoes, and red ties. Some wore little waistcoats and jackets, and hair that was usually wild and unkempt had been stuck to their scalps with Brylcreem.

'Look at Des! His ma's made him wear shorts! State of his big hairy knees. And that sailor suit! With a stupid ribbon tied in a bow!'

'Say that to me face!' Des cried, twisting round in the pew.

Evie turned abruptly away, giggling into her white lace gloves.

When the big moment came to crown the statue of Our Lady, the Queen of the May, with Carol Connelly fussing about straightening her long lace train, moved imperiously towards the altar, stood on a high stool and reached up to place the beautiful crown of flowers on the statue's head.

'Crown's wonky,' giggled Frankie, causing Carol Connelly to turn around and look at him sharply, forgetting that she was still holding the train, and that the train was still firmly attached to the Queen of the May's head. There was a gasp as the stool wobbled, teetering somewhere between heaven and hell, before the May Queen lost her balance entirely and shrieked 'Feck me! Carol, you clot!', as she fell backwards, and toppled into an ungainly heap.

Going up to the altar for communion, Evie joined her hands and winked at Frankie. Kneeling at the altar rails, she poked out her pink tongue. The priest's fat fingers came towards her holding the communion host; the wafer stuck to the roof of her mouth. Using her tongue to peel it off, she reflected that it wasn't much like bread at all, despite all those hymns about the Bread of Heaven. It was more like the texture of the flying saucers from the sweetshop that she so loved, but without the sugary taste.

She stood up from the polished brass altar rail, smoothed down her dress and, with her head held high, swished past Sister Boniface.

The Mass had been calm, and most had been well behaved. They had all walked into the church quietly and reverently, in pairs, but as soon as they came out into the sunshine and went through the small gate into the nuns' garden, seeing the trestle tables laid out on the lawn with the holy breakfast of a feast of jam sandwiches, peanut butter sand-wiches, butterfly cakes and jugs of orange squash, the pent-up energy flew off each one of them like sparks of electricity. They watched, fidgeting and slavering, as they were ordered first to stand under the magnolia tree to take a photograph with Father Donnelly, then to join hands as he led them to say grace. They had barely finished the sign of the cross before Evie grabbed a peanut butter sandwich, stuffing it into her mouth. She enjoyed the texture and the crunching sensation between her teeth, savouring the taste. She had heard so much talk of the GIs bringing this stuff over here during the war, but this was the first time she had tried it, and it was strange and delicious.

When every morsel was finished and the mothers had finished pouring out jugs of orange squash, they were allowed to charge around the garden. They played Tick and British Bulldog; Frankie and Evie were chosen to be the bulldogs. As everyone tried to run from the wall at one end of the garden to the row of green beans at the other, with Frankie and Evie grabbing and everyone screeching and yelping, Sister Boniface ran over in a fury. She told them that she was banning it – 'Eejits, you'd think you were babbies, not teenagers! Look at the state of you all, with grass stains all over your white clothes!' – and just then, Evie got kicked and rolled over clutching her shin and screaming. 'Not another injury from this blessed stupid game,' cried the sister. She ordered them to play Grandmother's Footsteps instead, which was boring; the whole point of British Bulldog, as Frankie said to Des, was that you could cop a feel of the girls if you were lucky. Instead, one of the boys found a football in the church shed and smashed it across the wall, and that was the end of that. 'Five Glory Be's, and off you all go!' yelled Sister Boniface.

When Evie arrived home, the house seemed oddly silent. 'Mammy!' she called, running from room to room. 'Look what I've got. Peanut butter sandwiches! Clotty gave me the jar and there's some left! I kept some for you! Mam!' She heard a sound from above, and ran up the stairs two at a time.

But it wasn't her mother. It was Linda from next door, standing on the landing looking pale and wan and clutching a set of rosary beads – the white pearl rosary beads with the silver crucifix that Clotty had left as a present for Evie. Linda wore an expression of such distress and sadness that Evie stopped short, alarmed.

'Is something wrong?' she asked.

Her father just shook his head.

'Oh, Evie . . .'

'Where's Mam?'

'Gone,' he said sadly.

Evie gulped air.

'Will she come back?' she asked plaintively.

'Not this time, love.'

'Wait, I don't understand. Is she dead, or has she just gone off and left us?'

'She's gone to . . . a better place. Took her last breath right there in that rocking chair,' Linda said. There was something about the way she kept looking shiftily at Da that made Evie suspicious; but her father seemed unable to say another word.

Downstairs Clotty, who had just arrived, was standing breathless at the door with her arms full of leftover food. She had seen Vic in the street earlier, angrily kicking a wall, and had known straight away that something must be wrong. Now she stepped in and went up the stairs, kneeling down to take Evie's hand. Holding it tightly, she spoke into the girl's tear-stained face, telling her that she was a child and some things in an adult's world were impossible to understand. Evie fixed her with a hard, dead stare. She knew her mother wasn't dead, and she prayed that Clotty would have the good sense to know that this wasn't the time to talk about Jesus.

When Sylvie started wailing, her father finally lost his temper and grunted that they would all just have to bear it. Sylvie stamped her foot and said that she couldn't, she wouldn't. If her mother was dead, why couldn't she see her? Meanwhile, Nelly stood with a thumb in her mouth, scuffing her white shoes against the wall. She had a pear drop bulging in one cheek and occasionally took it out of her mouth, regarded it gravely, then put it back.

'Is Mammy really dead?' she asked, twisting a ringlet of blonde hair round and round her finger.

'Shut up, Nell. Have another pear drop.'

Someone suddenly remarked that the children were too young for the funeral, so Evie would have to stay and look after them. But the oddness of that being said now, along with the looks that passed between Clotty and her father, only made Evie all the more certain that her mother's 'death' was purely imaginary, a way to hide the inconvenient truth of their abandonment. The lie was already stitching in and out of the family in a hopeless effort to stop it fraying around the edges.

'Take them upstairs to bed,' said Evie's father. So that was what she did. That night, and every night afterwards.

In the days that followed, everyone said how marvellous Evie was at accepting the situation, but she wasn't really accepting it. She was just covering up the gaping wound caused by her mother leaving, and everyone around her lying about it. She folded her sadness away deep inside herself, where it remained an open wound, an injury that the slightest trial or tribulation had her picking at just when it started to heal, until she began to bleed again. *What is moral virtue? Moral virtue is honesty, justice, purity and self-control.* Not when it came to her mother – the words came back to her from nowhere, seared into her brain forever.

Just like the empty wardrobe, with the bare hangers swinging gently when she flung open the door. Or the empty drawers: one by one she had pulled them all out, and each one told the same story. And just like the letter that Clotty pressed into her hand a few weeks later, when she stood waiting for her on the school steps at the end of the day.

'Read it when you get home. It's only right you should know. Your father gave it to me to destroy and I swore on Jesus' name I would, but on this occasion God will forgive me. Please don't tell him I have given it to you. Remember, Evie, your mother leaving has everything to do with her and nothing to do with you. Oh – and best not to say anything to your sisters and brother just yet. The time will come soon enough.'

Sitting on a low wall around the corner from the school, with her slender hands trembling like feathers, Evie pieced together on her lap the sheet of paper that had been torn into halves and quarters.

> *Dear Angel,*
> *This letter is very hard for me to write because I keep crying, knowing I can't be there to comfort you when you read it. But I need you to be strong and sturdy as an oak for your brother and sisters. The reason I have gone is not because I don't love you, it's that I can't think what else I can do. I can't stay at Coghlan Street, and I can't stay anywhere else in Liverpool either as I have your father's pride to think of. The gossips in this town would kill us all. I am so tired. Life is so hard and every time it has hit me and I have struggled to my feet, it has hit me back twenty times harder. But just because I can't fight anymore, doesn't mean it should defeat you. Decide to fight back. And never forget I love you and Vic and Sylv and Nell with every single tear I weep and every tiny piece of my broken heart,*
> *Your Ma*

Evie raised her head to the watery sky and blinked away the hurt. She had known from the very first moment that her mother wasn't dead, even if she knew better than to challenge the lies the grown-ups were telling. There was a story that had been spoken of before, in low, indistinct voices: of a distant cousin in Ireland, of her mam's nerves, of the drink, of a fella who thought he was the bee's knees. And how, if it wasn't for the kiddies, oh, if it wasn't for the kiddies . . . But even that hadn't been able to keep her this time.

Four

Spring, 1949

Evie sat in front of the range and allowed the heat to warm her face. She removed a brick from beside the coal scuttle, threw it into the fire and waited until it became hot. Then, after a few minutes, using the blackened tongs, she took the brick out and let it sit cooling on a piece of brown paper she had placed on the stone hearth. When it was cool enough to touch, she wrapped the brown paper round it, tied it with a piece of string and went upstairs to give it to her father. It was sooty and sharp-edged, but they couldn't afford hot water bottles, no one around here could, and the brick did the job just as well.

'Here you are, Da,' she said.

He took it from her.

'Ta, Evie,' he said, putting it under the bedclothes to warm his feet on it.

'It won't be long before the kiddies are up,' she said. 'But that'll keep you warm for a little while . . . I've made you tea.'

'Hope you didn't drown the pot.'

The ice on the inside of the windows looked

beautiful, making spectacular and intricate patterns across the cracked pane of glass.

'Stop daydreaming, love,' said her father. 'You'll be late . . . Now get off. Be a good girl . . .' She was the only one in the house working at Tate & Lyle now, since her dad had been sacked.

Outside, the pavements and the cobbled streets that took her down to the Dock Road had completely frozen. She had to step carefully to avoid slipping. Steam rose from the river Mersey as Liverpool waited for a watery sun to rise this cold March morning. Around the factory, it felt quieter than usual. Stanley let her in, keys jangling from his belt, along with the other five or six young women whom she met on the way: Mavis, Edna, Celia, Krysia, all of them just like she was, wearing colourful checked shirts and matching turbans, and the regulation rough and scratchy, ugly navy-blue overalls. Mavis was yawning. Edna was puffing on a cigarette.

'Cold this morning,' said Celia. 'Supposed to be spring.'

'Aye. Cold as a witch's tit,' said Stanley. His breath hung on the freezing air.

'No need for that,' said Edna. 'Evie's only a lass.' Edna was a few years older than the others, who were in their early twenties, much older than Evie. She had a protective streak in her. 'If I was your ma, Stan, I'd tell you to wash your mouth out with soap.'

'Well you're not, thank God,' replied Stan.

They were each handed a brush as they entered.

'Start sweeping the far end,' said Stan. It was still dark, but with a finger of light sloping in from the skylight above. The floor of the factory glistened an eerie white, like the frost on the window at home. The foreman snapped on the banks of factory lights: one, two, three. Evie blinked away the icy glare to readjust to the hard brightness. She could feel particles of sugar crunching under her feet as she walked across the floor.

'I'll do this row, you do the next,' said Mavis.

Evie began sweeping. She knew she had to do it well and cut no corners. Stanley Mulhearn had let her have this job because he'd felt sorry for her. Such a bright girl, he had said, shame, having to leave school to earn money for the family; and as if that wasn't bad enough, now her stupid father had been sacked for stealing a few wraps of sugar. The swish of the brush moving rhythmically across the floor was hypnotic. The electric lights fizzed and buzzed. You could taste the sugar in the air, taste the sweetness on your lips. When you licked your fingers, they tasted sweet as well. Evie knew that when she went home, it would have got into her pores and the cracks and dimples of her skin. She would sweat sugar, and it would sit on her eyelashes like snow.

The dustpan on a long handle collected the granules, which then had to be tipped into a large keg. It was only a fine dusting, but when you swept it up, piles of it heaped up in the corners and against the skirting boards – small mounds of white. Every last bit of the sugar would be collected and crushed to form sticky molasses. Nothing was wasted here. The foreman would see about that. Nothing was wasted and nothing was nicked, not even a single granule. He was ruthless. Smuggling anything out of this place was virtually impossible. All bags were rigorously checked at the end of each day for contraband – which was how her father had been caught.

Evie could see the throng of people through the glass in the door waiting to come through. A few had already made their way inside and started working at their stations.

Evie smiled and watched as a tanker rumbled through the gates and two young boys chased after it. She knew what they were up to. As it slowed to halt and its engine idled, they were hoping everyone would be too busy getting inside and starting the machines to notice when one of them ran forward and opened the tap at the back. Molasses spilled out. The boys yelped with excitement as they stuck their hands under the flow, licked their fingers and then ran off, leaving the tanker trailing a trickle of the sticky brown substance. A pack of dogs appeared from nowhere, sniffing and licking up the sweet liquid from the cobbles.

'Oi! Oi! *Git!*' cried Stanley, racing out into the yard and running after the boys. 'Bloody crown yer thieving tykes!' he said, collaring one of them.

Evie leaned on her broom and smiled as she watched everyone laughing and jeering. Fisticuffs were breaking out between Stanley and the skinny boy, whom he had caught by hooking a finger under his pullover and was now triumphantly holding off the ground by the scruff of his neck. The boy was kicking and screaming.

'Now scarper, and don't let me see your snotty face again, lad.' He threw the boy down onto the cobbles, watching as he dusted himself off and ran away licking his fingers.

'Eh, Evie, guess who've we got starting here next week? Frankie O'Hare,' said Edna as she swept by. Her wooden broom lifted a cloud of dirt. 'Hey, Ivy, can you spray the floor! This is getting to my chest,' she cried. Ivy came over with a bottle and pumped water onto the floor so that the moisture would prevent the particles of dusty sugar rising into the air.

'Frankie?' said Evie, stopping in her tracks.

'They might put him on the cradle.'

'That's dangerous work, that is,' said Ivy.

'Yeah, but well paid. And they're good on safety checks here,' said Edna.

'You'd still have to be a fool to want to do it.'

That's about right, thought Evie.

She spent the rest of the morning on the sewing machines, stitching the large hessian bags. Later, during their first break, she and Edna sat at a long trestle table, drinking steaming cups of tea. The mugs they nursed against their cheeks were fashioned out of Golden Syrup tins. Evie felt Edna slide along the bench to move closer to her.

'What's the matter, Evie? You seem gloomy,' she said.

'I'm all right,' she said, pushing away the tea, turning down the offer of the heel of loaf smeared with treacle that Edna had stuck in front of her.

41

Getting their hands on treacle during rationing had been one of the perks of working at Tate's during the war, and this was still a treat four years on, not available to most.

'No you're not,' said Edna, hands cupped round her tin mug for comfort, feeling it warm against her palms. She squinted at Evie. 'When I mentioned Frankie's name, you blushed. And I saw you with him the other day, coming out of the Luxe picture house. He take you to see the new flick? *Youth Runs Wild*? He find you a couple of seats on the back row? Hope you stood up for the National Anthem, or were you too busy kissing?'

Evie flinched. 'No. Not me . . .'

'Don't worry, I won't tell your da,' Edna winked, and grinned. 'But don't do anything stupid with him, Evie. I mean, in the bedroom department.' She paused. 'Oh, please tell me you haven't already . . .'

Evie blushed.

'You're seeing him. I know you are . . . He's a right Jack-the-lad. And pretty handsy, I'd say. Take my advice, love. Treat 'em mean, keep 'em keen, Evie. Don't give him a full English fry-up when he'd be grateful for a soft-boiled egg and soldiers. Evie . . . Evie? What? Are you all right? Say something . . .'

'I'm not seeing him. You must have mistaken me for someone else. I'm not stupid, Edna. We used to run around together when we were kids, but not now.'

Stanley appeared and sat on the table behind them with a plate of tripe, demanding to know what Evie and Edna were still doing there sipping tea instead of working at their stations on the factory floor.

'Chin up,' said Edna, instinctively grasping her hand and squeezing gently. 'Someone has to say it. I feel like your ma would want me to warn you about Frankie. You're so young, love.'

Evie looked at Edna with large, doleful green eyes, gave a half-smile. She was still grateful for the chance to hear the words 'your ma' said out loud, whatever the circumstances. 'Is everything all right at home?' asked Edna.

'I suppose,' she replied. 'I'm the ma in our house now. And I'm like me da's wife sometimes, the chores I do for him, the way he speaks to me . . .'

Soon after her mother left had come another subtle difference in their relationship that she had dumbly accepted – being responsible for her siblings' happiness. Only that morning, Victor had wandered in and asked her whether it was true that their mother had gone off with one of them three fellas.

'*Three* fellas?' Evie had asked.

'Luigi, Gal and Harry,' he had said.

'Oh, Vic,' she'd replied. 'Who told you that?'

'No one. I heard Da talking about it. I knew Ma dying was a lie, anyway. I remember those arguments they had when Da came back from war, and that time he threw a shoe at her and asked her how long she had been carrying on behind his back. I know she left us to be with one of those three fellas.'

'You shouldn't listen behind doors. Anyway, it's not Luigi, Gal and Harry, it's just Luigi. Mam's fellow was Italian. Do your sisters know Ma is alive?'

'No.'

'Well, let's keep it that way. I'll tell them in time.' She had put her arm round him and explained, in tearful, back-to-front sentences, that the grown-ups had obviously only been trying to protect them; even Ma had done what she thought was best. She had offered to show him the scraps of the letter that she'd kept pressed in between the pages of her old catechism book, but Victor had retorted spikily 'No ta.' He claimed he really didn't care – Ma wasn't coming back, so she might as well be dead, and a stingy old letter wouldn't make any difference to the situation.

'Look,' said Edna, dragging Evie back to the present. 'It's four years now since the war ended. This is a time for looking forward, not back. We're all getting back on our feet, and it's hard to believe how much this city is finally changing for the better. We're all moving on.'

'I don't want to move on. I'm actually scared I might forget me Ma. And you're the only one that I've told she's still alive, apart from our Vic. I can talk to you about her, thank God.'

'Oh, Evie.'

'Despite what she's done, I still hope she'll come back. What if she walks back in, and I don't recognize her?'

She hesitated, dropped her head and fiddled with the button on her dungarees. Every day she tried to remember her mother's face, wished she at least had a photograph of her; but her father had burnt them one desperate evening in a rage. How could I ever forget those eyes? she thought. But then her mind began to play tricks on her. How soon would it be someone else's eyes she was thinking of? How soon would her once familiar features become interchangeable with someone like flame-haired Greer Garson, who she had seen the other day on a movie poster outside the Luxe? It was all becoming so difficult. Terrified, she blinked away the awful thought.

'I don't know, love. In the meantime, try to make the best of things. I do know that's what she'd want you to do.'

'It's so hard though. Such a struggle. Like the other day, our Nelly refused to go to school because they were making fun of her hand-me-downs. And Vic was shouting the place down because he has holes in his shoes and the cardboard I'd put inside them just went all soggy because it was raining; and Sylvie just complains about being hungry all the time. Says she has butterflies in her belly.'

'Don't be afraid to ask to get that National Assistance. It's not like before the war, when we had to stick our hands out to any old passer-by. Charity is a cold, grey, loveless thing. That's what Clement Attlee said. Take him at his word. The Corpy will help you if you need it.'

'Sister Mary Clotilda sometimes comes to the house. Brings food parcels. Checks up on the kids. Makes sure they go to school. She even gives us clothes sometimes.'

'That's nice. Suppose she doesn't have to do things like that.'

'She's kind. I like her,' Evie said. 'She bought me

a dress once. For the Crowning of the May. Because my mam wasn't up to organizing it with her nerves, and we were broke as usual.'

'We're all broke, love.'

'Worse now that me fool of a da has lost his job. I've asked Stanley if he can get me any extra hours.'

Stanley approached their table. 'Evie, love. Can I have a word?' Evie stood. He was smiling. 'Now, pet, I couldn't help overhearing. I can't be seen to be giving you extra time here just because your pilfering da has lost his job.' Her face fell, but Stanley continued: 'But here's the thing. I do have a job for you. I want you to collect the cheques for some of our orders in town. Small businesses. Nothing flashy. But Mr Tate says it's important for us to be reaching out to our customers and supporting the community. Put a face to the factory. And what better face than yours?'

'Really? Me?' she said.

'You,' he answered. 'A shilling extra a week. Little birdie also told me you're good with figures, so that would be a boon.'

'Yes, Mr Mulhearn. I'll do it,' she said eagerly, excited at the thought of a change from the clatter of the factory for a few hours each week. How thrilling, how different from sweeping up sugar in the dead hours of the morning or on the machines, with the dreadful noise of clanking and rattling vibrating in your head. And it was hard to argue with numbers. They couldn't take a view. They were just as they were. There on the page. Intractable, immovable. They judged no one.

Edna nudged her. 'There you are. Told you things would begin to look up for you! Fresh start, love. Just remember what I said about Frankie – put him out with the bins. Time to think about tomorrow now.'

Five

Evie pulled her flimsy coat round her as she made her way across Williamson Square. It was a breezy spring morning, and she was glad to have ticked off the last few shops and restaurants on Stanley's list – the Kardomah, George Henry Lee's, Bunney's and Cooper's in Bold Street. Everyone had been friendly and delighted to see her as she doled out reminders and took cheques that were owing. But today she had a new name on her list: the Playhouse Theatre Cafe. The façade with its Grecian ladies, togas draped over their half-naked bodies; the posters celebrating the production of a Noël Coward play; the lanterns above the front door – it was all a world so far away from the greyness of Coghlan Street, the factory and the tatter's yard. It made her heart beat faster just to enter the building.

The foyer hadn't yet opened, so she went round the side of the building and in through the stage door, just as she had been told to do. It was the smell of greasepaint and chalk and cheap, sweet pomade that hit her first. Not like the smell when you passed the perfume counter at Blackler's, or the scent of Elnett hairspray and perm lotion at the hairdresser's. It was different. You could become drunk on it, she thought.

A mixture of Pan-Stik and powder, fresh, clean sweat, and musky bodies that hit the back of her throat.

'I'm here for Biddy Lloyd,' she said to the man sitting on a high stool. 'I'm from Tate's. She's expecting me.' He raised his eyes tiredly from his copy of *Picture Post* magazine. 'Go through the door that says 'STAGE' at the end of the corridor. Walk through the wings and down the steps at the side of the stage, and Biddy's office is at the back of the stalls. It's got her name on it.'

Evie nodded, and headed off down the corridor. Everything about this place was different. Even the paint on the sweating walls was a contrast to the dull, cream gloss they used on walls at school, the hospital and the factory. The rich, sumptuous yet faded colours here hinted at decadence. Bold yellows and reds were flaking and peeling off the walls; probably just practical, didn't show up the dirt, Evie thought, but nevertheless it made a strong impression on her.

A lanky, bookish-looking fellow wearing round horn-rimmed spectacles was lounging with his back to the wall, smoking a Woodbine. He nodded a hello and moved out of Evie's way to allow her to go down the corridor, where the plaster had chipped off in sections and she could see the exposed bare brick. When she went through the door, which she struggled to open and which then took her through the wings, she blinked against the dazzle of spotlights that flooded light onto the stage. A sturdy, manly-looking girl was dragging a basket full of props behind one of the flats; spilling out of the top were a papier-mâché elephant's head, a trumpet, and a single embroidered

49

shoe. Raising her head and looking up into the gallery, Evie saw that someone up there was doing something with a light. She took note of the dizzying array of ropes and pulleys. A boy, balancing precariously on top of a very high ladder, poked at an overhanging spotlight with a metal rod, and looked as if he was in danger of imminent death. He leaned over, cupping his hand round his mouth, and cried: 'Oi! Lawrence! You down there? Come and tell me if this pink gel will do the job.'

A tall, long-limbed young man walked onto the stage, squinted into the spotlight and shielded his eyes with his hands. He then stopped, shoving his hands deep into his pockets. He had wide-set eyes, decisively sharp, high cheekbones that could have cut ice, and fairish, silky-smooth hair swept off his face. He was like a man Evie might have seen at the movies, but never in real life; certainly never at the factory. He reminded her of some kind of beautiful rare bird. Lawrence raked his fingers through his hair.

'Too far down stage. And how about we try the old amber gel instead of the pink? Make me look more like Leslie Howard?' said the young man, with a raffish smile.

Of course, Evie shouldn't even have been looking at him. But she couldn't help it. She watched him pace across the stage, holding a script he had just pulled from his waistband. He was reading from it, and looked like he was murmuring lines. Suddenly he glanced up, walked further into the centre of the stage and said to the boy coming down the ladder,

'While you're getting that gel, can you see if my other script is in the green room?'

Amber gel. Down stage. Green room. The words just fell out of his mouth so naturally, so casually. She thought of the words that came out of her mouth. *Scouse. Totters men. Put wood in door. Scrub step. In the flaming club.* Blunt and brutish.

''Scuse me, lovey . . .' said a voice behind her. It was the boyish-looking girl who had been grappling with the elephant head. She was holding a lamp and a plastic bunch of roses.

Evie started, turned to go. But then the beautiful young man, shouted from the stage, called out to her. 'Hey, dearie . . . Yes, you, dear. With the red hair. I don't suppose you've got my other script with the notes?'

Stepping out from the wings and shading her eyes, Evie came forward into the light, squinting. 'Me? No . . . I'm sorry . . .'

'Not your fault, dear, if all the world's a bloody stage and all the people are merely players but no one knows where my flaming script is . . .' And then he looked at Evie more keenly. 'Can I borrow you, darling?' he said.

Evie could feel the red heat gushing up her neck and prickling her cheeks; she flicked away a stray curl from her eyes. 'What?' she said.

'Can I borrow you?' he repeated, smiling. 'I won't bite. I'm an actor. We actors are pretty friendly. Rather tame, most of us. Come on. I need you to help me with this scene for a sec. Won't take a moment . . .' And he swept over and led her onto the middle of the stage so that he was standing directly in front of her.

He moved her into the light. She could feel his breath on her face, the smell of cigarettes and the heady scent of his sweet, musky cologne, mingled with the perspiration that had appeared like fresh pearls studding his shining brow.

'Don't be afraid, sweetheart, you'll be marvellous,' he said, pushing her right and left, forwards and backwards. 'That better, Ken?' he said, speaking into the blackness of the auditorium. 'And how 'bout this? Further down stage?' he said, manoeuvring her towards the row of bright footlights cradled in brass shades shaped like flowers. 'If I'm a foot to my right, and Mabel is here . . .' he said, coaxing Evie to his left. 'How's that?'

He wiped his brow with the sleeve of his shirt, twisted her to him, took her in his arms and clasped her round her waist. She felt his body pressing against hers. Her frayed coat, flat hobnailed shoes, her dress made out of coarse brown material from the remnant bin at Lewis's embarrassed her. Then he stopped. Looked at her, smiled.

'Your hair. What's that stuff in your hair? It's kind of . . . like glitter . . . is it glitter? You one of the dancers from the Empire?'

'No, it's . . .'

'What?'

'Sugar,' she stuttered.

'Sugar?' he said with a smile.

'Oh. I work at Tate & Lyle. I'm a sugar girl, that's what they call us . . .' she stuttered.

'You are sweet, that's for sure,' he said with a wink.

Had he really just winked at her? The way he'd said it, so full of energy, of life – Evie gave a tiny, tremulous smile. He took her hand, squeezed it, sending an electric shock shooting through her body. 'Mind if I . . . ?'

She sprang back as if on a coil, withdrew her hand and let it fly up towards the exposed flesh at her neck. He grinned, tipped his head to the side, grabbed her hand again, jerked it back towards him, held it to his lips. And kissed it. Then he licked his lips.

'Oh, you beauty. You taste of sugar. Hey, Ken! We have our own Sugar Plum Fairy.'

She was so shocked, she could barely speak. 'I have to go,' she said. She felt a wave of heat spreading up through her chest and flowering her neck.

And she hurried away in desperate search of Biddy's office, leaving in a flurry of stammering and unnecessary apologies.

Six

'Toys for old rags! Toys for old rags!' a voice shouted from outside in the street. Evie went over and peered out of the bedroom window. Halfway down the road, the tatter's man was pulling his cart. 'Toys for old rags!' he cried, in his deep, gravelly voice, followed by the sound of a rusty bugle, before his phlegmy cough got the better of him.

They had always come down this road on a Wednesday and a Saturday, but since money was still so tight – despite the war being over four years ago now, everyone's purses were still empty, what with the ravages of it – the rag-and-bone cart, which had in the past usually been piled high with old clothes and bits of tat, now appeared with each collection looking more meagre than the last.

Victor came thundering up the stairs and running into the small room, squirrelled his head under the net curtains, pulled the sleeve of his jumper over his fist, and rubbed harder at the windowpane smeared with muck. His warm breath blotted the glass.

'Toys day!' he cried.

Evie knelt and took hold of his arms, speaking into his snub-nosed face as she tousled his mop of tangled hair. Since her mother had gone, she felt as if she had aged twenty years instead of three.

'Toys day!'

'It's ridiculous, Vic. They say new toys but there's no toys now, just bits of rubbish. Spinning tops made out of the bottom of treacle tart tins, whistles made of old twigs. They're desperate . . . Just like the rest of us. Besides, you're eleven now.' She looked outside at the washing strung across from one side of the narrow street to the other, frozen on the line, and sighed. When Vic tugged on her skirt and looked up at her with soulful blue eyes, she relented. 'Go on, then. If you want you can get that bundle of rags at the bottom of the stairs . . . you might get a few pennies for them, and then you could buy a couple of marbles. But let's not just end up with more old tat pretending to be a toy.' They lived up to their names, she thought, the tatter's men.

When Evie went downstairs, she found her father in the kitchen bent over the Belfast sink, coughing as he smoked, his braces looped around his thighs, shirt sleeves rolled up to his elbows revealing his strong forearms. He raked his fingers through his thick black hair.

'What's got into our Victor?'

'Second Saturday of the month. Toys day,' answered Evie.

Vic shot out of the door and was already halfway down the hill, as he followed the cart to Haight's Yard at the bottom of Coghlan Street. He raced the hundred yards down the hill, Evie following with her basket resting on the curve of her hip.

'Wait!' he called after it, waving, dropping a stray sock that had been darned to death and an old ragged nightshirt. 'I've got rags!' The cart slowed as it turned into the yard. The sign, in curving metal letters above the wrought-iron gate, read 'Haight and Sons'.

'Come with me, Evie,' he said, tugging on her skirts.

'I haven't got time, I've the shopping to do . . .'

'Please?'

Evie sighed. 'As long as we're quick. At least then I can make sure you get something for them rags. Might buy us a bag of fades from the greengrocer's.'

'I hate fades. They're mouldy and they stink,' replied Victor, making a face.

How Evie wished she could afford oranges and apples that hadn't gone off, or potatoes that didn't have sprouts growing out of them. 'Nothing wrong with fades. Just fruit and veg on the turn. Won't harm you.'

They made their way through the piles of twisted, rusting iron and old clothes on the forecourt. There were all kinds of paraphernalia: pots and pans of every size, horse brasses, bits and stirrups, old farm and garden tools, animal and bird traps, bullet casings, bits of fuselage, even a wooden leg and a surgical boot.

'Whoa, Dobbin. What you got, lad?' said the man on the cart, tugging at the reins.

The horse, with its oversized fringed hooves, stopped, shook its head, whinnied and snorted. The foreman was expecting Vic to have brought only bits of stuff he had nicked from some of the local houses that had fallen into disrepair, after their owners had moved out to safer parts of the countryside and never come back. There were plenty of derelict properties in the city now, ever since the Corpy had tried to move everyone out. Bill's boy already had that look, he thought: a scavenger. They got them every day – kids with bits of pipes, lead from the roofs. They would take their haul to the scrap or and rag-and-bone yard, where they would be weighed, and they might make a few pennies if they were lucky.

Vic held out the pathetic bundle of rags.

'Oh,' said the tatter's man. 'That it? Take 'em to the Sheriff.' He pointed to where a man sat on an upturned crate, wearing a battered cowboy hat with a silver badge. Vic ran over excitedly.

Evie watched from a distance as they chatted. The Sheriff nodded, smiled, went into his wooden hut and produced a yellow balloon on a stick in exchange for the clothes. Not even a goldfish. That took the biscuit, thought Evie. Thieves and vagabonds, the lot of them.

The Sheriff wandered over with Victor, ruffled his mop of tangled brown hair, then stopped and pointed at a rusting iron contraption.

'See that?' he hissed, tipping the brim of his cowboy hat so that it sloped back off his head. 'That ain't for fox or badger. A German was caught in that.'

'They've gorra man trap!' cried an enthralled Victor to Evie.

Heaven knows where that came from, thought Evie. Terrifying the kids like that. Shouldn't be allowed.

'Did he die?' asked Victor.

'Aye. Dead as a doornail, he is. Cut right in half.

Top half screaming in the trap, bottom half, just a pair of legs, thundering around in a frenzy . . .'

Vic's eyes opened wide.

'He's kidding, pet,' said Evie.

Vic beamed. 'Ah, eh, look,' he giggled, pointing at the sign above the lavvie door. 'No Ball Games Allowed . . . Get it? No ball games allowed,' he repeated, grinning. Evie raised her eyes, tutted, and shook her head. 'No fiddling with your knackers. And wait until I tell Da about the trap – and rifles, did you see them rifles?' he added excitedly. 'That's a Nazi rifle . . .'

'Come on. You get off home, Victor. You've been had, love. Flamin' balloon on a bit of twig . . .' Evie bent down, buttoned up the last button on his gaping shirt. Vic clutched the balloon to his chest – he wasn't going to let go of his precious new toy. But then, just as they were about to leave, a voice stopped Evie in her tracks.

''Ow do?' said Neville, coming out from the office into the yard, blinking into the sunlight with his uneven smile.

Evie shuddered. What was he doing here? He should have been in the yard, surely. Neville, whom she'd been at school with, with his flapping shoes poking out from under frayed trouser bottoms. She even noticed that he had used a bit of string for his belt. His sleeveless jumper, knitted and darned to within an inch of its life, was pulled low to conceal the makeshift belt, but she could see it poking out nevertheless.

'I'm not too bad, Nev,' she said, supremely indifferent to his obvious delight at finding her here.

He rocked back on his heels, hands thrust into his pockets. 'Grand. You look grand,' he said, winking at her and running his pink tongue over his bottom lip. 'You fancy coming out on the cart later?'

'Boy, you know how to show a girl a good time,' she said.

'What's wrong with cart?' he replied.

'Nothing,' she said. 'But no thanks, Nev.' Her cheeks stung. 'Got to get Victor to Boys' Brigade,' she lied, sounding faintly bored.

He nodded. 'Might see you some time.'

Some time never, she thought, her nose wrinkling at the lingering smell he left behind. He was persistent, this one, but Evie was stubborn. Our Evie. She's very bonny, and she's very stubborn, her mother used to say.

She left for the greengrocer's, bought a turnip and three potatoes and then a scrag end from the butcher's. She would make a Scouse stew, which would hopefully last for another three days. Coming back into the house half an hour later, she got the odd impression that something was different: a chair moved to an unusual place, a stool tucked neatly under the table. Her father's mug, which normally sat on the Welsh dresser waiting for her to rinse it out, was already on the draining board.

She took her coat off, hung it over a chair and left the room to head upstairs. But then she stopped. She was sure she heard voices. Her father's and, by the sound of it, a woman's. She pressed herself against the wall. And she was right. Through the crack in the kitchen door, she could see that her father was now sitting at the table, and opposite him, only visible to Evie from behind, was a woman wearing a velvet cloche hat.

'They don't call him the Snitch for nothing, this new manager. He'd tell on his own mother for pinching,' the woman was saying. 'You should have been more careful.'

There was a silence, then Bill shuffling in his chair. 'It was only a few twists of sugar.'

'Yes, but if everyone nicked a few twists of sugar, there'd be no sugar left, and then no factory and no jobs; and then where would we all be?' the woman said.

'Give over. A few twists?'

'I'll try and have another word. See if they'll change their minds. But I can't promise anything. For now, you're still sacked, Stanley said.'

Evie squinted through the crack in the door. She could hear the clink of a teaspoon against a mug, the swirling of the water in the sink, the whistling of the kettle. Then, avoiding treading on the bottom stair (which always gave out a creak like a dying man's last moan), she started to go upstairs. Suddenly the kitchen door was pulled open – it was her father.

'Kettle's boiled,' he said. 'Who's for a cuppa char?'

Sylvie and Nelly appeared on the landing. Evie stopped in her tracks. The woman stepped out into the hall, smiling, drying her hands on a tea towel. She had a serious-looking face, a slash of red lipstick. She'd taken off her hat, but her wiry black hair looked like it didn't belong on her head. She had wide hips and a huge bosom. And then it registered: Joan Hennessy. Holy Joan, everyone called her: the woman from the Legion of Mary, who usually came with scones and had once delivered a Bible. She was a right nosy parker. She looked different without her hat on.

'Oh. Hello, Mrs Hennessy,' said Evie.

'Call me Joan. Anyone fancy a brew?'

Evie looked at her, then back at Sylvie. But it was when Joan Hennessy returned to the kitchen and reached up onto the top shelf of the dresser for the tea caddy that Evie's heart lurched. How did she know where that was kept? Only a person who knew their kitchen inside out would know that. It was hidden out of sight, behind the breadbasket. An ugly tin, her ma had always kept out of the way, so they wouldn't have to look at it.

'Mrs Hennessy is so formal, isn't it, Bill?'

Bill, still in the open kitchen doorway, nodded and smiled. 'It is, Joan love,' he said.

And then Joan Hennessy did something so unexpected that it made the blood drain out of Evie's body. She took out a small linen handkerchief that had been tucked into the bottom of her sleeve, spat on it, and wiped a smudge of black soot from Bill's cheek. The tiniest of gestures, but a gesture that seemed so private and so out of keeping with her usual place in their lives. And it was enough. Enough to send waves of panic through Evie's body.

Evie looked at Joan, then back at her father. She didn't trust this woman. She didn't like the way Joan was rearranging her skirt, or her false smile; but most of all, the way Bill was looking at her with a strange expression of . . . *fondness*. Surely not? This woman, with her Our Lady pin and rosary beads spilling out of her purse, and a silver crucifix around her neck: what was she to him? A hypocrite, that's what she was. Making out she was so holy and saintly, and at the same time fawning over Evie's father. Who was still married, by the way.

'Joan's been telling me about some changes we could make here. What with the war draining us of every bit of our savings, and me losing my job,' Bill said.

'Changes?' Evie moved slowly, reluctantly, into the kitchen with them.

'You heard of a straw box?' Joan said brightly. She was bustling about the room, putting a dish away, rinsing it under the tap. Then she opened the cupboard under the sink, groped around and squinted into it, and took out a dishrag. How on earth did she know that was there? wondered Evie.

'There's no need to go wasting heat,' Joan continued, talking over her shoulder. 'You take the food out and place it in the box. It will cook in its own heat. I've told your father I can buy one at Paddy's market,' said Joan.

Evie looked at her father as if to ask what on earth was going on.

Joan picked up one of the bricks from the coal scuttle. 'And these bricks? What are these for?'

'Da's hot water bottle. He loves it. Makes me do one every morning and night for him. What with the crack in the bedroom window and the wind whistling in. It's the only way you can stay warm in bed, isn't that right, Da?'

'Well, not entirely. I can think of other ways,' he said, his face crinkling up into a smile.

'Bill!' Joan flicked the tea towel playfully at him. Evie felt sick to her stomach. 'All I'm saying, Evie, is it could be put to better use, dear.'

Later, after the woman had left, Evie said to her father: 'Why was Joan making us tea? What was that about?'

'Nothing, love. She's no one. Be a good girl. Just popped by to collect the mission box. Don't worry your head. Works outing tomorrow, isn't it? Go and get an early night.'

Seven

'Stop shoving! Everyone stop flamin' shoving!' cried the foreman.

Evie, waiting in the shade for Edna, squinted against the bright ball of sun that was riding high above the Mersey. She looked across Tate & Lyle's yard and smiled to see all the other sugar girls gathering for the Easter Sunday works outing to the seaside. Instead of their work dungarees, blue checked shirts and turbans, today they were hardly recognizable in best frocks, summer hats and newly peroxided hair. Noisy fellows in suits they hadn't worn for months, with their carry-outs and billycans, jostled and jangled with each other, all of them chattering and laughing excitedly. Evie repositioned her raffia summer hat on her head at a jaunty angle, secured the hatpin and tucked a piece of her red hair behind her ear. With her thumb and forefinger, she made two short, sharp pinches on the fleshy part of each cheek.

'Now line up over there by the gate,' shouted the foreman.

'Hey, Evie,' said Edna, coming up behind her suddenly. Evie twisted round. 'Don't you look gorgeous in that frock? Nice to see you showing a bit of flesh,' Edna laughed. 'You'll be lucky to keep Frankie away from you today. Especially if he starts necking down the beers. He'll be all over you like a bloody rash. He's soft on you, everyone knows.'

Evie felt herself blushing as she tugged up the neckline of the dress. She needn't have bothered with pinching; her cheeks bloomed a bright pink. 'Don't be daft. Frankie can pick and choose, he could have any lass he wants.'

Edna laughed. 'You've no idea, have you, pet?'

'What?'

'You're a looker, Evie, you are. Real peachy. Have you not seen the fellers getting all tongue-tied the minute they start to try and strike up a conversation with you?'

'Not Frankie, though.'

'Frankie as well. He just hides it with all that laughing and larking about, playing the idiot and doing those stupid things. I've told you he's sweet on you. Jesus, you're a green girl,' Edna sighed.

'And I've told you there's nothing between us . . .'

'Look out, here's Stan,' said Edna, gesturing at the manager walking across the yard. He was dressed in his Sunday best, but the trousers and sleeves were too short, leaving his bony white wrists and ankles exposed. 'He looks a right state. Couldn't his ma have stitched him on some cuffs and turn-ups?'

'Turn-ups is no good for here,' Evie pointed out. 'More bother emptying all the sugar out every night. Maybe that's why.'

Edna nodded. 'Let's see if Stan can keep this rowdy lot in order today. That's the trouble with losing all the good fellas to the war. There's a reason the ones that were left in Liverpool are useless. The ones that had anything about them, you didn't see for dust . . . They didn't come back here.'

Evie fiddled with the long plait that grazed her waist.

Edna nudged her, pointed at the gathering crowd. 'Hey, look at Stan trying to act all stern. Telling them to line up or he'll clock every one of them. Like they care what he says! That fella couldn't frighten the skin off a rice pudding.'

Stan turned to the crowd. 'Sarnies on the tables behind the charabancs. One packet each. Any sign of trouble, we'll turn right round and come back again. Sorry, that's the way it is.'

A boy shouted from the back, 'We'll be good as gold, guv'nor!'

Another stood up and saluted. 'Aye, aye, Sarge!'

Edna hollered: 'Any of you who ruins our beano, you'll have me to answer to! Spoil our works day out and Stanley'll dock your wages.'

A cheer went up from the crowd. There were shouts and scuffles, and more writhing and shoving to hear what Stan was saying. He clapped his hands to stay them. 'Get yourself your sarnies. And remember, it doesn't please me to be a killjoy, but you're still representing the good name of Tate & Lyle. You might be in civvies, but everyone knows who we are, that's all.'

Another shout went up and someone threw a hat in the air. 'Stupid silly article,' said Edna.

Evie felt someone come up behind her, warm breath

on her neck. Turning, she started when she saw Frankie chewing a match, hands thrust deep in his pockets jangling coins, standing close and winking at her.

'Leave her alone, Frankie,' said Edna.

Evie smiled and blushed. 'He's all right . . . I can handle meself . . .'

'Now, ladies and gentlemen, make your way onto the charabanc in an orderly fashion. When you get to Southport we'll park up down by the promenade. You're there for four hours. Miss the bus back, and it's your own flamin' look-out. Don't spend all your money on the slot machines and then have nothing left to buy yourself fish and chips and mushy peas. Jimmy Mack's is the best in the North-West. We'll meet at the bandstand for the raffle. You could be the lucky winner of a black pudding and sausage necklace. Mrs Parker here has organized a knobbly knees competition for the fellas, and if any of you ladies want to go into the best ankles competition, head to the bandstand in Floral Hall Gardens and sign up before you go. Father Leddy said he would do us the honour of judging it.'

'Well, there's a surprise. Leery Leddy,' laughed Edna, raising an eyebrow.

Outside the gate, the wooden trestle tables were piled high, groaning with towers of sandwiches wrapped in brown paper, just like the foreman had said they would be. Rationing meant that they were mostly tinned Spam, but there weren't many complaints. Anyway, most of them would be wolfed down on the half-hour journey; it was the fish and chips from the chippy, and cockles and whelks and candy-floss from the fair, that everyone was looking forward to.

'Best behaviour, sugar girls . . .'

Frankie leaned in to Evie, nudged her playfully with his elbow. 'You heard that, Evie? Best behaviour. No leading me astray, Evie O'Leary. Just saying, like. See you when we get there.' He gave her a wink.

'Move it, Evie,' said Edna, shoving her forward. Two men, hauling a crate of beer each, jostled them up the stairs to the top deck. The engine started and everything began to rattle. Someone started to sing, a small woman with a loud warbling voice. *'We are the sugar girls of Love Lane, Give us a kiss blue eyes, I'll always be yours if—'*

'You show us your drawers!' sang a boy who had already loosened his tie and taken off his jacket. Squashed up on the back seat with his friends, they slapped their thighs and rocked back and forward with glee.

'Aye, aye! Less of the potty mouth!'

There was more laughter.

Evie smiled. This was going to be a good day. A day for making memories and trying not to worry about her sisters and brother, or her da and that woman, Holy Joan. But then, looking around, she felt a wave of sadness come over her. There was Celia, who had lost her two brothers and mother in a bomb at the start of the Blitz, all the more tragic as they were both home on leave from the air force at the time; there was Harold, whose father had been killed when an incendiary blew up his face. Mysterious, neat, elusive Krysia had barely spoken a word since she'd arrived at the factory speaking only Polish; it was rumoured her father, mother and brother were all sent off to a camp during the war, where something so unspeakable had happened that she would never talk about it – or anything much else. Edna too had lost her sweetheart in the Normandy landings, and that was another subject that was never spoken about. It was still only four years since the war, but the memories were as painful and fresh in everyone's minds as if it were yesterday.

They arrived in Southport and spilled from the charabanc onto the pavement. It was a boiling hot day, with the sun riding high and only a few puffs of cloud hanging like angels' breath in the sky. The flagstones radiated a dry heat; some of the girls took off their straw hats and fanned themselves, undid their top buttons, blew on the flesh pillowing out from their cleavage to cool down. The men wiped their foreheads with handkerchiefs.

'Hey!' shouted someone, as Evie and Edna gingerly made their unsteady way down from the top deck. 'You all right, sweetheart?' It was Frankie, holding out a hand to help Evie step to the ground. His arms looked muscular and tanned, shirt sleeves rolled up above his elbows.

'I am. It's good to see everyone looking so happy.'

'They're a grand lot. Nowt could crush their spirits.' She smiled again.

'You look awful sweet. I like your frock,' he said.

She nodded seriously. 'It's not special or anything. It was me mam's.' She had added the flounce at the hem and taken the sleeves off, and she felt a prickle of pleasure that he had noticed. It had been one of the few things her mother had left behind.

'Well, you look a picture. She'd be proud.'

The buildings along Lord Street's Victorian promenade looked elegant, all black-and-white and swirling wrought iron. The largest of the buildings had graceful plate-glass windows, with gold letters that said BOOTHROYD'S DEPARTMENT STORE and, next door to it, GLADYS CARTER TEA ROOMS. This place had a delicacy about it, a finesse. Although the buildings in Liverpool that had withstood Hitler's bombs were noble and proud, it was plain that these fine, genteel terraces outshone them. As they walked past Walker's Arcade, they caught glimpses of ladies inside having tea; through the brass revolving doors of the shops and in the windows, they saw mannequins dressed in the latest fashions, pristine white gloves and handbags hanging off the end of arms in ballet dancer's poses. Evie wondered what it might be like to live here. She could never do without the rough-and-tumble of the factory, the girls and the gossip, the dances and laughs over the fags and cups of tea they had at lunch breaks, the camaraderie. But she thought it might be nice, once in a while, to breathe in sweet fresh air instead of choking your lungs with the dust and grime of the sugar factory.

Edna linked her arm. 'D'you want to go about with Blue Eyes or me today?' she asked.

'Me,' Frankie replied, snatching Evie's hand.

'I do not,' replied Evie, laughing, detaching herself from him and slapping his hand away.

Edna smiled. 'Let's go to the boating lake, then I

fancy a game of pitch and putt. And let's see if we can hook a few ducks at the fair. Ta-ra, Frankie. Bad luck, love.'

Frankie shrugged. 'I could take you a ride on the miniature steam train, Evie?' he called after them, as she walked off with a toss of her head, linking arms with Edna.

Half an hour later, after winning a goldfish and the plastic bag splitting and the fish slipping and slithering through her fingers, and then watching it nearly drown in a puddle on the floor – the funniest thing Edna had seen in her entire life, it would seem, as she scooped it up and liberated it by chucking it into the boating lake, so funny that tears were streaming down her face – and then playing a round of pitch and putt, they sat, exhausted by the heat, sunning themselves on a bench, feeling the warmth on their faces. When Frankie crept up behind Evie and poked her in her back, she was so startled she dropped her ice-cream cone into her lap. He laughed as she used his handkerchief to mop up the mess, and then without warning, he snatched her hat off her head and threw it right into the middle of the boating lake, as if it were a discus and hat-throwing was a sport, and he was the champion of all Liverpool.

Evie shrieked. 'What the 'eck? Why did you do that?'

'Look what he's done now! The bloody eejit,' cried Edna. 'It's ruined!'

'Go and get it, Frankie,' said Evie. 'It's me best hat!'

He laughed and kicked off his shoes. Then he took off his socks, undid his belt so his trousers dropped to his ankles, stepped right out of them and waded out into the lake until he was up to his thighs. He had a beer in his hand, cigarette drooping from his lip. Soon he came wading back out again, waving the sodden hat with its crinkled, candy-striped ribbon above his head.

'Come on, love. You wanted it, come and get it,' he said as he put his trousers back on and wedged the soggy hat down on top of his head, pulling it over his ears.

'Ignore him,' said Edna. 'What does he look like? Thinks he's Arthur bloody Askey.' But Evie knew this was a game, and so she picked up her skirts and raced towards him.

'Give it back!' she yelled.

'You have to come and get it!' he said, leaping onto a bench. She stood in front of him, jumped up to catch it. 'Finders keepers, losers weepers!' he said, snatching it away.

'I've not lost it, you nicked it!'

Throwing his head back in an open-throated roar of laughter, he darted off again towards the rosebushes, past the clock made of flowers, a dazzling arrangement of yellow and purple pansies. He rounded the corner, and she raced after him.

'Evie!' cried Edna. 'Come back!'

'Can I kiss you here?' he said, out of breath, as he stood panting, one hand leaning against a wall, another on his hip. 'No one can see us.'

'Frankie, you're a bloody case . . .' she said, pulling away from him as he took a step towards her. Picking up a convenient dry stick, she began peeling the bark from it.

'Ah, ey, Evie. Come on . . .'

She dropped the stick, smoothed down her skirts. The heady scent of roses filled her lungs and the sun was warm on her face.

'Go on,' she answered. 'But be quick. They'll start to suspect about us. Or Edna will, at least.'

He kissed her full on the lips, tongue pushing into her mouth, twisting around her teeth.

'Look,' he said, pausing for a second. 'I got this for you.' He took something wrapped in a tissue from his pocket and handed it to her. She opened the tissue. It was a trinket, a cheap bracelet, but with two charms hanging from the links – the letter F and the letter E.

'Oh, Frankie,' she said. 'It's lovely.'

He helped her fasten the clasp around her delicate wrist. And then he kissed her again, and she kissed him back as he began searching out her breast through the flimsy material of her dress.

'Stop, Frankie . . .' said Evie. 'What if Edna—'

He paused, pushed a strand of hair behind her ear. 'You don't think she's guessed? Six months now.'

'No. No one knows.'

'Then stop worrying.'

'I just don't want Edna to know. What on earth would she think? She'd tell the other girls, and it will be round like wildfire and back to me da in no time.'

He laughed. 'Evie's a one, Evie and Frankie kissin' in a tree, along came a baby and then there were three . . .' he teased.

'Stop it, Frankie.'

'I don't care. I know your da would kill you if he finds out we're courting, thinks I'm not good enough for his precious angel. But it's not going to stop me loving you. I love you like buttons love holes, and I always will. Jesus, Evie, look at me – I'm a right state, but there's nothing I can do about that. And . . . oh God, I love you. I can't . . . oh Evie. Please, will you let me?'

'What – *here*? Edna's right. You're a lunatic! You're loose in the head. You're as stupid as you always were!'

'Why not? No one can see us.'

'Of course they can!'

'Come with me, then.'

He grasped her hand and dragged her off behind a tree, through a gate where a small boathouse stood under overhanging branches at the end of a cinder path. She opened her mouth to say no, but between protests and kisses, kisses triumphed. 'In here,' he said, pulling her through a wooden door that squealed on its rusty hinges like a stuck pig.

Inside it was dark, except for strips of light that came in through the gaps in the wooden plank walls. There was a strong smell of musty sacks, newly cut grass, paraffin and engine oil. Frankie pushed Evie against a wall and started to kiss her.

'Oh, Frankie . . . I want to . . . of course I do. I can't help meself either. But have you bloody planned this? How did you know this shed was here?'

'Never mind. Just tell me this feels wrong? It feels about the only thing that makes sense to me in the whole of this mad, desperate world,' he said, tugging up the skirt of her dress.

'Frankie,' she sighed. 'Frankie . . . I love you. You know that . . . but . . . what if . . .'

'Then trust me. Trust me, love. I promise. Fella told me nothing will happen the first time. And I won't tell a soul. Our secret. Okay, love? If no one knows, what in the world does it matter what's going on in this shed? Door's shut. Straw's warm. Lie down on this pile of sacks with me for a kiss first. Please, Evie, let's do it . . . I know you want to as much as me . . . please say yes . . .'

Eight

When Evie arrived at the Playhouse she knocked on Biddy's office door and a woman's voice, tinkling and high-pitched, called out for her to come in. Twisting the knob, she found it wouldn't open.

'Give it a good shove, duckie!'

Evie leaned heavily on it, and it flew open. She got a shock at seeing not Biddy, but a pretty, curly-haired blonde girl with a creamy complexion and red-painted bow lips, dressed in a blue satin shift dress. In one hand she held a cigarette stuffed into a gold holder, and with the other she was furiously pulling at the handle of a locked drawer in a filing cabinet.

'I need petty cash, dearie. D'you have the key?' asked the girl.

'Me? Oh no, I'm just here to collect the cheque for Tate's.'

'You *must* have a key,' the girl said, rattling the cabinets, tugging at the handle whilst placing her foot flat against them. After a moment or two she gave up, sighed and sucked on the cigarette holder, the end of which was stained with lipstick.

'I honestly don't.'

'Just my bloody luck. You telling the truth? I'm desperate . . .'

'No. Sorry.'

'I'm Mabel, by the way. Pleased to meet you,' the girl said, sticking out her hand. 'Wait a minute.' She frowned. 'Tate's, you said? Are you the girl Lawrence was talking about? We were doing a scene the other day and he said, "Mabel darling, can't you be like that sugar girl that comes in to help Biddy? She's beautiful but has the air of being sweetly unaware of it." Did he mean you?'

'Oh well . . . I don't know . . .'

'Of course he did. Don't be shy. I'm rehearsing our Christmas show at the moment; he thinks of me as nothing more than a twirly but I love a bit of high-kicking. I find most of the Rattigan and Priestley stuff so bloody dreary, don't you?'

'I'm not sure,' Evie stuttered.

'You've got such a serious look about you. Soulful eyes. You'd make a good actress with those eyes. I can see why Lawrence was rather taken with you. Word of advice, though: our Lolly – that's what I sometimes call him – he's top-rate, but . . . how can I put this? He can be a bit frivolous at times. Some would say he's a little shallow.' Mabel paused. 'You've a pretty face under that little cloth hat. Want to go on the stage yourself?' she said, taking a few steps towards Evie and standing unnervingly close to her.

Evie touched the summer cap self-consciously. 'No. Like I said, I'm just here to collect the cheque from Biddy.'

Mabel reached out. She pushed the peak of the hat off Evie's face with the cigarette holder. 'That's better,' she said.

Did all theatre people feel they could just poke or prod at you without asking? wondered Evie.

Mabel's blonde curls shivered and she gave a tinkling laugh. 'What am I to do, then?' She sat on the chair, scooted it towards the desk on its wheels. She spun round in a circle, then smoothly placed one foot on the desk and the other across that one. 'The end of the week always comes round quicker than I need it to. I haven't got a bean. But then, looking at you, you haven't either – am I right, dearie?'

Evie shrugged.

'Oh well. I guess it's going to have to be one of the fellows at the bar again.' She paused, raised an eyebrow. 'What, duckie?'

'Nothing . . . I . . .'

'Don't look so shocked, love. All those boys love an actress. They think we're loose. D'you think I'm loose?'

'N–no . . .' Evie stuttered.

'Well, you're wrong. I am. And guess what? I don't care.'

Evie blushed. Thinking of what she had let Frankie do to her in that shed at Easter time, and what he had been doing to her ever since, she still felt ashamed. And yet here was this girl who didn't seem to give a fig about the world knowing what she got up to. When Evie tried to avert her eyes, Mabel gave her a small, conspiratorial smile and winked, which only made it worse. 'You're a pretty girl. Just not making the most of what God gave you. I'd die to have those big green eyes of yours. But a word of advice: don't waste it on Lawrence. He's got nothing. I could introduce you to a nice dentist? Or a councillor? Or a bank manager? You fancy that? Doesn't need to be anything too grand. As long as they take you out and show you a good time, and give you a few shillings to be going on with.'

'No. No, thank you . . .'

'Please yourself, darling. But you are really very pretty. Much prettier than that girl I'm meant to do scenes with. Phyllis the pre-Raphaelite football, I call her. Not to her face, of course. You've got wonderful cheekbones . . .'

'Oh,' said Evie.

'What do these letters spell: A, I, R . . . ?'

'Sorry?'

'What does A, I, R spell? Go on.'

'Air . . .' answered Evie, falteringly.

'And now this: H, A, I, R.'

'Hair.'

'Good. We're getting there. L, A, I, R.'

'Lair.'

'Now put those words together.'

'Air, hair, lair . . .'

'*Oh, hell-air* to you too! See?' Mabel squawked delightedly, clapping her hands together. 'I knew it! You could go on the stage. You're a natural for Noël Coward. Wait until I tell Lawrence! How unutterably charming you are!'

She danced about, making large sweeping gestures in the air, then slipped an uninvited arm round Evie's waist.

'Oh, no . . .' said Evie, squirming away.

'It's not bad. Chatting up the chaps. Nice to know

when you're broke that you can always make a few bob if you're clever. Where do you think I got this lot from?' She stuck forward her hand and gleefully showed Evie a gold ring with a large pink stone. Then she took the pearls around her neck, put them to her mouth and opened her kohl-rimmed eyes wide, batting her long false lashes. 'My heart belongs to Daddy. Daddies, plural. Don't look so shocked! I worked bloody hard for these baubles.'

'If you need money, couldn't you pawn them? I know someone who would give you a good price.'

'Pawn them! Ducky, I've done unspeakable things for these jewels. I'm not *pawning* them. You know what I've done to get these? As if eight shows a week is not hard work enough. I've had to go out night after night and pretend that I find these oafs and drips charming, and listen to their dreary stories and laugh and find them oh-so-funny and witty, when the truth is, they're all as dull as ditchwater. Still, I'm out of here soon. And you know how?'

'No,' said Evie.

'A fellow from London is coming to see the show. He said he's going to put me in the pictures. Apparently, after all the drama of the war, all these stories coming out now, there's work for us actresses. They're making films to raise the spirits . . . and the like. Could you imagine? Me? In pictures? Could you imagine how wonderful that would be? He says I've got *it*. And he had money in his eyes when he said it. Do you think I've got *it*, Elsie – Edith – whatever your name is?'

'I'm not the person to ask,' Evie replied flatly.

'Now don't be such a bore.' Mabel leapt to her feet and began to dance again. 'Watch this . . .'

Waving her arms about in strange windmill movements, she started to sing. '*I can't give you anything but love, baby* . . .' she warbled, and winked at Evie when she finished, looking pleased with herself.

'There – you see? I'm not bad, am I? D'you think I look like Jean Harlow? Lawrence says I'm the spit of her. He's not the only one. I'm wasted on this lot here. Soon as I get that offer from Mr Moriarty, I'm off. Take my advice, you'd do the same if you had any sense,' she said. 'Like I said, you're a pretty girl under that awful hat. You just need someone to take you in hand. Bet you scrub up well. Bet you could be the poppy in a field of grass if you wanted. But those shoes, dear – oh God, those shoes. The noise they make. You can hear the sound of your feet clattering down the corridor a mile off.'

Evie blushed at the thought of the nails that she'd hammered into the heels.

'Right, I'm off to the bar, seeing as I can't get any petty cash here. Let's hope it's not that ugly brute with halitosis who was hanging round the stage door the other night. A girl has to keep some standards. Toodle-pip, Cheery Bubbles. And with Lawrence baby? You've obviously made an impression. I wouldn't be surprised if he's been skulking round the corridors looking for you – so you be careful. You hear me?'

Nine

Vic appeared at the parlour door, socks drooping, twisting the cuff of his jumper.

'Don't do that with your pully. What are you still doing here? Shouldn't you be at school?' asked Evie. 'Get off now, love. You shouldn't be sagging off.'

'Miss says we can stay home if we want to today . . . It's a saint's day.'

'No she doesn't. And no it's not. Go now . . .'

Sylvie, still upstairs, began to cry.

'Sylvie's bawling . . .'

'Yes, I can hear her. And so will you be when I wallop your backside if you don't scarper. Go and fetch Sylvie and get on.'

Vic grinned, and made to leave. But before he did, he paused. 'Is Holy Joan Dad's new fancy woman?' he asked.

Evie shuddered. 'What makes you say that?'

'He lets her in the house when you're at work, and she bought him a jar of fudge from the Milk Bar in Cherry Lane. It had a pink bow tied on it.'

He was sharp, was Vic. Maybe sharp enough to pass the eleven plus.

'I haven't got time to be nattering about all this stuff. Go on.'

When she went into the kitchen, she saw the jar sitting on the table. Vic was right. There was the fudge and, tied around it, a pink gingham bow. Peculiar. Peculiar to do that. And suddenly Evie was filled with worry; it descended on her like a raincloud.

Her thoughts turned to the other people who had come to the house. Her father certainly hadn't wanted anyone to see how they were living. Apart from Sister Mary Clotilda, who would deliver food and clothes regularly, and Linda next door, who did a good job of minding the younger kids whilst Evie was at work, he hadn't let a soul come near. He was embarrassed. Embarrassed by the torn curtains, the worn linoleum, and the unanswered questions as to where her mother had gone. And yet he hadn't cared with Holy Joan. Why not? If only her mother was still here, thought Evie. But her mother wouldn't have been in a fit state for any situation, least of all this one. Her and Luigi Galinari, at it like knives. The horrible words came back to her.

She looked at the children's clothes hanging on the wooden clothes horse in front of the range, steam rising from the vests and petticoats. She thought of all the other worries going round and round in her head – and now there was Holy Joan to add to the problem.

That day after work Evie set off for Princes Street. Frankie would be waiting for her at the bend in the road. As she rounded the corner, she saw him sitting on the wall with that big grin on his face, cigarette drooping from his lips. It was a play street, a new idea of the council's where children could play safely in daylight hours. There were a couple of scruffy kids pushing an old pram with an overgrown twelve-year-old dangling his legs over the side of it.

'Evie!' Frankie cried. He jumped off and brushed himself down. He looked sunburnt, bright pink cheeks and freckling about his lips, flushed and happy.

'Let's not go to the Kardomah. Do you fancy a bottle of pop at that new club in town instead? They have jazz there,' he said. 'We could go dancing. You know – lindy hop, and stuff. I didn't much like the Americans being here, but I were glad they left their music in Liverpool as a parting gift . . .'

'Two of the girls at the factory were left with parting gifts an' all. A couple of buns in the oven from the GI Johnnies, they said.'

Evie could feel the wind in her hair as they walked down Mount Pleasant Hill. The late-afternoon sun was bouncing off the glass panes of St George's Hall. Frankie suggested they stop for a minute as it was still quite early, and they sat on the grass of St John's Gardens.

'I'm on the cradle again soon,' he said.

'The cradle?' said Evie, worriedly, taking the twig away from him that he had just picked up and was poking away at the weeds with.

'Some bugger has got to do it. Aren't you the lucky one now Stanley's put you in the office, with your head for adding and subtracting?'

He rolled onto his stomach. She did the same, felt the sun on the smooth velvety nape of her neck, supported herself on her elbows as an ant crawled over her hand. He shuffled closer to her, put his arm round her.

'Frankie . . .' she said, squirming, pushing his arm away, sitting up again, drawing her knees to her chest and pulling her paisley skirt over them.

'What?' he asked. 'What's wrong?' He propped himself up.

'I wish we hadn't, you know . . . done it . . .'

'You mean on the works outing? No one saw, and I promised I wouldn't tell anyone. So what's the matter?'

'Not just then – all the other times as well. I don't want to be thought of as a tart. Like that girl at the theatre.'

'What girl?'

'Doesn't matter. And I keep thinking of me ma . . .'

He sighed. 'How long is this going to go on, Evie? Love, whatever the story was about her disappearing, it weren't our fault. Not yours or mine. Just bad luck. You don't owe her anything. You don't need to be ashamed of what we've been doing. It's natural . . . Your body speaks to you and sometimes you just have to listen . . .' He traced a finger down the slope of her nose. 'Don't you like it when I do that?'

She squinted up at the sky.

'How about this,' he said, his other hand creeping up from her knee to her thigh. 'I know you do. That bit there, you like that, don't you?'

She pushed down her skirts brusquely, slapped away his hand. 'Give over, Frankie,' she said.

'Can I kiss you? With tongues?' he asked, his eyes twinkling.

85

'Is this why you brought me here?' she said, sharply. 'To lie on the grass and put your wandering hands up my jumper?'

'Shurrup. I want to marry you, that's why . . .'

'What?' she said, shocked.

'I've decided I love you enough to marry you . . .'

'Oh, you've decided, have you?'

'Yep.'

'Where's the ring?'

'Steady on, Evie . . .'

She paused, lowered her eyes. Then her expression changed. 'What about our Vic and me sisters? Who'll look after them if I'm to marry?'

'You're not their mam.'

'I have to stay in Coghlan Street. I have to think of them first. Besides, I don't want Holy Joan coming into the house.'

'Why?'

Evie sighed. 'Because I don't like her.' She rested her chin on her knees. 'I could kill my stupid da, trying to steal a wrap of sugar from the factory. Do you know what he did? Stuffed a stray kitten in his knapsack, hoping nobody would check inside too closely and the kitten would be a distraction from the sugar.'

'That's rotten.'

'It is. The only good thing about the whole debacle was that our neighbours felt sorry for us and invited us to theirs for tea. Kippers with melted butter and carrots and a block of Wall's ice cream for afters. That were nice,' she added mournfully.

'Is this nice?' he said, tracing patterns along the inside of her arm.

'Stop it.'

He groaned.

'Holy Joan sees it as a chance to be me da's saviour. Always buzzing around asking if he's all right. She should flaming buzz off.'

'Kiss me . . .' She felt his hand touching her thigh again. She pushed it away. This time he sighed more deeply. 'Loosen up, Evie.'

'*Loosen up?*' she said sharply. She thought of that girl, Mabel, at the theatre. She could never be like her. 'I don't want people thinking I'm *loose*. That's what they said about my mam.'

'Jesus, Evie. Always comes back to your mam.'

'No, it doesn't.' She wondered why Frankie couldn't see that this was a serious matter.

Sighing, he sat up, plucked a piece of grass from the earth and chewed it. 'Remember that time when you told me to stop hanging around you, when you were wanting to wear that flaming Crowning of the May dress and you wanted everyone to think you were pure? "Bugger off, Frankie, if you're with me people might think I'm a bad girl." Well, it's the same now, isn't it? Nothing has changed.'

'It's not that . . .'

He squinted into the distance. Evie could feel the depth of his frustration in the way he flinched when she reached out and touched his hand. 'Everyone says fellas only want one thing. Edna says it all the time about you. Is that why you're asking to marry me and saying you love me?' she said.

'No, Evie. Don't listen to Edna. She's got an axe to grind because she lost her fella.'

Evie paused. 'If you really love me, then, you'll wait.'

'Yer what?'

'I've got to sort the kids out with their communion and school tests and whatnot. And I'll use the time to find out what's going on with me da and Holy Joan. I'll not let you come near me for a bit. It's not much to ask.'

He moaned. 'A bit? How long?'

'Three months?' she said, randomly plucking a time out of thin air.

'Three months! I'll die, Evie.'

'No, you won't. Three months. You get on with your life, and I'll get on with mine.'

'What makes you think you can always call the shots, Evie?'

'It's not like that . . .'

'What is it, then? You seeing someone else? You seeing Neville? That why you want three months apart from me?'

'Neville!' Evie laughed. 'Don't be daft.'

'It's an awful big risk to take.'

She pressed her lips together. 'It shouldn't be. Here – take this,' she said, unclipping the nickel charm bracelet and pressing it into his hand. Thoughts tumbled through her head as he closed his palm around the trinket and slipped it into his pocket. 'It will remind you that I'm here waiting for you.'

'Then what?'

'We'll see,' she said, hoping it would be enough to mend the slight she had just inflicted. 'We'll see.'

*   *   *

Three weeks passed. To Evie's amazement, Frankie seemed to be taking it seriously: he nodded hello at her when he saw her on the shop floor, winked, gestured to his heart.

One morning he waved to her from up in the galley and blew a kiss, and she blushed; Edna raised her eyes again and flicked a tea towel at her. It was a busy day inside the factory, and the thrumming and clattering machines seemed louder than ever. You had to shout to be heard. Someone had put *Workers' Playtime* on the radio, and some of the girls were singing along to 'Whistle While You Work' as it was piped through megaphones onto the factory floor. Everyone knew the words about Hitler. It had been morale-boosting during the war and it still raised the spirits. A couple of the girls danced and swayed their hips as they loaded bags onto the conveyor belt.

Frankie had arrived at the factory earlier than most. The cradle slowed to a halt on the ground floor. It was rear-mounted to a steel column and had to be winched up on clanking chains and pulleys. Frankie climbed in. Behind him was his mate Jacky O'Hallaran, who had been waiting for him.

'Good to see you, Frankie,' he said. ''Ow's it going?'

Frankie wished he could tell Jacky how much he was missing Evie, but it wasn't a manly thing to pour your heart out about a lass to another fella. And any rate, it would get back to the girls before they were even out of the cradle. Jacky was a right slack-jaw.

'Not so bad. Still waiting for me promotion. They've put me in charge of checking the bags and organizing the rat-catcher's rotas, so it's a start. I'll be off the factory floor before the end of the month.'

'That what you want? Instead of the cradle? You frightened or summat?'

'Ha,' Frankie replied. Didn't want Jacky to think he was a milksop.

He undid the rope, twisted it into a knot to secure it around the handle. Pausing to unbolt the door, he waited until the cradle was suspended three inches above the stone floor, then stepped in. His weight caused it to swing back and forth, but there was nothing unusual about that. There was a small metal seat soldered into the back door and Jacky barged in after him, flipped it down and sat on it. A big, burly man came rushing forward. 'Room for a little 'un?' he asked. But he wasn't little. He was six foot two, and as broad as a bus.

'Not sure about that, mate. Not being funny and no offence, it says it takes three, but you're built like a brick shithouse. Read the sign.'

Three men only, it said. The cradle seemed like an insubstantial contraption, not really sturdy enough to hold even one man. The ropes and pulleys designed to take them up to the top of the warehouse floor, where they could check the sugar silos, clean out the guttering and the lips and take a look inside, seemed too flimsy to support their weight.

'This thing has taken six fellas and a hod of bricks,' said the big fellow.

'Gerrin then . . .'

The man stepped inside, and the cradle swung suddenly to the right. There was a burst of nervous laughter. Down below on the shop floor, one of the men pressed a button. Frankie pulled the door of the cage towards him. The cradle began to rise with each short, sharp yank of the chains below.

'I don't like this,' he said.

It was dangerous work, but you were paid an extra pound for it. Frankie was one of the few who was trained to work the machine at the top that scooped out debris from the circular lip round the circumference of the silo. But he would have been happier to do it on his own.

'Many hands make light work. We'll be done in no time with the three of us,' said Jacky. Frankie handed each of them a tool for scooping out the waste if the silo lip was clogged up.

About three floors up, the cradle lurched again as the big fellow shifted from foot to foot. By instinct, Frankie grabbed one of the ropes. 'Steady on,' he said. 'Stop shifting about.'

The fellow laughed, revealing a toothless grin. The cradle reached the top and the system of tracks and pulleys began to move them along into the centre of the large warehouse, jerking towards the silo.

'All looks fine,' said Frankie, peering in. The lip was clear. The glistening sugar looked pristine. 'Beautiful,' said Frankie. 'Not many get to see this . . . Chokes me every time. Checks done. All good, all correct. Let's go back down.'

The big fellow leaned back.

'Whoa! Stop moving about, everyone . . .' said Frankie sharply.

The man laughed. 'You're all right. If I just undo me safety belt and step back—'

That was when the door swung open. Jacky reached out in a panic, losing his balance as he lunged to try and close it, causing the cradle to tip.

Whether the catch had been left undone by the big fellow or by someone else, nobody could be sure. But there was no mistaking that when he took off his belt the door had fallen open, with the fellow following. All Frankie and Jacky could do was gasp in horror and watch as, flailing and crying out in what almost seemed like slow motion, he fell with his legs splayed and arms outstretched like an angel, into the sugar. They looked on, horrified, as he sank to his neck, his arms groping upwards for someone, anyone, to reach out and save him. Clutching and grasping at thin air, he screamed until he could only splutter and gag, his words choked into nothing, his cries muffled, mouth filling with sugar. Within seconds he was buried to the tip of his nose – then his desperate eyes – then only the crown of his head was showing, his bald pate almost indistinguishable from the white sugar. And then he was gone, sunk without trace.

All was still and silent apart from the creaking of the cradle on its chains. The surface of the sugar was once again eerily smooth, immaculate and glittering. It was as if the whole thing had never happened.

There was nothing they could do. Nothing anyone could have done.

'Call someone! Call the bloody foreman! Man's died. Bloody drowned in the sugar! Man's drowned in the bloody sugar!' cried Frankie.

*   *   *

News reached the factory floor from a stricken Edna, who poured out the story in a volley of words, and then Krysia, though hard to understand in disjointed Polish and English, who was crying 'Help! Help!' – the most any of the girls had ever heard her say. Celia, who was pushing a mop back and forth across the floor, dropped it in shock. Evie, meanwhile, saw the commotion from the office window and raced across the yard, where she met an ashen Stanley Mulhearn outside on the cobbles, pacing back and forth. 'An accident with the cradle . . . A fellow's been killed . . . Can't even say how . . . what happened, I don't know . . . Dreadful, dreadful,' he said, wringing his cap as if he didn't know what to do with his hands.

Evie came running through the front doors onto the factory floor. 'Frankie? Krysia, talk to me!' she cried, grasping the other girl's slender shoulders and shaking her. 'Where's Frankie?'

'He's fine,' said Edna.

'Oh, thank God.' Evie felt her legs buckle underneath her in relief and was instantly ashamed, as there was still some other fellow dead. 'How did it happen?'

'Can't say. All sorts of rumours flying around. But he wasn't wearing his safety belt,' said Celia.

And then Frankie's husky voice called out, 'Evie?'

'Frankie!' the girls cried. Seeing him pacing down the gangway, striding between the machines, Evie ran towards him, flung herself at him and clung on with her arms around his waist.

'You're all right, love . . . The whole thing tipped. I held onto a rope,' he said. 'That bit of rope saved my life . . .'

93

A wave of relief flooded through her. 'Oh, thank God. We thought something had happened to you.'

'It were the other fellow.'

'You were in the cradle with him when he fell out?' Edna asked.

'Aye, but I'm fine. I'm absolutely fine. Look at me. Hardly a scratch on me. Just a bit of a fright, that's all. Fella drowned in one of the silos. In the bloody sugar. That's a sight I'll never forget.'

Evie noticed Frankie's hands were blackened with soot, and there was a smudge across his face. 'Oh, Frankie,' she said, wiping the smudge tenderly with her thumb.

'Just watched him sink to his neck. His arms thrashing about. Then his head went under. Then the sugar choked him. And there was not a thing he could have done. Or anyone else could have done. They're trying to dig him out, but you take one scoop, one bucket, then another, and it just fills in with more sugar. It'll be a long job.'

She looked at him, the lines of her face etched with worry, and said, 'What if something had happened to you? What would I have done? What would any of us do?'

'I've nine lives, love. Haven't I always said that?'

She nodded.

'I've got to find Jacky,' he said, releasing himself from her grip. He kissed her on the lips. Edna raised an eyebrow, but Evie didn't care. She kissed him back, and shrugged at Edna as he walked off.

But then, just as she was about to return to the office, there was a noise at the far door – a cry, or more of a yelp. A young woman came hurtling through the crashing swing doors and ran past Evie towards Frankie's retreating silhouette. She was moving so fast that she was just a blur of blonde hair and swirling pink-and-yellow flowered skirts, racing towards him.

'Frankie, my love!' she cried. 'Thank God, thank God!' She threw herself at him, flinging her arms round his neck and clinging to him, much as Evie had just done.

It took only a moment for Evie to realize what was happening. There was no doubt. She would have recognized those blonde curls anywhere. It was Carol Connelly from school! What on earth was *she* doing here? What on earth was she doing, kissing her Frankie on the cheek – and on the *lips*! Slobbering all over him and clinging onto the lapels of his jacket, burying her head in his chest, crying and moaning and sobbing!

Frankie looked up worriedly at Evie over Carol's cascade of curls. He released himself from her arms and his gaze flicked from Evie's back to Carol's, then to Evie's again.

'I don't believe it,' Carol said. 'Didn't I tell you not to take that job on the cradle?!'

It was the way she smoothed down his hair and pushed a piece of it behind his ear, then pressed her hands flat against his cheeks, that did it. It was the way that Frankie *let* her. Evie's whole body started to shake. Waves of fury and shame came over her. It was as if someone had reached into her heart right there, squeezed and twisted it and wrenched it out.

What an idiot she had been! What an idiot! Her mind began to make dramatic leaps, running over their recent conversations. So *that* was why Frankie hadn't wanted to go to the Kardomah a few weeks ago. Didn't Carol Connelly work there? Vic had mentioned it – he'd heard it from Carol's brother, who was in his class as school.

Evie didn't want to think about how long the two of them must have been carrying on. She turned on her heel and walked away, numb and embarrassed, leaving the gaggle of panicked people behind her trying to work out what to do next about the man in the sugar. She could slip away now, barely noticed. Why hadn't she listened to Edna? Why had she been so stupid? Well, that was the last time she was going to make a fool of herself, she thought, determined and resolute. She was never going to see Frankie O'Hare again.

Ten

After a week of avoiding Frankie, refusing to answer the door when he came to her house, steering clear of the gossip and trying to lose herself in work at the factory, it was a huge relief on Saturday morning to be free of the worry of bumping into him. Evie straightened her clothes, tucked in her blouse, shifted her skirt round so the frayed hem was hidden by her light, summer coat, and set off to the city.

When she arrived at the Playhouse, Gordon the stage doorman barely flicked up his eyes as she came through the door. He was munching on a cheese and pickle sandwich and puffing on a fag at the same time, feet up on his desk. He blew smoke out of the window and nodded for Evie to go through.

She could hear someone practising the trumpet as she went down the corridor. Whoever it was, they were going over and over the same few notes. Clutching her purse, she turned off towards the small office.

'You the Tate girl to see Biddy?' said a man pulling on a rope in the wings, a cigarette drooping from his lips. 'She's waiting.'

Evie trod softly in her heavily shod feet. As she passed a room with a small glass window onto the corridor, she could hear a piano playing. It sounded joyful, enhanced by the sharp echo, and she couldn't resist stopping and peeping very cautiously over the sill. It was a young man; she couldn't see who. His nimble fingers skipped over the keys as easily as a child might skip flat pebbles across a still pond. She saw the slight arching of his back when he leaned upon a particular chord, and the hairs on his head shivering in a ballet of their own. She shrank back and moved away, sensing it would be dangerous to linger.

But when she hurried on down the corridor with its peeling yellow paint, graffiti'd here and there with people's names, there *he* was again: Lawrence. It was almost as if he was waiting for her. He looked an even more glamorous figure than last time, wearing a seersucker shirt unbuttoned to his waist with a white cotton vest underneath, hanging over his loose slacks. He was standing against a door jamb, sucking a lollipop.

'Here she is,' he said. 'The sugar girl.'

He had a clear, beautifully pitched voice and spoke without a trace of the northern vowels Evie was used to. But she wasn't going to be distracted by that. She frowned. He took the dove-white towel that was bunched up around his neck, wiped the perspiration off his forehead and face, and grinned. 'Come in here a minute . . .' He opened the door of his dressing room wider, pushed it with the toe of his patent leather shoe. A warm yellow glow coming from the lights around his mirror spilled out across the worn carpet.

'Oh, no, I can't,' she stuttered.

'Why not?' he asked. 'What are you frightened of?'

She thought for a moment. Should she tell him about Frankie? But then, *what* should she tell him about Frankie? How hurt she'd felt? That she could never trust a man again? Of course not – that would be ridiculous. 'I'm not frightened of anything,' she said, with a toss of her hair. 'I was taught by nuns.'

He laughed and raised an eyebrow. 'That's funny,' he said. 'Very funny. I like a girl with a sense of humour . . . Come on in, sugar plum,' he added, more softly. 'I need you to take something to Biddy for me. You'd do that for me, wouldn't you?'

Pausing, she tilted her head to one side, rolled the plumpest part of her bottom lip between thumb and forefinger. It was a habit she had formed, but she barely knew when she was doing it.

He gestured with the lollipop. 'Come on inside while I find it.' And then he smiled again, revealing perfect teeth and a flash of that pink tongue as he stuck the candy back into his mouth.

Evie peered round the door. Intrigued but trying not to show it, she took an inventory of the contents of the room. The walls were painted in smoky yellows and grubby reds. There was a shabby sofa pushed up against chaotic bookshelves, a row of lightbulbs around a mirror running along one wall. There was also a threadbare brown carpet from which your feet came away sticky, much the same as your hand did from the brass doorknob. Opposite the sofa was a desk on which there were heaps of papers torn into halves and quarters, and old newspapers. *The Stage*, she noticed. *Playbill*. In another corner of the room there was a wooden dance floor approximately five feet square, scuff-marked and worn smooth in the centre. Another large mirror, blotted by time, was propped up against a closed door. A red velvet curtain on a wire had been left open to partly reveal another smaller space, clothes on hangers hooked over a stained Chinese screen. A pale grey suit with the silvery sheen of money hung from one of them.

He turned his back to her, swept every useless item except what he was looking for off the top of the dressing table, scribbled something on a bit of paper and folded it in two. He handed it to her and said 'There you are.' She took it and turned to leave.

'Stay a minute, sugar . . . The wardrobe mistress has baked us this bread pudding. It's going round the dressing rooms. Have some. It's delicious,' he said, taking a glass bowl that was covered with a tea towel from a shelf. He sat on the table, crossing his ankles and swinging his legs back and forth as he scooped up the dregs with his fingers and put them into his mouth.

'No. I have to go,' said Evie.

'Take off your coat . . .' he said as he wiped his hands on the tea towel. 'You don't need that on in this weather.'

She pulled it to her, embarrassed about the threadbare blouse and plain skirt she wore underneath – like most of her clothes, the top was a hand-me-down and the skirt was one she had made herself from a pattern book that had belonged to her mother.

'I'm sure Biddy can wait. Please stay . . .' His hand accidentally brushed against hers as he moved past her to his dressing table, and a tiny shock went through her body.

'Sorry. I shouldn't. I can't.'

She worried about disappointing people. As she stood with the papers wedged under her arm, the smell of cologne as he sprayed himself filled the tiny room. She felt her hands sweating.

'How old are you, babe?'

'Seventeen . . .'

He was undoing the last few buttons of his shirt. She could feel herself blushing. 'I'm twenty-five,' he said.

'I'll go now,' she stuttered.

'No, wait . . .' he said, taking the shirt off, suddenly chucking it at her and causing her to yelp as she caught it. 'Well done,' he said. And she blushed more to see him standing there wearing only the white vest, lithe and muscular with smooth, sculpted arms.

He crossed the room, his movements easy and graceful, and removed one of the books from the shelves, producing a bottle of what looked like rum from behind it. He waved it triumphantly in front of her face.

'Have a drink with me. You'd like to have a glass? What's the matter?'

'Nothing. No, thank you.'

'Babe, you're blushing . . .' he said.

Why did that always give her away? How could she have been caught so off guard?

101

'Where d'you live?' he asked.

'Oh. Coghlan Street.'

His eyes widened. 'Coghlan Street? I know it. Sailortown? One of the dancers, Cyril, has digs there. Gay as a daffodil, Cyril. Not that we can ever say it out loud. Just have to watch him mincing around. He loves Carmen Miranda. Always prancing around with a basket of fruit on his head. You should see it.'

'That's good. That he's happy,' Evie said, confused.

He laughed. 'No, not gay as in jolly, you dope. No. Gay as in, bent as a nine-bob note. Dances up the other end of the ballroom to most other chaps . . .'

Good God. Surely he didn't mean . . . How could he say it? It was illegal. There had been a fellow at the factory who worked the night shift, and it was only rumours, but some said he had lost his job over it. He'd had to move to Preston. The police had been involved, as far as Evie remembered. It had been shocking – but here was this fellow laughing.

'How d'you get on with living down there by the docks? With all the lorries and cart horses and the dreadful noise?'

'It's not so bad,' she replied.

'It's not so good, I bet. All day and night. The smell of the stables. I bet it reeks.'

Evie was slightly surprised to find she suddenly felt defensive about the place she lived, and loathed on a daily basis. 'It's all right. The house is cosy . . . so it's fine,' she said lamely.

He pulled at either end of the towel around his muscular neck, which contrasted with his tanned skin. Topping up his glass, he slugged back the bronze-coloured liquid, his body curving into itself as he straddled a spindly arts and crafts chair. He pressed the glass against his face, cooling his glossy cheek. Rocking backwards on the chair legs, he said: 'You haven't even told me your name, sugar.'

'Evangeline O'Leary,' she answered. 'But they call me Evie.'

'They? Who's they?'

'Folks.'

'Well, I'm not "folks". So I'll call you Angel,' he said. 'Short for Evangeline, isn't it? Got a nice ring to it.'

'Evie's fine,' she said. No one had called her Angel since her mother had left.

Smiling, he stood over the basin and, without warning, ran the tap and filled a small jug, bent his neck and poured it over his head. He looked up from the sink, dripping.

'Oh, that's fresh, Angel,' he said, panting at the shock of the cold water. He tilted his chin for effect. She could have sworn he winked at her.

'I have to go,' she said. 'I have to find Biddy.'

She could hear the sound of the guns firing at midday from the docks. That was when all the dockers rushed to the pub for their lunchtime pints. She knew her father, now that he was trying to get dock work, would want to join them. He would be hoping to strike up a conversation with the foreman, and he'd be annoyed if she was late and he had to stay behind looking after Sylvie or Nelly. He would have to go and fetch Linda from down the road to babysit.

'Damn,' Lawrence murmured as he watched her, head bent, scurrying off down the corridor.

'Who is she, Ken? The sugar babe?' he asked later. Ken laughed.

'You leave her alone. She collects money from Biddy. She's a mystery, flits in and out. Tate's send her. I think there's a tragic story there. You can see it in her eyes. Maybe a broken heart somewhere along the way.'

'She's lovely. The real thing. Different to Mabel and the others, with all their preening and primping. No doubt Mabel would think Sugar Plum is plain as a pikestaff compared to her, with all her war paint and pin curls, but she's got a natural beauty. Proper natural glossy curls, not stinking of perm lotion like Mabel. If only Sugar would take the blessed hat off. I'd like to see what's underneath.'

'Aye, and a bit more than that . . .'

'Steady on, Ken,' he said.

Ken laughed. 'I thought you were in love with Mabel?'

'Mabel? Always practising how to cry somewhere. Or standing in front of the mirror quoting Noël Coward. The other day I caught her having a bash at fainting down a flight of stairs. In a way, I do love her . . . and it's true, only last week she said that she loved me. But there's only one person she's really in love with, Ken, and that's herself. Now that girl – Evie – could love, I bet. I can see it in her eyes. The next time she's in, you'll tell me, Ken? . . . Ken?'

'I will not,' Ken said. 'Sweet little Liverpool innocent. Pure as the driven snow, that one. Don't want
you getting your hands all over her. Corrupting her.'

Lawrence smiled. 'Would I?' he said. His laughter
gurgled, deep and throaty and low.

Eleven

Evie arrived back home half an hour later. Once Vic had gone off to play and her father had left for a pint at the Boot, she sat on the front step of Coghlan Street, lifted her face to the sun, and took the letter she had been writing out from where it was tucked under the cuff of her sleeve. Smoothing it out on her lap, she read it for a final time.

> *Dear Frankie,*
>
> *First, please do not reply to this letter. And please stop coming to the house. I was a fool. There's not many words need to be wasted on this matter. I want no more excuses. Carol is just a friend, you keep saying, and she threw herself at you and you let her kiss you to make me jealous – well, you still haven't told me why you never mentioned her in all the time we were courting. I have a pair of eyes, and despite you turning up at the house and protesting your innocence, I still do not see any reason to speak to you. I've listened to your excuses, and I just can't believe them. I saw the way she put her arms around you. She kissed you on the lips. On the lips! It's*

*not the fact that everyone at the factory
knew, it's not the fact that I trusted you with
the one precious thing I have, it's not the fact
that you took that away, it's the fact that I
swore to myself the world would not see me
with the same judging eyes it used to look at
my mother. I've let myself down, and my
father too.*

*Now on the practical front. One of us will
have to leave the factory. I am hoping I will
get a chance at a new job. I'll not say where.
But soon I will be gone.*

*I'm not even really angry with you,
Frankie. After all, I was warned. It's myself
I'm angry with for being so stupid. And
you're right, since the war, and since Mam, I
should move on. Everyone else has done. I
think this is probably what I should have
done years ago. So if there's any good to
come of what's happened, it's that I can
finally face that fact. Everyone says Liverpool
is at last dusting itself down and rising from
the ashes, so that's what I'm planning to do
too. You just watch me.*

*I wish you and Carol the very best. Please
do not make this any harder for me than it
already is.*

Evie

The pen wobbled. Move on? Evie stood up and went
into the house, her face flushed red from the sun,
holding the letter between finger and thumb as if it

were a dead mouse. Surely now this silly, stupid romance would be over? She'd been in danger of getting stuck in it forever like a wasp in honey, tired of beating her wings, finally losing the energy to fly and simply waiting for death to come.

But as to moving on . . . As she trudged upstairs, the words felt hollow. How on earth could you avoid living in the past, if it came back to haunt you every minute and second of the day?

Twelve

Frankie's mother lifted the bottle of stout to her lips and took a swig of the warm brown liquid. She let out a sigh as she heard the door slam. If she hadn't been so distracted, she would have noticed that lately there was something about her son's eyes: an unfamiliar look, a change. This was a different boy to the one who used to come home cheerful every evening, kicking off his shoes and grinning. The way he walked in now and hunched over the kitchen table, rocking back on the legs of his chair, sucking a burnt match, made the difference obvious.

'What's up, Frankie?'

'Nothing,' he replied.

'Well, I've some news. We've heard from the Favreaus in Canada. I cried buckets when our Dotty and your brother were evacuated there. It seemed such a long way away. But we've certainly fallen on our feet now,' she said.

Frankie looked at her, baffled.

'They say that there's work for all of us there. This is the news we've been waiting months for. It's a once-in-a-lifetime opportunity, Frankie. They say they would love to have us, they're missing the kids so much. Dotty will be beside herself with excitement.

I still can't get over how much they changed while they were over there. Ten years old, and she came back home knowing how to plough a field! Finally, we'll be able to taste that hot chocolate for ourselves, which apparently is made out of cocoa powder, and you get a biscuit on a leaf with it – a cookie, they call it, not a biscuit. Can you imagine! Dot seems excited about wearing bobbysocks again. Whatever they are.'

There was a pause. Frankie frowned uncertainly.

His mother jerked her head up and pushed her steel-grey hair back, raking her fingers through it. 'Who knows what's next for us?'

'But, Mam . . .'

'Why would we stay in Liverpool? What if there's another war? They said there wouldn't be after the one your grandad died in, but still the next one came around soon enough. I'm old enough to remember. What if there's another war, and there's even more of those doodlebugs like the ones they dropped on London?' She shivered at the thought of it. 'Silent bombs. You couldn't even hear them. Lethal, they were. Terrifying. Or, God forbid, another atom bomb? Let's get out while we can. We can't stay here. There's nothing for us. Half of Liverpool is still in ruins. And what the Luftwaffe hasn't destroyed, the Corpy is about to finish off. Bulldozers on every street.'

'Liverpool is all right. It's getting back on its feet. This town has got spirit. They've patched up so many parts, and they're finishing where they left off before the war . . .'

'Don't be stupid. You have no idea what you're talking about. This place is falling down around our ears. It's rotten. The floorboards are sunken and broken. There's holes in the roof. An actual hole. Buckets all over the place . . .'

'Corpy have said they'll help us find somewhere. A nice place.'

'They've said that to every poor soul I know. Our house was flattened, your dad dead, and they've put us in this godforsaken hole. If they think this is fine and dandy, I can't see where they're going to put us next that's anywhere better. I'm not moving out to one of them high-rise flats they're going on about. The Favreaus said we can rent a house on their farm in Canada. White clapboard walls. Don't ask. I have no idea what that is either, but it sounds lovely and clean. And there's work out there, for all of us. It's the fresh start we need.'

Frankie traced his finger down the bridge of his nose. His thoughts turned to Evie. For a moment he wavered. Maybe this *was* the distraction he needed. How many more times could he try and talk sense into her? To tell her there was nothing between him and Carol Connelly, despite how it looked? Every time he went to the house she would turn him away; every time he saw her at the factory, she would turn on her heel and pretend she hadn't even seen him.

'If we stay, they'll most probably rehouse us some-where in Knotty Ash . . . or Norris Green. They say they're going to build more of those prefab huts,' he said.

'Do I look like a flipping rabbit, Frankie? I'm not living in a hutch.'

'They're proper houses.'

'My eye, they are.'

'But Mam, I'm nearly eighteen, and they're already talking about promotion at the factory.'

His mother snorted. 'Don't kid yourself, son. Now that all the older fellows have finally returned from Africa and Cyprus, you're back where you started. Hauling bags of sugar onto the lorries, working on the cradle, pushing carts and pulling at the chains all day long. Dangerous work it is, cleaning the sugar silo. And they're the ones, the heroes coming back from fighting the Jerries, the ones who've been given the proper jobs again.'

Frankie smarted. 'Stanley said I might get a job doing the exports.'

'Stanley said nothing of the sort. Stanley's worried about his own job. I spoke to him myself not long ago and he certainly wasn't talking about promotion for you, Frankie. Anyway, you should set your sights higher than Tate & Lyle. Canada would open up so many opportunities for you. You're a bright boy. You could get a job as a clerk.'

Shifting from foot to foot, jangling the coins in his pocket, Frankie thought that the war had made his mother bitter. It had made many people turn mean and nasty when they'd been perfectly reasonable, easy-going souls before Hitler had decided to stamp his boots all over Liverpool. They now said things they would never have said in the old days. But then maybe, he thought, if you'd seen your husband killed, found him stone-cold dead with a lintel crushing his body in two, blood spilling out in a pool behind his broken skull and flowing from his eyes, ears and mouth . . . maybe you would now have the same unforgiving streak running through your veins.

'What's keeping you here? Why not try it? You can always come back if it doesn't agree with you. A new life, in a country that's not seen the ravages of war? Toronto is beautiful by all accounts. Pine trees and lakes. There's fishing and swimming. It's clean. You could eat your dinner off the pavements. What's here for you? This city has had its day. They're even talking about knocking down the tenements. Why not Canada? It's beautiful. The air is fresh.'

If only he could tell her about Evie – but that would be useless. It would probably make things worse than they already were. Besides, what would he say? I want to stay here to be with an impossible girl who's so set on her version of events that she won't even speak to me? A girl who wants to destroy everything that's good in her life because of her mam, because that's what she always has done, because that's what she will always do, most likely? A girl who hates the very sight of me?

Thirteen

Stanley, sitting opposite Evie in the canteen, began chasing a piece of tripe round his plate with a fork. Seeing it, she felt like vomiting. Standing up to leave, she felt herself swaying back and forth.

'Something you've eaten?' said Edna. 'You look green, love.'

'Maybe,' she replied, feeling another wave of nausea at the sight of Stanley eating his tripe. Just the thought of the sweat dripping off his forehead onto his plate – it was disgusting. Enough to turn anyone's stomach.

Edna frowned. 'Sure it's something you've eaten, love?'

'What d'you mean?' asked Evie. She played with the woollen tassel on her shawl, caressed it with her forefinger as though it was a pet mouse, and flipped it over in the palm of her hand.

'You know . . .'

Evie shrugged. 'I'm sure,' she said, quietly.

Edna nodded. 'Anyway. Just putting you in the picture, like. About Frankie leaving. I shouldn't worry. When the wrong people leave your life, the right things start to happen.'

Evie's gaze dropped to the floor and lingered there

a few moments, as though she couldn't bear to look at Edna. She felt as if there was some huge lump of sadness inside her that was getting in the way of every other feeling she had.

She turned to go back on the floor, where the sugar girls were at their stations beginning to start their afternoon at the machines.

Krysia sat at a trestle table, threading a needle. She was sewing a pile of hessian bags that had become frayed and worn but, with a little attention, could still be put to perfectly good use. When she thought no one was looking, when her head was bent as she sewed the bags, she paused and glanced over her shoulder before licking her fingers, taking pleasure in the sweetness of them. Her big, soulful brown eyes darted up to Evie's guiltily as she passed.

Once Evie was inside the office, after shooing out the last man to whom she was giving a chit, she shut the dimpled glass panelled door. As she was twisting the key in the lock of the metal tin of petty cash, she heard a knock on one of the office windows.

Frankie?

It was him. Standing in the door frame. Now stepping inside, bringing in damp air. 'I'm soaked through,' he said. She could hear the warm rain thrumming on the corrugated roof of the lean-to that ran alongside the office. He was so wet that his cotton shirt had stuck to his skin.

'Good to see you, love,' he said, moving from foot to foot. 'You've heard? Canada?'

Presenting an indifferent back, she pretended to

sort through papers, but the shock of it ran through every vein in her body.

'I'll not go if you say I should stay,' he said in a small voice.

She paused, shrugged, but inside she felt a rush of anxiety, as if she were suddenly becoming loose from her moorings.

'Anyway, it's not forever. Just to see if we like it. I don't expect our Alf will want to stay either,' he said to break the silence. 'Stuck on a farm in some godforsaken place. Miles from anywhere. He'll want to get back to his beloved Everton football team, I bet. They've barely even heard of footie out there.'

She nodded.

'I love you, Evie. That Carol Connelly thing. I only let her kiss me to make you jealous. To make you see some sense. That stupid three-month break idea was nonsense. I thought that if—'

'When exactly are you going?' she said, cutting him off and dropping her gaze to a pile of bags of sugar on a wooden pallet. This was all too painful and she could feel her eyes brimming with tears.

His brown hair flopped in a front lick over his face as he walked behind the desk, stood in front of her, bent forward and, with a finger, tilted her chin up.

'Evie. Look at me. Thing is. That's why I'm here. There's a ship leaving this evening. We got the last four passages. Mam's insisting we take it. We had the most furious row. But she got them for half the money. Someone's dropped out. Friend of her sister's. Been taken ill.'

Evie felt herself swaying with the shock of it. An awful sense of mistiming made her stomach lunge.

'She was on the phone to the War Office, sorting things behind my back . . .'

More tears filled Evie's glassy eyes. She reached out, steadied herself.

'I don't know how to make it better, love. To make you believe Carol Connelly is nothing to me. She set her sights on me after her father decided that she and I should start courting. It was all about money. Her da and my ma—'

'Not again. I don't want to hear,' Evie said. 'I'm tired of your excuses.'

He sighed. 'I do know if you let me kiss you, we might forget about it for a moment.'

'No, Frankie.'

'Come here . . .'

She fought tears. With beads of sweat meandering over her body, she turned and placed her hand gently on his arm. There was the sound of the factory klaxon starting up again, telling everyone to clear the fore-court for a delivery lorry that was about to reverse into the loading area. She stood up, peered out of the window. A streak of light flashed through the sky.

'Something's up.' Drawing the curtain aside, she heard the sound of a car's engine revving outside, saw the Austin Ten in the factory yard. 'There's a car arrived in the yard,' she said.

'Jacky. I asked him to bring me,' he said. 'I needed to get here quick. I love you, Evie,' he said.

Jacky was sitting at the wheel, his trilby perched at a jaunty angle, smoking a cigarette with ash curling from the end of it. He leaned over, opened the passenger door and pressed the horn with the heel of his hand. 'Come on, you two lovebirds.'

Evie winced. Frankie went out, turned up his collar and got into the car.

'Toodle-pip, love,' said Jacky, breezy and happy and blissfully unaware of the drama of the moment.

Watching the car roar off down the road and the sky turn blue-black, Evie wondered if picking up the pieces after the war was turning out to be a miserable affair for everyone, not just her. Too often, love went sour, and it was hard to get over the fact. She thought back to all the doomed love affairs of the war. Linda had fallen in love with a serviceman, but he had been caught kissing a girl in Bootle when he was supposed to be in a prisoner-of-war camp in Japan. When Evie had confided in her about Frankie leaving, she had said no man could be trusted; he'd find some girl in Canada with pigtails and clean nails soon enough. They all knew that Mrs Liddy down the road had had a fancy man knocking at her door whilst her poor husband was risking his life in the merchant navy, and that's why her husband was now drinking himself senseless every day. Edna's sweetheart had died. And Ivy's baby, well, it didn't make sense, the dates – who had a baby at five months that was so bonny and healthy? Maisy Gribble, well, she had remained faithful to her husband and he to her, despite them not seeing each other for five years whilst he was in Africa. It was just that she'd never expected him to come home in a wheelchair. She was only twenty-three; there were a whole lot of years of looking after him in front of her, and it was taking its toll, all right. And then there was her parents' marriage. Luigi Galinari had made his move whilst her father's bed was still warm.

But even so, was this a ridiculous thing she was doing? Pushing Frankie away like this? The strange thing was, she just couldn't seem to help it. And she wondered if she would ever be able to get the picture of Carol kissing Frankie out of her head, despite Frankie insisting he had only let Carol do it to make Evie feel jealous. The pain of it would remain with her forever.

Fourteen

'Sweetie!' said a squeaky voice. It was the unmistakable tones of Mabel. 'How do I look? What do you think of this get-up?'

She twirled, showing off a voluminous pearlized silk floor-length evening gown that shimmered and rippled over her curves. 'The wardrobe girls made it out of old parachute silk. Can you believe it? I wear it in Act Three.'

'You look pretty.'

'Pretty? Pretty's not enough. I want spectacular, dreamy, *gorgeous*, darling.'

It was the last Friday of June. The weather had got warmer and the bowels of the theatre felt stuffy and uncomfortably close. Evie had just arrived to collect the cheque, but instead of Biddy in the office, Mabel had been waiting for her. She perched on the desk, began painting her nails.

When Evie entered the room, Mabel squealed and started chattering away about movies, music and make-up. Had she heard about a new film on at the Odeon picture house? *Three Strangers*, she said it was called, and began babbling on about how Bette Davis had lost her precious part in it, which quite frankly, in Mabel's opinion, was worse than dying.

Oh, and didn't Evie think Perry Como was dreamy? Was he her type? Who was her type? Please God, don't say Lawrence! What colour varnish did Evie think suited Mabel best? Jezebel Red, or a Hot Pink? Evie had just nodded nervously in reply to each question, and Mabel had laughed at her as though it was some kind of sport.

'She making trouble? Leave her alone, Mabel.' The voice belonged to Lawrence, putting his head round the door.

'She doesn't mind. We were having a girly chat, weren't we?' said Mabel, blowing on her painted nails.

Evie frowned and shrugged.

'Actually, I need to speak to you, Lawrence,' said Mabel.

'Save it for later, lovey,' he said. 'It's Evie I'm looking for.'

Mabel snorted, waving her hands about to dry the nail polish. Evie was already scurrying past Lawrence, out of the room and off down the corridor.

'Wait, Evie,' he said. 'Don't run off . . .'

He caught up with her, began walking beside her, in front of her, behind her, turning backwards to face her, bobbing up and down, cantering down the narrow corridor, nearly toppling over a crumbling plaster bust of Shakespeare.

'I've been waiting for you,' he said. 'Biddy told me you were coming today. I should be going through a scene with Mabel, but she's such a floozy and she's driving me round the bend. Keeps complaining about her costume – but it's not the flipping costume that's not right, it's her. Nothing's right with Mabel.'

Evie stopped. Dry-mouthed, she looked at him, not knowing what to say and finding herself unexpectedly rooted to the spot as he wafted and chasséd around her. He reached out his hand. And though he had delicately cupped it when he held her arm, it felt like a manacle around her wrist. She felt the blood rushing to her head. 'Let go of me . . .'

He dropped her arm. 'Let me take you to Giotti's cafe in Bold Street. I've got half an hour off from rehearsals . . .' He smiled at her. 'You have beautiful eyes. I've never seen anything like them. They're such a gorgeous colour. Unusually green . . .'

'No. I can't go.'

She marched on ahead, out of the grubby fire door at the end of the corridor and down the stairs, gripping the greasy handrail, through a velvet fringed curtain and out into the foyer. The glass doors were locked with a chain running from one side to the other. Lawrence followed her.

'You frightened?' he said, giving her a dazzling smile.

Evie gave a short laugh. 'I told you. Nothing frightens me,' she said.

He grinned. He was really getting to like this girl, with her unstudied beauty that shone out from her fierce temperament.

'Anyway, what d'you mean? Frightened of what?' she said.

He came towards her, picked a thread off her coat and flicked it aside. It swirled in concert with the specks of dust glittering in a shaft of light. 'A milkshake with me.'

She adjusted her jacket and looked at him steadily with big round eyes. 'No.'

She couldn't do this again, no matter how much she would have liked to – no matter how much the thought of sitting in a booth at Giotti's, with the silver bowls and plastic cracked seats and fringed lampshades, and him sitting opposite her, made her heart race. No, this was exactly how it had started with Frankie – and look where that had ended.

'Sorry. I have to go.'

'Is it because of your chap?'

Evie froze.

'Were you jilted? Let down? People only let you down if you allow them to.'

What nonsense, she thought. She turned to leave, but a sudden noise beyond the curtain, a clanking and clattering, a tin bucket being kicked over maybe, made her start.

'Don't worry. It's just the theatre ghost,' he said in an exaggerated whisper, and grinned.

'Ghost?'

'No, you big nelly, it's just old Swainset, the theatre rat-catcher. He wanders about in the gloom back here when no one is around. You know how he kills them? Bites them on the neck.' Lawrence reached out to move Evie's hair back from her neck and whispered into her ear. 'Like this . . . aaaargh!'

'Rot.'

'Aye. It's true,' came a voice from the gloom. 'But this one, I'll let go.'

Swainset, an ugly man with beady eyes and a hooked nose, had appeared behind them. He held a hessian sack in one hand and a cigarette in the other. There was a sudden movement from inside the sack, and Evie gasped.

'This one's still alive. I'll let him go because I don't want to make meself redundant,' Swainset chortled, brandishing the sack as he exhaled a thin dart of smoke. 'If there's no rats to catch, there's no job for the rat-catcher . . .'

'You're a bloody liability,' replied Lawrence. He turned to Evie. 'He puts the rats in cages in the large water butt outside and drowns them. He also has a terrier that likes to chase the others he keeps alive, around the yard. Takes bets, don't you? All highly illegal, but you won't say anything, will you, Evie?'

'As long as he doesn't let them out anywhere near me,' she said. 'You keep that sack away from me, d'you hear? Horrible things,' she added with a shiver.

'Sure I can't get you to change your mind about that milkshake?'

'No,' she replied. 'Please don't ask me again.'

Evie made her way to Stanley's office when she arrived back at the factory.

'Stanley, I'm sorry, I appreciate you getting me the new job. But I don't want to do it anymore. I'll find something else. Bar work, maybe. I've heard they're looking for a girl at the Throttle's Nest.'

'Why not?' he asked, confused.

'I'd rather not say.'

'Come on. Out with it,' he pressed.

She sighed.

'Is it a fella?'

She felt the heat rise in her cheeks. 'No. It's just . . . some of the people I've met, they're so different to me. And it doesn't seem worth the bother. I hope I haven't let you down.'

He leaned back in his chair, folded his hands behind his head.

'Is everything all right, love?'

'Dandy,' Evie replied.

'Is it your dad? It wasn't my choice he was sacked. The fellas up top. A rule is a rule.'

'I understand,' she replied.

'So then, what is it? You're the kind of lass who lights up the room when you step into it. But lately you seem, I don't know. Worried? Something you want to get off your chest, love?'

She turned to go. Then hesitated. 'Stanley, you knew my mam, didn't you?'

He shifted in his seat. 'Yes, love.'

'I'm not a slut, Stanley.'

'Who said you were?'

She chewed her lip. 'I don't want people talking about me the way they talk about me ma.'

'And why would they do that, queen?'

She lifted her chin, looked him straight in the eye and spoke firmly. 'No idea. But they'll have me to answer to if they do.'

Fifteen

That Sunday morning, Evie dragged herself to church, taking her siblings with her. They would be making preparations for the feast of the Sacred Heart. The church would be full of flowers and it would remind her of the Crowning of the May.

Her heart felt heavy, knowing Frankie was on the other side of the Atlantic. The walk past the bomb sites – the hollas, as everyone was beginning to call them, because of the huge, gaping hollow wounds that scarred the city – felt longer than usual. Roads were now cordoned off, corrugated-iron fences known as 'the tinnies' boxing in and boxing off familiar routes, and everywhere bulldozers and wrecking balls filling the air with dust. She covered her mouth with a handkerchief, clutched her sisters' small hands whilst her brother ran on ahead. In the distance, the church steeple seemed to wobble in the heat. The sound of the bell rang softly and told her that they were late.

Suddenly Victor dashed across the road, just as a lorry thundered by. 'Vic! What d'you think you're doing!' she cried.

'Look!' he said, pointing to a piece of wreckage that was sticking out of the ground. It was a lump of metal, glinting in the sun. 'Reckon that's a bit of fuselage. From a Jerry plane. Can I go and—'

'No! You're going to church. It's probably just a bit of an old tin can . . .'

'Aw . . .' he complained.

Evie sighed, pulling him along. He had developed an unhealthy preoccupation with all things war-related. These new movies he was so fixated on, *Tokyo Joe*, *The Sands of Iwo Jima*, *Twelve O'Clock High*, didn't help much.

When they got to the church, there was a small group of people on the steps. The doors were wide open and the strains of the opening hymn, 'Soul of Our Saviour', seeped out into the street. There was a heavy scent of flowers in the air. Evie could see huge vases of yellow and white roses, bunches of posies tied to the end of the pews with ribbons. The people began to move through the doors. She and Victor and the girls joined the throng, with Victor sticking his fingers into the holy water font and vigorously crossing himself.

'Never mind that,' hissed Evie, genuflecting at the end of the back pew, then shoving him along the bench. 'There's a space in the middle,' she said, directing him to move further up, apologizing as they barged into people and tried not to step on feet as they shuffled along and climbed over bodies. '*In nomine Patris et Filii* . . .' murmured the priest.

There was the sound of hymn books flapping open, making thudding noises. She glanced up to the organ loft. There were people up there, squashed up against each other, hanging over the wooden rail.

The organ began to play. Father Donnelly sang out in a booming voice.

Evie squashed into a pew and began to sing. She had no idea how on earth belting out 'Angel Voices Ever Singing' was going to help matters, apart from perhaps bringing some comfort from the knowledge that there were others like her in this situation and they weren't completely alone. The priest stood on the altar under the frieze of stone saints, their sorrowful faces looking down on the scene played out before them.

They knelt down and joined hands, said a quick prayer. But when Evie opened her eyes and went to stand, there she was – Sister Mary Clotilda, kneeling in one of the wooden pews on the other side of the aisle, eyes shut, head bowed, hands joined in prayer. Evie, with Vic fidgeting beside her, took another glance in her direction. She watched her lighting a candle in a side chapel. And then suddenly there was a surge of people going up to the altar to take communion.

Outside on the steps, as was customary at St Augustine's after Mass, Father Donnelly was waiting. He had walked in steady rhythm with his altar boys down the aisle, all swishing white linen and starched lace, to the back of the church, so that when they reached the end of the processional hymn and the congregation came out onto the steps, he was standing there to greet them one by one as they emerged blinking into the sunlight. As Evie stepped out, she felt a hand under her elbow.

'Evie!'

'Sister Mary Clotilda,' she replied.

'My, you look bonny, Evie. Haven't seen you in a while. You do look well. I hardly recognized you, dear. How's the family? How are you all doing?'

Evie looked at her, round-eyed. She had always been so kind. 'We're not too bad. Though Dad lost his job . . .' She started to speak, but couldn't think what else to say; the words fell silent on her lips.

When she got home, the house was empty. The children had gone off to play at the reccy. She was hungry. She had never felt a hunger like it. Searching through the cupboards, she found a tin of Spam. There was a jar of pickle on the back shelf. Piccalilli. Reaching for it, she screwed off the lid, scooped the bright yellow gherkins and onions onto a plate.

They tasted good. Strange and delicious.

Searching right into the back of the cupboard when she had gobbled them down, she brought out another jar, dusted it off. It was treacle. She stuck a spoon in it, put it in her mouth, licked it, and went to take another, then paused. What on earth was she doing, wolfing down a whole jar of pickles, and now spoonfuls of treacle? Almost simultaneously, another thought crashed into her head. *Bonny*, Clotty had said. Yes, she was bonny. But was bonny just another word for *fat*? Her heart lurched. And suddenly, the actual truth of the situation came slamming into her brain.

She counted on her fingers. But this time she counted properly, didn't push the terrible fear aside, and decided she must confront it. Her heart thudded. Weeks. It must be weeks now since she had had the

Curse. God, *months*. Could it be months? She thought back to all the times when the dreadful horror – she could think of it as no more than horror at this moment – when *it* might have happened. Getting herself up the duff, in the club, knocked up, in the family way . . . had it been that time after everyone had left the factory and Frankie had pulled her into the cupboard in the office? It wouldn't be the first time a couple had had sex in there, he had said to her, laughing, and she had laughed back. Or the time when her father and Vic had gone to Paddy's market and the girls were with Linda and the house was empty and Frankie had leaned her across the kitchen range and it had felt warm across her thighs and she had arched her back and asked him to do it again. All the times when he'd promised that – as long as they did it standing up, against the wall in the passage one dark night, against the park railings – there was no way they could make a baby. All the times he'd begged her to say yes, and she had said no, but then given up the fight because it had felt so damned sweet and natural and good. In the end she hadn't even bothered to say no, but instead *yes please, more, Frankie, more, I love this, I love you, it's the one thing that makes me happy in my life, the one thing that helps me forget.* What on earth had she been thinking of? *Had she been out of her mind?*

Oh God, no, please God, she thought, trembling and in shock as she ran upstairs to the bedroom. This can't be happening. Not to me. That wouldn't be fair. The stupid thing was, she'd already had to bear such sadness in her life, with her mother leaving and her father struggling to find work, and being so poor, and now this awful Joan sniffing around – she had just felt it wasn't possible. She had thought that it was reasonable to trust God had only so many cards to hand out, and she had already received so many duds – it just wouldn't be fair that she had been dealt the very worst of them, on top of everything else.

But no, slowly unbuttoning her dress, smoothing her slip over her full breasts and stomach, letting her hands slide over her new curves, she finally had to face the fact that hers was a cruel God after all. There was no getting away from it. No free passes for Evie. She had played with fire, and now she had got burnt. She was having a baby.

And now, more than ever, the past came back to haunt her: her mother and Luigi Galinari, and her decision to push Frankie away. She slipped her arms out of the dress, let it fall to the bedroom floor, stepped out of the crumpled heap of linen and winced at her reflection, running a hand over her tender breasts, feeling the swell of her belly.

Sixteen

She sat up all night writing the letter to Frankie, but in the end decided to make it short and to the point.

> *Dear Frankie,*
> *I'm not sure where to send this letter to, and I really do not want to break this news this way, but I have something important to tell you. Unfortunately, I'm afraid it's not the news that you probably want to hear. I only wish I had realized before you left, but the fact is, I was in such a muddle about everything else, the business with Carol, you and everyone else telling me one thing and my eyes telling me another, I seemed barely to notice. That might seem incredible and so I should come straight to the point now. I'm having your baby. Please don't be angry and please write to me with news of when you might return home so we can decide what to do.*
> *Evie*

She couldn't think of what to do except go to Frankie's house and see if there was anyone there who could give her his new address. She remembered he had an aunt who lived with them. She had already made enquiries at the factory, but nobody there seemed to know where exactly in Canada Frankie's family had gone. Jacky had a vague idea that they'd moved to somewhere outside Toronto; but when he'd begun to ask too many questions, Evie had ended the conversation quickly.

When she got to the grocery shop, there was a man putting up a sign at the bottom of Coghlan Street. *Danger: Demolition Works*, it said. Evie's heart lurched. Were they starting to tear down the houses here as well? Surely they couldn't do that? 'Out of the way!' cried a voice, as a wrecking ball smashed into the side of a building and it collapsed in a pile of bricks and dust.

She stopped and looked around her. This place was becoming like a ghost town. There were great holes in the ground appearing overnight, whole areas flattened. It was like a wasteland. It had a lost feeling, a feeling of complete annihilation; where once it had been crowded with houses, it was now a piece of desolate open land. A bus, with men's faces peering through the back windows, trundled across the vast empty space, dust rising from its tyres in great clouds. Probably being ferried out to the new flats in Kirby and Fazakerley. It reminded Evie of one of those wagons in the cowboy films she had seen at the movies, trailing across the prairie. The sun appeared and the windows of the buildings flashed. Frankie had been right to get out of here, she thought sadly. Who would want to come back to this awful place?

She made her way down the street. But as she

rounded the corner, she gasped. The words didn't come. Nothing could have prepared her. She shook her head disbelievingly as a scraggy little wind blew a strand of hair across her face.

Just like the open land she had walked through to get here, there was nothing. Everything about this place, only a few moments' walk from her home, was suddenly unfamiliar. Things that had been so much a part of her childhood – the lamppost they would tie a rope around, knotted at the bottom, and swing around for hours; the high wall they'd had so much fun throwing a rubber ball against; the railing they had clung onto as they made their way down the steep hill – were all gone. Liverpool's court houses had never been places anyone would choose to live, but now that this whole area had been destroyed, it seemed like a terrible loss.

Did this place even have a street name now? How could it? Nothing was recognizable. A little further away, Evie could see a collection of stubby terraces. There was now nothing to the side of them, nothing in front of them, rubble underfoot, particles of dust swirling around . . . she might have been standing on the surface of the moon.

A group of children who were playing with a hubcap and an old tyre stopped and looked at her quizzically. They had made a small fire and were dancing round it, yelling rhymes. It looked like a great game, chucking bits of metal, wood and debris into the flames, hoping for bullets they had scavenged for, old bits of casing, shrieking and dancing away in delight when some of them popped out from the flames.

'Do you live here?' Evie asked one of them. The smaller child stuck a grubby thumb in his mouth. 'Any of you know the O'Hare family?'

'No one knows anyone round here anymore. All shifted out, Mrs.' The child's eyes flicked away, back to the fire. The others just stared at her blankly, then went back to burning the remains of a door. There was a dreadful sense of foreboding about this place. It had nothing much in the way of vegetation or other buildings. No trees or grass verges, just rubble and sandstone and jagged lumps of concrete with broken bottles stuck in it. It looked the way Evie felt.

'I should clear off, kids,' she said. 'It's dangerous, what you're doing. Your mams wouldn't like it.' They ignored her, laughed as a firecracker spat out. 'And if you're not from round here, stop making this place more of a bomb site than it already is.'

The children glared at her, challenging and obdurate. The war had done something to people, she thought sadly. Made them wild and untamed.

She took the letter to Frankie out of her pocket. It was useless now, she thought. No street. No house. No letterbox. No family left to ask. She walked over to the fire, scrunched it up, threw it onto the small pile and watched it burst into flames.

Seventeen

Edna looked shocked.

'I didn't think it would actually happen to me,' said Evie.

'Why not? I warned you often enough. Have you told your dad?'

'No!' she said.

'So tell me again. Frankie's in Canada, but you want him to come back.'

She nodded. 'I feel a fool. Letting him go. That was my ma's fault . . .'

'Eh? How is it your ma's fault?'

'Never mind,' she said.

'I would forget him, Evie. One thing you can be certain of, if he were to actually get your blessed letter telling him you're in the club, you'd probably never see him again.'

Evie sighed deeply.

'Do you think he was carrying on with Carol?'

'No, love. How many times do I have to tell you? Carol had her teeth into Frankie, her da knew his ma through the dockers' strike fund and they somehow thought they should marry and move to Birkenhead to run his seed business. Carol's da had engineered the whole drama, getting her to turn up at the factory and throwing herself at him.'

'That's what he told me, but I didn't believe him. He said he'd let her kiss him to make me feel jealous,' Evie said sadly. 'I never expected him to go to Canada. Not for a moment.' It pained her to hear the shattering details. Amongst the fog of information, it was too overwhelming.

'You wouldn't have listened to anyone. You sent him away.'

Evie crumpled. 'I need to tell him about the baby, but I don't know how. I've tried. I've even asked Stanley.'

'You could ask Carol?'

'I've tried that as well. But they've been moved out to Birkenhead. Everyone in this flaming town has gone.'

Edna sipped her mug of hot tea. 'And you won't hear of going to the mother and baby home and giving the baby up for adoption?'

Evie looked shocked. 'No. I don't trust nuns. Apart from Clotty.'

'Why not see if she can help you, then?'

'Clotty? She's still a nun. She'd hate me. She'd think I was disgusting.'

'Oh, love . . .'

'You haven't actually asked me if I want to keep the baby. Whether I want to . . . you know . . .'

'You mean – get rid of it? Do you?'

'Yes. No. I don't know.'

'How far gone are you?'

'Not sure.'

'How many of your monthlies have you missed?' Edna asked kindly.

'Three.'

'Come with me,' Edna said, grabbing her coat. 'We haven't got much time. But I think I can help you make up your mind.'

A small, winding alley, squashed between two rows of houses, led them to dizzying criss-crossing narrow lanes through back-to-back court houses and the recesses of dark, dank terraces. A woman threw a bucket of water into her back yard from an upstairs window. A cat mewed as it leapt from a pile of bottles and tried to avoid the splash.

'Looks like someone's had a good night,' said Edna, stepping around the bottles. They went down another tapered passage to a small flight of stone steps with a handrail to steady yourself. The smell of stale air hit the back of their throats in these streets. If there was any way to shock Evie into the seriousness of her situation, this was it.

They stopped for a minute at the bottom of the steps. 'You all right, Evie?'

Evie nodded.

'That's the spirit,' said Edna, reaching out to Evie and tucking a piece of hair behind her ear.

The building they finally arrived at reminded Evie of a teapot her grandmother had once had. Tall and thin, the teapot roof was the lid that you took off to put the tea leaves in. The little square dusty black windows hinted at something awful behind them. When Edna rang the bell, it was opened immediately

'Hello, Edna, love,' said the smiling woman who answered it. She wore an apron and was tall and thin, with long curtains of shiny black hair; her eyebrows were plucked into exaggerated arches. But she was friendly and cheerful. Edna had told Evie that this woman had once been a nurse, but as the babies had kept coming she'd eventually had to give up work. Now, with eight kids and counting, this was her way of bringing in a few extra bob. The way they hugged each other, it seemed as if they were old friends.

'You look nice, Ed. You done something different with your hair? It suits you.'

'One of them pin-up perms. Did it at home. You should try it.'

'Oh, I wish. Can't do a thing with mine. Poker straight. I've learned to live with it.'

Evie frowned. How could they talk about something as insignificant as hairstyles when she felt as if she was almost dying of torment right in front of them? But they carried on chattering as the woman took them into a room where there was an upside-down table and chairs piled up precariously in the corner. The heat was smothering. The air smelled of sour cheese.

'How are you?' said Edna to the woman.

'I'm not so bad. Paddy's driving me round the bend. Bone idle, that man. I've asked him to fix our back door so many times. Kids nearly do themselves an injury every day. I said to him, Paddy love, behind every nagging wife is a fella like you not doing what you're supposed to be doing. Who's this, then?' she said, turning to Evie.

Evie flinched.

The woman winked at her. 'You don't have to tell us your real name, ducky.'

'Oh,' said Evie. She drew her eyebrows together. 'Oh. Then I'm . . . I, erm . . . can't think . . . who should I be . . .' Why was it she couldn't even think of another name to call herself? 'Can I be Edna?' she blurted.

The woman laughed, not unkindly, but it made Evie blush and feel ridiculous. 'That might be a little confusing, ducky.' Evie nodded. 'Come into the back room and we can have a little chat. How far gone are you? You look about three and a half months to me.'

Evie followed her. The woman sat down on a battered velvet sofa, rearranged herself, and patted the seat beside her. There was an overpowering smell of Omo washing powder and a clock on the mantelpiece that ticked loudly. The corner of the room was curtained off with a piece of flowered material on a sagging nylon wire.

'Love is all fun and games, isn't it, until someone gets poked in the eye or ends up in the club,' she said. 'Don't worry. We'll sort you out, dear. Now, you understand how it works? Has Edna told you?'

Evie shrugged. 'Not really . . .'

'We all have our own way of doing things. But here, I will do the procedure behind that curtain, and then you'll go home, you'll start to bleed, and hopefully that will be that.'

That will be that? thought Evie with disbelief. She had heard plenty of stories. There had once been a girl called Maggie at the factory who had never come back; rumour had it that her parents had been so ashamed after finding her in a pool of blood on the cold stone floor of the lavvy that they'd buried her at night, with only the coffin, the priest and the church mice in attendance.

'I will give you a telephone number, and if anything goes wrong—'

'Wrong?' interjected Evie.

'If you have an infection, if the bleeding doesn't stop, or you're in pain, don't come back here, you understand? You must ring the number and describe what's happening to the person on the end of the line. If it's bad, they will probably tell you to go straight to the hospital. They have wards full of girls like you, especially on payday. The doctors and nurses probably won't even tell your parents, if they can fix you up.'

The way she spoke, as softly as a lullaby, chilled Evie. She felt her blood running cold.

'The, erm . . . what did you call it?' Her head swam.

'Procedure?'

'Yes, that's it. The procedure. What exactly will you do to me?'

'We all have different methods. I prefer to insert something through the cervix to pierce the amniotic sac, which will induce labour, leading to the expulsion of the foetus.'

Evie frowned.

'I don't know what you mean.'

'Don't worry. You're not the first girl who's come in here who has no idea what I'm talking about.

Your cervix is above your vagina, the bit between the neck of the womb and the uterus. Don't they teach you anything in school?'

'They showed us with a rabbit in biology. Sister made us cut one in half, but I couldn't look.'

'God help us . . .' The woman steepled her hands, turned them upside down. 'See here? Imagine the amniotic sac is at the top – here. Usually the baby will stay in there, snug and safe, for nine months. But if that sac breaks, your body rejects the foetus. You do know what I mean by the foetus?'

'Yes. The baby,' Evie said in a small voice.

'I don't like the soap-and-water method. Any cavity that fills with something that shouldn't be there – generally, it ends in tears.' The woman talked on. She looked like an ordinary housewife with her pinny and flowery slippers, but she certainly talked like an ex-nurse. Her voice seemed to grow loud and then soft. She also had something of the teacher in her; in fact, she reminded Evie of Sister Mary Oliphant.

'Inserting something into the cervix is by far the best way. It's all natural. Your body naturally expels the baby. Much safer than hot baths or gin. Or the dreaded knitting needles and coat hangers. We've got all sorts of things here to help us along.'

'Like what?'

The woman frowned. 'Well, a cervical dilator, for example. We can use a screw to gradually build up the pressure. That works very well. Opens you up. Gets things going quite nicely.'

Evie felt her eyes fill with tears, but she blinked

them away. She felt as if she had been clubbed around the head with all these unfamiliar words that she was struggling to picture. *Cervix, uterus, amniotic sac.* She had no idea. Even *vagina*, which she'd only ever heard called a tuppence, nunny, or minnie – she didn't really have a grip on what one looked like, not even her own. She knew Frankie had liked looking at it and how it had felt when he touched it, and that was why she was in this mess, but everything else was just guesswork.

'Now I'll leave you alone for a minute to gather your thoughts, and you can ask me any questions when I come back. Remember, though, we have to be discreet, Evie.'

'I thought you didn't know my name?'

'Oh sorry, dear. Edna must have let it slip.'

The woman glanced at the dark blue of the hem of Evie's threadbare coat, a tell-tale sign that it had been let down to get more wear out of it, probably because she couldn't afford a new one. She wondered if Evie had enough money for her services, even with the generous discount she usually gave to friends of friends. She left the room.

Evie sat miserably on the sofa. All this talk about 'the procedure'. Far from feeling relieved that she had found a solution to her 'problem', it had made her feel sad and frightened and ashamed.

There was a table pushed against the wall, and on it she could see a jug of water and a tray covered with a starched white linen cloth. Poking out from beneath the cloth was something glinting – a pointed metal instrument. Evie went over to take a closer look, and couldn't resist lifting a corner of the material to peek underneath.

The steel-pronged instrument was just like the fork they had at home for picking pickles out of a jar. Theirs had a wooden handle, but this one was made of metal. Lying next to it was a silver rod that looked rather like a long, thin bullet. There was a roll of gauze, a rubber pipette, curved scissors with long handles and an instrument with flat silver ends. Then another metal rod, long and thin, with a hoop at the end. And a glass syringe with a curved handle. Krysia and Edna had once talked about knitting needles, and how they could kill a girl. This woman had said she didn't use them, but Evie could have sworn that was exactly what was lying next to the syringe: a long, thin knitting needle.

There was a gentle knock on the door.

She dropped the cloth and moved in front of the table, white and shocked, as the woman bustled into the room.

'All right, honey? Happy? Take your knickers off, there's a good girl, and pop yourself on the couch.'

'Why?'

The woman faltered as she went to draw back the curtain. 'Well, because I have to examine you. We don't know how far gone you are.'

'Don't come near me!' Evie shot back at her.

'Now, now, love . . .' She moved nearer, reached out to calm Evie.

'Get your flippin' hands off me!' Evie yelled.

'Evie!' said Edna, flying into the room. 'What's going on? Why are you shouting? What's wrong?'

'Don't keep saying my name in front of her!' Evie, flailing, backed away towards the table like a trapped animal. She was so frightened and panicked, it was as if she might start hissing and spitting at any moment.

'Careful,' cried the woman, 'the tray!' But it was too late; it toppled off the table, crashing to the floor, the jug of water spilling. Pieces of steel slid off, slithering over the floor. One of the glass instruments smashed.

'Oh, love, look what you've gone and done . . . We're only trying to help you,' said Edna.

'It doesn't matter, Evie,' said the woman kindly, bending to pick up the things scattered all over the floor. 'It doesn't take a minute to sterilize them again.'

'I'm not Evie!' she cried, and stamped her foot. And as she crunched her fists into her eyes, she thought, I'm not Evie, I just want to be *Angel*. I want to be Angel, like my mother used to call me. I want to hear her say my name, and I want all this to go away. I want this *thing* inside me to disappear. But not like this. It can't be. Not in this cheerless room with the feeble fire in the grate, those sharp, pointy, sticky-out cruel objects and the smell of steamed cabbage, the sound of a girl crying through the wall and that woman's pitying coos and simpering smiles.

When they were outside they headed off down the street, out of the dank passage. It was a huge relief to be in the fresh air. Edna lit up a cigarette. 'Why d'you think I brought you here? I didn't actually want you to do it. Not when you might die. Even though my friend was a nurse, there are still risks.

And there are other ways, you know. You could have the child adopted.'

Evie sniffed. It was as if even breathing was an effort, she felt so downhearted.

'I just want you to understand how serious this is, Evie.' She patted Evie on the arm.

'So what now?' said Evie, mournfully. 'What's going to happen to me now?'

'Well, I would have thought that was obvious. You're going to have a baby. Babies have a habit of taking their own course, no matter what the world might think. So I don't see there's any way round telling your da, love,' Edna said, handing her a handkerchief.

'Then I guess it's time to go home and face the music,' said Evie sorrowfully. And, exhausted with the effort of it all and for lack of finding any more words to say on the matter, she sank to the cold gutter and sat on the edge of the pavement, dropped her head in her hands, and wept.

Eighteen

'A baby! You're having a baby?'

After a week of worry and dread, she had come home to find the house quiet. She knew she couldn't put off telling her father any longer.

He was standing with his back to her, supporting himself with his arms as he leaned over the range, head bent, hunched with the shock of what he had just been told. The bread and dripping he had prepared for himself lay untouched on a plate.

She looked at him dolefully.

'Take your coat off.'

She looked down at her stomach.

'Take it off!'

There was no hiding it now. Slowly she undid the buttons. As she pulled it off the shape of her belly was obvious, rising like a small hill below her breasts.

'Oh, Evie. If your mother—'

'Don't bring Mam into it.'

'Who's the father?'

'Frankie O'Hare.'

'Jesus. Jesus, Evie. You bloody stupid girl! The O'Hares are halfway to Canada.'

'I know . . .'

'Well, you'll have to get him back. You have to marry him. He'll have to come back and make an honest woman of you.'

'No.'

'What d'you mean, no?'

'I don't think he loves me anymore. I'll have this baby on my own.'

Her father banged his fist on the table. All his fury came out in the energy of the gesture. '*Love!* Don't say that word to me! How many times did your mother say the same! You wouldn't know what love was if it hit you in the face, Evie. It's not about feelings and swooning about the place, it's not Frank Sinatra and the movies, and Perry flippin' Como. It's about sticking to it, it's about keeping a family together, not about the Luigi flaming Galinaris of this miserable world . . . ' He stumbled, tried to row back what he had just said. 'If your ma hadn't gone and—'

Evie felt the words like a slap across the face.

She flinched. 'Gone and what? Died? Because I know that's a lie.' He looked ashen. 'I've known for years she went off with her bit on the side,' she said sorrowfully. 'Vic knows as well.'

He drew himself up, became angry again. 'Doesn't matter if she's dead or alive, makes no difference, you can't have the baby on your own! You have no idea, you have no idea at all. Little Miss Know-it-all.' He pointed a finger at the side of his head. 'What goes on in there?'

'I'll not have the same life as me mam had,' she muttered.

Her father slumped into a chair, dropped his head

into his hands. And then he did something she'd never seen him do before, through all the heartache and sadness she had watched him suffer. He began to cry.

She watched him for a moment, the tears splashing onto the oil tablecloth. It was awful to see. She would have found it easier if he had slapped her, hurled a dish across the room, yelled at her.

'Don't, Da,' she said, touching him gently on the shoulder. 'Don't. I'm sorry. I can't bear it.'

He bowed his head, smeared a finger under each of his eyes. 'A man shouldn't be crying,' he grunted. He pressed the palms of his hands against his temples, took a deep breath, swallowed down more tears. His fury seemed to have been overtaken by a sadness that hinted at the past.

'Why not? I think it's okay to cry,' she said, quietly.

'So what's it to be?' he said gruffly, blinking away tears, gathering himself.

'I don't know.'

'The nuns? Adoption?'

Her face clouded over. 'I'd rather die than go to one of them places.'

'What else are we to do? You've no choice.' He sighed. 'I'll ask Joan. She's in Ireland with her sister who's not at all well, but I hope she won't be there long.'

'No, Da!' She fell to her knees, tugged the corner of his shirt, and gave in to huge gulping sobs.

'So what are we going to do?' He moistened his dry lips with his tongue.

We, she thought. It was only now that she was

149

realizing this was as terrible for him as it was for her, and it hurt her to see it more than anything.

'I don't know just yet. Please don't tell Joan, though. She doesn't need to know if she's not here.'

'She's good in these situations.'

'Please don't. Not yet.'

'When is this baby due?'

She shrugged helplessly. 'Five, six, months, I reckon . . . Oh Da, I want to die,' she said, sobbing, collapsing into the chair and burying her face in the crook of her elbow. 'I hate myself.'

He shook his head sadly and finally went over, placed his hand on her shoulder, drew her to him gently. 'Pet. Don't cry. What a bloody mess.'

Evie sniffed, taking some comfort in the smell of his tobacco and Brylcreem, and in the fact that he wasn't telling her never to darken his door again. She knew plenty of girls whose fathers would have done just that, if the same had happened to them. It was what Edna had said would happen.

She sighed. 'So what now?'

He shrugged his drooping shoulders sadly, raised his palms. She tried to make sense of the gesture.

'What about if you try and find another fella to marry you? You're a bonny girl. I can think of half a dozen at the factory who would jump at the chance to have you as their wife.'

'Who?' she asked, bewildered.

'Jacky?'

'Jacky! He's your age, Da! He's got no front teeth!'

'Stanley, even.'

'Oh, Da,' she said. 'Stop it. You're not talking sense.'

Crestfallen, he pressed his fists into his eyes, took her by her sagging arms. 'Love, it's late. Let's try and sleep on it. We'll come up with a plan in the morning, shall we?'

She nodded, weak with shame and sadness. At the door she stopped, turned. 'I'm sorry, Da . . .'

He looked up at her, could barely meet her eyes.

'I lost your mam to that lounger,' he said, raspy and taciturn. 'I'll not lose you, love. Go to bed. We'll decide what to do in the morning. And one more thing. Don't do anything stupid.'

'What d'you mean?'

'I've heard about those places. That's all I'm saying. Girls die,' he grunted.

'I know,' she said quietly. 'I'll not do that.'

He hadn't really given her much hope on any front, but then, it was late and they were both exhausted and upset. It would be easier to talk tomorrow.

Evie rose before the sun, but went back to bed and stayed in her room until after the children had gone to Sunday school. She spent the time just lying there, staring at the crack in the ceiling. Percy Rathbone had turned up with fresh warm eggs laid by his hen. He lived in one of the few remaining court houses in Liverpool – dreadful Edwardian tenements, four storeys high, built on all sides around a small, airless, dark back yard, but useful to keep a chicken in as there was no route of escape.

Evie sat on the corner of her bed, listening to Percy and her father talking downstairs. A few minutes later, after she heard the sound of the door slamming

151

and Percy saying 'Best be off,' she heard the pan sizzling and could smell her father cooking an egg.

She straightened her pretty blouse, did up the buttons. She had never liked the way Rathbone turned up unannounced, and she decided she didn't want it to happen again. She had never liked the way he looked at her. Pushing the thought aside, she went into her father's bedroom, folded hospital corners into the bed sheets, tucked them into the straw mattress and then went downstairs.

'Tea,' her father said, when she came downstairs and found him waiting for the kettle to whistle. 'Proper cuppa. I'll not drown the pot . . .' he said, smiling at her.

He sounded surprisingly chirpy. And pulling the chair up to the table, he even had a gleam in his eye. 'I knew I'd feel better in the morning. I've had an idea, love. Auntie Renie,' he said.

'Auntie Renie?' echoed a bewildered Evie.

Nineteen

My dear brother Bill,
I received your letter. It took me a little while to take it all in, but from what you said, if anyone can deal with this situation, it's Evie. She's got spirit and vim, that girl. We all saw how well she coped when Josephine left. She became like a mother to Vic. And at thirteen. She was barely a child herself. I'm not one to judge, so I'll leave that to other folks and pray for her soul.

I was upset to hear about the father. Run off to Canada, you say? And the baby is due in five months' time? Well, a family crisis brings folk together, I think, which is why I'll be coming to see you as soon as she has the child, as you have asked.

Other news. Davey is working all hours at the factory. It's going as well as can be expected and they say that a job as manager is on the cards. Mind you, these southerners are a different breed to us northerners. I prefer it when people say it as it is, call a

153

spade a spade. They talk around the subject down here, an awful lot of dancing around the blackberry bush. Leaves you feeling out of sorts sometimes.

That aside, we are happy with the move. It's a long way to come for work, but it had to be done. There's certainly more money down here, and being a seaman is no job for a family man. But you don't need me to tell you that. The Ford factory treats the workers well. They have dances each week at the club and last month Denny Dennis came to sing. They have a nurse on site, check you've not got nits or the start of rickets, small things like that, and if you're feeling a bit dicky, they'll send you to the doctor or put you in a room until you're better. And we are renting a little prefab in Dagenham, so a bit different from home, no upstairs! Which is a boon, I think. And cleaner, brighter, newer somehow. They've made such a big effort to improve things down here, to get back on their feet after Hitler bombing them to pieces. And with a garden!

We've even got a budgie, can you believe. A green one with a black beak, in a cage in the living room. He's different to the canary at Wilmington Street. They say that if you keep at it, you can teach it to say words and speak to you. The children are thrilled to bits. Lots of new-fangled ideas down here. We have a toaster! I'll tell you more about the toaster when I see you. Anyway, all things considered, it certainly beats standing in the pen on the dock road, or waiting at the corner of Aintree Road with all the other poor fellows in desperation for someone to come along with a job. Is it still the same at the docks? Still not many ships? It's no time to be a seaman when there's not much work, but of course you knew that years ago.

We miss the family. We miss Evie. Remember when she was little? She always asked me to hard-boil her an egg, and I could never persuade her to try my soft chucky eggs no matter how hard I tried. Stubborn. Let's hope she doesn't dig her heels in like that when it comes to giving up this baby.

Perhaps we can persuade you to come and visit? The other day we had a trip to Southend. The kids had a grand time at the fair. Just like New Brighton. Except paddling in the sea is a lot warmer, and a lot less mucky than the Mersey. I am so looking forward to meeting the child when it arrives.

Your loving sister,
Renie

P.S. Everyone is talking about Clement Attlee down here. What he's going to do next. How he's doing a grand job of getting us all back on our feet again now this war is over. And his Children's Act for orphans and deprived kiddies was a wonderful idea, wasn't it? Have you read about it in the paper?

Bill scanned the letter for a third time. Why was she talking about the Children's Act? Was that anything to do with Evie and her baby? He propped the envelope up on the mantelpiece. Renie hadn't mentioned how exactly, or when exactly, she would take the child back to Dagenham. But these were minor details and arrangements, maybe too complicated to put down on paper. And it gave him heart to see that the words were there on the page. They were a family that pulled together in times of crisis. And this was a crisis if ever there was one. Renie knew now the dire straits that they were all in, and she was the one who could save them – not some useless article buggered off to Canada who poor, resentful Evie would only have had to stare at over a bowl of chicken broth for the rest of her life.

On reflection, he decided he should put the letter away in a drawer. He didn't want Evie reading too much into it. Besides, he still hadn't entirely put aside the idea of finding a fella for Evie to marry – but failing that, Renie adopting the child was the best solution yet. He felt certain that Renie would take the child straight back to Dagenham when she came. He felt sure that if the baby looked anything like Evie when she was born, with those big, mournful, searching eyes, she would find it impossible to refuse.

Twenty

'Mabel's going to leave soon, you know,' Ken said to Lawrence when he found him sitting on an upturned packing case going through his lines on stage. Ken was standing behind a spotlight clamped onto a metal pole. He suddenly swung it round to face him head-on, causing Lawrence to squint against the hard glare. 'She might have another job.'

Lawrence shrugged indifferently. He didn't seem that concerned at all.

'Going off to London. Some fellow from the Smoke saw the matinee and decided she had the right face for a movie. Something about playing a munitions girl who falls in love with a soldier. Sorry, pal. You all right?'

'What? Turn that blasted thing off,' Lawrence said.

Ken pointed the light in the opposite direction.

Lawrence would miss Mabel, of course, but the fat man in the suit with chubby fingers, smoking a fat cigar, had no doubt promised her the world – and that made the Playhouse repertory company pale in comparison. 'To tell you the truth, I always knew she would trade me in, Ken. Just didn't think it was going to be for such an ugly brute as him. I saw him sitting in the stalls. Red-faced, fingers like bloody sausages. Thought she would have a bit more taste, but hey ho: that's actresses for you. Unreliable, and fickle to boot.'

Ken nodded in agreement.

'What's happened to Sugar Girl?' Lawrence said. 'Not seen her for weeks.'

'Not sure. Biddy said she didn't really need to come and collect our debts. Besides, it was Tate's idea. Sugar Girl was a kind of walking advertisement. They have fellows in rooms thinking all this stuff up now.'

'Well, I need her. I miss her. Miss seeing her little turned-up nose, and them freckles. Maybe I'll see if I can get her back.'

'How?'

'I don't know. Find a job for her, maybe? Proper job. She could work in the box office. We need some fresh young blood around the place.'

Ken raised an eyebrow. '*You* do, you mean. Now Mabel's off.'

'Mabel's a game girl, but I'm coming to the conclusion that the key to a happy life would be to marry an ordinary, unremarkable young woman. Like Sugar Girl.' Lawrence took a rolled-up script from the back pocket of his trousers, removed a pencil from behind his ear and began idly to scribble notes. 'After five years on the road, I've realized that. Theatre people . . . well, one minute we're one big family, and the next we're at each other's throats. And my God, *actresses* . . .'

'Are you complaining? Being surrounded by girls like you are? You turns – you're so bloody jammy.

I wish I had your life, Lawrence. When I see you up there on the stage, I'm green with envy. I'm hauling sets and flats and lights all day whilst you're fighting off your leading ladies, who always seem to fall in love with you and leap into bed with you three days into the first week's run. No one looks at us fellows behind the scenes.'

'Let me tell you how it works, Ken,' Lawrence said, putting down his script and offering Ken a cigarette before lighting one for himself. Ken knew he was in for one of Lawrence's speeches. He really ought to be a writer, not an actor, he thought.

'When you walk onto the stage and look out into the auditorium, you can just about make out shapes and pairs of eyes in the first few rows – just grimaces and smiles – and you can hear the rippling of laughter, intakes of breath, gasps. You look back at the girl, and you soon feel quite separate from everything out there. Like it's just you and her.' He gestured, painting the scene with his cigarette in the air. 'You're bonded by terror, that rush of adrenalin. You have this special connection, whispering in the wings, adjusting her costume, looking into the whites of her eyes as you struggle to remember your lines and she saves you from sudden death; and then you go over and over the near-catastrophe as you share drinks in the pub after the show. It brings you together – nothing else comes near it. And of course you end up in bed with her.'

'Like I said, where's the hardship in that?'

'Ah well, you see. It's all smoke and mirrors. Because the minute the show is over you go off and lead your separate lives, and if you've been stupid enough to promise to a girl that there can be more to what you've just shared on stage, out there in the real world it all falls apart. And then you try as hard as you can, but you can never get that magic back. This business is cruel, all right.'

Ken wondered if Lawrence was expecting him to applaud.

Lawrence crossed one leg over the other and ran his finger down the crease in his trousers. 'Sugar Girl is not like that. Perhaps I need someone normal in my life, someone who's not ridiculous,' he mused. 'A normal girl who's used to a factory where people have works outings to Blackpool, exchange a kiss and then marry, have children. Perhaps that's where I've been going wrong. You'd have liked the way she spoke to the rat-catcher. Mabel would've just screamed and run away. God, she's such an actress. Put a mirror in the bottom of a swimming pool and that one would drown herself, that's for sure.'

'Sounds like you've fallen a little bit in love with the factory girl. But from where I'm standing, you actor types are pretty unreliable and fickle an' all. You be careful with that lass. She looks to me like she's carrying the world around on her shoulders. She doesn't want another dollop of drama from you to add to whatever grief she's already suffering. Don't you go playing cat and mouse with that poor thing.'

'Would I?'

'You would, Lawrence. You would.'

Twenty-One

The evening had slowly descended; the kitchen utensils lay about and glinted in the light of the gas lamp outside. Her father's mess was everywhere. Every surface was covered with split bags of flour, eggshells courtesy of eggs from Rathbone's hen, overflowing ashtrays. Empty bowls, unwashed, lay in the sink. A glass of brandy was on the table, a piece of tripe congealing in a dish.

Evie sat down, rubbing her tired eyes. Vic was at the Boys' Brigade and the girls had just gone upstairs to bed. Her father, now that he had found himself another job on the guy ropes at Stanley Dock and helped out on a stall selling cans of paraffin at Paddy's market on a Saturday, would be spending his wages in the pub. She had planned to clear up, but she was exhausted. Six months into her pregnancy, and she was finding it tiring in a way she had never imagined. She soon dozed off in the armchair.

'Through here,' said a voice outside in the back yard, waking her suddenly and making her sit bolt upright with a gasp. How long had she been asleep? Quickly she jumped up from the chair, rushed upstairs to her room.

'Evie! Evie! Get down here,' cried her father,

banging about downstairs, scraping chairs across the floor and slamming doors. She could tell he'd been drinking more than usual by the slurring of his speech.

'Wait on,' she answered.

She came back down the stairs to find him standing in front of the range, rubbing his hands together and then holding them up to warm against the fire, laughing. There was Neville Reilly standing beside him, skinny as a toothpick and looking terribly tall in their small, squat house.

'Hello, Evie.'

She was shocked that her father had brought someone home. Couldn't he see she was pregnant and not fit for company? What was the point of him taking two jobs so she could hide indoors, if he started bringing people to the house? Slightly flustered, she discreetly fastened her shirt when she noticed she had left the top button undone, and pulled her thick crocheted shawl tighter round her shoulders.

'Hello, Neville.'

He didn't look so bad, lit only by the flames of the fire and the gas lamp; he was strong and broad-shouldered, a tall, youthful boy compared to her father, a small pale man in his fifties. But when he grinned – well, that *smile*. That toothless smile. What was her father thinking of? This one really was worse than all the others.

He stood there, twisting his cap.

'Sit down, Neville,' said her father.

Evie could smell drink on both of them. She turned her back, widened her eyes at her dad, and mouthed

'No!' Then she spun back around to face Neville. 'I was about to go to bed.'

'Bed? Surely you've half an hour?' said her father, knitting his brows together, signalling his displeasure. 'Nev has been telling me stories of what happened to him in France. Killed a German. Don't you want to hear them?'

'Another time. I'm dead on me feet, Da.'

'I'll go. Don't want to keep you.' stammered Neville. He was as dopey as he was ugly, this fella.

Evie twitched a smile. She felt bad for him. Another one of her father's grand ideas. Why couldn't they just wait for Auntie Renie to come and take the baby? She'd become resigned to that idea. After all, what choice did she have?

Her father pulled out a chair. The legs scraped across the stone floor. 'Stay, Nev, lad. It's early yet. Have a drink . . .'

'Right . . . Right y'are.' He sat at the table. Evie's father poured out a beer, pushed the glass towards him. He slurped it down in practically one go.

Evie stared down at the table. The silence yawned into a chasm; she glared into her lap, then moved an invisible coin on the floor with the toe of her foot.

'What did I tell you?' said Bill. 'She's got a nice pair of ankles. Nice hair an' all . . .'

'Who's *she*? The cat's mother?' said Evie, jerking up her head, her green eyes flashing.

'Well, if you're going to sit here like the dumb man of Manchester, someone's got to kick things off.'

Neville blushed to the tips of his ears.

'You're embarrassing the poor fella,' said Evie.

'No, I'm not. You embarrassed, Nev?'

Neville squinted into his glass. His eyes looked fixed and glazed. He finished the last dregs. The drink repeated on him, a little belch, the smell of beer escaping into the room, escaping into the same air Evie breathed. If she couldn't even bear to breathe the same air as him, what hope was there?

'No, Mr O'Leary . . . But I best gerroff . . .'

He stood, nodded, smoothed down his lank hair so that it sealed against his forehead, and left, skirting around the single ceiling bulb they could never afford to switch on, ducking under the door frame as he left the room.

'Good God, Evie! So what was wrong with Neville Reilly? Don't tell me you're still hankering after Frankie O'Hare? And him ruining your life. Disappearing into thin air and leaving you with a flaming baby.'

Evie stood, startled by his tone.

'Not thin air, Da – Canada.'

'Neville's a nice lad.'

'Neville is as wet as a haddock's bathing costume! You're not really suggesting I should let him anywhere near me. He smelled. He actually smelled . . .'

'Nowt wrong wi' a bit of muck. That's from the stables at Haight's yards, that's all . . . Poor fellow can't help it.'

'I just can't. No.'

Bill hunched his shoulders, banged his fist on the table. 'Beggars can't be choosers, love. I'm beginning to wonder if Renie is serious. I've not heard from her for months. Neville would have turned a blind eye. He said as much . . .'

Her mouth fell open. She looked shocked and upset. She felt the heat gushing up to her neck and prickling her cheeks. 'I thought we were trying to keep this a secret. I thought that's why you made me leave Tate's!'

'Secret? You told Edna. I had to tell Stanley, to explain why you'd left. Neville wouldn't care . . . fella like him. He'd look the other way. Let's be serious. How else is he going to get a beauty like you?'

Evie winced. 'But *I* care that you told Neville about the baby! It's just tittle-tattle. And to think how much trouble we've been to, so we could hide it! You know how gossip gets around. Ooh, have you heard, Bill's Evie's gone and had a babby. She's one of them fallen women now. What would her poor mother say about that!'

'Look, love. I've done the best by you, haven't I? I'm trying to find your ma to tell her, but no joy. I've got myself a job at the docks, working day in, day out to get enough money to put food on the table. And I agreed we'd stay away from the bloody nuns and wait for Renie. But you still keep going on about Frankie coming back from Canada. Well, he's not going to. Not ever.'

'He might have done already. How would I know?'

She smarted. This dreadful thing she had done. It had picked at the seams of their lives, and she knew before long everything would start to unravel.

'We don't know exactly when Renie will get here. So you'll see Neville just in case. What have you got to lose? You might take to him. Then you wouldn't have to go to St Jude's to have the baby. You might

165

be able to have it at a proper hospital, with a ring on your finger and Neville on your arm.'

'St Jude's? What's St Jude's?'

'The home for fallen girls.'

'Why would I go there?'

She knew that he was getting angry when his brown eyes seemed to fleck with black. 'Well, where d'you think you're going to have the bairn? Whether Renie takes it or not, you still have to push the damn thing out of you . . . You can't do it on your own.'

'Thing? Don't call it a thing,' she said sadly.

'You'll let Neville start courting you, and in time you'll be grateful. He's got a room in Upper Parly Street . . . We all want to feel like we're starting afresh. Like we all had to do after the war.'

Starting afresh! she thought. She wished she could imagine that: a future. All she could think of right now was hiding in the back bedroom the minute anyone knocked at the door, to keep the gossip at bay. She crossed the linoleum to join her father. Sliding an arm around his waist from behind, she rested her head on his shoulder. 'I'm sorry,' she said, coaxing him out of his black mood. 'But I can't. Just give me a little more time. I'll think of something. And, as you said, what about Auntie Renie?'

'What about her?'

'You wrote to her again, yes?'

'Yes, but . . . I don't know. I don't know now.'

'She'll come to Liverpool and take the baby back to Dagenham with her. I have an instinct for these things.'

'You! An instinct. Bloody baby about to come

slithering out of you, ten toes, ten fingers, and a bawl that will probably be heard other side of the Mersey, and you up to no good with Frankie O'Hare morning, noon and night, no doubt. Didn't have much of an instinct then, did you?'

Evie's face crumpled and she started to blink back tears.

'Oh God, now, love. I never meant to say that. Come here. I'm sorry. That's not going to get us anywhere.' He sighed. 'When Joan comes back from Ireland, I won't be so quick to rise to a temper. Your mother always said that was my weakness . . .'

Evie sniffed. Joan again. Thankfully, he had kept off the subject of Joan since he had waved her off to her sister's in Dublin, and for that Evie was grateful. She did love her dad, despite his gruff manner and his exasperation at the 'situation'. She was only too aware that most other fathers, and some mothers even, wouldn't have done that for her. He could have turfed her out. He could have so easily sent her to the St Jude's place already.

Twenty-Two

Evie spent months at home behind closed doors, hardly going out, not even to the shops, all the time amazed at how her body was rapidly changing. Pink marks mysteriously appeared like fish swimming under her skin, on her tummy and on her breasts; her back hurt, and she couldn't sleep. Her swelling belly meant she was finding it difficult to move. Holy Joan still showed no signs of returning from her sister's in Ireland, and that was one thing she was grateful about. But the children had been aware of something strange going on in the house. It was November now, and they seemed to have accepted the secret behind the doors of 33 Coghlan Street without having to be told to keep it. Vic had moved into the third bedroom to share a bed with his sisters and left Evie the box room without a word of argument.

One evening, Clotty had turned up in the kitchen.

'Oh, Evie, what's happened now?' she had said, unable to take her eyes off Evie's belly. But she hadn't been disgusted at all, mostly sad, and even kind, telling Evie that a life was worth celebrating no matter how tragic the circumstances. She had said, wasn't it perfect that her aunt was going to adopt the baby, and she had made that clear to the sisters at St Jude's.

The good news was that they were happy for her to go there six weeks before she was due, and they would deliver the child. Evie insisted that this baby would be going home with its mother – no nuns would get their hands on her little one (present company excepted, of course). Clotty had told her not to worry, that it happened a lot more often than you'd think these days, plucky girls without a husband, returning home alone with their baby. Plucky? thought Evie. I'm not plucky. Just desperate.

Clotty left, and Evie went upstairs. The pain was sudden and startling. Should she fling open the window and call her back? She pressed her fist into her side, but by the time she heaved herself off the bed, the pain had vanished. She slumped back down, pulled the covers over her head, and shifted from side to side, dreading another night with the baby kicking and squirming, and waking up every hour to face the next day exhausted from lack of sleep.

It was three o'clock when the twinges started again. It was four in the morning when they turned into real pain. It was five o'clock when the pain disappeared, six when her father put his head round the bedroom door. Evie reassured him that she was fine. No, the baby wasn't coming, her body just kept tricking her into thinking it was. It was too early.

But it was eight o'clock, daylight slicing across the parlour floor, when the children had left for school and her father had long gone to work, that there was a gush of water from between her legs – and then such agony, so terrible, as though she were being split in two, so awful that she thought she was dying.

'Jesus, Mary and Joseph!' she cried. 'Help, someone!' But she barely had time to gulp another mouthful of air before the child just slithered out of her onto the peg rug. And she was *so* shocked. Shocked that despite all this blood that had come out of her, staining the rug, sopping her nightclothes, pooling in the grooves of the stone flags, she wasn't dying after all. That instead she was just having her baby. And there he was: her son. His little face squashed up in velvety folds. The colour of a ripe plum. Bawling so loud that she imagined the Liver birds flying off over the Mersey in fright. And there she was, huddled on the cold floor, cradling her perfectly formed, slippery infant in her arms and gazing into his eyes, thinking he was the most beautiful thing she had ever seen – and thankfully not within a sniff of St Jude's, but with no clue what she was going to do about it.

'Where are you, Evie?' said a voice.

'Sister Mary Clotilda?' Evie said, turning her head towards the door. The nun's blurred, gently moving silhouette sharpened into focus.

'Ssh . . .' she said, coming over and mopping Evie's brow with a handkerchief. 'Oh my word! The baby! Your father asked me to check on you. Didn't like the sounds that were coming through the bedroom wall in the night. But he had no idea you were this close! Let me get a bowl of soapy water and some towels . . .'

Evie heard a tap running. Sister Mary Clotilda left the sink and wiped the mewling infant clean with a flannel. She had a leather bag with her that fastened with a clasp, and from it she took a pair of scissors.

'Oh, look at him,' she said, misty-eyed, as she cut and tied the snaky gristle that both revolted and mesmerized Evie. 'He's a beauty, Evie.'

After a short while, under Clotty's guidance, Evie put him on her breast, his mouth searching out her nipple.

'Like this,' said the nun. She touched the top of the baby's head, coaxed him to clamp his lips onto her breast. Evie could feel the strange prickling sensation of her milk filling the child's mouth.

'Now what?' she murmured, looking down at her baby.

Clotty smiled, pushed a piece of damp hair behind Evie's ear. 'In a minute I'll ask you to push and we'll deliver the placenta. And that's it. You're done. Then all you need to do is sleep. Sleep Evie, dear. Rest well and may God bless you both.'

Twenty-Three

The child was in his makeshift cot, a bottom drawer emptied of old petticoats and stockings. When she looked in to check on him, Evie could see the rise and fall of his chest. In the few short weeks that had passed since he had come into this world, he was getting to look more beautiful each day. Leaning down, she kissed him gently on his forehead and stroked a lock of hair with her finger.

She had decided to call him Terence. It had a ring to it, she thought: an air of better things to come. Unfortunately, her father was beginning to call him Curly, he said it was because of the curl of hair that fell over his forehead. The name was beginning to stick – Vic and the girls were starting to use it when they cradled and fussed over him, and Evie didn't like it much.

It was the middle of the day and the olive-green curtains were closed, though low shafts of light still bled through at the gap between window sills and the frayed and worn curtains, which meant particles of dust jitterbugged in the sunbeams. Lately the girls were becoming more difficult to keep at bay with their constant questioning and badgering about the baby. Vic understood that this was about the worst thing that could happen to a girl, but he had been told that soon it would change. Everything would be resolved before Christmas, which was fast approaching. The new decade would bring a fresh start. The baby would be adopted, or Evie was going to marry a boy – it was just that nobody was sure which boy yet.

'But I hate that it's always so dark in here. Can't hardly see my hand in front of me face. The oil lamp is making me feel sick all the day,' he'd said that morning.

'Why do we have to keep the curtains shut half the time? It's daytime,' added Sylvie as she got ready for school.

More often than not, Evie swept away these comments by gesturing vaguely in the air and saying 'It's not forever,' but that was beginning to wear thin. How much longer? she had thought, bustling the girls out of the door with a glance at her father. How much longer hiding like this, waiting for Renie?

The only time Evie had left the house had been to do a little bit of grocery shopping and to register Terry's birth. She had dealt with that by disguising herself in an old coat of her father's and an old cloth cap pulled over her ears, with her red hair pushed up inside it. She was frightened of anyone who might knock on the door or turn up unannounced, or worse, with an idea in their head that they might know what would be best for her and her child. Though of course, with each hour, each minute she spent with her baby, she grew less keen for Renie to come. She dreaded her aunt's arrival, even though she knew it was her only choice.

173

Evie took the fireguard and placed it in front of the fire, draping Victor's shorts and her father's long johns over it; before long, steam rose from them and filled the small room. She prodded the fire with a poker whilst sitting on a small wicker chair that her father had brought back from abroad during the war.

She missed that sometimes, the house full of treasures and trinkets he'd produced from his deep pockets after returning home from his travels with the merchant navy. Curtain rings from Egypt. A tin whistle from Jamaica. A pair of small carved birds from Norway. It had all stopped when, halfway through the war, her mother got ill and suddenly disappeared for a week to somewhere mysterious for 'rest and recuperation'; or at least, that was the story. Bill had wanted to be a part of the war and do his bit, but as everyone had said, he could hardly have gone off to sea again and left four children in the house alone – especially with what was going on between their mother and that Italian. Didn't he have to 'do his bit' for his family? For a while he had continued to enlist as a merchant seaman, just short trips to Scotland or Southampton, but soon someone had come knocking on the door. *You can't leave these kiddies on their own without a mother. Look at the state of them!*

Bill, sitting by the range, took an onion from his pocket and started to peel it, placing the outer skin on a plate. Then he bit into the onion whole. Evie couldn't help wrinkling her nose as the fierce smell of raw onion filled the room.

'What, love? Best remedy for a cold,' he said, his

eyes watering and choking slightly. 'Now, I have some news,' he added. 'I've finally heard from your Auntie Renie.'

Evie's heart lurched. She sat up ramrod straight on the wicker chair.

'She's coming to Liverpool in a few weeks' time. I didn't talk too much over the phone. I called her from the Exchange. I thought it was best not to, with the operator listening and the line crackling. But good news, eh?'

Evie didn't reply. Good news? No – terrible news.

'You need to put things in order, Evie. And you need to do it quickly. The child needs christening. Renie's a God-fearing woman, never missed Mass on a Sunday, holy days of obligation, saints' days, Benediction. It'll be the first thing she'll ask . . . Curly is three weeks old now . . .'

'Don't call him Curly. He has a name. Terry. Call him Terry.'

Her father grunted.

'I can't bear the thought of them nuns and priests shaming me when they find out I haven't got a husband. I'm just not sure I even want to step foot in a church.'

'I've told you, they'll want to make Terry one of their own. Make sure he's baptized. That's all they'll be thinking about. Not you. Now, sit down . . .'

Evie dropped a dish into the Belfast sink. Water slopped over the side and onto the draining board. She sat down, scraping her chair across the stone tiles.

Now clasping a tankard of beer tightly with both hands, her father raised it to his lips. Seeing his face reflected in the glass of the window, Evie thought he looked a little more tired these days, a little older. She sank further into her chair opposite him. On the table was a tureen. In the silence she took off the piece of frayed linen that covered it, tore a hunk from the stale loaf on a plate, and dipped the crust into the skim of the cold vegetable stew. She swallowed a mouthful. Three weeks since she'd had the baby, and she still couldn't eat properly. Food just clogged her throat and made her feel slightly sick.

'Love, you knew this day was going to come. I know it might break your heart in two; I'm not made of stone. But at least this way you'll still be able to see him from time to time. You'll be able to watch him grow up, albeit from a distance. Besides, Vic might have been sworn to secrecy, but the girls are beginning to ask questions about where the baby came from. What am I supposed to tell them – the stork brought it? Found it under the blessed gooseberry bush?'

Too late for the truth to come out about that now, Evie thought bitterly. Perhaps if he had told her how you actually make babies, if he had told her that the nonsense about doing it whilst you were standing up was just an old wives' tale, they wouldn't be in this mess. But that wasn't a father's job, she thought sadly. If only her mother had been around to have that conversation.

'Flamin' onion,' Bill said as a tear rolled onto his cheek and meandered down the grooves in his face, following the deep, craggy lines etched into his jowls.

Evie's tea turned cold in her mouth. She could see

a pigeon hopping about out in the street. Its plumage was dirt-black, like everything around here.

'Well, off you go. I changed him whilst you were doing the grate,' said her father. He pointed to the terry cloth soaking in a bucket. 'Man shouldn't have to do this,' he muttered.

'I know, Da,' she said in a quiet voice. 'I'm sorry.'

'Bit late now for apologies,' he said. Moisture brimmed in his eyes. She didn't know whether it was the onion or the desperate matter of the baby, but seeing his baggy, wet eyes and his crooked arthritic fingers raking through his pepper-coloured hair was almost too much to bear, and she glanced away. The guilt was awful. It hurt her to meet his gaze these days – she felt as though she had let him down so badly. And it had taken such a toll on him. Still square-jawed, he was now gaunt with hollowed-out cheeks, his scraggy neck showing lavender veins underneath the crepey skin.

She could hear the faint mewling of her baby, the sound of his crying seeping through the walls and floorboards. She could feel the milk in her breasts prickling and knew the rags that she had put down her liberty bodice wouldn't be enough to sop up the moisture. Pulling her cardigan round her, she shivered, dreading the wet patches appearing on her blouse. 'Baby's crying, Da,' she said, getting to her feet.

Padding upstairs, she opened the door of the darkened room. There he was. The boy in a drawer. Her heart ached just to see him. He had a look of Frankie about him. Seemed to grow more peachy each day. He was pinker than ever, his cheeks rosy. His fat, kicking legs stretched out, pointing his toes to their tips in happiness as she lifted him from the cot and pulled him to her. And oh God, the smell of him. Still so creamy and new. And that smile, such innocence. She unbuttoned her blouse, allowed him to nestle in to her and search out her nipple with his mouth. She could feel his tiny hands grasp her flesh, smiled at his yearning as he clutched at her, dug his soft tiny nails into her skin, and fixed his large round eyes on hers. And with each one of his snuffles and nuzzles and tender breaths, the burst of love that hit her like a train – an actual physical jolt to her body – made the thought of giving him up even more impossible to bear.

Twenty-Four

Mabel, standing on the top steps of Lime Street station, pulled her fur stole around her tiny shoulders. Christmas had been and gone in a whirl, back-to-back shows – *A Christmas Carol* and *Cinderella* – with barely time to draw breath. Ken had invited her and Lawrence to his little flat in Penny Lane on Christmas Day and cooked a turkey 'with all the trimmings'! 'What a feast!' Mabel had cried. They had exchanged gifts, worn silly hats and played charades. She had bought everyone at the theatre trinkets. But things were always lean after Christmas. Besides, this fellow was one of *her* fellows. He was a lonely chap, and quite content to shower her with pound notes for the thrill of an hour dancing and drinking with a beautiful girl – the kind of girl she knew full well that he wouldn't ever expect to brush up against, even in his wildest dreams.

He was waiting for her on the forecourt. Stanley Mulhearn. As she trotted up to meet him in her high heels, she smiled and waved.

'Stanley!' she said. 'You look smashing, sweetie! You got the money for a taxi cab?'

He nodded, and they made their way to the cab rank behind the Adelphi Hotel. She pecked him on the cheek, and he blushed as she snuggled up to him on the back seat.

'Warm my hands,' she said.

The very thought of this girl linking her arm in his, chattering away with him, letting him blow on her fingers and rub her palms – it was enough to make him faint with the pleasure of it. And she knew all right, she knew the effect she was having as she pressed her thigh against his, the way she kept touching his knee, straightening out his collar, speaking into his face, breathing on him and calling him darling, as she asked him how his mother was with her dicky ticker, how was his job at Tate's? She hoped Christmas hadn't been too lonely, she knew it was hard for a chap like him.

'What you need is a proper girl in your life,' she said.

'Why would I want anyone else when I've got you?' he said. 'Not worth the bother.'

'Oh Stanley, am I enough?' she said. 'It's all very well taking me shopping for silk stockings and to the occasional tea dance, but a chap needs more. I'm only sorry I can't give you that.'

'You have no idea, love . . .'

'Please God, you're not falling in love with me. This is nice, our *arrangement*. And I love our trips out. I like our cups of tea and choosing lipsticks in Owen Owen's. But don't you need a real sweetheart?'

He looked at her, touched her cheek.

'No.'

She kissed his rough hand. 'Well, I'll not complain, dearie.'

After they got out of the cab, they headed towards Blackler's department store. The Christmas sale had started. People were already coming out of the brass revolving doors with bags full of shopping.

They made their way to the fifth floor in the elevator, newly refurbished with oak panels and brass buttons. In the restaurant, with its black and white tiles and potted aspidistras on stands, there was the gentle sound of cutlery on fine china. A string quartet was playing a Brahms lullaby. Mabel thrust out her chin and, aware that the *maître d'* was giving them sideways glances as they walked in, almost dared him to look her straight in the eye. They did look an odd couple: Stanley was a lot older, and he clearly couldn't take his eyes off her. His hand was on the small of her back, guiding her between customers, while she, young and glamorous, seemed like she didn't care a jot. The head waiter handed them both a menu and showed them to a table.

After tea and delicious scones, Mabel said, 'Shall we try a waltz today?'

Stanley nodded. As he guided her round the floor, she was struck as usual by how good a dancer he was. And although his breath smelled of tobacco and his hand felt clammy on her tiny waist, he didn't look too bad. He always made an effort – his shoes were polished and his hair swept back tidily off his face.

'Steady on, love,' she said as she felt a hand slide down over her hips.

'Sorry,' he stuttered.

Why does he put himself through such torture?

181

she wondered. But that's men for you. And she had met her fair share in her time. The fellow who paid her to have dinner in Cooper's dining rooms, dinner with a strange sort of twist – when he gave her the nod, he liked her to shout at him that he was a good-for-nothing cad, and he would squirm with pleasure at the humiliation while everyone dropped their mouths and stared. What on earth that was about, she had no idea. Or the chap who just liked to curl up and cry in her lap; or the one who would come to her dressing room and massage her feet after a quiet matinee.

Some, of course, wanted to take it up a notch, but even Mabel had her line in the sand, despite the impression she sometimes deliberately gave off. 'You're very respectful,' she would say to Stanley with a smile. 'Probably because you know I'm not *that* kind of girl. Here, let me do that,' she added, unbuttoning his top button. 'Oops,' she said, as her skirt slipped up her thigh and threatened to reveal the top of her stockings when she leaned forward and crossed one leg over the other . . . and she could see the blood rush to his face, rush to every part of him, probably.

'Some of the girls at the factory . . .' he said, stuttering. 'No morals. The girl I sent to the theatre – can you believe it . . .' He leaned forward and whispered. 'I had to let her go. She was unmarried and clearly pregnant. Now she's had the baby.'

'A baby! Evie? No! Really? Do tell . . . Tell me *all*!' Mabel's eyes became as big as saucers with the drama of it all.

Twenty-Five

Evie slid her feet into her worn boots. She put on her coat and left the house with Terry bound by a shawl to her chest. Sitting at the back of the tram, she held the baby close under the folds of the loose-fitting coat. He began to cry, just a small bleating sound, but she thanked God for the noise of the light bulbs rattling in their cases and the wheels squealing and screeching along the metal tracks that drowned out his mewling.

When they reached Victoria Parade, she set off towards the greengrocer's and bought a bag of carrots and a turnip. On the short walk to the tram, the light quickly filtered from a bright orange and pink, the beginnings of a sunset. Glancing upwards, she saw that dark clouds had filled the January sky. There was a sudden chill in the air, followed by dramatic forks of lightning and a loud crack of thunder.

'Blimey. That was ferocious,' she said to Terry. It began to rain, heavy and hard, and soon great hailstones were pelting the earth and bouncing off the pavements. She made sure Terry was covered up before she put up her collar and ran to take shelter. She watched as more black clouds bulked up on the horizon.

'This blasted rain . . .' she murmured to her son. She adjusted the makeshift sling that she had tied around her body to make sure he was safe and as dry as he could be in such foul weather. The rain continued to drench the pavements. It splashed her hair, and she could feel the water rising up through her flimsy boots. She shrank back, and then stopped suddenly. She was standing in the doorway of a church. The building, with its gothic turrets and gargoyles, was black with soot. Its huge wooden door was half open. 'Can't stop outside here getting soaked. It will ruin these boots, and I don't have another pair.'

The church was empty. It was sombre, dimly lit apart from the flicker of candles, and dank. The statue of Jesus with his arms outstretched, his head drooping under his crown of thorns, seemed to be looking directly at her. And it wasn't a forgiving look. It was the same look of disappointment that so many people had been giving her lately. She remembered once, as she sat at the kerb, a complete stranger had given her a halfpenny, telling her what a lovely little girl she was. Evie had been so taken aback that she had promptly dropped it down the drain. 'Oh, you stupid girl,' the woman had said, and walked off, annoyed. She felt the same now. A complete disappointment.

Terry gurgled contentedly. Evie felt a sudden pang of sadness. Soon, when Renie came, she would never see this little face again. But dwelling on that would get her nowhere, and she shivered and tried to push the awful, desperate thoughts aside.

The votive candles on their rack of metal spikes quivered and bent towards her when she approached the pews; it was as though they had been expecting her. She looked in the direction of the christening font. Standing in her leaky boots, wet and water-marked from the brown slush outside, she wondered what she should do next. She genuflected, a quick, glancing sign of the cross, and shuffled along the bench. The confessional boxes were on either side of the nave. Suddenly, from nowhere, a nun appeared at the end of the pew and genuflected. Evie stopped, gulped air. Her heart leapt to her throat.

'In the name of the Father and of the Son, and the Holy Spirit. Blessed be God, blessed be the Mother, blessed be the Father . . .' the nun murmured, striking her chest gently with her clenched fist.

Evie looked around. She was conscious of the baby; conscious of the cheap wedding ring she'd bought from Woolworths to wear on the few occa-sions she ventured outdoors; conscious of her burning cheeks. She crossed herself and stood up to move out of the pew. She felt a tug on her coat.

'Do I know you?' said the nun. She was smiling.

'No . . . no,' she stuttered.

Of course she didn't know her. That was why she had come here. Three miles away from their home, so no one would recognize her.

'Are you here to take confession?' the nun asked.

'Oh. Yes, I suppose I am,' Evie stammered.

'Well, go in quickly, child. You're the last. Father will be getting hungry now. It's nearly his teatime.'

The nun gestured towards the confessional. A

woman was coming out. She looked peaceful, calm. Perhaps the priest was one of the kind ones. The nun came up behind her again, noiselessly. Evie started. She prayed that the baby wouldn't make a sound. She had been grateful that the child had fallen asleep as she walked around the park in front of the church, jigging him up and down. He did that. Went spark out like a light after bawling his head off. Fell dead asleep, and sometimes it scared her so much, she had to wake him just to see if he was alive.

'Father won't bite,' said the nun. 'Go on, dear. He hasn't got all day. Would you like me to hold the baby?'

Evie gasped inwardly. The nun reached out a hand speckled with liver spots.

'Baby?'

She was instantly ashamed. Of course the nun could see Terry under all the swaddling. What was she thinking of? The lick of hair that had given him his name, Curly, had escaped and was poking out over the top of the blanket. Could the nun tell that Evie had no right to wear her cheap wedding band?

'The baby under your coat? You can give him to me if you want . . .' she said.

Faltering, Evie answered, 'Oh . . . I don't know if . . .'

But the nun was persistent, and she repeated, 'Come on, dear. Give him to me. It will be easier not to take him into the confessional.'

Evie looked at her child, bundled up in the blanket, hesitated for a moment, and instantly regretted it when the nun reached out and peeled it back rudely.

'Oh, what a beautiful little thing he is. It puts all your faith in God and in his creation when you see such a bonny baby as this little one,' she said.

Evie nodded, but then, feeling a bristle of annoyance, she said, 'Actually. He's sleeping, and I'd rather keep him with me. Can I?'

The nun just looked at her with a dead stare. It was impossible to tell whether she was angry or not. Nuns confused Evie, mainly because she never knew what they were thinking. For every awful nun, there was a nun who radiated kindness; only it was often difficult to tell which one was which on first meeting. Was it something to do with the wimples that stretched their features into a blank canvas?

She slipped inside. She could hear the familiar rustle of linen, the sigh of the priest. The clearing of his throat. It was the disembodied voice that floated out from the other side of the grille that she prayed she wouldn't recognize. What if it was the priest who used to come to her school – or Father Donnelly, who had helped them with her mother? What if, even worse, *he* recognized *her* voice? She had been hauled in front of priests in her life so many times, and yet still their disapproval was a thing she dreaded.

'Bless me, Father, for I have sinned. It has been . . . erm . . . five months since I last came to confession . . .'

A blush rose to her cheek. Five months? Over a year, more like. Here she was in a confessional, and she was already lying. She hadn't been inside a church since it had proved too difficult to hide her pregnancy. What kind of person lied in a confessional? Maybe the kind of person that she was. A dreadful person.

'Speak up,' said the priest. 'I haven't got that long.'

'Sorry, Father, sorry.'

'Go on, child,' he said. 'Stop apologizing and confess. You're not here to say sorry to me. You're here to say sorry to God. I'm simply God's vessel. It doesn't matter what I think. So you can tell me anything.'

'Father, I have done things that I'm ashamed of . . .'

'Things? What do you mean, things?'

'I'm embarrassed to say, Father . . .'

'God does not have blushes. The Lord welcomes sinners. Indeed, the Lord *loves* sinners.'

She could feel her palms sweating. Go on, say it. Just say it, she told herself. Things couldn't be any worse than they were already. So she gritted teeth. 'Father . . . Father . . .'

She prayed silently to Jesus to help her say out loud the dreadful things that she was thinking of when, as if on cue, the baby gurgled. She could feel movement from beyond the grille. She froze.

'Child, do you have a baby in there?'

The priest's face peered closer towards the mesh, marking his features out in small blurred diamond shapes, revealing a knotty face and squinty eyes.

'Yes, Father. This baby. My baby. He hasn't been christened. And he'll be two months old soon,' she blurted.

She sat there, twisting the baby's shawl.

'We will have to do something about that. We can do it now, if you want. Come outside, child. So that's why you haven't been to confession? Because of the baby.' He stood up, and she heard the bang of the confessional door.

She came out to join him in the church, and answered with a nod.

'And the father?' he asked. 'The father? Where's he?'

'The father died. Pneumonia. He worked at Huskisson Dock. It's just me and the child.' She hoped God would forgive her the fib, if it got Terry christened.

'I see,' he said, nodding and casting a glance at her left hand. He recognized a lie when he saw one. Being in the business of forgiveness, you got to know the signs. Blushing, eyes cast to the floor, the slight stammering, the downward tilt of the chin. He had it down to a fine art, and still got a thrill each time the truth spilled out and he was able to dole out his penances.

There was the sound of more mewling from beneath the scarf.

'Come with me.'

He led her across the marble floor, guiding her by her elbow. Standing in front of the christening font, he rearranged his vestments, made the sign of the cross. Then he disappeared, returning with a jug of oil, a white chasuble, a small lace square of linen.

'Give the child to me,' he said. Evie handed him the baby. He removed the covers, peered into the

189

baby's face. The baby blinked up at him, stared at him under long dark lashes, screwed up his face, stuck his tongue out, and smiled. Evie's heart broke.

'Sister, bring me the oil . . .'

The nun appeared from the shadows. She was carrying a silver tray on which there were two glass bottles. She silently handed one at a time to the priest as he said, 'In the name of the Father and the Son and of the Holy Spirit, amen.' He poured the water over the baby's head, dabbed the oil on his forehead. Droplets splashed over the font. Evie felt tears gather, and she worked a finger under each eye as the priest now stood before the altar table, murmuring prayers in Latin that were unrecognizable to her. When it was all over, the nun asked Evie if she would like a cup of tea. Perhaps she was one of the kind nuns after all.

'Remember, the Lord loves a helpless child,' said the priest, as he swept off in search of his Fray Bentos pie and boiled potatoes.

What about me? Am I not helpless? I'm still only a child myself. Does the Lord not love me? Evie wanted to scream.

'Dear, if you ever need us, you know where we are,' said the nun. 'You will always have a home, in every town, city, village on this earth. You might not have a roof over your head or shoes on your feet, but you will always have a home. You understand that?' She leaned in to Evie, and in a warm, soothing voice, she said, 'You *belong*. There are people here who love you. Never forget that. You may have no parents or family, but you will always have us.'

'I'm very sorry, Sister. I do have a family.'

The nun nodded and smiled.

'Thank the Lord,' she said.

Evie made the sign of the cross, bobbed her knee at the altar rail and whispered, 'Except I'm not sorry about you, Terry. Whatever happens to us both? How could I be sorry about a thing as beautiful as you?'

She felt a wave of relief when she stepped out into the cold air. At least now Terry had been christened, which would please her father; he had been pestering her for weeks, even though it would have been impossible to have the family christening most babies on their street seemed to have. Terry was still a secret, though it was hard to see how he could remain so for much longer.

The fresh air invigorated her. She made her way to the overhead railway – the docker's umbrella, as everyone called it – seeing the letters and images that took shape on the hoarding advertising Bisto gravy and Pears soap, and an old peeling poster from the war: 'COUGHS AND SNEEZES SPREAD DISEASES', and a promise of better times.

Looking into the baby's face, his eyelids becoming heavy, she thought of Renie's imminent arrival. How could anyone not fall in love with this baby? And Renie was a good person. A kind person. A pious person. It would be the first thing she would ask: *When was the baby christened, dear?* She wouldn't take a heathen child. And now, if anything were to happen to him, Evie didn't need to worry about him floating around in limbo forever with all the other heathen babies. She worried constantly about scarlet fever or the croup. At least there was one small thing now, amongst her sea of troubles, that she could be thankful for.

Twenty-Six

The next day, Evie took the pram that was hidden under the coal sacks in the back yard, placed the baby in it and walked all the way, nearly six miles, to a park on the outskirts of the city. Her feet ached by the time she got there, but it killed a few hours. It was a blustery, fresh February day and the sun was shining. She had taken a back route through the maze of terraces in Bootle, hoping no one would see her. Coronation Park, it was called; no one would know her here. She looked at a boulder that was fenced off by railings and wondered why it was there and what was so special about it; she bought a bag of chips and then wheeled the baby around the beds of roses in his pram. For a while she sat on a bench rocking him, marvelling at his little squashed-up peachy face. She left as dusk brought soft sepia tones, and finally arrived back home as it was getting dark. But while she was out, a visitor had arrived.

'Auntie Renie!' Evie said in shock. Renie looked different, dressed smartly in an A-line pleated skirt and a neat bolero. Her silhouette was backlit with the gaslight, blurring the edges of her. 'You've come early!'

'Couldn't wait.' Renie beamed a smile and took off her gloves. 'Oh, Evie. Can I hold him? He's beautiful. He's called Terry?' she said, coming over, pulling away the blanket and peering into the bundle that Evie was holding.

'Dad calls him Curly,' she said.

'He's darling,' Renie said. 'He's a lovely little thing.' She stuck her thumb into his mouth for him to suckle. 'So tell me everything from the beginning.'

Evie frowned. Renie seemed rapt by the baby. Every time she craned her neck and looked down at him, her pudgy face dissolved into smiles and she became momentarily distracted. It hurt Evie to see it.

'Little over two months ago, I had him. Nobody knows. Well, not many people. We've tried to keep the gossips at bay, haven't we, Da? He came early. I had him at home, but he seems fine and healthy.'

'He certainly does. Thank the Lord. Your father said you have both been trying to hide him upstairs. That won't work, will it? At least, not for much longer. Not when the other kids know the truth of it. What about when he starts crawling? Babies don't stay babies forever.'

'I know that,' Evie answered.

'We've no spondoolies, Renie,' Bill said from his armchair. 'Can't have a baby that needs feeding when you're skint. Grim, things are. You can see it in the city. Did you notice on the tram ride? Buildings disappeared, whole streets gone. All because of the flaming war.' He shook his head. 'There's not much work. We're all waiting to see what's going to happen next.'

All the time, Renie rocked the child back and forth, shifting from one foot to another, pushing his forelock gently to the side, touching his nose, letting his little fingers clasp tightly around her thumb.

'Aye, the docks have been quiet, all right. That's why it's so good to see you, Renie,' continued Bill. 'We really didn't know who to turn to.'

Renie nodded, took one of Evie's hands with her free one. 'And the small matter of the father, dear?'

Evie frowned.

'Still in Canada. He's not coming back,' interrupted Bill.

'I thought he was my sweetheart. He always made me laugh. He threw my hat into the boating lake once, and then he said he wanted to marry me.'

'Really, dear?' Renie sounded slightly taken aback.

'He was always doing that kind of thing. He was kind, would always walk me home.'

'Kind? Once he knew that she was having his baby, he was off,' said Bill, his eyes darkening. 'I reckon that was it.'

'It wasn't exactly like that,' said Evie.

Renie looked at her pityingly. They were sitting opposite each other now. The baby slept in the crook of her arm. Across the table, she reached out her hand. 'Oh, you poor lamb.'

'He was a useless article, could have told you that from the beginning. Throwing hats into the boating lake. What a load of nonsense. Anyway, he was a bad 'un,' said Bill. 'When I found out what he'd done to our Evie, I went round to knock seven bells out of him, but he was gone.'

'He wasn't that bad, Da . . . he was kind to me.' She glanced at her father.

195

'Look at him, fast asleep in the land of nod. He really is lovely,' said Renie.

'You're a natural, Renie.'

She smiled up at him. 'I was born to have babies. It's the one thing I knew how to do. Just took to it. Like shelling peas. Lovely child . . .'

There was a silence. Bill shuffled about a little and for the lack of something to do, he took out a cigarette from a small tin that had once contained cough drops, tapped the end of it onto the table, sucked at it and then used his fingers to remove a piece of tobacco that was stuck on the end of his tongue. He struck a match, held it to the cigarette.

'Folks will be unkind when they find out. They used to say our Evie had an evil eye. Evie! Evil. She doesn't have a bad bone in her body. Do you, Evie?'

Evie blushed. She did, of course. There were so many parts of her that were bad. The nuns had taught her to feel that. It was just that being bad had felt so very good at times, and that's why she had got herself into this mess in the first place.

'So anyway, we were wondering –' Bill said, sucking on the Woodbine – 'I know you've got all your kiddies. But we were wondering, well, seeing as Evie has made it clear that she doesn't want to give the child up for adoption, and she doesn't want the nuns to take the baby, well, who would? Never to see him again. But of course it's just not practical for us. Well, would you be able to take the child back with you when you leave? How long are you staying? A few days? Evie would probably need a little time to prepare him. To say goodbye, sort of thing.'

Renie's mouth fell open in shock.

'*Me?*'

Bill glanced at Evie, whose brows knitted together in confusion. Her cheeks flamed with worry suddenly.

'Me?' Renie said again.

Twenty-Seven

'You didn't actually think that . . . I couldn't possibly. That's why I'm here, I'm afraid. To tell you that it's an absurd suggestion. I couldn't put it in a letter, so I thought I'd come. No, if you don't want to keep this child – well, you must have him adopted immediately. St Jude's mother and baby home. They would be able to help you. They're not all monsters, you know, Evie. They would only have the child's best interests at heart.'

Fighting back tears, Evie glanced at her father with a look of anguish.

'You mean you don't want to take the baby back with you to Dagenham? Ever? *Not ever?*'

'Oh, Bill.'

'You keep saying how much space you have there. And look at you. You look so different. Like you've got a bob or two. You keep going on about how much better things are down south. And it sounds so lovely. With the new budgerigar. We'll pay you,' said Bill desperately.

Evie had heard enough. 'Of course we can't pay, Da. We have no money.'

'We'd find it.'

Renie turned to Evie. Placing a hand gently on her

forearm, she said: 'You do understand why I can't have the child, dear? It's not realistic. I've got three kids of my own. There is just not enough room.'

Evie frowned and stared at the floor. She felt as if she was looking down on herself. Her whole body began to shake. She still couldn't quite believe what Renie was saying. Did she really mean she wouldn't have the baby *at all*, not under any circumstances? Had her father lied about her response to the letter and the telephone call, or had he just heard what he wanted to hear in Renie's words? Had he just been stringing her along these past few months, with his promises of sorting everything out with Renie? *Wait until we talk to Renie, Renie loves children, one more won't make a difference for Renie. You'd still be able to see him sometimes if Renie took him . . .*

'I . . . I think you have been getting ahead of yourself, Bill. I came here to talk about the nuns.'

Please, please, please, don't bring the bloody nuns into this, Evie wanted to yell. She could hear Renie's words as she spoke of childless couples and a better future for Terry, but they were just coming out in back-to-front sentences.

'Is it because your house is too small? The bairn is no trouble. You've got room for a budgerigar,' said Bill.

'Budgerigars and babies are not the same thing. Don't be daft, Bill.'

He humphed. 'What are we supposed to do now? Don't you think I've tried with the nuns? Evie won't have it.'

'Well, that's not my fault.'

'It's a bloody mess. Thank God Josephine's not around to see it,' he said, red-faced now, and then suddenly turned round to Evie. He jabbed a finger fiercely in her direction. 'You stupid, idiotic girl, Evie. What are you going to do? I'm damned if I can think of anything. There's enough gossip as it is. You made your flaming bed, you can lie in it now.'

Renie frowned. 'Oh, Bill, don't be so hard on the girl. She's a good child, really. This could happen to anyone. Good grief, it probably has happened to half the people in the street, if you knocked on the doors and asked any mother to tell you the truth. I reckon there wouldn't be one person who was able to cast a stone.'

Evie, sitting at the table, struck dumb with worry, dropped her head down onto her folded arms. Renie, still holding the baby, placed one hand on top of her slender neck and up onto the crown of her head, which only made Evie give in to sobs.

'I couldn't help it. I had no idea. It wasn't my fault, Frankie just, he just . . .' She sat miserably and cried into the crook of her arm, her back heaving as she tried to control the crying.

'Stop, duck,' Renie said. 'Instead of going on about what happened before, let's think about what's going to happen next.'

'What d'you mean?'

'The baby . . .'

'So, Renie. Can I just get this straight? Will you not at least take the child until we think of something?'

Renie looked at him, frowned. 'Bill . . . How many times? Will you give over asking?'

200

'Will you have him for a few weeks? Just to see how you get on?'

'Bill, this is a baby, not a mutt to be handed around. I can't have the child. What are you thinking of?'

How could they have been so stupid? Evie thought. Of course Renie wasn't going to have the baby. Why would she? It was an enormous thing to ask of anyone. She blamed her father. If he had been straight with Renie, then Renie would have said no from the beginning, and Evie would never have allowed the idea to take shape in her head. They clearly hadn't even had a proper conversation about it.

'Terry will need feeding,' said Evie. 'Can I take him, Auntie Renie?'

'Of course,' her aunt replied. 'And before you go – I've brought something for you,' she added.

'Oh no, Auntie. I don't need anything,' Evie said flatly.

'Don't be ungrateful,' muttered Bill.

Renie rummaged in her bag and produced something wrapped in tissue.

'That's nice,' said Bill. 'That's kind.'

No, she wasn't kind.

'It's just a gesture. Take it, love,' Renie said, handing the gift over to her.

Evie opened the tissue. Lying there, nestling in the crumpled tissue, was a hard-boiled egg.

Evie was speechless. What was she supposed to do with that? It was ridiculous. A hard-boiled egg! Renie was looking at her, smiling.

'Just a little something. I knew you would like it.'

Evie just stared at her, open-mouthed. Thank God

this woman hadn't agreed to take her darling precious child. Bill made a face at her from the other side of the table.

'Are you forgetting your manners, Evie?' he said.

'Thank you, Auntie Renie,' she stammered. A boiled egg! A flaming hard-boiled egg. She'd thought she was at least going to give her some money, or a brooch. Or a set of buttons. Anything. But *a boiled egg*. She was fond of them, but that took the biscuit!

'Remember, I know a lovely sister at St Jude's.'

Evie let the words wash over her. All her father's hopes had been pinned on this woman, her aunt, for the last two months; and now it had just disappeared into nothing, floating away like a piece of gossamer, floating away like Frankie had floated out of her life, just spinning away into thin air. And she was left with a hard-boiled egg, the prospect of Neville, and her baby.

Evie couldn't help but smile. At least she still had Terry. But the question was, for how long?

Twenty-Eight

'Joan's back from Ireland!' said Sylvie, when Evie came downstairs. Nelly, wearing a tea towel on her head, danced around her. Vic looked across the table with serious expression.

'Is it true, Da?' said Evie.

'Yes,' he replied.

Evie snatched the tea towel from Nelly's head and hung it over the range. Neither had thought that when Terry was three months old, they would be in exactly the same position as on the day he was born. A month had passed since Renie's visit, and nothing had changed except for the secret beginning to take shape into something as concrete as an out-and-out lie. Evie had grown so attached to the child – but this was news she dreaded nearly as much as her aunt coming to take the child away.

'Thank goodness she's back. I got a nasty gash when I scraped my arm in the scramble this morning in the pen. Joan'll put me back in one piece, all right.'

'Make sure she uses the Dettol, Da. No use if you don't make sure it's not going to get infected,' Evie said pithily.

'Of course,' said a voice behind her. It was Joan! Sauntering in from the kitchen as if it were hers, drying her hands on a cloth.

'I have to go upstairs. Would you excuse me?' said Evie, panicked.

'Don't worry about running off,' said Bill. 'No need to be hiding up there. Bring the bairn downstairs. Joan knows everything.'

Joan looked at Evie and smiled. Evie felt sick to her stomach.

'What if he's sleeping? I'll not wake him up,' said Evie, short and brusque, and not at all sure what was going to happen next.

'I can hear him,' said her father.

Evie wavered, and then went upstairs. She couldn't stand being in the same room as that woman a moment longer. As she lifted the grizzling baby out of the cot, he looked at her from under his dark eyelashes. Rubbing his eyes with his tiny fists, he smiled.

'Shh . . .' she said. He laughed. His thumb found its way to his mouth. Holding her to him, doing an elaborate dance of rocking from foot to foot to keep him happy and gurgling contentedly, she went over to the window and drew back the curtain. When's Holy Joan going to leave? she murmured.

The baby laughed again, this time a tiny burbling sound escaping from his lips. She put her hand gently across his mouth, but he only stuck his tongue out further, searching her knuckle as if it was her nipple. Stroking his head, finally she heard the latch on the door.

'Bye, Joan,' she heard her father call out. She listened for the door to shut.

Gone. Thank goodness. To the pub, probably. And she supposed to be a teetotaller. She was always telling people she was in the Pioneer Association and she'd made a pledge to God not to drink, wore the stupid pin of the Sacred Heart on her lapel so everyone knew; but Evie had noticed the empty gin bottle and two glasses on the kitchen table. Joan was a liar and a hypocrite – not only for that, but for carrying on with a married man.

Terry began to cry. Sitting on the bed, Evie unbuttoned her blouse and offered her breast. Reaching in to the pillow of her chest, the baby was grasping at her flesh now and put his mouth on her nipple. She could feel the milk coming through in prickles. Feeling the tenderness in her swollen breasts subside, she put the child, his eyelids heavy with sleep, back down in the cot and went downstairs again, not worrying about the embarrassing patches on her blouse now that a more serious worry had taken over. How long before Joan started sticking her nose in and going on about sending Terry off to the awful St Jude's?

Evie dreaded each day with Joan coming in and out of the house unannounced and fussing about the place. It felt like all Evie was doing was feeding Terry, putting him to sleep, waking him, feeding him again, and waiting for disaster to strike.

The next evening, sitting in front of the range, she put a piece of muslin over her chest, undid her blouse and let the baby suckle. Soon he was fast asleep on her breast.

'We need to talk about Lionel,' said her father, coming into the room. 'Neville's going steady with a lass from Jacob's biscuit factory, so that ship has sailed.'

We need to talk about Joan, Evie thought.

'I've put up with months of you turning up your nose at fellas I've suggested.' Obviously he had got talking to Lionel in the pub the night before, thought Evie, and no doubt he had swiftly become the latest solution to her predicament.

'Da, I'm not turning up my nose . . . Is this because of Joan?'

Bill humphed. 'Where d'you get that tanner, Vic?' he asked Vic, who had wandered in and sat down, spinning a coin at the table.

'Evie give it me.'

'Evie flush, is she?'

Evie frowned at her father. She didn't want another argument, not today. She stood and rubbed her aching back. 'Tanner's only for the messages. Not for him. Thought we'd make some currant buns later.'

'So back to Lionel, Evie. It doesn't do, a man like me fussing over a baby whilst you refuse to face what's happening to you. I cannot. Not any longer,' he muttered under his breath. 'Lionel is waiting for you at the end of the road. A quick half with him in the Boot is all I'm asking. Give him a chance. I'll look after the bairn. He's spark out.'

She nodded, sighed; anything to avoid a row. And especially one in front of Victor. Lionel would soon change his mind when he saw how thin and tired-looking she had become, she thought, as she got out of the chair and gave the baby to her father. Pushing her arms into the sleeves of her thin, threadbare coat, she went to leave.

'So, Lionel. You look dapper,' she said, wondering

when Lionel had got so fat. His gut was spilling over the top of his belt.

Their steps fell into a steady rhythm. Even keeping as much distance between them as was polite, she could smell his sweet alcoholic breath. They reached the Boot Inn. He pushed through the throng of people. There was a gaggle of men, one of them barking loudly across the group. As Lionel barged past two young girls sitting at one end of the bar, the buxom one snorted with laughter into the crook of her arm. Evie was aware that she was being looked at lustily by weary, bleary-eyed young men in ill-fitting suits drinking after working a shift in the Cunard office.

'Thanks for bringing me here.' Why she said it, she had no idea, but she didn't want it to get back to her dad that she hadn't at least made an effort. This place was grim. They were sat in the snug, but she was the only woman apart from the two at the bar. And she didn't like the way they were looking her, either. Did they know? Gossip got around this place, and it was hard to hide a baby who was now getting on for three months old.

'Knew you'd like it. You can have a meat pie if you like. I've heard in London they have it with eels, but I like mine with tatties and tripe.'

He clicked his fingers. The barmaid came over with a plate of food that evidently had been waiting for him.

'Got me name on it, love,' he said to Evie, winking at her with his baggy eyes. The tripe slithered off the fork. It made a strange rippling feeling in her stomach just to look at him shovel the food into his mouth as though he hadn't eaten for weeks. No wonder he was so fat.

'You'll have some?'

'Just a bit of bread. The heel is fine.'

Was this man really the answer to her problems? Lionel Rafferty. With one collar of his crumpled shirt stuffed in his sweater, in serious need of darning. The tie, like a worm, sticking out boyishly from the bottom of the sweater. Could this man not dress himself? Was this why he needed a wife?

There was a silence. She shifted in her seat.

'Shall I show you me party trick?' he said suddenly.

Evie winced. A residue of saliva gathered in the corners of his mouth. And without answering, he gurned, baring his half-toothless smile, and began to blow. The whistling sound that emanated from him caused heads to turn.

'Go on, Lionel!' cried one of the women. 'Give us a tune . . .'

And he began to sing 'The Fields of Athenry' and whistle at the same time as he stamped his foot. Some of the people at the bar began to clap their hands in rhythm. Evie had no idea how he did it, but the girls thought it was a hoot, and he puffed his chest out with pride.

'Lionel, you're a bloody marvel. You should go on the stage. Shouldn't he, Elsie!? He should go on the stage . . .'

'You wouldn't be the first to say that,' said Lionel. And he laughed and slapped his thigh. Suddenly he stopped and pulled his chair closer to Evie, legs splayed.

'How am I doing so far?' he asked, grinning.

'Sorry?'

'How am I doing? Marks out of ten.' He flicked his tongue again, along the fleshy parts of his bottom lip.

She stuttered, shook her head.

'Go on. Marks out of ten.'

'Oh well. Seven . . .' she blurted.

'Seven! Only a flipping seven! Eh, Elsie, she's only given me a seven outta ten . . .'

'Seven! Bloody hell! Lionel is a fine catch. He's a ten out of ten, any day of the week.'

'No, no . . .' Evie stuttered. 'I meant the whistling . . .'

'I didn't mean my whistling, I meant, this . . . *us* . . .' Lionel said, gesturing first at himself and then at her.

'Our Lionel is a ten out of ten on every front, aren't you, love? You're a lucky lass to have him buy you that rum and black.'

'Disgrace . . . Who does she think she is?' muttered the girl's friend. 'And I thought beggars can't be choosers . . .'

'What d'you mean?' asked Lionel, who was sat close enough to hear the comment.

'Well, haven't you heard? She's just had a baby . . .'

Evie could feel her cheeks burning.

'Baby?' said Lionel. 'What you on about?'

Tears welled in Evie's eyes. 'I don't know what she's talking about,' she said. Though she was surprised her father hadn't made her circumstances clearer to Lionel. Why else did he think she had agreed to this date?

'Hasn't she told you?'

'Told me what?'

The girl got off the stool. 'She's got a baby. Frankie O'Hare's, who up and left her when he found out. Think of her poor mother.'

Hot, angry blushes rose from Evie's throat to her cheeks.

'Her mother wouldn't care. We all knew your ma. We all knew about Luigi Galinari. You're just like her, and now you've ended up with a baby out of wedlock. Should go to one of them homes for fallen women, but you won't go, will you? Bet you're too brazen or too stubborn. Time you went now . . .'

Lionel saw Evie pucker her forehead, saw a tear spill onto her cheek.

'Is this true?' he asked. 'You've a baby?'

'I'll not talk about that here. Not that I need to talk about any of my life to you. It's no business of yours . . .'

'And no, it never will be, love. Wait 'til I see your dad. Does he think I'm some kind of fool, walking up a blind alley with me eyes shut?'

But she was gone, in a flurry of temper and rage.

'You didn't know?' said the girl, draping her arm across Lionel Rafferty's shoulder. 'Bloody stupid Bill O'Leary, trying to set you up with his slut of a daughter. Seven out of ten, she gave you. What a flaming joke.'

And Lionel nodded, but then reeled slightly at the smell of sour beer on the girl's breath, and the sight of snuff on her teeth and her pockmarked skin, and the fact that he would have to pay for the affection she was showing him. He wondered if he shouldn't go and find Evie, after all.

Scurrying down by St George's Hall on her way to Lewis's to buy some remnants to patch up Vic's school trousers, Evie reflected on the disaster that had been her encounter with Lionel the night before. She had only gone along to please her father; no one could have reasonably expected that anything would come of it. Lost in thought, it was the motorcycle's engine she heard first, before the sound of a voice calling to her above it.

'Sugar Girl, is that you? It is you! Ha . . . I've missed you!'

Evie turned. 'Lawrence!'

He had pulled up to the pavement, and steadied himself with his feet on the floor on either side of the bike. She blinked against the afternoon sunlight that flooded the steps in front of St George's Hall. It looked like an old military motorcycle; she could see the insignia had been painted over with black paint. Unfastening the chin strap, he took off the helmet and put his leather gloves inside it, then raked his fingers back through his fair hair. The jacket he was wearing, the trousers and boots, all made him look impossibly glamorous. He reminded her of one of the movie stars in *Picture Post* magazine.

'She's a beauty, isn't she?' As if to demonstrate, he twisted the handlebar. 'Keep it in the back yard at my digs, but I thought I'd bring her out for a spin to stop her getting rusty.'

'Oh dear,' Evie said. She knew how strict the

council was about what you could and could not keep in yards.

He grinned. 'I know what you're thinking. You're a girl who does things right. Don't tell anyone. Don't shop me to the filth,' he said in an American accent, and nudged her and winked. 'I've taken the door off, there are chickens in there, and a small glass greenhouse where the landlady grows tomatoes and vegetables. I know, I know, don't look so serious, I'm for it if the housing manager comes round. Council says we're not allowed to mess with the house. Not even allowed to put up the greenhouse. But I reckon my bike isn't going to make much difference, and I'll take a chance.' There was a pause. 'Sorry about my mucky hands. It's lamp oil, can't afford petrol, and it gets everywhere.'

'Oh,' she replied, worries tumbling around in her head.

'Where've you been?' he asked. 'I've missed having you around.'

She faltered. 'I left Tate's.' She pursed her lips, contemplated telling him her awful story. But she couldn't. She just couldn't. It was the momentary pause he needed. He put his hands on the handlebars, then jumped down furiously on the pedal until, after a few more cranks it roared into life and spewed clouds of smoke. A noxious smell filled the air.

'You ever been on one of these?' he asked. 'Ten minutes down to the Pier Head and back . . . what d'you say?'

Evie coughed; her eyes were watering, and it covered her hesitation. He looked like some kind of film star in his sheepskin jacket. Even more so in comparison to Lionel . . . Should she say yes? But that was madness. That was crazy, and she was ridiculous to even consider giving him a second of her time, let alone going for a ride with him. She knew where that would lead, and she had made a promise to herself that she would never make the same mistake again – never get herself all tangled up with a man just because she liked the flick of his hair, his broad shoulders, or his lopsided smile.

'Come on, sweet?'

'No thanks,' she replied.

'Give a fellow a break. My legs have gone to jelly just looking at you. Make a sad actor very happy, won't you? Go on – I'm off on tour with Mabel soon. Though I'm sure no one wants to see me and Bug prancing around on a stage doing a dreary Priestley play. I suggested we should be doing something more cheerful to raise the spirits. Mabel will be hopeless. She's got a part lined up in a movie afterwards, and that's all she thinks about. Wonder what she did to get that,' he said with a knowing smile. 'I don't dare think. Good, you're still listening to me. Haven't run away yet.'

The faintest of smiles played across Evie's full lips, and it was the chink of light he needed.

'Go on. Come for a ride. You know you want to . . .' he said in a low voice, leaning in close to her. She could smell the heady scent of tobacco and Old Spice. 'You'll love it. Promise. Come on, live dangerously, Sugar Girl. You were the one who told me that nothing frightened you. Not even nuns.'

And there it was: the voice in Evie's head that she knew would get her into trouble. A voice that said every moment was unique and precious, and life was so difficult right now – awful Lionel, and her father and brother and sisters, and what to do about Terry, and Holy Joan – and the bike looked such fun, and everyone out there was having a good time, the pubs and bars full of people making up for lost time after the war. And just the very sound of the roaring engine – and he looked so, so handsome . . .

'All right,' she said, with a shrug.

'Well, I'll be damned! Jeepers Creepers, *she said yes!*' he cried, and pumped his fist in the air. 'You said yes, Angel!' he shouted.

'Just once round the block, mind,' she said, alarmed by his ebullience and over-excitement, quite out of keeping with the moment. That's actors, she thought to herself.

He beamed. 'Hop on, then, love.'

She lifted her skirts, straddled the bike. Her father wouldn't be expecting her back for a while yet; why shouldn't she have fun? The smell of the lamp oil filled her nostrils. She shoved her hair up into her woollen hat, held it tight down over her ears.

'Put your arms around my waist,' he said.

She gripped him firmly.

'Where to?' he said.

'You decide. I'm in your hands,' she replied.

'Hi-diddly-hee!' he cried. They set off, picking up speed as they roared down the streets. Feeling the wind in her face, seeing the buildings rushing by as they rode down past St George's Hall with its noble columns blurring into one another, and then towards Lime Street station, down the incline past the Adelphi, and then a detour to the theatre – she supposed Lawrence was showing off, as there was a huge poster outside with a picture of him looking brooding in a dinner suit and smoking a cigarette.

As they swerved round corners and whizzed along the roads, the way people on the pavements stopped what they were doing and looked at them gave her a thrill. She felt butterflies in the pit of her stomach. As she tightened her arms about him more securely, she thought of her father, thought of Holy Joan, and even dreadful Sister Bony Face, and imagined what they might say about this if they could see what she was doing. Imagine what Neville would say! Or the awful Lionel, or Edna and the girls at the factory! And Frankie . . . oh, Frankie . . .

The bike roared as it skidded in the direction of the river to where they had started.

'Lawrence!' she shouted into his ear. '*Lawrence!*'

He turned his head and spoke back at her. 'More, Angel? Faster, sugar?'

'No! And keep your eyes on the bloody road!' she shouted. 'I want you to stop!'

They drew to a halt. The engine idled. Breathless, she swung her leg over the side.

'Don't tell me that wasn't exciting? I can see it in your face.'

She narrowed her eyes. 'Too fast. You could have killed someone . . .'

He grinned. 'How d'you fancy another spin, another time, maybe out to the seaside?'

215

'Oh no, I couldn't,' she said solemnly.

'Why not? You enjoyed it, didn't you?'

She looked towards the horizon, fixed her eyes on the tangle of cranes and the river. 'Yes. But . . .'

'Come here,' he said. 'Your hair's come undone. One of your pins has come out . . .'

'I can do it . . . No . . .' she said, shrinking away.

'Let me,' he said, pinning the stray piece of hair behind her ear. The small gesture sent an electric shock through her body; the feel of his fingertips brushing her face, the feel of him gently pushing the pin into the side of her head. Much more of this, and all reason would seep out of her pores.

'Let me drop you back home,' he said, desperate to eke out another few minutes with her.

Home! I will never allow you to see where I live! she thought, horrified – the houses with their doors removed and burnt for firewood, the narrow street, the run-down tenements, fetid smells, the washing lines strung from window to window, hung with frayed nightshirts and ragged, embarrassing under-wear – and the baby. Of course, there was the small matter of the baby.

'Another time,' she blurted.

'Really? You mean that? That's made me very happy, Angel. We could ride out to Freshdale, make a day of it, take a picnic and have it in the sand dunes. Go somewhere nice for a cuppa after. I know a little place by the railway station. You're not just giving me the brush-off?'

She shrugged.

'God, I could wrap you up in one of them Tate

& Lyle wrappers and pop you in my mouth. The sweetness of you, Sugar Plum Fairy,' he said in a low, breathy voice.

Then he moved towards her again. She gasped inwardly. Was he about to kiss her? But then, actors were always kissing each other; was this just what actors did, going around kissing people whenever they felt like it? She held her breath as he gently brushed back her hair again.

But then suddenly he paused, took a step back, frowned and pointed at her chest. 'What's that, love? Have you spilled something on your blouse? It's all wet, honey. Do you need a handkerchief?'

Horrified, she glanced down and saw that an ugly wet stain had seeped through the flimsy cotton material, growing into a dark patch.

'God,' she said, her forearms flying to her breasts to cover them. 'Sorry, I – oh God, yes, I must have spilled something.' She gathered her coat around her and hurriedly clutched it to her. 'I'm really sorry. I have to go.'

'Don't forget our trip to the seaside! You've not changed your mind. You'd like that?'

'That would be lovely,' she said.

Not a cat in hell's chance, she thought as she walked off in the direction of home, stinging with embarrassment and shame that she had for one brief instant forgotten Terry and her predicament.

'Guess who I saw, Ken! She's thawing. I gave her a ride on my bike. Sugar Babe is sweetening . . .' Lawrence said, unwinding the fringed white scarf from

217

his neck. 'I swear I could have kissed those luscious lips.'

Ken, sitting on an upturned packing case at the side of the stage with diaphanous material spilling out of it, paused in fixing the light he was adjusting with a screwdriver. His expression was serious. 'Lawrence – a man came to the stage door. He was asking for you.'

'And what's that to do with me?'

'Nothing, if you're serious about this Tate girl. Are you really? Serious enough to send a chap like him packing?'

'I'm falling in love with her. I've never been more serious in my life, Ken.'

Twenty-Nine

It was getting dark. There was a smell of smoke in the air, and Evie was glad that soon she would be home after nipping out to the butcher's to buy a scrag-end of mutton. Stepping aside, she made way for two boys smashing a football against a wall, but the ball curved towards her and by instinct she caught it.

'Ay, missus, give us back our ball!' one of them cried.

She chucked it back in their direction. Two young girls came along the street pushing a battered old pram. She thought about Nelly and Sylvie playing real live dolls with Terry, as though it was perfectly normal for their sister to have a baby out of wedlock, but a baby they weren't supposed to talk about with their friends.

The kiddies round here, she thought. Look at them. Shorts with no arses in them. Frayed, unravelling jumpers. Who would want to stay here? Despite what Mr Bevan was saying, there were still plenty of kids going to school in bare feet round here, filthy dirty. No wonder they didn't want to turn up for classes and instead spent their whole time skiving. Who would want to be seen like that? How could you walk to school in snow with no shoes or socks? Would she want the same for Terry? Was this the life she would save him from if she were to give him up? The thought made her sad but resigned.

Evie arrived at home to find the door on the latch and the curtains open. She hesitated on the front step. Moving a foot to her right, she looked in the window. It was the electric light burning that she saw first. Since when could they afford that? And then she saw that sitting at the table was Holy Joan, with Vic beside her. They were hunched over the table. She saw Vic beam as he opened his arms out wide and unfolded a chain of cut-out paper men holding hands, made from the *Liverpool Echo*.

But then she saw something far worse than this: peering in through the side pane of glass, she saw that Joan had Terry sitting on her knee, nursing him in the crook of her arm.

Evie rushed into the house and dumped the mutton wrapped in newspaper on the table. 'What's going on?' she asked. 'Where's Da? He said he would look after the baby . . .'

'Pub. Linda came. But I sent her home,' said Joan. 'Gave her a tanner. She was happy to get off early.'

Evie's cheeks flamed. A moth fluttered against the light bulb, which was unusual for this time of the year and, as far as Evie was concerned, a bad sign. She could see Victor's eyes dart back and forth worriedly, from her to Joan to the baby.

'Look what we made!' he said, trying to lighten the atmosphere. 'Paper men chains. We're going to

pin them over the window so everyone can see them.'
Evie's heart lurched.

'You shouldn't have sent Linda home.'

'Why ever not? I was only trying to help. Save
you a few coppers. That girl is too stupid to know
what to spend it on, anyway.'

'Linda's not stupid . . . just a bit—'

'Slow? Besides, we're expecting a visitor,' said Joan,
cutting her off.

'Who?'

As if on cue, there was a sharp knock on the door.

'That will be Sister,' said Joan.

Evie jolted. 'Don't answer the door, Vic.'

'Don't be silly. Sister knows all about the baby.
There's no need to go running up to your room and
hiding. Now go and answer the door.'

'I won't,' said Evie.

'Now then, Evie. We can do this two different
ways. You can kick and shout and scream, but you
will still be left with the baby, hiding upstairs in the
bedroom whenever anyone comes to the house. Poor
Linda and your father covering for you, and no clue
as to what's going to happen to him or you. Or you
can talk to Sister Consilio in a sensible manner and
we can decide what we can do to help you and baby.'

'A nun! I'm not answering that bloody door.
Anyway, what's it got to do with you! Give me Terry!'

'Have it your way, then. Don't answer the door.'
Joan thrust the baby into Evie's arms and turned
away from her. 'Vic, you go and do it, then. And
here – take a penny to go off and buy yourself some
gobstoppers, there's a good boy.'

Vic leapt up, took the coin, and squirrelled it into his trouser pocket.

As he opened the door, the nun, who had been standing on the doorstep wondering why no one was answering her, nodded a hello. Vic pushed past her.

'Now there's a young man in a hurry,' she said, smiling as she came into the room. Her long black habit swished out behind her, and she brought in a rush of cold air and leaves from outside.

Tears welled in Evie's eyes.

'And oh, what a beautiful baby. I've never seen such a beautiful little thing. All that hair. My, isn't he the best little chap? Now, dear. Don't get upset – what on earth are you crying for?'

Evie slumped into a chair.

'Joan has told me all about you. You have to understand that we only want the best for you and your baby.'

Looking at her nodding and smiling, Evie was confused. She looked almost kind. She didn't look like one of those cold, unfeeling nuns. She even had the same eyes as Evie's mother – smiling Irish eyes – and she spoke softly and kindly.

Holy Joan took a small crystal glass from the shelf, poured sweet sherry into it from a bottle on the dresser, and handed it to the nun whilst congratulating herself as she indicated the goody-goody Pioneer pin on her lapel. What nerve, thought Evie.

'Now, can I ask, has he been christened?' asked the nun, sipping from her glass.

'Yes,' said Evie.

'That's good. There's plenty of girls out there like

you who wouldn't have bothered. It shows you're a good girl deep down. Some of the girls who have come to us haven't even thought about it. They just want their children to be put on a ship and sent off to Canada, and they don't even want to wave them off. It's the furthest thing from their minds.'

'Canada?' said Evie, firing a look at Joan.

'I know – there's an irony. Frankie O'Hare gone all the way there, and his child following . . .' said Joan, in a flat tone.

How could she be so cruel! thought Evie.

'There are so many couples in America crying out for babies. I know it's hard to imagine, but a lot of the girls just want to get rid of their babies, hide their shame away. It's as if they have no feelings at all. They just want to get back out there as soon as they can and make the same mistakes all over again. But I can see how dreadful this is for you. Which only goes to show how much you care about your child. You're a good mother, Evie. I could see that the minute I walked into this room. Even though you're still so young.'

Joan reached out and touched Evie's arm. Evie withdrew it as though she had just received an electric shock.

'A good mother only wants the best for her child. And when we look back at what we've achieved before we enter heaven, if you're a mother, that's going to be our children. After all, dear, everything we do here on earth is only so that we can stand proud before the Lord at our death.'

'Sister, you speak so beautifully. I couldn't have put it better myself,' said Joan.

'I suspect that what you want more than anything, Evie, is to be a good mother. Believe me, I meet so many who couldn't care less.'

'Sister, I – I . . .'

'Now, Evie, don't fret. I know how you feel. I don't need to have had a child myself to understand the pain of being a mother. I've been the mother of so many. So many girls come to us for help; so many babies. And Joan here – she might not have a child of her own, but she will be a good mother in her own way to Vic and Nelly and Sylvie when she gets married to your father. As I say, it's about looking God in the eyes as you approach death, and knowing you've done your best.'

The words hit Evie harder than the slammer at the factory. 'Married?' she yelped. 'Married *to my father*!? He's not even divorced!'

'Didn't your da tell you, love?' said Joan. 'Good news. Your mother has finally agreed. Divorce papers are coming through any day now.'

'Divorced?' said the nun, shocked. 'I thought Josephine had died?'

'No, Sister. I'm afraid the ugly truth is that she left Bill and her poor young children to run away with a man. No wonder Evie has got herself into bother. But we all deserve a second chance at happiness, don't we? I'm sure God would forgive Bill for that. Now we just need Evie to do what we say, and life will take a turn for the better for everyone.'

'Not for me and Terry,' Evie shot back.

'For you and Terry most of all,' replied Joan, flatly.

Thirty

The following morning, a flustered Evie came downstairs to find her father standing in front of the
range. There was no sign of Joan. Terry was awake
in Evie's arms. He wriggled and kicked his legs and
she kissed him on the forehead, nestling into the
warmth of him.

'I'm starving, Evie. Lock-in last night at the Boot.
Can you go and get us some Spam from O'Dwyer's?
Get a bit extra.'

'Is it true?' she asked. 'Are you and Joan getting
married?'

He looked up at her.

'Mebbe . . .'

'You and Mam are divorcing? Have you spoken
to her? Do you know where she is?'

'Evie, I'll not talk about this now. Not in front of
the kiddies. And not until I decide what's what. Now
go and pawn this . . .' he said, throwing a package
at her. 'It's my old suit. Take our Vic with you . . .'

Evie paused. It was the suit he had worn on his
wedding day. And every special occasion since. Had
Holy Joan told him to get rid of it?

'Da, about this getting married. If Mam—'

225

'Evie. I said I'll not talk about it! Now are you going to the pawn shop, or do I have to do it meself?'

She humphed as she gathered up her things.

'And take our Vic with you,' he yelled.

She set off, dragging Vic behind her, coming out into the morning air with the smell of the gasworks prickling their lungs.

'Evie, can I have a tanner for some ollies?'

Evie sighed. 'Now where am I going to get a spare tanner from?'

'I hate it. They're always making fun of me . . .'

She paused. 'We'll see what we get for Da's suit,' she said. 'Don't get your hopes up, though. He might not give us more than a few bob for it.'

'Push likes you. All the fellas like you,' he added with a grin.

'Well, he was good to us last time, so it might get us some grub for tea and a few pennies left over. Let's see how we get on, shall we? We're here to get money for food, not ollies.'

Spall pawnbrokers was on the kink in Scotland Road where it veered towards the docks. They passed a line of shops and noticed in the window some strange foods had started to appear at the same time as rationing had finally begun to end. Apple rings, eggs that were powdered, cheese and bacon that came in tins, meats as well, corned beef in jelly. And then Spam. Evie liked it fried, with a bit of salt and in butter. Liver and a sheep's head lay on a silver platter, taking pride of place in the window display.

'Pig's hooves!' cried Victor.

'Makes good soup,' she said.

'And hearts!' he said, his breath blotting the glass as he stopped to look, pressed his nose up against the window. 'Actual hearts, with those tube bits sticking out.'

'Ventricles, they're called love. And that's an aorta, I think,' she said, dimly remembering some of her schooling. Did people really want to see a bloody heart in a shop window? But more than four years after the war, meat was still in short supply.

'Good for soup,' she repeated, urging him to get a move on.

The pawnbroker's bell tinkled when Evie pushed the door open.

'Evie!' The man behind the counter greeted her like an old friend. 'Well! I haven't seen you in best part of a year.'

'Hello, Push,' she replied. He was called that because of the sign on the door to his office saying 'Push'. No one knew what his real name was; those that had known once had long forgotten.

Vic leaned his chin on the counter, looked at the pawnbroker with wide, soulful eyes. 'Evie's going to get us something nice for tea tonight. Sick of Spam and bread that's rock hard.'

'So you're looking to make a bob or two?'

'Yes, we're brassic, Dad says,' said Vic. 'Because Evie can't work because of the baby, and . . .'

'Shurrup, love,' said Evie, blushing, pinching him hard on the flesh of his upper arm. Push smiled knowingly, and she felt her cheeks becoming hot.

'You come to pawn something?'

'Dad's suit.'

She carefully untied the string of the parcel. The suit was wrapped in another layer of tissue paper inside the newspaper. The tissue was like gossamer and seemed as if it might float away as she removed the jacket, then the trousers. She slid everything over to his side of the counter.

Push took a pencil from behind his ear, picked the jacket up, raised it to the light.

'It's from TJ's . . .' said Evie, referring to T. J. Hughes department store in the town.

'I can see that,' he replied. 'Says so on the label.' He flicked open the lapel. 'Oh dear, love . . . How am I going to get rid of this? Moths have been at it.'

'Oh. I thought . . . I thought . . .' Her brows knitted together in a frown. She glanced at Victor, idling in front of the shelves, nose pressed to the glass, looking at the canes and watches and gold chains. Leaning forward over the counter, she said in a low voice, 'Just give me what you can. And I'll be back within the week for it. Or the month . . .' she lied.

'I'll give you five bob,' he said. 'That's all I can do.'

Five bob. Well, at least that would buy Nestle's milk for the baby, and they might have Scouse for tea with real meat, and cherry pie. There would be money for the electric, and maybe even some ollies for Vic after all. He was the only one without a new bag of marbles in their street. So often Evie watched him hang back whilst the other lads ran off without him. It pained Evie to see her boisterous eleven-year-old brother able to do no more than look; his only other unhappy choice to go and play with the button box.

Push wrote out a chit, took the suit, and laid it carefully over a chair. Evie took the coins, trying not to snatch as it would have looked rude, but she couldn't help scooping them up in one quick, sweeping gesture.

'And I'd like to buy Vic something . . .' added Evie.

'What? Not the violin?' There was a violin in the glass mantle of the front door. It had become a standing joke. *Not the violin?* was what Push said to all his customers. One day someone would buy it.

Evie, still distracted, added, 'I might surprise you one of these days. But for now, Victor – would you like the shoes on that shelf? They look like they might fit. You deserve it for passing your school tests . . .'

Tests? What tests was she talking about? wondered Vic. He hadn't taken any tests in months, and those that he had, he'd done pretty badly in.

'A little scholar, this one. Here. Take them, Vic . . .'

Vic's eyes widened. He couldn't believe what she was saying. The shoes were shiny patent leather. They had laces that were thin and smooth, like liquorice. He had never seen anything as beautiful as these shoes. These were the type of shoes that didn't leak, and probably never would.

'Can we have them? He'll wear them now . . .'

Vic slipped them onto his feet. Push gave him a paper bag to carry his old shoes. He gasped. They really were beautiful.

'Go on . . . I'll knock a shilling off. Well done,

Victor . . . Keep up the good work . . . Latin eh? *Bona, bonus, bonum . . .*'

'Yer what?' said Vic.

'*Mensa, mensae, mensam.* See, not as daft as I look.'

'Thanks, Push,' Evie said.

'You're welcome.'

They went outside. Vic danced along, admiring himself in the reflection of the plate-glass windows of the Spall's. But as soon as they reached the corner, Evie knelt to meet his eyes. 'Love, take them off.'

'Why?'

'Because we're pawning them at Watson's.'

'What? I've only worn 'em for two minutes . . .'

'We're pawning them. I can get twice what I paid . . . He gave me a shilling more because he thought they were for you and he felt sorry for us.'

'Why did he feel sorry for us?'

'Never mind.'

'Ah ey, Evie . . .'

'Don't ah ey me, love.' She strode on ahead.

Ah, well – it was nice while it lasted, thought Victor.

'Run on ahead,' Evie said to Victor after they'd visited Watson's. 'Tell Da I'm popping to town to swing by Blackler's. I'll be half an hour.'

As she made her way across Williamson Square towards the Playhouse, she pulled her flimsy coat around her. A low fog was prowling the streets. The whole place was shrouded in mist, but as she approached the theatre, it blazed with fuzzy, blinking dashes of colour. Evie asked if she could leave a letter for Lawrence at the stage door. Gordon barely raised his eyes, as was his way, but told her to go and slip it under his dressing-room door.

'Thank you,' she said. She made her way quickly through to the foyer and down the corridor. Head down, she tried to scurry past Mabel's dressing room, but the door was open. Mabel, facing the winged mirror, was smearing the cold cream that had congealed in ridges on the frown lines of her brow. 'Evie!'

Evie stopped, stood rigid, not quite knowing what to do next.

'Well, here's a surprise! Haven't seen you in a while. You all right, sweetie?' Mabel said, beaming, as she swivelled her chair.

Evie nodded.

'Where are you going in such a hurry? I shall have to call you Road Runner, always dashing about. Hey, lovey, you're snowing down south . . .'

'Sorry?'

Mabel nodded at her hemline. 'Your slip's showing.'

'Sorry,' Evie murmured in answer, yanking at her serge skirt. 'Just wanted to leave this letter for Lawrence.'

'You can give it to me, if you like. Lawrence is rehearsing.'

'Oh,' replied Evie.

'I might not see you again, or not for some time. Lolly and I are going on tour next week and then straight to London afterwards. But come here – I hoped I might bump into you, and I thought you might like this.'

Evie went a step further into the room. Mabel handed her a small velvet pouch.

'Open it . . .'

Evie carefully unzipped it. Inside were various bits of make-up: two lipsticks, an eyeshadow palette, brush, and a small round tub of rouge. 'I have tons of the stuff, and I'm planning to buy some more. That lipstick's a good one. Chanel. I bought it from George Henry Lees. Don't ask me why I want you to have all this, I hardly know you. But I like you.'

'Thank you,' said Evie.

'No – wait. I need to speak to you. You see, I have a fellow. One of my *fellows*. Stanley Mulhearn is his name.'

'Stanley?'

'Yes, Stanley. Works at Tate's. Takes me dancing. What else is a chap like that going to spend his wages on? Actually, I like him. Gentle soul. You should have seen everyone staring at us when we took to the floor . . .'

'I bet,' said Evie.

Mabel stopped. The silence yawned into a chasm.

'Got a little squiffy. Got a little slack-jawed . . .'

Evie felt her cheeks blaze. She glanced down at the floor.

'Talked about a chap. The one in Canada. Told me why you left your job so suddenly.' A frisson of excitement rippled through Mabel at the thought of a bit of real-life drama.

Evie felt her eyes swell with tears. 'Please, don't say anything,' she said.

'You mean to Laurie? Does he not know about

232

this baby? I should tell him, if I were you . . . I've kept it from him for now, but not for much longer. He needs handling carefully, that one.' Mabel smiled, chucked Evie under the chin, and said, 'Have a good one, darling, and you be careful with Lawrence. He needs taming, that's for sure. But then again, maybe you're the girl to do it.'

Mabel headed out in her velvet coat and fur muff. She was quite a picture, blonde curls shivering and her silver-flecked tasselled shawl shimmering.

Thirty-One

Evie had washed her hair in Oxycol washing powder, and her scalp was beginning to itch. She was self-conscious about the white flakes that sometimes flecked her shoulders afterwards, but better this than to have horrible greasy hair. At least she felt clean.

She had woken as the morning was getting itself up, and flung open the curtain to see everywhere covered with ice. She pulled her coat around her frail body. Head bent, her woollen hat pulled over her pinking ears, she made her way along the promenade, taking each step carefully as she pushed Terry in his pram. The Mersey stretched out in front of her. It really was beautiful. Dragging up the hill meant that it took a good deal longer than it should have done. Her calves ached and she squinted, blinded by the sunlight that dazzled her eyes. She had told Lawrence to meet her at the Victorian bus shelter. Hurrying along the undulating promenade, Terry kicking the blankets off with his stubby feet, she fixed her eyes on the horizon where sea and sky blurred together in an indistinct haze. On the walk from the station, she had noticed that the new flats the Corporation had started work on now looked like the builders had suddenly left and gone home in a hurry. There was a bag of cement on the pavement, split open, the contents spilled out and gone hard. A shovel lay flat on the floor. Everyone had been so optimistic about these new flats and tenements. Lives were going to change for the better with the new architect's scheme so Liverpool could rise out of the ashes after the war, but money was short all of a sudden – no one had expected rehousing and recuperation of soldiers and their families to be so costly – and everything had ground to a halt.

She rocked Terry in his pram. Was she doing the right thing?

And then she realized that even if it was the wrong thing, it was too late to do anything about it. Because Lawrence was coming towards her, grinning, his coat blowing out behind him, waving his hand at her. Her heart lurched. And as she expected, with the hand held aloft, he paused. From the beaming smile, his forehead puckered into a puzzled frown.

'What's this, Angel? A baby?' he said as he jogged towards her. His silk scarf, tied in a loose knot at his neck, flapped in the blustery wind. He could make clothes look beautiful just by wearing them.

For a moment she panicked, contemplated whether she should lie or not. She was so used to lying. She was becoming an expert at it. She had perfected the art of presenting a version of herself that was so far removed from the real worried, hurting, panicked, desperate Evie – but today she had decided that it was time for her to be truthful.

'Lawrence, there's something I wanted, needed to tell you . . . about . . .'

She gestured towards the pram. 'You see, this is my, this is my . . .' She faltered; the words 'baby brother, friend's child, nephew' played on her lips.

Lawrence squashed up beside her on the bench in the Victorian bus shelter. 'He's a smasher,' he said, distracted by the baby blowing bubbles with his fat lips and gurgling. He leaned in, pushed back the hood of the pram and jiggled the fringes of his scarf in front of Terry's face.

Meeting his eyes, Evie blurted out: 'He's the reason why I can't be your girl. He's *mine*. My child. My son . . .'

'Oh,' he said, looking a little downcast. 'That's a shame. No one told me that you were married. I'm sorry. If I had known, I—'

'I'm not married.'

The realization showed on his face as it began to dawn on him what she was saying. 'Ah, so that's what this is about. Is that what you wanted to tell me? Your letter didn't make much sense. But I see now,' he said. 'You don't have a fella – but you have a baby? Is that it?'

Her eyes met his worriedly. She plucked at the child's threadbare coverlet, nodded her head sadly. 'It's a mess. I don't know how much longer I can stand it,' she said, sadly. A tear splashed onto the back of her hand.

'Stand what?' he said.

'Living in shame . . .'

'Oh, Angel . . .' he said, putting his arm around her shoulders.

'You see, my mother left us, just up and went one

day. All sorts of rumours about another fella, although my dad has just pretended to everyone she died. But I don't know where she is, so I have no one to help me. Even if I wanted to keep my baby. So now you understand why there can never be anything between us. Even if . . . well . . . I never dreamt someone like you would even speak to me. I'm shaking,' she said. 'Look at my hand . . . I'm shaking like a leaf . . .'

She held it out and showed him the tremor.

'Can I hold him?' asked Lawrence, pulling the cover away from the pram. Terry smiled up at him.

'Of course,' she said, momentarily confused.

Lawrence stood, took the child out of the pram, cradled him in his arms, moved from foot to foot and kissed the top of his head, breathing in the smell of him. When Terry smiled and gurgled back at him, he sat back down and bounced him on his knee. Evie had never seen such tenderness in a man.

'What a kid,' he said, as Terry babbled and giggled. 'What's his name?

'Terry.'

He stood him up, supporting the baby under his arms and singing a rhyme into his face. 'Little Terry went to France, to teach the ladies how to dance, first the heel then the toe, then the splits and around you go!' he said, lifting him into the air. 'Salute to the captain, bow to the Queen, blow a raspberry at the Nazi submarine . . .' He sang and laughed as the baby burbled again, then sat down, crossed one foot over the other and jigged him up and down as if his thigh was a horse. 'He likes it. Look at his big smile. He's a beaut.'

'You're very good with him. Most fellas he's met, well, he usually cries when he sees them,' said Evie, through misty eyes. 'Probably because he stays at home most of the time.'

'Ah well – my grandfather was Italian. And us Italians are crazy for kids. We don't take with all this "children must be seen and not heard" nonsense. Never have done.'

She smiled. And as she watched him continue to gurn faces at her son and try to make him laugh, she thought, I've never felt like this. I've never felt like this for anyone. Am I falling in love with him? But it's impossible. He's never even kissed me, this is stupid.

'Angel . . .' he said. 'Earth to Angel . . .' She made a half smile. 'Tell me what the heart of the problem is.'

She sighed. 'My dad's lady friend says I should give him away. She doesn't want him in the house. She doesn't want me, either. She'd be happy if I just left for good today, but where can I go with a baby? No one would take us in. I feel so ashamed. She knows a nun, and she says they want babies like Terry to send to America. Or Canada . . .'

'America! Crikey! That's a bit bloody drastic,' he said.

'I know. And it looks like my da is getting married again. The divorce papers from my mam are coming any day now. And it's true, I have no way to look after him. We're poor . . . you probably don't know what that's like . . .'

He laughed. 'All actors are poor. Apart from the

famous ones. We just make a good show of pretending we're not.'

'Really?'

'Really. It's all an act. I know what it's like to feel hungry, but I'd spend my last few bob on a tin of Brylcreem rather than a loaf of bread. That's how ridiculous and vain us actors are.'

He'd said it to make her feel better, nudging her in the ribs gently, and she smiled.

'Well, I can beat that – we're so poor, my da had to burn some of the doors in our house for firewood just to keep us warm last Christmas, because we couldn't afford coal. That's after he got done for nicking sugar from the factory. Now he works at the docks, but they pay you a pittance . . . Still, the house is nice and roomy now.'

'Ah well, I can't beat that,' he said, smiling at her dark humour.

'We had a bit of a drama this morning, me and Da. It's getting worse each day. Holy Joan – that's my dad's fancy woman – is taking over, all right. She's got her feet under the table and sticking out the other side, for sure. She also hates Terry. I think she wants to shame me into giving him away. I've decided I'm going to get rooms somewhere if I can't stand it.'

'Oh, Angel,' he said. 'How can you afford that?'

'I've got money saved up. Not much.'

'Sounds a bit grim.'

'Yes, it is. But so is everything else. I hardly know you, Lawrence. But I just wanted you to know about Terry, before you go away on tour.'

239

Still with the child on his knee, he put one hand flat on her cheek and then pushed a lock of hair away from her face, tucking it behind her ear.

'Can I kiss you, Angel?'

'Oh, I . . .' Tears welled up in her eyes. She looked at his face; his skin was lustrous, his pale blue eyes searching and hopeful. His slender hands were beautiful and had veins that pulsated under his lightly tanned skin.

'Good God, that wasn't supposed to happen,' he said. 'You don't have to kiss me if it will make you cry . . .'

Evie sniffed into the crook of her arm. 'Hay fever,' she said.

'Hay fever? There's frost on the ground.'

'Oh, he's falling asleep . . . here, let me . . .' she said, taking Terry from Lawrence and putting him back in his pram.

'Can I?' he asked again. 'I've wanted to kiss you since the minute I first saw you . . .'

She sat back down next to him, felt him touching her forearm. It was the smallest of hesitations, the smallest of nods but he needed no more. First he brought her hand to his mouth and kissed her fingers one by one, and when he put his lips on her lips, dove his tongue into her mouth, twisted it around her teeth, and stopped only for breath and to tell her she was the most beautiful girl he had ever met and how all he wanted to do was to make her happy, she began to cry.

'What is it, Angel?' he said. 'What's the matter?'

She thought of her father, who wanted her to marry

Lionel or anyone who would have her, and if he had his way would consign her to a lifetime of missed opportunities. A lifetime of drudgery and sadness, all because of one stupid mistake. What would her father say if he knew what was going on in her head – knew that right now, all she wanted was to breathe in the same air as this man, touch him, kiss him? After all, she thought, why should one stupid mistake mean I'm not allowed happiness? The nuns, her father, thought she only deserved a man like Lionel – or Neville with his stutter and face full of boils, and that annoying thing he did sucking his teeth, and saying sorry all the time. No, there was something in Lawrence – a charm, sophistication, a femininity – that the other men she had met in her life seemed to lack. Just imagine what it might feel like, making love with this creature. No matter that her father and Joan wanted her to live the life they wanted for her; they could never take away her imagination, and feelings, and more, experience. Frankie had given her that, at least.

'I'll marry you. I'm going to marry you, Angel. How about that? I've done with all the flouncing about and histrionics of girls like Mabel. I need something real in my life. A purpose. I'm leaving in two days to go on tour, but the minute I'm back I'll come and find you. How about that, Angel? How about it? I could look after you and the baby.'

The next day, Edna sat with Evie in the Boot Inn. Evie was grateful to have someone to talk to. Edna would be able to tell her what she should do about the marriage proposal, even though she wasn't quite sure how to bring it up. They each had a glass of stout in front of them. Edna was puffing on a Player's No. 6, sitting back, wearing her Tate dungarees, with one leg stretched out on a bar stool. She didn't care. She was done with being a lady. It hadn't got her anywhere, so why bother?

'Any news on Frankie?' said Edna.

Evie sighed. 'I don't know. I went to his house months back, hoping I might leave a letter for him, and there's nothing left. The whole place has just been flattened.'

'What about his family? Uncles, aunts?'

Evie blushed. 'No idea. I guess, though, I can't keep Terry a secret much longer.'

'Everyone knows, Evie. But so what? Anyway, it takes two to tango, doesn't it? Does Frankie's ma have a mother? A father?'

'Don't really know much about his family. Chances are they won't want to know me anyway, once they find out I've got a baby. His mother hates me. I think that's why she was trying to get Frankie away from me. She had grand ideas for him with Carol Connelly. That's why she took him to Canada after the accident at factory.'

'Talking of the factory,' asked Edna. 'Have you asked any of the lads there if they know where he is?'

'I've asked Stanley, and Jacky. They have no idea either. It seems Frankie left without leaving a trace behind him.'

'Love, isn't it time now for you to perhaps try and forget and move on, to start a life with someone new? I heard—'

Quick as a flash, Evie interrupted. 'You heard what?' Her green eyes stared at Edna fiercely.

'Stanley told me.'

Evie winced.

'Actor at the Playhouse, I heard,' Edna continued. 'What's he like?'

'Good-looking, like a film star.'

'Good-looking like you, you mean?'

'I'm not good-looking. You should see his friend Mabel. All blonde curls and cupid's bow lips. That's good-looking.'

'Fake. You've got that rare Irish beauty that your ma had . . .'

There was a moment's silence.

'He is caring, even if I'm not sure he's my type,' Evie said thoughtfully. 'We're so different. Lawrence is his name. Ridiculous name, I know. And we're like chalk and cheese. I think he's just in love with the idea of being in love. I mean, he's already asked me to marry him. Isn't that absurd?' She didn't know what to make of it herself. In many ways it was the answer to her prayers, but it still didn't seem real.

'Look, love, even if you find Frankie, who's to say what he might feel about you having a baby? It might not be all wine and roses. And as for this Lawrence. In love with being in love? Well, couldn't you get used to that? If he doesn't mind about the child? Theatre types have a way of looking at the world

243

differently to others. Quite the exciting thing, I'd have thought. Does he have a friend?' she added, with a wink.

Evie smiled and sipped at her drink. Thank God for Edna. Where would she be without Edna?

Thirty-Two

So that's why Joan was wearing that stupid hat, Evie thought. She'd never believed it could have happened so quickly. It seemed such a cruel thing to do. They explained it had been practical, her father not really saying much on the subject, just shuffling about and unable to meet her eyes.

She didn't know what felt worse: the fact that he had gone off and married Holy Joan without telling his children, or the fact that her mother had finally given him the divorce he wanted and he hadn't told her that either. They said they had done it quietly because they also didn't want people to go to much fuss, or to travel. They told her they had asked Seamus the flower-seller to be their witness. And not even married in a church! Holy Joan! But there would have still been arrangements. There would have been forms to fill, surely. Evie thought of asking to see the divorce papers. Until she saw her mother's handwriting, she still couldn't quite believe it.

'All done through a solicitor,' Joan had piped up. 'We haven't even set our eyes on your mother. I've traipsed the length and breadth of Ireland looking for her.'

'So that's what you were doing in Ireland? I thought you went there to be with your sister?'

'What? Well, yes, that as well.'

'Where's me mam?'

'Somewhere on the west coast. We still don't have her address. Josephine doesn't want you to have it, either.' Her mother's beautiful name sounded wrong in Joan's mouth. Still smarting, she thought of writing to Renie. *She* wouldn't be that impressed.

Suddenly she heard a commotion in the street. It was the boys selling the *Echo*, one voice trying to outdo another; they sounded hoarse from shouting. And then the words: 'Liverpool City Centre to be completely demolished! New road running right through Liverpool!'

So it was true. It wasn't just gossip. Evie made her way into the street, rocking Terry in the pram in the fresh air to help him fall asleep and hoping she wouldn't bump into anyone. It seemed natural to be outside. Down by the river, looking towards the dock, she could see five or six men grappling with guy ropes as they tried to bring in a container of tyres.

Evie pulled her coat round her. She didn't want Joan moving around her, filling the spaces that had been left by her mother, sitting on the battered chair with the dent in the cushion, lying on the right side of her father's bed – that lonely bed that had for so long made Evie ache with sadness. Already Joan was bustling about making the blessed straw box, chucking out the hot brick, telling Evie how she needed to make plans about the baby; had she written to the sisters yet? Evie had put up with it for these past few weeks, but now everything seemed to be closing in on her. And Edna was right: this war had ruined everything. The destruction all around them seemed like a fitting backdrop to her own troubles.

Terry had begun to doze. Evie wheeled him back to the house. Sitting down and shifting in the spindly wooden chair, she tried to think what she should do, took her hairpins out for want of something to busy herself with, and slipped them into her pocket.

'Well, I'll go to the foot of our stairs!' Joan said, bursting in and bustling around the kitchen. 'Look what I've found! A shoe! Under the sink! We're going to have to make some changes around here. I've put a lid on the bath, put a mattress on top of it and a coverlet over that, so it'll be grand. That's where you'll sleep from now on, love. Your brother shouldn't be sleeping in the same bed as his sisters. It's not right. We're lucky to have a bath. Might as well put it to some good use for now.'

Whatever was she talking about?

'That's my ma's shoe. Can I have it?' Vic asked, in a small voice.

'What on earth do you want an old shoe for?' said Joan, handing it to him. He placed the shoe on the table.

'Well, I don't know why you've put the shoe on the table,' Joan said. 'We don't know where it's been. It's going to be full of germs, Victor.'

'We do know where it's been; you found it under the sink. Anyway, there's nothing wrong with a bit of dirt. It builds up your immune system, Ma always said,' muttered Evie, turning away to fill the kettle.

'Aye. And it means you can grow potatoes in your ears. When did you last have a bath, Victor? Cleanliness is next to godliness, have you not heard that saying?'

Vic glanced up and exchanged a frown with Evie. He slipped his thumbnail under a piece of wallpaper that was coming loose from the wall. 'I go swimming in the Scaldies.'

'Exactly. Disgusting. The canal might feel nice and hot to jump into, but it's only because the water is flushed straight from Tate's refinery. So stop it. Don't do that,' Joan said. 'I'm going to start on that front step,' she added, and left.

Evie went back to the sink as Vic finished his liver and onions, mopping up the greasy plate with a bit of bread. 'I hate her,' he muttered under his breath.

That night, when Evie tried to sleep on the lid over the bath and the hard mattress with Terry lying in a drawer beside her, she could hear her father and Joan talking through the thin walls. She could hear his muffled footsteps as he crossed the room, a window being pushed open, the sound of her father's hacking cough, and then Joan's low, throaty laughter.

Shouldn't she allow her father this happiness? After all that he had been through, didn't he deserve it? But it seemed it was at the expense of her own. She knew that this woman coming into the house would mean everything was going to have to change. Beginning with Terry. But then, as if to compound her worries, the conversation she could overhear grew stern and serious.

'What's the matter?'

There was a sigh, and a rustling of the eiderdown.

'She's going to have to give up this baby, you know . . .'

'Aren't we being a little hasty?'

'Sister Consilio is already making arrangements. For America. Or Canada, maybe.'

Evie heard the bedsprings creaking. Perhaps her father sitting up, or settling himself into bed. It made her feel a little queasy.

'She's bold, our Evie. She won't give the child away.'

'Aye – bold as a pig, Bill. You said you'd tell her she had to. It's all very well having the baby around whilst he's an infant, but what about when he starts talking?'

'Give me another few days.'

'If you don't do something about it, I will.'

'She'll hate you for it.'

'No, she won't. She'll realize that we're doing it for her own good.'

'We?'

'You agreed. You said so. And what about our plans? Now come here. Give us a kiss and a cuddle . . .'

Evie shrank away. Plans? What plans? Much as she wanted to know what that meant, she didn't want to hear any more, especially not the sound of tonsil tennis between Holy Joan and her father.

The following morning, when Evie yawned and opened her eyes, it was still quite dark. The light normally woke Terry. But as she turned back to look at his cot, her heart stopped. It was empty.

She gasped.

'Terry! Where is he?' she cried.

She rushed downstairs, found her father smoking a Woodbine in front of the range. He coughed up phlegm, swallowed it back down, scratched his head, thought hard and shrugged.

'Where's Joan?' Evie said, her pupils darkening.

'Mass. Feast of the Annunciation.'

'Terry's gone! Do you think Joan could have come into my room whilst I was sleeping and taken him with her to church?'

'Would be an odd thing to do,' he replied.

'Well, where is he, then?' Fear gripped Evie, panic clutching at her heart. 'I'll knock next door,' she said, desperately. It was as if she was having trouble breathing.

Evie spent a good half-hour walking up and down the street pointlessly calling Terry's name. The woman next door came out onto her front step, and there was even talk of the police. Evie was genuinely astonished to see Joan wheeling the pram down the road and smiling. She was so surprised she ran out into the street and realized she had managed to forget to put her skirt on over her petticoat, or tie the laces on her boots.

'Look at the state of you,' said Joan.

'What are you doing?' Evie cried.

'Getting him a bit of fresh air.'

'Give him back,' she said, tugging at the handle of the pram. 'Where were you taking him? What are you doing with him?'

Evie thought how much she wanted to strangle

Joan, put her hands around her neck and squeeze until her eyes bulged out.

'Just a walk down the hill, you silly girl.'

I don't trust you, Evie wanted to cry.

'You haven't taken him to see that nun, have you?'

'Evie, dear. As a matter of fact, no. But what if I had? Where would be the harm in that? We're all on your side, Evie. We only want the best for you.'

'I'm not letting that nun take him to America. I'll move out. Get a room. There's even someone who . . . who . . .'

'Finish the sentence. There's someone who what?'

But she couldn't say it out loud. She knew in her heart that it was probably ridiculous, the idea that Lawrence would take her in along with the child. How could he? Was he just making promises he wouldn't be able to keep? So she said nothing.

But half an hour later, when she had put the baby to sleep upstairs, her rage at Holy Joan for taking the pram, marrying her father, refusing to tell her where her mother was – was that even legal? – bubbled up and spilled out as she stood in the kitchen washing the pots. The argument started over something so small, it would never be remembered. But the screaming, the shouting, the yelling of obscenities, the slamming of doors, the tears, the short, sharp slap across the face, would never be forgotten.

'You need to smarten up your ideas, young lady. This can't go on. Has your father told you the Corpy are finally rehousing us? We're moving out to the countryside. St Helen's. He's got a job at Pilkington's glass factory. We can take Vic and the girls with us, but it's only three bedrooms, so there's no place for you and a baby in any case.'

Evie dropped the pot into the sink and it landed with a clatter.

'Just talk to Sister Consilio. Just give her ten minutes of your time.'

'Sister Consilio! No. I know what she wants . . . She wants Terry.'

'No, she doesn't. She wants to help you . . .' Joan's voice sounded bitter; she seemed twitchy and spiky all of a sudden.

'I don't want anyone's help! You're not my mother! You're cruel. Why don't you mind your own business? We were fine before you came along.'

'Fine! You with a baby, and no idea what to do with him!'

'I just need time to think,' Evie said, pushing her fists into her temples. My father would thump you if he could hear what you're saying, coming in and ruining our lives, she was thinking.

'Well, Jesus might love a sinner, but he thinks you're a little whore,' Joan spat. 'Good job your ma ran off with Luigi Galinari so she's not around to see this, you . . .' She waved her hand at Evie in up and down motions, as if she were painting a picture of disgust, and rolled her eyes. 'A fallen woman. Red-haired, brazen hussy, you are, and bold as brass.'

The sad diminutive figure at the door, the white nightgown, the mess of curls, appeared from nowhere. 'I thought our mam was dead,' said Sylvie in a small voice, clutching at her rag doll. 'Is Mam alive?' she added, round-eyed and hopeful.

'No, love, she's not dead. She's living with her fancy fella across the water,' said Joan, cruelly.

Sylvie's eyes filled with tears.

'Now look what you've done! How could you do that?' yelled Evie.

Joan shrugged.

It was the casual nature of her response that made Evie run at her, head down as though she was a charging bull, her voice leaping to a cry of fury. For a moment, they wrestled. Joan tugged at Evie's hair and looked amazed to see she had pulled out a clump of it in her fist. Evie, screaming in pain, used her hands to lash out at Joan. Then she darted away, grabbed the poker from beside the fire, and raised it above Joan's head. And though she might not really have been intending to hit her, it made Joan cry out in terror, crouch to the floor and cower. At that very moment, Evie's father burst into the room.

'What the bloody hell are you doing, Evie! Fighting Joan, like a flamin' alley cat! Why's everyone yelling and crying? Curly's bawling his head off upstairs!'

'She started it!' cried Evie.

Her father telling her she should apologize to Joan immediately would be etched into her mind forever. It was clear that she and Joan Hennessy were finished before they had even begun. There could be no coming back from this.

'I'm going. I'm taking Terry and I'm leaving. Tell the girls the truth about Ma, Da. But don't let Joan do it,' she said, springing to her feet. Outside in the hall, she thumped her fist and slammed it into the wall, then nursed her bruises, sucking on her knuckles.

And when she ran upstairs and buried her head in her pillow, sobbing, it wasn't just the walls closing in on her, with their peeling paint and creeping damp making it hard to breathe. It was the whole world that was collapsing in on top of her.

And it was then she decided that if Lawrence was true to his word, when he came back from his tour, she would be an idiotic fool not to accept him.

Thirty-Three

NO BLACKS. NO IRISH. NO DOGS. NO ACTORS.

No actors? That was something she must tell Lawrence when she saw him again. But that's what the sign said in the window. Evie wondered if she had the right address. The curtains twitched, and a face peered out. Evie gave the woman a half smile.

'I saw the advert in the *Echo*. I need a room.'

The woman, wearing tatty overalls, moved away from the window, came to the door and opened it an inch, still with the chain on it.

'Is that your baby?' she drawled.

Evie nodded. 'It's only for a short time. Just a few weeks or so. Whilst my husband is away. We won't make any noise. You'll hardly know we're here . . .'

The woman didn't even reply, just slammed the door shut in Evie's face.

The next house, a two-up, two-down that looked onto the docks, was more miserable than any she could remember seeing before. And there was the sign again, only this time it just said NO IRISH. She knocked, decided to try and take a different approach, and moved away from the window so that the pram couldn't be seen. The wind whisked her skirts up around her thighs and her loose hair whipped across her face and stung her cheeks. Eventually, the door opened.

'I saw you have a room to rent. My husband has sent me . . .'

The man was puffing on a cigarette. He opened the door wider to her. She went in. The smell of damp hit her first. The whole house was fetid, airless. Damp sweated through the fungus-infested walls.

She could hear a baby wailing, the sound coming from a room upstairs. There was the noise of a woman cackling, then a cry of *shurrup*!

A cat slinked around the banister; its fur had bald patches, and it was mangy. It hissed at her when she put her first foot on the bottom step.

'Don't touch him,' said the man. A young girl, straggly hair plastered to her dirty face, no shoes, blackened feet and scaly scabby knees, and then a young boy who looked like dirt stuck to him, appeared on the landing. Evie noticed the ragged hems of their skirts and trousers. This was 1950: there was television, cake mix that came in a box, irons that permanently hissed steam – it wasn't Dickensian Britain, thought Evie, shocked to see what a state they were in. The man opened the door to the room. She could never have imagined such poverty. Her own family was poor, but she could never have dreamt how people lived like this. A small range in the corner, an iron bedstead with a filthy dirt-stained mattress. A chamber pot in the middle of the floor with some noxious green liquid in the bottom of it. In the dim light of an oil lamp, strange shadows hollowed out their cheeks and eyes.

'Cooking facilities on the landing, love . . .' he said. 'Where did you say your old man is?'

'Oh. He's at sea.'

He nodded. She didn't know whether he believed her.

'Three shillings a week,' he said. She nodded. Terry began to cry.

'Can I move in tonight?' she asked.

'Come back later,' he said. 'You're pretty. I say three shillings, but . . . well, if you'd like to come to an arrangement . . .'

He reached out, placed his hand on the curve between her neck and shoulder, let it lie there for a minute. The hollow-eyed young girl, with her hands curled around the banister, just stared. He grinned and the girl cocked her head quizzically, waiting to see what Evie was going to do next.

'You don't look like the kind of folks we usually get here. You in some kind of trouble, queen?' he asked, leering at her.

'Just need a room,' she replied, shuddering at the thought of this man breathing into her face, blowing smoke, his braces, his fat stomach. 'Just need a room.'

'Come back later. I'll see what I can do, la.'

She walked the two miles home, thoughts twisting around in her head. Standing on Coghlan Street, she shifted from foot to foot on the cold pavement slabs. How could she go back in after making such a dramatic exit? Fingering the change in her pocket, she wheeled Terry towards the Pier Head to sit on the bench – Evie and Frankie's bench – just to think for a moment. Perhaps she should go to Edna's? She might know what to do. A gentle breeze blew the hair from her face. A lorry trundled up, stopped, and two builders got out, with buckets of sand and spades with long handles.

'Cheer up, love. It might never happen,' one of the men shouted.

Evie dropped her head and knitted her eyebrows together in a pinch. It already has, she thought miserably.

Thirty-Four

Edna had welcomed her into her tiny one-roomed flat above Grady's corner shop, made her a cup of tea and gone to collect a bag of clothes and Terry's bottle from Coghlan Street.

'Evie will be staying with me for a few days. Just until she's sorted,' she'd said to a surprisingly flustered Joan and a bewildered Bill. 'I'll be glad of the company,' she added briskly. 'I know it's six years ago, but since my Archie died, well he was always up and down the stairs to see me in my little flat and the place still feels awful quiet without him. You'd think I'd have got used to it by now, but not a day goes by when I don't think of him weighed down by those guns and whatnot, drowning before he even stepped foot on the Normandy sand. What a waste.'

That was enough for an embarrassed Bill to start bustling her out of the door for fear of another tragic conversation about love, war and death. They had all had enough of those to last a lifetime.

Evie spent an uncomfortable night sleeping on Edna's battered old sofa. When she woke, Terry, lying on a cushion wrapped in her overcoat, was happily kicking his stubby legs and chewing on his fist.

Evie rubbed her shoulder, trying to smooth out

the crick in her neck. After Edna had gone out to buy milk, she picked up the envelope that Edna had brought from Coghlan Street along with her small bag. 'Your da told me to give it to you,' Edna had said.

Lyceum Theatre, Crewe
Dressing Room Number One (!)

Dear Angel,
While the Sun Shines is turning out to be pretty cloudy. They replaced Mabel with the assistant stage manager for yesterday's matinee as she's got a bad cold from the damp in the dressing room. But the girl has got legs like tree trunks and looks like a man, if you ask me. She can barely get into Mabel's costumes, so it's all bit of a shame. Let's hope The Tinker's Wedding, which we start rehearsing next week, will not prove to be such a damp squib.

I am writing this in my dressing room, where as you know, I am about to get changed into a rather dashing uniform (I'd much rather dress up as a soldier than be one, you get all the adulation without being shot at) and ready to go on stage. Everybody keeps popping in and out, the stage manager, the dresser, Ken, so I've had a job to get it finished and now I have to go on stage as we've had our five-minute call.

I keep thinking about our meeting on the

promenade. I meant every word, Angel. I know how hard it must be for you, what the world thinks of girls like you. It's so unfair. Especially when there are folks like us theatre types who couldn't give a damn about things like that. Some of us behave abominably and the sky hasn't fallen in, nor have we been struck by a thunderbolt. At least not yet! Besides, you are much the best girl that I have ever known. I can't help thinking you were put on this earth for me. I know that Terry must never be separated from you. But I would like to take you both away and marry you. And next time when I go off on tour, come with me, we could take Terry around in a wicker basket and you could sit in my dressing room whilst I'm on stage. I understand this is so very rushed and sudden. But you can't stop feelings.

'Evie. I've been going out of my mind,' said her father, coming straight up the stairs and into Edna's flat through the door.

Evie quickly folded the letter and slipped it under the chipped blue willow-patterned plate on the sideboard.

'What are you hiding?' he said, quick as a flash.

Evie picked up Terry. 'Nothing,' she replied.

'It didn't look like nothing. Is it that letter that came for you? Sylvie thought it was from your mam, and Vic said that just because Mam's alive doesn't mean she'd suddenly write after all this time. What a mess,' he added, sadly.

Evie sighed. 'I don't know why Joan told her.'

'She didn't mean to. Evie, you can come with us to St Helen's, you know. Joan just gets a little hot under the collar. She's very sorry. We'll just have to figure out what to do about the baby . . .'

Evie sat back in her seat, took a deep breath. 'Da, I think – I think I've met someone. He's not in Liverpool at the minute. But I've decided that when you go, I'll not come with you. I can't live under the same roof as Joan. Not another day. And if she'll put up with our Vic and the girls – and as she's your wife – I don't want to make you unhappy either, Da.'

'Think on it, love. Think on it. Who's this chap, then? Frankie finally come back from Canada? Some hope. Is it Neville? Finally decided you could get over the manure smell? Or Lionel? Lionel's an honest sort of fellow. Maybe a few bricks shy of a load, but decent enough.'

'Stop, Da. I won't say now. But please trust me.'

Kissing her tenderly on the head, he said, 'Good of Edna to take you in.'

When he had gone, Evie picked up the letter again. '*I love you. I loved you from the first moment I set eyes on you, my sweet sugar girl.*'

Terry was hiccupping. She rubbed a soothing hand on his back in a circular motion, nuzzling into the top of his velvety head. 'What d'you think about me marrying Lawrence? Hey, love? Am I crazy? Or should we give it a go?'

Thirty-Five

'Evie! What on earth has happened now?' said Sister Mary Clotilda.

The convent, adjoining Evie's old school, was dimly lit. It was built onto the back of the same building. There was a porch light and it threw a soft glow onto the wooden front door, lighting up its brass knocker. Evie breathed deeply, jigged the pram in which Terry slept. She had knocked softly. When Sister Mary Clotilda had answered the door, Evie had been shocked and relieved to see her. She couldn't imagine what she would have done if Sister Boniface or Sister Mary Oliphant had opened it.

'Evie? Are you all right, dear?' prompted Sister Mary Clotilda.

Evie swallowed down the familiar panic. Clotty's gentle, kind smile made her genuinely pleased that she had come all this way. Leading her into a small, functionally furnished room, Clotty pulled out one chair from a small round table and sat down in the other.

'What's the matter, dear?' she said. 'What can I do for you? How is the little man?' She smiled into the pram.

Evie pulled back the blanket. Terry smiled up at them.

'Sister, I have nowhere to live. I'm staying with my friend Edna, but I can't stay there forever with the baby. And I don't know where to turn . . .' she blurted. 'Da is going to St Helen's with Joan and Vic and the girls, but I can't go with them. I won't,' she said, earnestly.

'Oh dear,' said Sister Mary Clotilda quietly.

Evie spilled out, in a tumbling avalanche of words, how Joan had been trying to persuade her to go to St Jude's; how they wanted her to have the baby adopted. How she just needed time to find a job, earn some money. Before her fiancé came home.

'Fiancé? Frankie? That's good news.'

Evie blushed. She couldn't bring herself to tell the truth. She squirmed inside, knowing it would sound preposterous and faintly ridiculous to say that she might be about to marry an actor with whom she had barely spent even one whole day; it was easier to let the sister believe it was Frankie she was talking about. What did nuns know of romance, after all?

'He's coming back in two months' time.'

Sister Mary Clotilda paused, knowing not to ask any more questions. 'I wonder, I wonder . . .' she said, thinking aloud. 'St Sylvester's – that's an orphanage about five miles from here – they've just lost Sister Ignatius after she returned to the missions in Dembi Dollo. I wonder whether you could go and work there for a little while? You could teach the smaller children arithmetic. You were always good with numbers. Sister David was only saying the other day that she needed a replacement.'

'But Clotty – I mean, Sister Mary Clotilda – what

about my baby? I don't want to give him away,' said Evie, urgently. She glanced at Terry, feeling anxious and panicked.

'He will be no bother. We are used to babies at St Sylvester's. We have a beautiful nursery. One more won't be any trouble.' Clotty smiled serenely.

'And they'll let me keep him?'

'Of course. Seeing how you'll soon be married. St Sylvester's is just the place for someone with a child: they have dormitories and cots in rows, and plenty of people around to look after wee ones. Just what you need. As well as, right now, a nice cup of tea and a biscuit. How does that sound?'

'Oh, Sister . . . Thank you. So long as you're sure that I can keep Terry.'

Sister Mary Clotilda took both her hands, spoke directly into her face. 'I'm making a promise to you. Believe it or not, it's our job to keep families together, contrary to what the world might think.'

'And then, when I'm back on my feet . . .'

'Yes, dear. When Frankie comes back and you marry – I presume he's going to marry you?'

'Yes, Sister.'

'Well, when you're married, everything will be just fine. Now, we call our girls our angels in aprons. There are a few others like you. They normally help with the laundry, menial tasks, but it would be wonderful if you could run errands for us and do a few hours' teaching.'

Evie's eyes swam with tears. She hadn't wanted to lie to Clotty, but it was hard to be noble and honest under such circumstances. Clotty would find out the

265

truth soon enough. Her mind leapt back to the conversation she had once had with a nun who had said that wherever she was in the world, she would always have a home when she walked through the doors of a Catholic church. She still didn't trust the idea of that; whatever it meant, she wasn't quite sure. But for the moment, she felt grateful – grateful that she would have a roof over her head, grateful that St Sylvester's would be happy to have Terry, grateful to Clotty that the tea and her kindness had probably saved her. At least for now.

Thirty-Six

The next morning, just as Evie had asked her, Edna broke the news of Evie's plans to Bill and Holy Joan. Cheerily declaring that St Sylvester's seemed like an ideal solution for them all, Joan said she had meant no harm – she just wanted the best for Evie and Terry. Bill seemed to be singing from the same hymn sheet, even though his eyes shone with tears. *We just want the best. A change is as good as rest*, they said. *This will get you back on your feet, we're sure of it.* Thank the Lord for Sister Mary Clotilda, and the prospect of a husband for Evie in Lawrence.

Clotty had told Evie to make her way to the road adjacent to Lime Street station, where she would be met by a man driving a black sedan car. Sure enough, there he was, in a Morris Oxford with its shiny bonnet throwing back liquid reflections.

'Gerrin, love,' the man said, dropping his cigarette butt and grinding it into the pavement with his toe.

A woman got out of the passenger side. She was wearing a navy-blue gabardine coat and had a white armband around her upper arm, just as Clotty had said she would. She didn't look like a nun, but she had the same inscrutable face as most of the nuns Evie knew.

'In the back, dear,' she said.

Who were these people who were available to drop everything and drive her all the way out to Freshdale? With its beach that stretched for miles and a tide that never came in except when it crept behind you in order to drown you, and inhospitable pinewoods.

They drove out of the city, first past the docks and then the factories, then neat houses with window boxes, and through fields and hedgerows. Eventually they went through the gates of the red-brick gothic building, their silver-hubcapped wheels crunching on the gravelled drive. Evie saw that there was a nun standing on the step to welcome her. She was smiling as she greeted them. Evie lifted Terry out of the back seat of the car in a battered portable bassinet.

'Well, hello, Evie!' said the nun, coming down the sandstone steps to meet her. 'This must be Terry. Sister Mary Clotilda told us he was bonny. What a little champ he is.'

She reached out a hand to shake Evie's, and Evie returned the greeting, putting the bassinet down on the top step.

From the double doors there appeared a girl wearing a tunic, with tumbles of dark hair falling about her shoulders. 'Sister, can I take her on the tour?' she said excitedly.

The nun smiled. 'Go on then, leave the baby with me,' she said. 'Oh, I do love babies . . .'

'I'm Ellen. Don't look so worried. Sister David is one of the nice nuns. Your wee one will be fine. This is one of the dormitories,' the girl said as she flung open a door. The rows of cots with mobiles hanging above each one, stars and moons eerily bobbing on the ends of thin wires, seemed a little tragic to Evie. 'Most kiddies don't want to be in separate rooms, so they're quite happy to sleep here,' she said, gesturing towards the rows of small beds. 'These are the classrooms,' she continued, opening another door. There was a large hinged blackboard on wheels in front of the lines of single desks. In front of the large window, a girl with long brown hair tied in a pony-tail was standing on a stool, cleaning a silver rose bowl with a rag.

'All right, Trappy?' Ellen said with a grin. 'We call her that 'cos she doesn't talk much, do you?'

The girl turned, laughed, and chucked the rag at her. Ellen ducked.

'Shut your cakehole, Mattressback.'

'You shut yours, Rat,' Ellen retorted, giggling. She turned back to Evie. 'We call her that sometimes too, because she just sniffs her food. That's why she's so skinny.'

The girl threw back her head and laughed again. 'I won't say why we call you Mattressback, Ellen. But you can make a guess, love . . .'

'Tch,' replied Ellen, smiling.

The convent interior was divided functionally into wings. A residential wing held the dormitory halls, where children were separated by age group. Then there was an isolated wing for the nuns, and a service wing that contained the dining hall, kitchen, storage areas, offices, halls and rooms for social activities and, at the back of the building, another classroom. As in all convents, the sisters' pride and joy was the chapel, a small, high-ceilinged room. The domed roof above the altar was painted pale blue, with a frieze of angels blowing trumpets and sitting on white clouds.

At the top of the stairs, Ellen shoved her fingers in her mouth and whistled. Down below, a girl came out from under an arch, looked up and beamed.

'Hey! Hottie! This is the new girl! Evie!' said Ellen.

Hottie? thought Evie. She was startlingly pretty, long blonde hair, thick eyelashes, brown eyes, and did have nice breasts, curves, and a tiny nipped-in waist. 'There's only one thing you need to remember, sweet. Hottie is mine – isn't that right, Hottie!' she said.

Hottie winked up at them. Evie wondered if they were trying to shock her. 'You're my girl, aren't you?' said Ellen, blowing a giggling Hottie a kiss and making the shape of a heart with her forefingers and thumbs.

Eventually, after Evie had eaten a supper of bread and chicken broth in the kitchen, Ellen showed her to a tiny room at the end of a long, narrow corridor where she would be sleeping with Terry. In the neat, bare room there was a chipped enamel bowl on a stand and a square piece of linen lying on the small metal bed. Ellen remarked that it was already getting late so she should get ready for bed. Half past seven surely isn't late, Evie thought, but she supposed she should do as she was told. 'Try and get some sleep,' said Ellen.

'Thank you,' she said.

'You'll be a big help here,' Ellen said. 'There's only five of us. Trappy and Hottie are a right laugh. And you'll get along with Beryl and Julie.'

When she had gone, Evie fed Terry and laid him in the cot beside the bed. 'Sleep tight, don't let the bedbugs bite,' she whispered, luxuriating for a moment in his dimpled knees and cheeks, tucking the swaddling blankets tightly round his little pink body. How she could have even contemplated giving him away to her Auntie Renie? she thought, with a shudder. Not that Renie had wanted him, in the end.

She felt lucky to have Terry with her in her own room, in the small cot next to her bed, but even so she hoped that this wouldn't be forever. Before she closed her eyes, she took out Lawrence's letter from under the thin mattress in the carrycot. '*Angel, I should be back in four weeks' time. Until then, my precious sugar girl . . . Until then, my precious sugar . . . until then, my precious . . .*' she repeated as her eyes grew heavy, and she drifted towards sleep.

She slept well, but was woken at five thirty by the sound of a gong banging in the corridor. She guessed it meant that she was supposed to get up, so she blew on her hands to warm them and then swung her legs over the side of the bed. Even though it was spring now, maybe because the bed was uncomfortable, the room felt freezing cold. She dressed in the set of clothing that had been left for her to wear, and pushed her feet into the clogs. The stone floor felt hard.

She went downstairs to the refectory with Terry on her hip, stopping to peer more closely at a notice

271

on the back of the door saying that there was to be no talking in this room after six p.m. A girl much the same age as her came bowling in, dressed in the same type of outfit. Sister David had called this tunic a jibber, like the one Evie had had to wear to school as a child. They must all wear a jibber, and it should come to no shorter than their calves. Evie wondered if the other girl was wearing the same itchy navy-blue knickers, too. She noticed the girl had rolled up her waistband, though who she was doing that for, she didn't know. Maybe she was doing it for Hottie? This girl had rosy cheeks and plump lips and an upturned nose. Her hair was shoved into a cap just like the one Evie was wearing.

'Hello, I'm Beryl. You the new angel? Sister David says I'm to take your baby to the nursery?'

Evie nodded.

'I'm also to show you the ropes.' She whisked Terry from Evie's arms and moved off, with Evie jogging along behind and a frightened Terry looking over Beryl's shoulder. Beryl nodded to a room off the corridor. 'That's where you and I have to take turns to play with the children. There's three toddlers. They're lovely, but I'll warn you, they're terrified little things . . . The little girl is deaf. The boy has a harelip and he doesn't speak. Not sure about the other boy, but he'll have something or other . . .'

Evie noticed that there weren't many toys, just the odd limbless and mostly bald doll lying around. The toy trains were broken, with wheels missing. There was a blackboard with the words 'Hello, my name is Tommy. Hello, my name is Pamela' written on it.

After Beryl deposited Terry in a rickety wooden playpen with a wave and a pinch of his chubby cheek, she led Evie through into an area where there were a few books on a shelf, as well as the obligatory crucifix. A statue of the Sacred Heart sat on the mantelpiece above the fireplace, and there were vases of flowers on either side of it.

'Us fallen girls are useful. Well, we're free. Some help with the laundry and sewing. Cheap labour.'

'Oh, I'm not a fallen girl . . .' Evie stuttered. 'I'm not giving my son away. I'm here for R and R . . .'

'Eh?' Beryl said.

'I have a husband . . .' she lied. 'I'm here for rest and respite. I was going to go into rooms. But that's not easy with a baby. Apart from the places that are really dreadful. At least here is clean. I'm looking forward to running errands and teaching a bit of maths.'

'Oh,' replied the girl, flatly. 'Didn't know that was a thing. Is that why you're allowed to have your baby stay here with you? Pretty unusual.'

'Yes.'

'Well, you won't get much rest around here. As for respite . . .' she laughed. 'Just make sure a few weeks is all it is.'

'How did you end up here?' asked Evie.

'I'm a nurse. I was at St Jude's down the road, but they moved me here when they found out.'

'Nurse?'

'I work here in the san. There's two kiddies in there right now with scarlet fever. Some of the nuns here don't have a clue what to do. There's even still some war babies here, can you believe it? Five years after we crushed Hitler. Generally these are the kiddies no one wants to adopt. Look around. Haven't you noticed? There's a good few wearing callipers. Hearing aids – polio's a disaster. Withered arms and the like. But can you believe folks will even turn down kiddies with glasses? The nuns make them wear those awful NHS specs, but even so.'

'That's dreadful. Poor kiddies.'

'Yes. And each year they get older, it makes it harder for the nuns to get rid of them. Everyone wants a baby that's freshly baked.'

They walked through a maze of corridors as they talked. Evie could barely take in what she was hearing. It sounded so dramatic and sad.

'Ellen's kiddie is a war baby. One minute Ellen's mother was dragging her around Liverpool, proudly telling everyone how she was the best shorthand typist in Knotty Ash, seventy words per minute. Next thing, when she finds out she's knocked up, she slings her out and says never to darken her door again. And then there's Julie, who doesn't even live here. She lives in the village now. Comes here to work so she can see her baby. Been doing that for the last four years.'

'Four years!'

'Yes. Never mind. Time flies when you're enjoying yourself,' she laughed darkly. 'She's useful for the nuns. She's strong and can shift things. Stacked a whole pile of tables on top of each other the other day. Not afraid to get up a ladder or stick her hand down the lavvy.'

'Why is her baby here in the orphanage?'

'Well, see, she met her fella at the Locarno. Ronnie. He buggered off the minute he found out she was preggers, of course. If it hadn't been for the colour of his skin, she might have had a hope of getting her baby adopted. Shame, the kiddie is the most beautiful thing you've ever seen. Still, there's now a plan to send her off to America. Brown babies are not such a problem there as here. It's a new thing, but seems to be working.' She drifted off into a thoughtful moment.

'And you, Beryl?'

'Me? Well, here's the thing. I have a baby too. She's at St Jude's. Had her five weeks ago. My fella scarpered an' all, so what could I do? Someone will adopt her soon. She's perfectly healthy but right now her face is all spotty from a milk rash, so no one wants her. I'm hoping she'll stay that way so I'll have a few more weeks with her.'

They clacked over the linoleum, both of them in the clogs that slapped the floor and the soles of their feet. Heading downstairs, Evie heard a child's voice call out repeatedly for Sister David. Why was no one answering? she wondered. Then a girl with one leg in callipers, about ten years old, seemed to appear suddenly from nowhere, standing on the landing in a white linen nightdress. She waved at them, her eyes following them intently.

'Come back to your room, Kitty!' said another disembodied voice.

When they got to the classroom, there was a woman at the door, wearing a tweed pencil skirt and a coral jumper that showed off her curves. She was standing, neck bent and nodding, in deep conversation with Sister David.

Beryl dragged Evie by the sleeve, pulled her aside. 'She's come to look at one of these kiddies. The child is deaf but they've given him a hearing aid and he's a little better. Why she doesn't want one of the pink healthy babies from St Jude's, I don't know. But he's got an awful pretty face, this kid. The nuns try. They bring the couples who want to adopt a baby here first, but then they so often end up down the road at St Jude's. This woman's different. She's been back twice. I'm glad. I'd rather she was here looking at the kids, than over the road looking at my Kimberley.'

'That's a nice name.'

'The sisters made me call her Hilda, after St Hilda. But I call her Kim. Didn't want a religious name. They can stuff their St Hilda crap.' Evie looked shocked. 'My ma said I had to be brave and never look back. Never ever look back. Remember that when it's your turn.'

Evie's heart lurched to her throat. 'My turn? I don't need to. Like I said. I have a fella. And there's not a chance I'm giving Terry away.'

Beryl cocked her head full of curls.

Evie faltered. 'I couldn't stay at home. I had nowhere to go. My husband is away but he's coming back soon.'

'Pooh. Aren't you the lucky one?'

She blushed, and whispered, 'Truth is, he's not my husband, we're not married. Yet . . .'

'I'm not one to talk. I don't care, love. No one cares about anything like morals around here. You've met Hottie and Ellen, haven't you? The nuns don't have a clue,' she laughed. 'Sneaking into each other's bedrooms. Mind you, Hottie is gorgeous, isn't she?'

Evie blushed.

'The sister who organized for me to come here, she was kind to me. The sister I met yesterday was kind as well,' she said, changing the subject.

'Can't have been Sister Annunciata, then. Yesterday was another one of her hairshirt days. Spent all day praying for our souls.'

Evie heard a whimpering noise on the other side of the wooden dividing panel, turned her head to the sound of it.

'Don't worry. It's morning nap time. They have nightmares. Happens all the time. Sometimes in the night, the older kiddies cry out as well. Or if they have a fever they talk in their sleep. It's our job to get up and see to them.'

'What about the sisters?'

'You're joking. They're too bloody lazy. Anyway, remember this. They'll do you a favour if you're useful to them. Sister David is a lovely woman. It's Humilitas you want to watch out for. There was one girl years back who had a baby with a German soldier, so no one wanted to adopt the kid when they found that out. She was at St Jude's. The nuns flit from there to here. Apparently, Humilitas made her shave her head so she would stand out from the rest of the girls as a traitor. At least we didn't sleep with the enemy. Now let me introduce you to my favourite, Trixie. Trixie's a mongoloid, but you wait. What a kid.'

As she spoke, a small girl of about five wandered

277

in. Smiling a radiant smile, she ran over and buried her head in Beryl's skirts, and Beryl hugged her. Trixie giggled. 'Trixie's my special girl. Aren't you, lovely?' she said. 'Trixie makes all our lives worth living.'

Beryl had hardly drawn breath, but when she stopped to kneel and tie the loose ribbon in Trixie's hair, she said wistfully, 'I don't want to go anywhere whilst I can still see my Kim. So until she's adopted, I'm nursing here. But when I get out of here, I've done with nursing. I'm going to open a little sewing shop.'

She hauled a Ewbank push-along carpet sweeper out of a cupboard. Outside, there was a noise coming from the refectory. 'Jesus! I feel so sorry for these kiddies. Can you hear the little ones next door? There's always a lot of pushing and shoving the minute food is put on the table. Mind you, I guess if you've been starved in your life, you'll always be grabbing a crust.'

Evie folded sheets of paper into squares, then used a ruler to rip them into smaller squares again. Beryl finished rolling the Eubank back and forth over the carpet.

They walked together into the classroom. There were children sitting at desks in rows. She looked around at them, at their bowl haircuts, serious, anxious-looking faces, the ones wearing ugly metal and iron callipers that made their legs stick out at odd angles from underneath the desks.

'Seems cruel to bring you here with all these babies in the nursery, and leave yours next door,' said Evie.

Beryl laughed as she straddled a wooden chair.

'Well, Sister Humilitas isn't in the business of kindness. Despite the way her name sounds. They don't want us to get too attached to our babies.'

'I see . . .' she murmured, trying to take everything in.

Sister Humilitas bustled in. 'Nice to have you here, Evie . . . Beryl . . . For pity's sake. Sit with your legs together . . . You're supposed to be setting a good example. You're like a wanton washerwoman, and with those huge bosoms of yours bursting out of that shirt. Do up your top button!'

'Sorry, Sister . . .' said Beryl, exchanging a wry smile and a wink with Evie.

That night Evie had trouble sleeping. It was a challenge to adjust to the sounds of the constant shuffling of the nuns in the corridor above and the children whimpering, now that she had a clearer idea of what went on here. The next day, after she had left Terry in the nursery, Beryl explained more about the 'wanton washerwoman' exchange, as she and Evie walked to the classroom. 'They're obsessed with chastity here. These kiddies, they're taught how to dress, undress, and bathe without exposing their bodies. Some of them find it difficult, especially the little ones, as you can imagine.'

Evie nodded. She was now standing in front of the class with a chalkboard and an abacus. The coloured wooden beads clacked as she pushed them back and forth along the metal rods. She started on times tables. The children repeated by rote.

'One times ten is ten, twice ten is twenty . . .'

She asked a question about division. Little hands shot up into the air. There was a girl of about ten, sharpening pencils, sitting at the front desk, sticking them into a small metal box and turning a handle, mesmerized by the curling pencil sharpenings fluttering into her lap. She clearly couldn't hear what Evie was saying, and when Evie tapped her on the shoulder she looked up vacantly and smiled.

Later she and Beryl went down to the nuns' corridor to deliver back the times tables books. There were yellowing pictures of the saints hanging from picture rails, some of the images coming loose from the frames and curling up around the edges. In the distance you could hear the sound of singing and the bells that called the nuns to the midday Angelus, ringing softy. They met Ellen coming the other way down the corridor.

'Look out, Sister Mary Menopause is on her way down . . .'

'Thanks, love,' said Beryl. 'She means Sister Annunciata. You don't want to be around her when she's in one of her moods. Let's go for a smoke.' They went to go through the back door. A small girl was hanging from the rails of the staircase. She swung back and forth, but when she saw Evie and Beryl, she quickly lowered herself down to the mosaic tiled floor. The girl blushed and ran off, but not before giving Beryl a firm, testing look.

'You know what my plan is?' said Beryl, puffing dreamily on a cigarette. 'To keep my baby and get out of here with her. I want to keep her so badly. Shall I tell you something awful? I've been feeding her milk from the dregs in the slop bucket to stop her getting better. Just put a little bit of the sour stuff on my finger and let her suck it. I know it's a terrible thing, but it won't harm her. If it doesn't agree with her, though, well, maybe it will make her a bit more spotty. Who wants a kid with a face full of spots?'

For a moment, Beryl's eyes filled with tears. But then she recovered. She ground the cigarette into the floor with her clog.

'Fancy a biccy?' she said. 'I know where they're kept.' She smiled mischievously.

'Will we get into trouble?'

'Who cares? What's a few tears over a custard cream? I'm prepared to take the chance. I always say it's much smarter to ask for forgiveness than ask for permission.'

They headed back inside. 'Hear that?' said Beryl. She nodded up at the ceiling. There was the sound of scraping, someone moving over the wooden floor.

'What is it?' Evie asked.

'The old biddies, the ancient nuns. They push chairs about when they're saying their night prayers . . . They're the worst. Let's get them biccies.'

The next morning, they were in the playroom. Beryl stood on a high stool and began to flick a duster over a statue of Our Lady. There were flowers stuck into the holes of a silver vase at her feet. Beryl sneezed, then clutched at her side.

'Jesus, I've peed myself again,' she laughed. 'I thought I'd be back to normal by now . . .'

Ellen was sitting on a low three-legged stool with

three young children crowding around her, a baby in her arms. The children giggled as she dangled a red ribbon strung with cotton reels in front of the baby's face as it squirmed on her lap. There were two other babies sleeping in bassinets, one of whom was Terry. The room was stuffy – heated by a roaring fire, unnecessary for this time of year – and Evie worried to see that Terry's tender curls were stuck to his head. A toddler rattled around in a walker on wheels with a small wooden seat, and kept bashing himself against the wall. 'God love us, Daniel, you'll take someone's eye out!' Beryl said, laughing as she gave him a hefty push with her foot so that he went whizzing across the wooden floor to the other side.

Evie wasn't sure it was funny, even though Daniel giggled. She looked around. There was one pale-eyed boy with a flat head who stared vacantly, his hands pressed solemnly against the glass window; he seemed a little older. He just looked peculiar. She could see it in his sad face. Even asking him to follow her into the classroom made him flinch and stare at her, round-eyed with fear. No one would want to adopt him. She wanted to put her arm around him, but she knew he would just wriggle away.

A couple of girls sat studiously at their desks, waiting. She could see one glancing at the other, then shielding her notepad with her hand. She was competitive, this kid, the fiery one who had gold stars next to her name – Pamela. She was streets ahead in her times tables and long division and always first in the queue for orange juice and biscuits. Evie had already noticed. But perhaps if survival was the only thing on your mind, you learned to look after yourself here.

'When you have finished long division, we will start on spelling . . . Would you like to begin, Tom?' she asked the boy.

'No,' he answered fearfully. He pulled his sweater over his head and made a hood of it.

They went through the alphabet, writing letters on the board, Evie urging them to spell out each word aloud, then seeing if they could write them on the board themselves before she assigned them a task.

'Now back to maths, can anyone tell me the product of this equation?' she said. Pamela's hand shot up and she displayed an understanding of the question that none of the others had. 'You have a good brain, Pamela,' Evie told her. 'You could do so many great things in your life.'

The girl smiled shyly.

An hour later, they all put away their sheets of squared paper. Suddenly the door was opened by Sister David.

'Put the wireless on. Quickly.'

'What's the commotion?' asked Beryl.

'They've just made the announcement! Her Royal Highness Princess Elizabeth will undertake no public engagements after the end of this month! That's the commotion. It means she's having another baby!'

There was a ripple of interest. Everyone ran forward to the wireless, pushing and shoving, as if the closer they got, the closer they would get to Princess Elizabeth herself. The gossip ran through the place, and within minutes there were four more nuns at the door. The nuns parted the sea of children and gathered around the wireless excitedly.

'Royal announcement or no announcement, babies still need bathing and feeding,' said miserable Sister Humilitas, looming in the doorway. She clapped her fleshy, liver-spotted hands like a seal and made clicking noises with her tongue. Her black habit flared out around her.

The children were excited by this news of the royal baby, even if they didn't quite understand why. They really did live for today, Evie thought, because they had no idea what tomorrow might bring. But for now, with a cotton reel, hot food and a soft bed to sleep on, and now news of the Princess and her new baby, they seemed contented enough. Perhaps she should take a leaf out of their book? But she had seen enough to know she wasn't sure about this place. Please God she would hear from Lawrence soon.

Thirty-Seven

'Lovey,' said the woman behind the cash register. 'Can I help you?'

It was a Wednesday, and Evie was in the village doing the messages. She had placed the order for Spam, cornflower and Carnation milk and now she was supposed to be buying cotton reels for Sister Humilitas at the haberdasher's. Instead she stood rigid at the entrance, her heart thumping against her chest.

'*While the Sun Shines* – The Garrick Theatre – For one week only – Liverpool Playhouse brings Terence Rattigan's play to Southport,' announced the small flyer stuck in the window. Southport! Was Lawrence in Southport? It was so close! He had mentioned Crewe, Chester, Bangor, Preston, but he hadn't told her that!

'It's awfully good,' said the woman. 'The actor is very handsome and very talented. A young Montgomery Clift. You a theatregoer yourself?'

'Yes,' she replied.

'Well, don't miss it. You're in for a treat.'

Sister Humilitas had frowned when Evie gave her her sob story. 'Sister, it would break my heart in two if I missed our Nelly's Holy Communion. God spoke to me in the night and the Holy Spirit was calling to me in the voice of an angel, saying that I must be there with my family. My heart was bursting into flames, and I saw a strange, glowing vison floating above the sink. *Go, Evie. Go to Nelly's Holy Communion, and—*'

'Oh, for heaven's sake. D'you think I was born yesterday? Go. I don't care. But you're not taking Terry,' the sister said, shrewdly.

The following day, Evie walked out through the iron gates of the convent with a small triangular headscarf covering her hair, wearing her favourite paisley flower-patterned tea dress.

She took the train to Southport and headed towards Lord Street. The floodlights of the Garrick Theatre lit up the brown brick building, with its stone zig-zag motifs in Art Deco style and impressive colonnade. When she saw Lawrence's picture on a poster outside, Evie felt a thrill in the pit of her stomach. After buying a ticket and taking out the note she had written before she left, she went around the corner of the building. Were all stage doormen the same, she wondered as she saw the man sitting in the small booth, cigarette drooping from the corner of his lip. He barely looked up at her. She scanned the note that she was clutching: *Lawrence, I can't believe it. I'm actually here watching the play. I'll come to find you after the show. Break a leg. Your sugar girl, Angel.*

'Can you make sure Mr Childs gets this?'

'Leave it there,' he said in a tired voice.

There was a smell of damp in the auditorium,

which was filled with rows of red velvet seats tilted towards the stage. The ceiling was curved with a huge chandelier, and the yellow, green, gold and black-painted walls threw back a golden glow. As Evie made her way into the stalls, the woman playing the grand piano on the corner edge of the stage finished with a flourish, jumped up and took her seat at the end of the aisle. The gold-braid-fringed curtains jerked open, and the bright lights directed from behind the proscenium arch flooded the stage. There was a ripple of excitement and a round of applause. Evie gripped the seat so hard that her knuckles turned white.

She scanned the programme. Mabel was obviously still ill, or perhaps she had fled to London with Mr Sausage Fingers. When her understudy, the assistant stage manager, came on, Evie was amused to see that she *did* have thick ankles; Lawrence had been right. And then there he was: Lawrence, *her* Lawrence, sweeping across the stage, as he found his light, showed his best side and delivered his lines flawlessly. By the end of the first scene, he had really made Evie believe he was in love with the dumpy, short-sighted understudy, who kept bumping into the furniture and trying to shuffle onto the T-shaped sticky tape marks stuck on the floor as the follow spot swung wildly about to find her. Evie thought her heart would burst with pride. This man loves me. How is that possible? she thought.

The first half went by in a whirl. The woman who had played the piano got up, played all through the interval, then made her way back to her aisle seat again. Evie wandered through the audience and listened to the comments. *Isn't he divine? What a smashing performance. Why does that girl keep tripping over the rug?*

The second half began with Lawrence, hair greased back and now wearing a uniform. He swooned, laughed, cried, and died of heartbreak a little too realistically all the way through the next hour; and then it was over. He came forward to take a bow. Evie leapt out of her seat and clapped so hard, she thought her hands would never recover from the stinging. Had he got her note? He certainly seemed to be looking in her direction. And my God, he must have done! He was smiling right at her, winking, blowing her a kiss. She pressed two fingers gently to her lips and blew a kiss back, thinking she would die with happiness.

Lawrence took a final bow and left the stage. The fat woman started up at the piano again with a rendition of 'We'll Meet Again'. Happy and flushed, some of the giddier members of the audience started to sing along to it. An impatient Evie wanted to leave but the woman started playing 'God Save the King'. Finally, it was over. She tried to push past people as politely as she could as they all started to move towards the exits.

'I'm here to see Lawrence,' she blurted to the stage doorman, out of breath and excited.

'You and every Judy in Southport.'

'No, you don't understand. I'm Evie O'Leary. His fiancée,' she said, smiling.

'If I've heard that once, I've heard it a hundred

times. Girls coming round here trying to get into the dressing room of some turn with roving eyes and octopus hands. Word of advice, he's too old for you. Anyway, half the time these fellas dance up the other end of the ballroom. Them words that come out of their mouths up there on the stage are not their own. You do know that?'

She chewed her lip. 'Just let me see him. Did he get my note?'

'Yes,' he sighed.

'Let me through, then.'

'Well, I would, love. But the fact is, he's already gone.'

Her blood ran cold. There must be a mistake, she thought, and she argued to be let through, even thought of barging through to the dressing rooms. The doorman finally lost patience and told her to leave, remarking that Lawrence was probably halfway to Preston by now. Evie didn't believe him and sat for an hour on the cold stone wall outside the theatre, her bottom going numb; but Lawrence didn't appear. At last, realizing that the last train back to Freshdale was leaving soon, she reluctantly gave up and set off for the station.

But no, she wasn't going to believe it. Lawrence had *seen* her. She was sure he had. He had blown her a kiss. Why hadn't he waited? It was a question she didn't want to answer.

'You're late!' cried a furious Sister Humilitas, waiting for Evie in the porch when she got back.

'We decided to stay for evening Benediction after the Holy Communion Mass. I'm full of Jesus' love.'

'Sure y'are,' she replied. 'Aren't you the little glorified soul? Aren't you just bursting with holiness and goodness, with all that horrible sin relieved from your body. *Saint* Evie. Now get inside!'

Thirty-Eight

The following day, Evie sat in Sister David's room. The nun had lovely, kind almond-shaped eyes, thought Evie.

'How are you settling in, dear?'

Evie decided not to mention the bats that had flown in through a smashed window in the dormitory and squealed and fluttered about in the rafters. Anyway, she assumed the sister was talking about teaching the children.

'I must say, the change in your complexion is miraculous . . .' the sister went on.

'I think it's the country air, sister. The hawthorn bushes are in flower. And you can smell the sea. I can taste it on my lips.'

'Have you been to Freshdale before?'

'When I worked at Tate & Lyle, we used to come to Southport for our day trips, works outing. The fair and the prom and the like.'

'We're very lucky,' replied Sister David.

'The children seem very well behaved. Considering how difficult it must be for them, not having a mum or dad.'

'Yes, they will be rewarded in heaven, these little ones,' Sister David remarked, shuffling and reshuffling the arithmetic papers Evie had just placed on her desk. 'So you're happy here?'

Evie could hardly tell her she was leaving this place – she had no idea where she was going yet, but she wasn't going to sit here waiting for Lawrence much longer. 'Yes, Sister,' she said.

'And you had a good day, I heard. At your sister's communion?'

'Yes,' she replied, blushing. She needed to move the conversation on. 'Sister, one of the girls. She told me about her baby. How she doesn't want to give her baby away.'

'That's not unusual. Who?'

'I think she's upset about it.'

'Who are we talking about?' she repeated.

Evie stood awkwardly, with her arms dangling at her sides as though she didn't quite know what to do with them.

'Beryl.'

'Ah, Beryl. Thank you for bringing it to my attention,' Sister David said.

The next day, Evie woke to the sound of a fist slamming into the side of the bed.

'Thanks very much, love. I've just had the medicine!' said Beryl.

'Medicine?'

'The bitter pill. The bloody paddle on me arse from Humilitas.' She lifted up her skirt. 'See those red marks? You told Sister David I want my baby back? What the hell did you think you were doing?'

Evie sat up in her bed, rubbing her eyes, trying to

make sense of what she was hearing. She pushed her hair aside and squinted up at Beryl, standing over her with her hands on her hips. 'What?' she answered, trying to rouse herself.

'She said I didn't deserve to have a child, poisoning my baby like that.'

The words began to take shape in Evie's head. 'But I didn't tell her that. I just said you wanted to keep Kim.'

'Yes, and so she told Humilitas, who decided to do a bit of snooping. And then one of the girls at St Jude's snitched and said they'd seen me giving Kim the slops. So it's all your fault,' Beryl replied.

Evie dropped her head into her hands. 'I didn't mean to. I thought I was helping you. I thought I was doing you a favour.'

'Some favour! If you hadn't stuck your nose in where it wasn't wanted – look at this!' Beryl cried, pointing again at the red welts on her backside.

Evie shuddered. 'I'm sorry. I'm sorry, Beryl, please forgive me. I had no idea.' She slumped back onto the bed.

'You need to wake up to what goes on with some of these nuns. Sister David's as bad as Humilitas and Annunciata.'

'Oh, Beryl. I'm sorry. How can I make it up to you?'

Another four days passed in much the same way as the previous three. They spent the mornings in the classroom after starting with cold porridge and prayers, and in the afternoons there was sewing, playing with the babies, more lessons, then joining the other 'angels' in aprons to clear up. Sister David swept in and banged the bottom of a saucepan with a wooden spoon. All heads turned, and the children traipsed into the dining room. Standing at the top of the table was Sister Humilitas, who told them to join their hands together. 'For what we are about to receive, may the Lord make us truly thankful.'

'Amen,' everyone chorused. Then there was a surge forward as they all pushed and shoved their way to the table full of bean stew congealing in metal trays, and a large tureen with lumps of gristle floating in gravy. 'Who would be thankful for this?' Hottie whispered to Ellen.

'I'm thankful I've got you, Hottie,' Ellen whispered back, and Evie saw her squeeze her thigh under the table.

In the afternoon, Evie was allowed to take Terry out in his pram and wheel him around the grounds. Sister Humilitas appeared at the end of the path from behind a pink flowering rhododendron.

'Hello, Sister . . .' she said warily.

'May I walk with you? You are doing so well here. The children are fond of you and they are improving in leaps and bounds. And in such a short time! Three weeks! Some of them are doing long multiplication and long division – whoever would've thought that was possible so soon? I'm glad Sister Mary Clotilda found you for me. Now, I need to talk to you. We have received a letter from your stepmother.' Evie flinched. She still couldn't get used to the word *stepmother*. 'She wants us to speak to you about the child.'

'Which child?' asked Evie, puzzled.

'Terence, of course. I know you have a terrible feeling that he might be taken away from you without your blessing. But that's not how things operate here, dear. No one would take your baby away without your permission. What's the matter, dear? You look a little pale.'

Evie frowned. 'I'm all right, Sister.'

'We're soon going to be full to the brim with more children that no one wants to adopt. I'll come straight to the point. We had a family here earlier to look at one of our deaf children . . .'

She must be talking about the immaculately dressed couple Evie had seen walking down the corridor that morning. He with steel-rimmed spectacles and in a beautiful double-breasted suit with shiny slip-on shoes; she wearing a yellow dress, her white-gloved hands clutching a snakeskin handbag with a polished gold clasp.

'But the fact is, Evie, when we walked them through, well, your boy was standing in his cot – and with such a smile. And they said what a beautiful child he was. And we were wondering . . . Don't worry, it's not Canada, dear. But we were wondering: would you like to meet them? Really, they are a lovely couple. Terry would have such a wonderful life with them.'

Evie froze.

'But I came here because this was exactly what I *didn't* want to happen. No one said anything to me about this. I thought I was here for rest and respite.'

'Really, dear? It's been weeks now. What d'you suppose is going to happen to you?'

Evie didn't know what to say. She turned clumsily away, shocked, frightened and betrayed. Did Clotty know about this?

'Think about it. Unless of course your fiancé comes back. That will solve everything, won't it?' she said.

When she went back inside, she found Hottie and Ellen in the corridor with arms linked, walking along with yellow dusters tucked into their belts. Hottie, in her overalls, looked just like one of those girls the Americans had painted on their aeroplanes during the war.

'What's the matter?' asked Hottie.

'Beryl was right,' said Evie, panicked and slightly breathless. 'They want me to have Terry adopted. I have to get out of here.'

Hottie looked away. 'You're lucky,' she said.

'Lucky?'

Ellen sighed. 'No one wants Hottie's Trixie.'

'Trixie? She's yours?' Evie couldn't help but look shocked.

Hottie shrugged. 'I'd keep her if I could,' she said in a small voice.

Ellen chattered away. 'We all would. The sun shines when your Trixie comes into a room. But no one wants a mongol baby, do they? Trouble is, Hottie got awful attached to her because she had her for a whole year. She had no idea for a *whole year* there was anything wrong, did you, my poor Hottie? Didn't have a clue. Married an' all. You and Sid just thought your baby was sort of funny-looking, didn't you, love? It was only when her sister wouldn't let her daughter share her pram with

Trixie that Hottie realized she was different. That's when she went to the doctor with her – what a bloody way to find out.'

'Mmm . . .' said Hottie, picking at her nails.

'I'd punch her right in the face, your bloody sister, if I saw her. What a cow. And your Sidney, leaving your Trixie to the nuns,' Ellen said, squeezing her hand.

'Sid doesn't exist for me, not since the day he told me I had to choose between him and Trix. One day . . .' said Hottie. 'One day I'll get out of here with her. People are so horrible about her. I hate it. Should have heard my Sid. "The child will never be able to speak, the child will never be able to dress herself. She'll always be backward and ugly."' She paused. 'Such a cruel thing to say. And it's not true, either. She's beautiful. Don't you think, Evie?' she said, quietly.

'I do,' said Evie, touching her arm and wondering what fate awaited her and Terry. She would die rather than have Terry adopted, no matter how 'lovely' the couple were, no matter how expensive the woman's handbag might be, or how spotlessly clean her white gloves. It didn't mean they would give Terry a better life than she could. She had mountains of love for this boy of hers. But how on earth was she going to avoid the same thing happening to her as Hottie and Beryl – with nowhere to go, and now that Lawrence's marriage proposal seemed more uncertain with each passing day?

Thirty-Nine

'Oh, Evie! Think what I can do with this! I can make us some silk knickers instead of the awful hideous bloomers that Sister Mary Menopause makes us wear. I can do something beautiful with it,' Beryl said, as she unfolded the beautiful pearlized coloured silk that Evie had just handed her.

'They use old parachutes for the costumes at Lawrence's theatre. I got this from the haberdasher's bin in the village. There's some holes in it and some stains, but mostly it's fine.'

'Oh Evie, that was thoughtful. And I'm sorry I got so cross. I know you were only trying your best. Just a little naive, aren't you?'

'Beryl, you were right. They want to take Terry away from me. My stepmother wrote to them,' said Evie, in a small voice.

'Told you . . . They'll be thinking they want to save Terry, that's all.'

'I can't let that happen. I *won't*. I'm getting out of here as soon as I can.'

'Good luck with that,' sighed Beryl.

Later that night, Beryl found Evie in bed. She yawned. 'Can I get into bed with you? I've got to be up at five thirty for the laundry. I need to be getting

298

some sleep, but I don't want to be alone. I'm glad we're pals again.'

Evie pulled back the covers, and Beryl climbed in. It was good to feel another person, alive and warm, the smell of another body, the comfort of steady, shallow breathing. But that night Evie had trouble sleeping again. Her eyes wouldn't shut. All day her thoughts had kept wandering off. It felt like people were gently moving around her, their voices becoming indistinct and unfamiliar. Why hadn't Lawrence come to rescue her? Should she go back to Edna's? How would she live if she did? Should she go to the theatre and try to find Mabel? How long could she go on waiting for Lawrence? Surely the tour must be over by now. Would Joan and her father take them in, after all? But how could she bear that? Things felt so bleak. She needed some air, needed to go back to Liverpool and stand under the city sky and see the silver river to try and feel alive again. She was thinking about all of this as her eyelids grew heavy and she began to fall asleep. With Beryl's arms around her waist and her head laid on her shoulder, she sighed gentle, worried, uneven breaths, right through until the morning.

The first thing that Evie noticed when she went downstairs into the refectory was that the table had been laid with a white linen cloth. The sisters were fluttering around the room like moths. A frisson of excitement was in the air. The first nun came into the room and clapped her hands. Her face was flushed.

'Now, girls, now, *girls*. You're making a right *kludge* of it! Make sure you do that properly. We have a visitor today. A very special visitor: Father Murphy from God's own country, the Emerald Isle. He's not much time, as he's passing through on his way to Preston. Girls, we are so *lucky*. Novenas all round to give thanks.'

Beryl noticed that the nun's cheeks were crimson and that there was a purple rash on her neck. Beads of sweat had broken out on her brow, and she nudged Evie.

'Look at the state of her. You'd think Frank Sinatra was about to turn up, she's that flustered. It's only a feckin' priest.'

The sisters had already started lifting up candles and vases and dusting underneath them, flicking tea towels onto the high shelves, running fingers over the tops of doors.

'Never seen such a performance,' whispered Hottie to Evie. Evie giggled.

Another sister appeared with what looked like a briefcase on a tray. She put the case on the table, opened it. It was full of beautiful cutlery that looked as though it was hardly used. She started laying out the silver knives, forks and spoons. It was cutlery that none of them recognized. Silver handles, engraved and embossed with tiny flower markings and spoons that you could see your face in. A vase was emptied down the sink and the pungent smell of stale water filled the room. And then Sister Humilitas arrived with armfuls of newly cut flowers, dahlias and roses, brought in from outside. The vase was filled with fresh water and there was the sound of taps gurgling and gushing. The stem cuttings were scooped up and wrapped in newspaper. The curtains were flung open. A pregnant girl came in with a duster, a new girl. She started loping about, began dusting down surfaces half-heartedly.

'Put some oomph into it,' said Sister David. The girl looked like she was about to drop. She held the bottom of her belly and sighed. 'Quickly now. Father could arrive at any moment.'

'So could me bloody baby,' muttered the girl.

Evie noticed the sister regarding herself in the side of the silver teapot, pursing her lips, then baring and rubbing her teeth with her fingertip. She pushed a straggle of hair up into her coif.

'Get on, girl,' she muttered when she saw Evie watching her, and gave her a contemptuous look that said everything – she didn't need to utter a single word more.

Suddenly there was a commotion at the window. 'Is that him? Jesus, isn't he handsome! And young! Bloody hell, he's like a film star,' cried Hottie.

'A proper film star, all right,' said Beryl, rushing over and pushing her out of the way.

'He's coming up the path. Isn't he just gorgeous!' said Hottie.

Evie went over to the window to have a look, but by then the nuns had shooed the girls away.

'Stop gawping! Have you not seen a priest before?'

'Not one that looks like that,' laughed Beryl.

'What was he like?' whispered Julie.

Evie shrugged. 'I didn't see . . .' she answered. 'He'd gone by the time I got to the window.'

'I did. Sex on bloody legs,' said Beryl.

'Beryl! You can't say that about a priest!' said Hottie.

'Why not? They're made of flesh just like we are . . . It might shock you to know they have a pair of balls and a willy as well, under those vestments. A willy that works an' all.'

'Good-looking?' asked Evie.

'Silky hair blowing up into a peak. Shoes all shiny and polished. Young, too. Long swishy vestments with little purple buttons all the way down to his feet and a purple sash.'

'A bishop?' said Julie.

A voice cut through the excitement. 'Quickly! Will you move that chair over here? Have you made the tea yet? You've not left it stewing in the pot, you eejit girls? And did you remember to warm it?' cried Sister Humilitas.

'Yes, Sister,' Evie lied.

'Where are the biscuits?'

A worried crease appeared in Beryl's brow. The nun went over to the tin. 'Jesus, Mary and Joseph!' she cried. 'Who's ate all the feckin' biscuits?'

Evie blushed beetroot red.

'Jesus, what'll we do?' whispered Beryl, wryly.

'Father is walking up the path and we've no biscuits! Lord bless us and save us!'

'Perhaps you could give him a wee drop of whiskey instead?' said Beryl. 'Priests love the booze, Sister.'

'Don't be ridiculous, impudent girl. Now get out. Shoo, shoo . . . Father doesn't want to see you brazen hussies. That's not why he's here. Get down to the nursery and keep out of sight until he's gone . . .'

*   *   *

302

Half an hour later, the door opened, pushed strongly from the other side, and the priest came into the room to be greeted by a simpering Sister Humilitas. Caught in a beam of dusty sunshine, it was as if the doorway was framing a thing of utter beauty. On entering, it was as though his presence filled every particle and every atom that made up the space in the room. It was true, his cassock had purple velvet buttons that started at his neck and went all the way down to the hem. His white dog collar stood out stiffly and starched under his strong jawline. His shoulders were broad, and in perfect proportion to the rest of his body.

'Father. So good of you to come and see us,' said Sister Humilitas.

'Not at all, Mother . . .' he said, with a warm Irish lilt to his voice. He took Humilitas's hand, squeezed it and held onto it for a moment. The priests that came here were normally ancient with old, gnarled hands, but this one was young, with long, slender fingers, and the nun allowed herself to enjoy the rare sensation of a beautiful person's touch. He smiled, revealing perfect teeth. Some might have said it was a waste, such dashing good looks, but these nuns thought he was perfection put on this earth to give glory to the Lord.

'Will you have a cup of tea, Father?' said Sister Annunciata, her brow sweating and damp patches appearing under her arms. 'We're still trying to search out a custard cream.'

'Don't mind if I do,' he said.

'Now, Father, to what do we owe this visit? We

303

have been working tirelessly with the diocese. Since the war, war babies and whatnot, we have been inundated. But we would love to show you what progress these children have made.'

'Ah, to be sure, the orphans. I've also heard you have a beautiful chapel,' he said.

The nun puffed herself up. 'Yes, Father. It's our pride and joy.'

'And we have a priest hole,' interrupted an over-excited Sister David.

'A priest hole? Well, that's a good thing,' he said, laughing. 'Quick escape if I need it!'

The nuns grinned at each other over their china teacups.

'We're so honoured to have you here today. Sister will be delighted to show you around. We've a new statue of the blessed St Francis, and if you could bless him before you left, well, that would be heavenly . . .'

'Sure, I'll bless St Francis.'

'Oh, Father . . .' Sister Annunciata giggled like a teenage girl. 'That would be grand.'

'One more thing. The girls?' he asked after a pause.

The nuns glanced at each other. 'Yes, Father?'

'What about the girls?'

Sister Annunciata paused, her brows knitted together in a look of puzzlement.

'I would like to hear confession from the fallen girls working here at the orphanage.'

The nun looked nervous. 'Right you are . . .' she said, her smile tightening, nostrils slightly flaring.

'Sister, lead the way,' he said.

They went into the small chapel. There was a nun

laying out the hymnals on the benches. Another, after sprinkling holy water with a brush that she had dipped into the font, went off to sound the bells.

The priest went into the confessional, and when the nun gave a signal, Beryl and Evie, who had been waiting in the nursery, went into the chapel and were told to sit in a pew. Beryl went in first. She knelt down and joined her hands, resting her elbows on the wooden kneeler. 'Bless me, Father, for I have sinned. It has been a month since my last confession. I have sinned—'

'Shush, my child,' the voice whispered from behind the grille.

Beryl stopped mid-flow, her mouth falling open as if on a hinge.

'Sorry, Father?'

'I don't want to hear your sins.'

'Why not, Father?' she stuttered.

'Because, love, you're not a sinner. The Lord will forgive you, anyway. You have nothing to be ashamed of. Getting knocked up, well, it could've happened to anyone . . .'

Beryl frowned. This wasn't what she was used to from a priest, or from anyone else for that matter. It certainly wasn't what she had been expecting. And she was confused. What had happened to his Irish accent? There was a shocked silence from her side of the grille.

'How many Hail Marys should I say?' she asked.

'None,' he said. 'Like I said, this could happen to anyone. Just a bit of bad luck. Now off you pop, petal.'

She stumbled out, dazed and bewildered.

Evie, waiting in the pew, tugged at her skirts. 'What

did he say?' she asked. Beryl had come out looking so happy, she felt she had to ask her.

'I'll not tell anyone. That's between me and God. But Evie, that priest was the loveliest priest I've ever met. I feel like I could fly straight to heaven now, so I do,' she said.

Evie frowned. Sister David nodded at her to go in and take her turn.

'Bless me, Father, for I have sinned,' she whispered, screwing up her eyes, hands pressed together tightly with her fingers interlocking. 'It has been three months since my last confession . . .' A silence hung in the air.

'Father?' she said, after a minute. 'Are you there?'

'Evie?' said the voice beyond the grille. 'Open your eyes.'

She gasped. 'Lawrence!? Lawrence! *What the flipping heck!*'

'Shush!'

'Oh, good God,' she cried. 'Bloody hell! Oh God, now I'm swearing in a confessional!' She could feel her heart beating so loudly, she thought it was going to burst.

'Your friend Edna told me you were here. The foreman at Tate's, the one Biddy knows, he found her for me and said you were pals. I wrestled it out of her that's for sure, but I had to see you,' he said, reaching out and touching the grille with his fingers. 'Getting into this place is like Fort Knox. There was no other way . . . I called, and then I tried another three times. Thank God the nun who kept turning me away wasn't here today.'

'My God!' she whispered. 'You're crazy! Aren't you scared?'

'Scared? No. What do you think they can do to me? Put me in jail? Anyhow, they've all fallen for me. I'm a good actor, Evie . . .'

'I can't believe it,' she whispered, breathlessly. 'I came to your play in Southport. I thought you didn't want to see me. Did you get my note?'

'You came to *While the Sun Shines*? You couldn't even imagine the number of silly little notes and starry-eyed letters I get from the stage-door Johnnies. I get my dresser to put them in a big bag and never read them until I finish the tour. Makes me feel less guilty about not replying.'

'Oh, Lawrence! You didn't know I was there? But you blew me a kiss?'

'I do that every night. Can't see a thing beyond the front row when you're on stage because of the lights. Just a black pit. I had no idea.'

'I thought you didn't want me.'

'Don't be cuckoo.'

'Where did you get that get-up?' she asked, still gasping with the sheer bloody nerve of what he was doing.

'We're in rep with *The Tinker's Wedding* and I'm playing a priest. It's my costume. I couldn't stay away, Angel – I missed you. God, I want to kiss those lips. Kiss me through the grille. Kiss me . . . Go on.'

She giggled as she pressed her lips against the mesh and he did the same.

'You had enough of this place? Well, if you say the word, Angel, I'm ready to bring you home.'

Forty

'Sister Annunciata, this girl. I want to see her child. She has confessed her sins to me and I need to bless the baby,' said Lawrence, when he came out and joined Evie in the pew.

'Well, that's highly unusual . . . I'll see what Sister Humilitas says . . .' she stuttered. 'Wait here . . .'

'Get your skates on,' he whispered to Evie. 'Get a bag with your things. I'll meet you outside. Fetch Terry from the nursery and meet me under that ash tree at the front gates. And Angel, I love you. You melt me like sunshine, you do,' he whispered.

'You're mad as a bag of ferrets,' she answered. 'But I'm glad,' she said. 'I'm so glad you are . . .'

Evie watched as he made his way out of the chapel. The nuns were waiting for him by the statue of St Francis of Assisi, and they danced about him like moths fluttering round a candle as he walked down the corridor, telling them he was just going to take a wee breath of fresh air in the garden while Evie fetched her baby so he could bless him. There was a moment when he turned and, seeing Evie standing as he looked back over his shoulder, winked. Evie could hardly contain herself. Then her mouth crinkled up into a smile.

She felt waves of gleeful happiness bubbling up inside as she sneaked out of the back door, crept up to the dormitory and kissed each child, then left armfuls more of the parachute silk under Beryl's bed. Hottie and Ellen weren't there for her to explain what was happening, they were hiding in the refectory, anything to get out of confession no matter how handsome the priest was, but she would make a point of writing to them in time. The little boy with the flat head and Trixie were in the nursery with Terry, and when she slipped in, she kissed them both and said goodbye. If only she could take them with her. Thank goodness Terry had fallen asleep and she was able to lift him out of the cot and into his second-hand pushchair without him waking.

She drew a deep breath as she passed out of the back gate and down the passage by the side of the house that led to the front gates. She was free. Free to start a new life with Lawrence.

Meanwhile, Lawrence was making his excuses, and telling the nuns that after blessing the baby and a brief prayer with Evie, who was waiting for him in the chapel, he would be on his way. He had had a lovely time – the children were lovely, the chapel was lovely, the tea, to be sure, to be sure, begorrah, was the loveliest tea he had ever had – but he had to leave to catch the next train. One of the nuns pressed a set of rosary beads into his hand; a second offered him more tea; a third suggested he might like to go and look at the grotto of Our Lady Queen of Peace in the garden.

'Oh, but Father, the Blessed Virgin is beautiful, sure she is. We have the gorgeous Sacred Heart in the chapel, and divine St Francis, but she's our favourite. She has little flowers planted around her, daffies and pansies and the like. And Sister Humilitas has made a beautiful rockery, with the little candles in old jam jars. We did it all ourselves,' said Sister David.

'Be quiet, Sister. I'm sure Father has seen plenty of grottos in his time. Put ours to shame, no doubt,' Sister Humilitas said snippily.

'Well, 'tis true, I have. I've seen a fair few grottos in my time, and I'm sure yours is the loveliest, but I do have the baby to bless and a train to catch.'

'Of course. Of course you do, Father. Sister, you should've known better. Well, you'll be welcome to return at any point. The door will always be open for you here, Father. Let me take you to the chapel.'

'You don't have to trouble yourself to come with me. I can go there on my own, Sister.'

He smiled and couldn't resist placing his hands on hers, squeezing gently, and making a small sign of the cross on her forehead with his thumb.

'May God go with you and St Christopher guide you,' he said. 'Sisters, it's been an absolute pleasure.'

'No, no, Father. The pleasure was all ours,' the nun said, smitten, overcome by a delirious rapture that made pearls of sweat stud her brow like fresh dew.

When they met at the gates, Evie laughed, and he laughed, and they both laughed harder, and she clutched her sides and he slapped his thigh.

310

'The sisters fell for you, all right,' she giggled. 'Jesus, I bet any one of them would have given up her vocation right there and married you, given half the chance.'

'To be sure!' he laughed.

They quickly made their way to the station, where they sat in a corner of the waiting room, Terry asleep in the old metal pushchair she had found at the back of the laundry. Taking her hand in his, Lawrence leaned in to her.

'Kiss me,' he said.

'Not here. Not in that get-up,' she said. 'What if someone were to see us?'

It felt electrifying, just to have his skin touch hers.

He grinned. 'Don't say just a little bit of you doesn't find this exciting, to see me in this dog collar?'

She slapped him playfully. And suddenly he turned in to her and kissed her on the crown of her head, traced his finger down the slope of her nose, tilted her chin and then put his lips firmly on hers. She kissed him back, allowed him to bury his face in her hair.

'Now, Evie,' he said. 'I've got something serious to ask you. I really do want you to marry me. I love you. I fell in love with you because I couldn't stop thinking about the million things about you that you have no idea of. Your voice, your smile, your eyes, your laugh, your stubbornness, your sheer bloody grit and the way you have been so determined to keep your baby. I can't sleep or eat for thinking about you. I'm taking you straight back to my new flat tonight. You do want to leave this place, don't you?'

311

'Oh, Lawrence, of course I do,' she said, pushing the pram rhythmically back and forth as Terry's eyelids flickered. She tucked the blanket under his cheek, then looked back at Lawrence, his long eyelashes, his slender hands. 'There's an awful lot of sadness behind those walls. And I actually felt sorry for the couple who wanted Terry. That whole place is built on the misery of the girls, but there's also the misery of those poor people who are so desperate for a child of their own. No amount of handbags with gold clasps can make up for that. But I made some friends, and most of the nuns were civil to me. The children are all lovely. And they're amazingly resilient. But I'm still scared stiff about what they wanted to do with Terry – and me, for that matter.'

'By the way, Mabel says she will be your bridesmaid. Sausage Fingers' offer is off for now. She couldn't go through with it,' he said, grasping her hand.

'Through with what?'

'Never mind,' he replied.

Despite her joy, Evie felt her stomach tighten slightly. This was becoming real. She was thinking about what it meant for both of them. Did he know about nappies, and sleepless nights, and never being able to do things at a moment's notice? And the shame? Weddings didn't happen overnight, which meant they would be living in sin. There was still the shame to think of. Though oddly, Lawrence didn't seem to care much about that. Frankie suddenly crashed into her thoughts, but she pushed him aside.

'That's kind of Mabel to do that for us,' she said.

'Yes, well, as you know, she was probably only

thinking about herself. Mabel loves the theatrics and the chance to buy a new dress. You couldn't keep her away from anything that might have a little bit of drama to it. She thinks she's in a play half the time. Acts out her life rather than lives it, and sometimes, God, it's like a bloody Greek tragedy. You and Mabel couldn't be more different.'

'There's all those poor children and poor girls at St Silly's who really have lived tragic lives,' said Evie sadly. 'Like Beryl. And Hottie. And their kiddies.'

'I know, dear,' he said. 'Let me taste those lips again.'

He pushed her tangled hair out of her eyes and began to kiss her again, this time pressing against her, his hand moving up over her flimsy linen blouse, cupping her breast, searching out her pea-hard nipple.

'God, I love you, Angel,' he said, breathless and dizzy with love for this girl, and finally with a picture of what his future might be.

The nun, who had run all the way clutching a pretty Saint Agnes prayer card she wanted to give to the handsome priest as a parting gift, stopped outside the smeared window of the waiting room. Her hand flew to her mouth when she saw the two of them – he pushing his knee between her legs, then she with one foot off the ground, her leg wound around him, both engrossed in the kissing and touching and writhing spectacle, constrained only by what decency allowed at three o'clock in the afternoon in the corner of the empty waiting room of a sleepy train station. She gasped in horror when she saw what was happening.

'Oh, God help me! Jesus, Mary and Joseph! Oh my God,' she cried, staggering backwards. She could barely breathe or stand. No – it couldn't be! Not the handsome Father Murphy! And Evie. The little harlot! The *whore*! What did she think she was doing, whoring away with that beautiful man!? And to think she had wanted to give him her prayer card! Saint Agnes was the patron saint of chastity! She couldn't believe what she was seeing. She pressed her fingers hard against her temples. Maybe she was imagining it. But no, there they were. Him leaning against her, pressing his hips into hers. She moaning. And in broad daylight with a baby in a pram beside her! She had no idea what she was to do. Should she tell someone? Of course she should.

Picking up her skirts, she began to run. All she could think of was to blame the girl. Wait till I tell Sister, she thought bitterly. 'Wait until I tell her about the little slut tempting poor Father,' she murmured as she ran towards the house.

When she told Sister David, the nun was so stupefied, so appalled, that at first she didn't believe her.

'I saw it with my own eyes. The new girl, Evie, was kissing the priest.'

'But this is shocking,' said Sister David.

'Not too shocking to be true, Sister.'

'Are you sure?'

'I've never been surer of anything in my life,' she said. 'They were sat there. Under the sign for Pears soap. You know the one. With the little curly-haired baby. In the waiting room. And she was as brazen as anything. Kissing him. On the lips. And his hands

314

. . . Sister, his hands . . . they were like snakes all over her.'

'And did you say anything?'

'No, Sister. I was too embarrassed.'

'Well, let that be an end to the matter. You tell no one, you say nothing. But the girl must go, do you hear? The girl must leave immediately. And she must take her child with her.'

Forty-One

But Evie had already left. It was a warm summer evening. Lawrence's flat was at the better end of Paradise Street. It was a sturdy, elegant Edwardian building, and although its walls were still black from the grime and soot of the bombing, its façade retained a grandeur that even the Corporation wouldn't dare to meddle with. Inside, however, was a different story.

On entering, her eyes swept the room. Its ragged bohemian character made her pause. She hadn't been expecting such a contrast to what she was used to. There was a murky picture on the wall, an oil painting of a woman in a state of undress. In the corner there was a screen – it looked Oriental, Japanese maybe – that had a jacket and several fringed scarves hanging over it. There was a battered, moth-eaten chaise longue and a huge ornate gilt mirror on one wall that dominated the room, blotted with rust that seeped out from its edges. The ceiling seemed to sag a little with the weight of the floor above. Evie frowned.

'Don't you like it here?' he asked.

'Yes, yes, of course,' she replied. As he talked, he walked around the room, gesturing broadly, making plans to replace the stove and the curtains, even repaint the walls if the landlord would let him, and repair a few of the loose floorboards.

She listened as Terry, squirming on her knee, tugged at her hair. What she was doing was trying to imagine him in this place. In between the windows, which were adorned with faded satin drapes – whores' drawers, as her mother would have called them – was a spiral staircase of swirling wrought iron that led up to a mezzanine floor, where there was a bed with a moth-eaten eiderdown and feather boa twisting around the bedstead. Soon Terry would be walking. She imagined him tottering down these stairs, tumbling from the top to the bottom. She imagined him tangling himself up in the feather boa. She wondered, without an outhouse, where she would soak his nappies – was there a back yard, a washing line to hang them on? Of course, she shouldn't be ungrateful; of course this should be everything that she'd dreamt of. And yet . . . and yet. And yet what?

She walked over to a door, opened it, put her head inside a cupboard.

'Everything here that you need?' Lawrence asked. He came over to her and put his arm round her waist.

'One thing missing,' she said. 'A cot. There's no cot for Terry,' she said.

'Well, we'll go down to T. J. Hughes tomorrow. For tonight, he can sleep in the bed with us.'

With us? She looked at him, chewed her lip. She could feel her cheeks reddening. But she knew that now was not the time to be embarrassed. She had decided that if she was going to make this work,

317

there was no room for coyness or worrying about what other people peeping from behind their curtains would think. They were going to have to be practical, despite the fact that they would be living in sin. At least no one knew her here. She was determined to make it work – why wouldn't she be? He was someone who loved her. He said he would marry her. And in time she would love him, she told herself.

But as the evening drew in, she felt herself panicking. She undressed behind the screen and came out shyly in her floor-length nightgown, her hair, the colour of autumn leaves, tumbling about her shoulders, the clear outline of her body visible beneath the flimsy cotton. When Lawrence saw her, he gasped. 'You are a beauty. And what's more, you're *my* beauty, sugar.'

She blushed, busied herself with settling Terry into the drawer that Lawrence had made into a makeshift bed. As she was leaning over the baby, Lawrence came up behind her, leaned over her back and nuzzled into her.

Immediately he felt her body tense.

'You all right?' he said.

'Yes. Just, sorry, I'm . . .'

'What?'

'Can I ask you something?' she said in a quiet voice, turning to him.

'Of course.'

'Do you think I'm a loose girl? Because, well, I might have Terry, and I know what people think about that – that I'm a slut, or a fallen girl – but actually I'm not like Mabel . . . I don't want you to think I'm . . .'

'Oh Evie, stop, dear,' he murmured, pulling back her nightdress so he could kiss her bare shoulder. 'You couldn't be more different from Mabel.'

'But Lawrence, this has happened so quickly . . . you and I. We haven't even . . . we haven't even . . .'

'Even what?' he said.

'I have a whole life you know nothing about,' she went on, not answering his question. 'You don't know anything about my family. You don't know anything about my mother. Or my father. I have a brother and sisters. Did you know that? How can someone fall in love so completely, so quickly, and know so little about the person?'

He smiled. She seemed so innocent and other-worldly, with those huge soulful green eyes, and so beautiful, like the girl in the painting floating in a flower-strewn pond he had seen at the Walker Art Gallery.

'The day I set eyes on you, my life became better,' he told her. 'The more I tried to fight it, the more I kept falling in love with you, even when I wasn't with you. It got worse and worse when I was away on tour with Mabel. You're like no girl I've ever met. And isn't that the most important thing? That I love you? Not about our families. Not about my awful, snobbish cello teacher sister in Brighton. Or about my father, who turned his back on me because I refused to go into the army and went on the stage. Or about my school friends, lovely, by the way. Bertie and Freddie, real cards, both ended up working for a bank. For a while I was their entertainment, but when they met their wives, well – those fine, upstanding women didn't

want their husbands hanging around with some
lounger like me. Who can blame them?' He paused,
drummed his fingers on his lips. 'What else do you
want to know about? My dreary minor public school?
The lavatories with no doors on them, cold showers
and floggings, and the bullies who taunted me? Boys
and masters alike. My mother. God, my mother! I
wouldn't wish my dear mother on anyone. Drink is
the only thing that makes her truly happy. How about
my flat feet, that got me out of the war? I pretend I
don't mind about that, but I do really. I wanted to
feel a man as much as the next fellow . . . Do you
want me to go on? Or have you heard enough? We
have the rest of our lives for all this stuff.'

Evie dropped her eyes to the floor. 'I know you
say you love me,' she said. 'And this is the most
romantic thing that has ever happened to me . . .'

'So, then? Does anything else matter?'

'No, Lawrence. I suppose not.'

He pushed a piece of hair behind her ear. 'If you
want, I can leave you here tonight. You can stay here
with Terry on your own. I can go back to the theatre
– no one would know if I slept on the dressing-room
floor. Happened all the time during the war. I've a
little mattress that I can roll out and lie on under
my dressing-room table.'

'Lawrence, you don't need to do that. Of course
I want you to stay here with me and Terry. I don't
care about what people think. I have had enough of
being ashamed . . .'

She could hear the sound of her son's gentle
breathing, and glanced over at the drawer.

'Good. Thank goodness for that, sugar. I'm telling you, it's a new world out there and I'm desperate to show it to you. You like stuff in the hit parade? No one gives a fig about what anyone thinks. Just take a listen to the music they're playing. You heard Dinah Washington singing "I Know How To Do It"? Frankie Laine, "That's My Desire"? You should hear what they sing about . . . it's strong stuff . . . make your toes curl, it would . . .'

'The nuns at school and at St Sylvester's didn't allow us to listen to the hit parade. Devil's music, the sisters called it. Then I found out Sister Bony Face loved Bing Crosby, and had a gramophone and a secret stash of his records in her office.'

'That figures,' he said, smiling. 'In the movie *Going My Way*, Bing Crosby played a priest. But I wouldn't expect the nuns to be in touch with popular music.'

'They're not. There was a girl at my school who loved Frank Sinatra. She wrote his name on her pencil case and when Sister Oliphant found it on a bench, she announced in assembly that if any of us knew a boy called Frank Sinatra, he should come and get his pencil case from her office.'

He laughed, enjoying seeing Evie's smile break out as she told the story. 'So now I've told you a little about my life, do you want to tell me about yours?' he said, tenderly running a finger down her nose as they sat on the edge of the bed.

'Not really. It's pretty grim. I have some good friends. Edna from Tate's. And my new friend Beryl, who I met at the orphanage. And if it hadn't been for Sister Mary Clotilda, who I turned to when my stepmother wanted to throw me out, I don't know where I'd be.'

'Stepmother?'

'Holy Joan, we call her. She was the one who didn't want me and Terry around. I have an aunt in Dagenham who we thought might want to adopt Terry – but it turned out that was just my father's wishful thinking.'

He looked at her in the flickering candlelight, pulled her to him. 'I believe in love at first sight, don't you? I think there's something pretty romantic about living in the moment, like this.'

The glow from the dying fire licked their faces. She smiled and let him take her hand. Turning it over, he made small circular motions with his finger in her palm.

'That's nice,' she murmured.

'Shakespeare puts it pretty well. "Of the very instant I saw you, did my heart fly at your service." It's from *The Tempest*.'

'That's lovely.' She had never heard such thing. Never heard someone speak like this. It was still unimaginable that he was saying these words to her, Evie O'Leary, the sugar girl from Coghlan Street – that she was sitting here with this ridiculous, sublimely beautiful creature. And he was telling her that he loved her.

He led her to the bed by the hand and lay her down on it. For a moment, she froze. Despite what he had just said, she suddenly felt a little embarrassed again, awkward. Why didn't he care? she wondered. Because people like him don't care, she told herself.

Not like the small-minded people she knew. She thought back to how ashamed she had felt when she'd had to tell her father she was having Frankie's baby. How it had spread around the factory like wildfire. The gossip. The looks. The whispers behind her back. Lawrence simply wouldn't have cared. He was so different to her, and her people.

Lawrence pushed fingerfuls of fair hair back over his head, folding his cuffs up to reveal muscled forearms. He reached a hand up, placed it on the crown of her head and stroked her hair. 'I love you, Angel. But if you want to wait until we're married, I won't lay a finger on you. I can wait.'

He took her face and kissed her. Full on the lips. Pressed hard and yearning against her mouth. His skin was warm.

'Oh, Lawrence . . . I'm sorry,' she stuttered. 'Maybe that's for the best . . .' The feel of his cheek against hers comforted her.

But damn it all – there it was again. The thought of Frankie. She couldn't help it. She thought of Frankie's hands going over her body, Frankie's smell, the shape of Frankie, every part of his body – muscular legs, arms, even the slight curve of him that she was conscious of as he entered her, and his broad, strong shoulders. And yet this man who wasn't Frankie, with his constant protestations of love – her body ached for him as well. Was that right? To have the two of them so mixed up in her head? It was all so confusing.

'Why are you sad, Angel? Those beautiful sad eyes of yours. You have a great lump of sadness in your heart. Let me make you happy. Please, Angel. It would be my life's work. There would be no better thing in the world but for me to make you happy. D'you think you could let me?'

But that was a question Evie couldn't answer. She gazed at a space above his head, fixed her eyes on a small stain on the peacock-patterned wallpaper.

After a moment's pause, he said: 'Angel, I'm not even asking you to say you love me now, but do you think in time you might? If you think that's too much to ask of you, then I'll walk away now. I'll leave you to get on with your life without me, if that's what you want.' His forehead puckered into a frown.

Suddenly he changed from being so sophisticated, so in control, so confident, to so vulnerable – like a child, almost. Such a little boy, she thought. How unexpected.

'No, no, I don't want you to do that,' she said urgently.

'I know you're not ready,' he said. 'Physically, I mean . . .'

She felt her cheeks reddening again.

He heaved himself up onto his shoulders. 'But look, like I said, if you want, we can sleep together in this bed but I'll sleep on top of the eiderdown. I want you to be happy,' he said. 'I'll not do anything that upsets you. And if that means waiting until we're married, that's fine, Angel. You tell me as soon as you're ready to set a date. I'm in no rush. You do understand that, don't you?'

She felt waves of relief wash over her. 'Thank you,' she said in a small voice.

And when she wriggled into the bed, curling under the eiderdown, with him beside her, an old coverlet wrapped around him as he lay on top – as she heard his gentle breathing in the dark – for the first time in months and months, she felt warm and safe and happy.

Forty-Two

Canada

Out on the back porch of the small wooden shack that Frankie had made his home for the past year with his mum, brother and sister, he shared a final bowl of split pea soup with his mother, washed down by a glass of warm beer.

'Do you have to go back to Liverpool?' his mother asked plaintively, draining her glass.

'Mam, I do,' he said. 'But I'm not saying it's forever. Just got some business to do.'

Dotty, his sister, in dungarees and hobnailed boots, humphed, ran over to him and hugged him tightly. He sloshed more of the drink from the jug into a glass, and a deal onto the wooden floorboards.

'Hits the spot,' he said, banging the empty glass onto the table.

He then hauled his knapsack (full of bottles of maple syrup) onto his back, waved goodbye, and headed up the path towards the truck that was waiting to take him from Barry's Bay back to Toronto. It took him hitching rides in three different pick-ups, with an overnight stop at a hostel in Peterborough, where a woman offered him a meal and an hour in her bed for five dollars. He politely refused, but there was something in her sad, worried smile that made him think of Evie. After a letter from Jacky had brought news of Evie leaving her job at Tate's suddenly, suggesting some kind of trouble, he felt that it was more urgent than ever for him to return to Liverpool and try and persuade her to see him one last time.

He wished he had a photograph to look at. Evie had come to him in dreams so many nights since he had been here, but that wasn't enough. He also wished she had answered his letters; but, undeterred, he was now coming back to Liverpool to find her and get to the bottom of the 'gossip from the curtain-twitchers', as Jacky had described it.

The girl at the ticket office in the harbour smiled at him, covering her mouth to hide the gap in her teeth. She too had a look of Evie, but somehow without the cares of the world showing on her face.

'One way?' she asked.

'Open return.'

'Come on, boy!' yelled the man who was ushering people down the promenade to the ship. 'Boat leaves in an hour. Stop daydreaming, lad!'

Forty-Three

Paradise Street had so much coming and going, with the clattering of builders putting up scaffolding, the rumbling of lorries, wrecking balls demolishing whole streets on either side of them, that people barely noticed what was happening at number 24. The bumping of the Silver Cross pram down the steps and the sounds of a baby crying through the floorboards went uncommented on, and no one asked any questions. Lawrence was soon back working at the theatre, three plays in as many weeks. Evie would help him learn his lines, sitting in front of the fire, and he would be charmed as she put on exaggerated accents, imitated Mabel's lisp, or dropped her voice to pretend to be a man.

Over the coming days, much to her amazement, as she ran small errands and took pleasure in simple chores like darning a sock or using a pumice stone to try and make the ugly stains in the sink go away, Terry seemed a calmer, happier baby, crawling around the room, using his stubby hands to pull himself up on pieces of furniture and stamping his feet gleefully. For Evie to see the joy in Terry's face when Lawrence came back from the theatre and stood over the

328

bassinet and jiggled the mobile Evie had made out of silver bottle tops, was indescribable. Lawrence was beginning to love this child, and she in turn vowed she would try to love him.

'How amazing it is that people are so kind and generous when you allow them to be,' she said, showing him the bag of mushrooms that the woman at the grocer's had given her for a few pennies. They ate them fried with shoulder bacon and full of food that night, a Sunday, they went to bed early. He flopped onto his back and lay there staring at the ceiling in the dark.

'You happy, Evie?'

Yes, she decided. She was. There were a few things, like the way he'd bring back frocks from the theatre for her, sometimes tell her what to wear or not to wear, the way the other day he'd put her hair up when she wore it down, the way he'd sometimes ask her to turn in a circle in front of him before they left the house; but these amounted to nothing, minor things, soon forgotten after a moment or two.

'Yes, I am,' she replied. And yet, true to his word, he hadn't laid a finger on her, and a very small part of her was wondering why on earth he hadn't.

The next morning, under a blue sky, they wheeled Terry in the pram down the hill and into town. 'First thing we need to do is go to TJ's,' he said. 'Then we'll go and have tea and scones at the Kardomah on Bold Street.'

Evie nodded. Terry began to gurgle contentedly. Lawrence knelt at the pushchair and plucked at

Terry's nose, then, bending his thumb back, he curled his fingers over and performed his trick that made it look as though the tip of his thumb had detached. Terry laughed as Lawrence slid the disjointed thumb back and forward. He was laughing and kicking his chubby legs all the way to the tram.

'He's a good audience,' said Lawrence. 'I'm in love with him, Angel.'

That night, after an uninspiring and rather tedious performance of Shaw's *Arms and the Man*, he arrived home tired but happy, kicked off his shoes, had a short moan about his ridiculous costume and strange clogs with pom-poms, then went to the neat cot with a woollen blanket tucked around Terry's body and smiled down at him. Evie got out of bed and padded over to join him, yawning.

'Don't wake him,' she said.

'Too late,' he said, leaning in and stroking Terry's soft, velvety head. Beaming and rosy-cheeked, Terry struggled to his feet, his fingers curling round the bars of the cot.

'Da da!' he cried. 'Da da!'

Evie's heart leapt to her mouth.

Lawrence turned to Evie. 'Daddy! He called me Da,' cried Lawrence. 'You hear that, Angel?'

'I did,' she said, taking pleasure in Lawrence's delight as he lifted Terry out of the cot and hugged him close. Evie embraced them both.

The next evening, she waited up for him to come home, sat up all evening in the chair. When he came in and took off his mackintosh, she said, 'Let's get married now, Lawrence. I'm sick of feeling ashamed.

And you've been so good, waiting all this time. It's not fair to you.'

'You mean it?' he said.

'I do, Lawrence.'

'Oh, Angel. God, how I love you.'

I love you, she wanted to say back. But she still couldn't quite do it. The words just wouldn't come. And she refused to lie. But she hoped and prayed that in time they would, and it would be the truth.

Forty-Four

Two weeks passed, and autumn leaves carpeted the ground with red and gold. Lawrence had gone to the Town Hall and booked the first date that was available. When he wasn't rehearsing, he and Evie would spend the day making lists together on scraps of paper of the things they needed to do before the wedding. They would spend each evening when Lawrence returned, exhausted but still lively and full of adrenalin, talking about the play and the things that had gone wrong: him forgetting to put his braces on properly, which had made the other actors giggle when he'd played a scene with them looping about his thighs; and Mabel's tantrums with dressers; and Ken pressing the offstage doorbell at the wrong time in the middle of Lawrence's big speech. Each day, if he wasn't rehearsing, they carried out a small task like painting a piece of furniture, planting flowers in the window boxes, or patching up an old eiderdown, and miraculously it felt like they were beginning to fashion a life together. And there was a lot of kissing and caressing, skin on skin, passionate embraces, touching and stroking and sucking flesh – without doing the actual thing itself, as Lawrence was now rather taken with the idea of waiting to make love until his wedding night. He wondered how divinely exquisite that must be: a taste of what so many normal people must enjoy, but he could barely imagine. And gradually, with all this pulsating ardour going on behind the doors of Paradise Street, for Evie, even Frankie faded into the past tense.

Evie started to feel more confident, stronger each week. Confident enough one evening to let Lawrence slip her into the back of the stalls so that she could watch him and Mabel performing in *Private Lives*. A performance that was so real, the kisses and protestations of intense love, so believable, it was almost unnerving.

'Jesus, Lawrence,' said Ken quietly afterwards to Lawrence. 'You really going to do it? You really going to marry Sugar Girl?'

'I am,' he replied. 'Three weeks' time.'

Ken raised an eyebrow, but he knew it would be a waste of time offering his opinion on the matter. Besides, she did look awfully pretty.

Every morning Evie would walk Terry to the park in his pram and buy him a piece of cinder toffee to suck on, which she would always finish off, enjoying the prickling sensation on her tongue the more she sucked it and the more it filled with holes. She began to feel with increasing certainty that she had made the right decision. Could it be that she was finally beginning to fall in love with Lawrence?

Meanwhile, she wasted no time writing to her father at his new address and telling him the news about the wedding. He was flabbergasted, but firm with Joan when she reacted with open-mouthed shock to him saying how delighted he was that Evie had found happiness, and though he didn't expect to be walking her down the aisle, he would be asking if he and Vic and the girls could go to the wedding.

Beryl, meanwhile, had left St Sylvester's shortly after Evie, and with the most beautiful finely stitched and embroidered dress that she had made out of the parachute silk, had managed to get herself a job as a seamstress in a small dressmaker's shop in Bold Street. She was living in a room above it. But the best news of all was that she had taken little Kim with her, persuading her sister to have the baby while Beryl was at work. She had made Evie a pair of silk bloomers. 'Everyone needs decent frillies on their wedding day,' she had said.

Krysia had clapped her hands in delight when Evie turned up at the factory gates and broke the news. It was the first time Evie had seen her really smile, and the first time she noticed quite how beautiful she was. That morning, Edna had said she would go with Evie to town whilst Lawrence made the final arrangements for the wedding at the St George's Hall registry office.

When Edna and Evie arrived at the little dressmaker's where Beryl now worked, and the bell tinkled above the door, the dress was already hanging on the back of the door. It was ivory tulle, with a pretty white sash that tied in a bow in the small of Evie's back. It had a sweetheart neckline and scalloped sleeves, and it came to just below her knees. It did the job of not drawing too much attention to the fact that she was getting married – after all, with a child in tow, that wasn't something a girl would want to advertise – but it still looked stunning in an understated way.

Beryl, it turned out, really *was* a wizard with a needle and knew how to do the delicate lace panels and the embroidery around the hem, all the fashion right now; and Krysia in turn had recommended a Polish woman who would help them with finding a pair of seamless satin shoes to match.

They all gasped when they saw Evie come out from behind the curtain that hung on a sagging wire in the corner of the shop.

'You look like a film star . . .' said Beryl, her hands flying to her mouth.

'No, I don't. You wait until you see Mabel. She's an actual film star . . . or will be one day soon.'

Edna smiled. 'Just think, you could've ended up with that daft 'apeth Frankie. And now look at you.'

Frankie? thought Evie. Why are you bringing him up?

Forty-Five

Frankie, still tired after an uncomfortable night's sleep at the Anchor Boarding House with a view of the Mersey from his room and the sound of the docks waking him early, set off through Sailortown and past the jumble of tenement houses and warehouses, the dance halls and pubs, and the Seamen's Mission. He was headed towards Pitt Street. He paused at the fortune teller's booths, had a moment's thought about going in, and then continued on. Looking around the piece of wasteland between the station and the docks where Evie's house had once been, he saw that the place was barely recognizable. The greengrocers had taken over and expanded into the fruit stalls next door, and they were now also selling fresh milk and strange new foods like tinned peaches and chocolate spread. The tailor's shop had become a ladies' clothing store and there was a mannequin in the window wearing a slim-fitting, two-piece dogtooth checked suit and a pill-box hat. The blacksmith's sign now proudly announced that you could have your new keys cut and shoes cobbled on the premises. There was even a shop selling records, its windows adorned with posters of the Ink Spots and Nat King Cole. The park gardens, apart from the newly pruned shrubbery, had now been laid out with grass seed on the slopes, and green shoots were springing up. There was the noxious smell of tarmac; steamrollers were already starting work, trying to roll out a new road over the filled-in potholes. A small fire where the sticky black stuff bubbled up in a larger metal cylinder gave off strong fumes, making the air around it wobble in the fierce heat.

But when he turned the corner and walked down the hill, it was a different story. No renewal here, just more devastation. In place of the municipal garden was a flat, reddish piece of ground. Beyond that, the rest of the place, even though these were the streets where he had grown up knowing every curve and corner, was strange and unfamiliar. The weed-choked path winding over the barren patch of earth he could barely remember, and yet he had walked up and down it every day for years of his life. A scrawny pack of dogs came up to him; one of them, with a milky eye, pushed its wet nose against his leg. He pushed it away. Then the dog tried again, and this time Frankie allowed it to snuffle into his palm and lick his fingers. Walking over to the row of partially demolished houses and boarded-up shops, reminders of the devastating legacy of the war in this bleak wasteland, he tried to get his bearings.

Amongst all of this, Tate & Lyle's stood rock solid, rising up on the skyline like a beacon of hope. Frankie headed over to the large red-brick building, with smoke spewing and steam belching from its tall chimney.

*   *   *

'Is that you, Frankie!' cried Edna, carrying a pile of sugar bags, her chin resting on the top one to keep it steady. She had spotted him hovering about on the pavement on the other side of the wrought-iron gates, twisting his cap in his hand, eyes searching around, and she put down the bags of sugar and went over to him. 'Good God. What are you doing here? You look very different, Frankie O'Hare!'

'Do I? Farm work is hard. Takes its toll . . .'

He had muscles now, and his voice seemed also to have developed a subtle Canadian lilt.

'Never thought you'd come back,' said Edna.

As he shifted nervously from foot to foot, it was clear he couldn't wait a minute longer. 'What news of my Evie?' he said.

Edna's smile faltered. She glanced away.

'She took it hard, Frankie,' she replied seriously. 'Your silence.'

'*Me?* I wrote, then I tried again, and then nothing. I've heard nothing from Evie since the day I left.'

Edna frowned. 'What?'

'I can't tell you how many times I tried to get in touch with her. I even sent Jacky O'Hallaran knocking on doors. But then I heard she wasn't at Coghlan Street. They've moved out to St Helen's, haven't they? That's what Jacky heard. That's why I'm here. To find her.'

'Oh, Frankie. She was convinced someone had written to you and told you about the baby. She thought that was why you'd decided to stay away.'

'Baby? What baby?' he said, the blood draining from his face.

Edna frowned. 'Have you not heard?'

He wore an expression of complete and utter shock. The clattering sound of the machines, the hissing steam, the thundering and clanking of pulleys and chains, was a fitting backdrop to the tumult going on in his brain.

'Wait. You're saying Evie's had a baby?' he asked.

'No,' Edna said quickly. 'I mean, erm, her step-mother's had a baby . . .' She stuttered and lied badly – it sounded so implausible – a lame effort to try and row back her question. The minute the word *baby* had left her mouth she had regretted it, and more so now as he began to fire questions at her. *Baby?* Stepmother? Was Edna sure? Where was Evie living, was she at home with her da? Was she still working at the factory? *Why* wasn't she? Had Edna explained to Evie that Carol Connelly was a fraud and a liar? *Baby? What the hell! Baby!* 'It sounded like Evie you were talking about, not some blessed stepmother.' Edna lied and insisted that in all honesty, she had no idea where Evie was. From the wild look in Frankie's eyes, from the tensing and separating of every bone in his body, nothing would persuade her to tell him.

He sucked in air, then puffed his cheeks out, leaned back with his hands behind his head, and raked his fingers back and forward through his hair.

'I've got to find her before I leave. I'm only here for a week, Edna,' he said, wildly pacing back and forth. 'Where's Stanley? I need to speak to Stanley Mulhearn.'

'You won't find her. I'd let it go, love. Let her live her life. You wouldn't want to know. And I wouldn't bother with Stanley. Stanley'll be no good to you.'

Forty-Six

There were always a handful of Mabel's stage-door Johnnies along with a few shop girls hunting for autographs after the show. Some plays attracted them more than others. Mabel and Lawrence were still performing to reasonable houses in *Private Lives*, playing husband and wife. It irked Lawrence that sometimes it would mean he would get back home later than usual because of the time he would have to spend signing their little books, and chatting with these people at the stage door. Which also meant that Evie would have fallen asleep in the chair; which meant the next morning she would wake up with a crick in her neck, and if Terry had been teething in the night, she wouldn't be much good to anyone.

Tonight there was a smaller crowd than usual as it was a matinee day, and most had come to see the play in the afternoon. Mabel had sneakily pulled on her cloche hat, stuffed her curls inside and quickly slipped out through the foyer and the front doors of the building; she got changed so speedily that she was able to mingle unnoticed with some of the audience who had lagged behind, smoking cigarettes and muddling up cloakroom tickets.

As Lawrence came out from the stage door, two

excited middle-aged women, one with a daughter who was even more rotund than she was, were brandishing their programmes, which he duly signed.

'Mr Childs, this is my daughter. She wants to be an actress. She's ever so good,' she said. 'We're thinking of trying for the RADA . . .'

'The RADA?' echoed Lawrence, glancing at the girl's thick ankles and her unusually large nose. 'Marvellous,' he said. After five minutes talking, he hoped he had spent enough time answering their dull, predictable questions, enlightening them on how learning lines was quite the easiest part of the job, and smiling graciously through gritted teeth as they told him that his performance was their fourth favourite they had seen at the theatre that year, and that maybe one day he might become as famous as James Mason. Ever so talented, James Mason, didn't Lawrence think? Eventually, after he'd suffered silently for another ten minutes, they left him alone.

The man standing in the street under a buttery arc of light looked different to the usual kind of person who would wait this long on a cold autumnal night. He stepped forward out of the light, the shadows scooping out the hollows in his face. Lawrence had developed a sixth sense for Mabel's stage-door Johnnies, who would turn up even when they hadn't seen the play, and he resented it. Once or twice he plucked up the courage and asked to see their tickets. This chap hadn't watched the play, he was sure, and there was something peculiar about him, so he moved off quickly. But when he turned around, the man seemed to be following him down the narrow passage that ran alongside the theatre. Eventually, when he came out and turned right along the street that ran all the way down to the station, Lawrence suddenly stopped walking. Turning left, the opposite way to where he was going to catch the tram, and looking over his shoulder, he saw that the man was doing the same. Finally he turned on his heel, spun around, squared up to him and faced him, speaking to him directly.

'Look here,' he said. 'Can I help you?'

The man shifted from foot to foot.

'Wait,' he said.

'I'll do nothing of the sort. Who are you?'

He didn't reply, but he came forward, stepped into the light and thrust out his hand.

'For your wife,' he said.

Perhaps he had seen the show after all. Almost certainly one of Mabel's fellows. She shouldn't have left the theatre through the foyer. Grudgingly Lawrence took the trinket, casually glanced at the cheap nickel jewellery – some kind of bracelet.

'Next time leave presents and flowers at the stage door. No good giving them to me. I'm not married to her in real life. It's make-believe,' he said, in a bored tone. He was tired of receiving gifts on behalf of Mabel. He must tell her to stop this stunt of sloping off and leaving him to deal with the wretched autograph-hunters.

'It's for your real wife!'

But at that very same moment, the screeching of the tram wheels on the tracks pierced the night air and his words were lost in the din, just twisted into the dark, as Lawrence turned up his collar and slipped the bracelet into his pocket. Then he jumped up onto the board, and it rattled off into the night.

'Bloody nuisance,' murmured Lawrence.

Forty-Seven

A week later, an excited Mabel stood on the steps of St George's Hall looking every inch the film star she imagined she would one day be, in a tight, shimmering cerise décolleté dress with a plunging neckline and a white feather boa. The day of the wedding had finally arrived. Teetering in red sequinned court shoes and beaming out from under the brim of a huge hat with a matching red silk rose pinned on the side, setting off her blonde curls, she waved at Lawrence. He was striding towards her wearing an impeccably tailored suit that she recognized from their tour of *An Inspector Calls*. The river Mersey was all ruffled up, small peaks of white foaming on its surface; the sun was out, and the sky was a brilliant, cloudless blue. They made their way past the lions and the statue of Disraeli and up the wide flight of steps, to the impressive fluted Corinthian columns and huge open thick wooden front doors. Inside, in the foyer, their heels clacked on the swirling mosaic floor tiles decorated with leaping fish and sailboats on tossing waves.

Evie's father was sitting with Joan in the Minton Room, with its awe-inspiring domed ceiling and neoclassical pillars. Beside them were Victor, his cheek bulging with a gobstopper, and Sylvie and Nelly in matching pale-blue lace frocks. They huddled together and spoke in hushed tones, fidgeted and pointed wide-eyed at the friezes, the ornate gold leaf, the magnificent lamps held aloft by Greek gods. When they became aware of the handsome young man striding purposefully towards them, they twisted excitedly round in their seats.

Lawrence went over to them, smiling broadly. 'You must be Mr O'Leary,' he said, shaking Evie's father's hand firmly. Joan lifted a pencilled eyebrow. He did look magnificent, with his white carnation in his buttonhole, polished shoes, and that wonderful suit. He must have a bob or two, she mistakenly thought. 'I know this is a little short notice, Mr O'Leary. Things have been so rushed, thrown together so to speak, and we were going to write again; but the thing is, it would make Evie so happy if you would walk her down the aisle. Only if you want to.'

Bill hesitated. Joan nodded. Lawrence was a charmer, and she wondered how anyone could say no to this man. 'Call me Bill. Lead the way, sir,' said Evie's father, beaming, as they dodged past Krysia, with a translucency to her complexion that no one had seen before, making an entrance down the centre aisle. She was dressed in a pencil skirt with a split up the back and a pretty, close-fitting cream jacket with shoulder pads.

Evie, meanwhile, who hadn't seen Lawrence since the day before, as he had stayed at Mabel's flat the previous night, was sitting outside in Ken's Austin Ten car with Edna. She looked beautiful, her hair twisted and tied in a loose knot, wearing the ivory satin dress and nervously fingering the teardrop crystal earrings that Edna had lent her. She clutched a posy tied together with a curling white satin ribbon.

'You look so pretty,' Edna said. 'Come here.' From her bag, she took a lipstick and fashioned Evie's lips into a cupid's bow. Evie blushed.

Ken opened the car door and they came out, blinking, into the sunshine. On the pavement, Evie's father stood waiting nervously.

'Da!' she said. 'You'll walk me down the aisle?'

His eyes misted with tears seeing how radiant she looked, especially with the sun picking up flecks of gold in her hair. She was as beautiful as a rainbow after a storm. 'Of course,' he answered. 'You're my girl, aren't you? Come on now, Evie.'

Linking his arm, she took a deep breath, and they went up the steps and through the doors of St George's Hall. Preparing to enter the beautiful room, they marvelled at the graceful pillars, the alabaster statues in alcoves along the walls, and the meticulous, tiny, colourful pieces of glass and stone shimmering under their feet.

For a moment, Evie faltered. Edna rushed forward to meet her, straightened the ribbon in her hair. When she squeezed Evie's hand, she felt it shaking.

'Are you all right, Evie?'

'Yes,' Evie replied.

Was this typical wedding nerves, Edna wondered, or something else? Suddenly the thought of Frankie crashed into her head. Should she at least have told Evie he was in Liverpool? If Evie was having second thoughts – if she was a good friend – shouldn't she have told her she had seen him?

'You can turn back,' she whispered.

'Don't be stupid,' said Evie.

As she walked up the aisle on her father's arm to Artie Shaw's 'Frenesi' – a piece of music that Lawrence had chosen, and Gordon the stage doorman had agreed to make a stab at playing on the impressive organ – she saw Vic, a foot taller, it seemed. He waved at her and she winked back at him.

And there was Holy Joan. A triumphant smile played across Evie's lips, although she tried to fight it. There was Mabel, beaming at her wildly, with her nipped-in waist and breasts heaving out of the pink dress. Trust Mabel to try and upstage her. She was the kind of girl who showed no mercy, not even for a bride.

Lawrence was at the front of the rows of chairs, waiting nervously. As she joined him he had to catch his breath. 'You look divine, Angel,' he said. Ken took the rings from his pocket.

The registrar started the ceremony. When he got to the vows, Lawrence squeezed Evie's hand so tight that it hurt. He smiled lovingly at her.

'Do you, Reginald Hardbottom, take Evangeline O'Leary to be your lawful wedded wife?' said the registrar.

There was a ripple of laughter around the front pews. Mabel giggled into her gloves; Edna widened her eyes at Beryl, and they exchanged smiles.

Evie faltered. Reginald Hardbottom? She felt a

slight constriction in her throat. Tried to swallow. Lawrence had taken care of the forms, but it still seemed a little shocking to her that she was hearing his real name for the very first time, even though he had told her before about stage names.

Nevertheless, she was prepared to move past it. Now was not the time. 'I do,' she said, and as Lawrence slipped the ring onto her slim finger and whispered that he would love her forever, she whispered back, 'And I you,' amazed that this creature had just married her. He had actually wanted to marry her, and that was actually what had happened.

And she hoped it would be good enough for now.

'Well, Evie,' her father said, just before they went off to sign the register. 'Your ma would be proud. And my God, you look just as beautiful as she did on our wedding day.'

'Thanks, Da.'

'Where's Terry?' he asked.

'My friend, Beryl, her sister has got him for the night.'

'I'd like to see him.'

'You will, Da.'

She wanted to say she was sorry. She had always imagined a church and a long white dress, and bridesmaids, and him walking her down the aisle to give her away to . . . well, who? Certainly not some gadabout actor, eight years older than her. But then, this was so much better than the bleak future that had lain ahead for her when she had stormed out of Coghlan Street, and her father seemed happy enough.

'Vic, you've grown!' she exclaimed. Victor held out his hand and shook hers, as if he were a proper young man. 'Come here,' she said, ruffling his hair. And she yanked him towards her, wrapped him up in her arms and kissed the top of his head.

The man who had done the ceremony was coming up beside them, gesturing them to follow him into a side room where they would sign the register to make things legal. When Evie's hand shook as she took the pen, Lawrence rested his on hers to stay it.

'You all right, Angel?' he asked.

'Yes,' she said. 'I've never been happier.'

Lawrence smiled, and with the gold fountain pen, he wrote his name on the piece of stiff white parchment paper.

She looked at the page. 'Reginald Hardbottom? That was a bit of a surprise,' she said, thinking how odd it was that she had just married this man, and she hadn't even known his name.

He looked up at her, still smiling.

'That's really your name? Reginald? *Reg*?' she asked.

'Yes. Dreadful isn't it? Haven't used it for years.'

'And you didn't think to tell me?'

She looked at him, and he just shrugged.

Lawrence and Evie came walking out, linking arms, squinting against the sunlight. They stood on the steps of St George's Hall as Ken took a snapshot of them with an old camera he had borrowed from the theatre. Lawrence looked at Evie and kissed her on the bridge of her nose as they all stood milling about, whilst Ken, wanting to take more photographs, shouted directions as to where they should stand and who they should stand with.

'Evie!' called Edna. 'Come back inside.'

Mabel was standing in the doorway, waving. 'We want a picture with you and us gals by the statues inside. Come on, Ken!'

'You go,' said Lawrence.

Mabel linked Evie's arm. 'I want Ken to take a picture of me with the chap who did the ceremony. As handsome as a thirty-guinea pony, don't you think? What d'you think my chances are?'

Lawrence was standing at the top of the steps, breathing in the warm summer air, when somewhere off to the side of him he was vaguely aware of a noise, a raised voice. Squinting in the direction of the commotion, he saw a man gesturing to a second man – a doorman, it seemed, as he was wearing some kind of uniform. He was pacing back and forth wildly, twisting his cap, then suddenly he was bounding up the steps, two, three at a time.

He looked oddly familiar. No, it couldn't be. But yes, it was. Lawrence was sure of it. He might not have known his name but he would have recognized that serious, desperate face anywhere, those eyes, that square jaw. This was the same man who had been hanging about the stage door. The man who had tried to follow him home and given him the cheap bracelet for Mabel. He looked dishevelled, upset. What the hell was he doing here?

'Am I too late?' the man asked Lawrence, panting and gasping. The fellow had run as fast as his legs could take him, and they were wobbling underneath him. Lawrence, unnerved, turned away quickly, but he felt the man tug his jacket rudely. When he turned back he saw the man's cheeks flame.

'Evie O'Leary. Where is she? I love her, please God, I'm not too late, am I?' Then he paused. 'It's you, isn't it? The actor?'

Suddenly there was another person beside Lawrence. It was Bill, standing rigid on the steps.

'Get out of here, Frankie O'Hare!' hissed Evie's father. 'You have no place here. Leave now . . . Git!' he snarled, stepping forward aggressively.

'Bill? Just a minute with Evie . . .' gasped Frankie. 'I need to see her. Can I talk to her? Am I too late?'

Bill grabbed the lapels of Frankie's jacket. 'Sod off and leave.'

But as Lawrence stood there, open-mouthed in shock, Bill realized he was going to have to do the only thing he could think of to get rid of this fool. So he loosened his grip on Frankie's jacket, dropped his hands, then drew back a fist and punched him square in the face.

Frankie's legs buckled underneath him. He dropped to the floor like a stone. Bill dragged him to his feet, pushed him away down the steps. 'If you care about my daughter, you'll leave her alone!' he growled.

Frankie's whole body began to shake. Lawrence watched as this dejected creature faltered, swayed unsteadily, and staggered off like a lame dog, the strength of his desperate feelings showing in his crumpled body as he gave in to the pain and pressed a hand against his bloody nose.

'If it's my child . . . I have a right to—' he blurted, turning back, tense and angry, as he tried to stem the flow.

Lawrence, watching, didn't know what to think. Evie's father charged after Frankie, shoving him in the chest again. 'You bloody idiot, you don't know what you're talking about. It's too late. You had your chance.'

Frankie looked at him. 'I'm not finished yet,' he said, wiping his nose on his sleeve. 'I'm not finished with any of you yet . . .'

'Please don't tell Evie,' whispered Lawrence to Bill when Frankie had gone. 'Will only put a dampener on proceedings, don't you think?'

'I certainly won't,' said Evie's father bitterly. 'That boy has ruined her life once, and he's not going to do it again. I'll kick his arse all the way across the Atlantic if I have to. Our Evie must never know about this; I'll not risk her running back to him. I swear he has some kind of hold over her. Don't ever let his name be mentioned in your house. This marriage is doomed if you do.'

He turned to see his smiling daughter, looking truly happy for the first time in many years, skipping down the steps towards him.

'Mabel just draped her feather boa around one of the statues,' she said, giggling. 'The poor registry chap was frightened out of his wits.'

Then she paused, frowned, rubbed at something

on the steps with the toe of her shoe. 'It looks like blood. A tiny spot. Where do you think that came from?' she asked, as Lawrence exchanged a look with Bill and glanced furtively away.

Forty-Eight

The wedding party walked together, a small, vivacious band that made people smile when they saw them. Three women cheerfully poked their heads through a window on the fourth floor and waved. It was a short distance from the hall, past Liverpool Lime Street where the sun reflected off the glass roof and dappled the grass with yellow and green, a dazzling backdrop to their happiness, past the gleaming hansom cabs. When they arrived at the Adelphi Hotel, they went into the magnificent foyer. Miraculously, the building had remained largely unscathed during the war – unlike Lewis's opposite, which had been reduced to a hollow, blackened shell but was now covered in scaffolding.

Evie could hardly believe she was here. Edna had saved some rice, and threw a handful of it over both of them as they went through the revolving glass doors. The brass fittings and the elegant furniture, marble-topped tables with their clawed feet, the bar that stretched down the whole of the far wall, meant Evie had to pinch herself again that this was happening to her. She went up the long winding staircase. Part of the hotel was decorated with relics, or supposed relics, from the *Titanic*. There were huge marble pillars and long velvet drapes cascading down to the floor with gold-braided, tasselled ties. She had never seen such opulence. The bottles behind the bar threw back reflections along the polished surface. Men stood with their feet resting on the brass rail as a teenage boy circled the tables playing Scott Joplin medleys on a violin. But it was the staircase, with its polished brass handrail and wide steps, that was the most magnificent.

'Drinks on me!' cried her father. Evie wondered how on earth he could afford it.

After drinking and more drinking, with Mabel ordering one Red Witch after another – 'One more Pernod and black coming up!' the barman kept crying, as she giggled drunkenly – there was dancing. Victor stuffed a pickled egg into his mouth sideways and went running round the bar, grinning at his younger sisters, who collapsed in laughter. Holy Joan presented Evie with a carefully wrapped gift. Cautiously, she opened it. 'A statue of the Virgin Mary?' she exclaimed, and didn't know what to think, but thanked Joan politely. Joan told her every house should have one. Meanwhile, Ken was standing on a table, starting to perform a drunken version of the 'Egg Song'. Edna made a stab at an impression of Vera Lynn singing 'White Cliffs of Dover', but Mabel practically shoved her out of the way and gave them all a rendition of 'Every Nice Girl Loves a Sailor' in her wobbling soprano. Finally, some slumped into chairs and others staggered off into the night.

Evie and Lawrence were on their way to their hotel room. She gasped on entering to see that the bed was a four-poster, with satin drapes hanging down each side. There were plush cream carpets and aspidistras on stands in brass tubs. She had never seen anything like it.

'How can you afford this?'

'Got the theatre rate on the room. Dirt cheap. Hotels want us actors hanging out in their bars. At least, they do if we're the leading man and devilishly handsome.'

She slapped him playfully.

'It's true!' he said. The large urn-shaped vases were full of flowers, lilies and white roses. 'Your friend Krysia organized that,' he said. 'And, look . . .'

There on the bed was the most beautiful nightdress, embroidered with cream hearts and flowers, ruched, elasticated under the breasts and with a long cream ribbon. 'From Beryl.'

Evie turned to him as she picked up the nightdress and buried her face in it, luxuriating in the feel of the fabric. 'I'm so lucky to have these people in my life,' she said.

'And I'm so lucky to have you. The luckiest man in the world,' he said.

Outside, the moon shone brightly. Evie could hear music coming from somewhere far off. It was probably Beryl, still dancing downstairs.

'You see Mabel chatting up that fellow at the bar?' she said, slipping off her shoes.

'Showing off her cha-cha,' he laughed. 'Sit down,' he said, and when she perched on the edge of the bed, he knelt. Taking her foot in his lap, he began massaging her heel with his thumb.

She was feeling a little woozy as he leaned forward and kissed her on the lips, pushed her skirt up her thighs. The feeling in the pit of her stomach spread through her body to her toes and fingertips in tiny ripples.

'Should I put the nightgown on?' she said.

'Yes,' he said.

She faltered. She didn't know why but she was suddenly nervous. Standing, slowly she began to undo the buttons on her dress until her pretty camisole underwear was exposed. But she hesitated once again; she felt oddly shy and didn't want to undress in front of him.

'Shall I turn off the lights?' she said.

'Whatever you want, darling,' he said.

She nodded, relieved that he wouldn't see her blushes. She felt her heart race and her palms sweat, as she turned away from him, moved off into the bathroom. Taking a deep breath, she undid her hair and let it fall loose across her shoulders. 'What's the matter with you, Evie?' she said to her reflection in the mirror. She heard the sound of him taking off his shirt, the sound of the poppers on his braces, the sound of him untying his laces, *thwack, thwack.* Then the sound of the bed creaking as he sat on the side of it, creaking again as she heard him stand, and then his footsteps moving across the carpet, then the striking of a match.

She stepped back into the room. She was surprised to see him smoking and with a glass in his hand, sitting on the banquette seat in the window, staring out at the city. The shoulder strap of the nightgown had slipped down her arm, and she pushed it back up shyly.

'Come here,' he said. 'You are the most beautiful thing I've ever seen.'

'You must have seen so many beautiful women,' she said.

'Not like you, Evie. You're so natural. Kind of a real girl. Not a fake girl.'

She smiled, shyly.

'Wonderful. Come here . . .' She joined him and sat down beside him. He put one hand around her waist. She could feel his touch through the gossamer-fine silk. And then he did something strange: he just rested his head on her shoulder. She remained staring out at the shell of Lewis's building opposite. People coming and going. A couple, maybe Mabel, getting into a taxicab. She felt his hand grasp her waist tighter. And then he released it, turned her to him, put both of his hands flat on each cheek and stared at her.

'What?' she said.

'Nothing, Sugar Girl,' he replied.

He had a far-off look in his eyes.

'Are you all right?'

'Yes,' he replied. 'Come on, dear.' He took her by the hand and led her to the bed. He stood at the foot of it and began to undress. She could see the shape of him as he took off his trousers, then his shirt. Looking at his sculpted, lithe body silhouetted against the light, his smooth hairless chest, his silky hair pushed back off his face, it was as though she was seeing him for the first time. Pulling back the goose eiderdown and revealing the crisp white sheets, he said, 'Get in, love.'

They lay there together in the dark. She concentrated on his breathing and waited for something to happen.

After a few moments he pulled her towards him. She could feel his hands moving down her body, over her breasts, the small of her back. And then he stopped. He rolled onto his back. Resting his hand on the marble skin of her flat white stomach, he said, 'Would it be awful if we just slept?' She twisted her head on the pillow, turned her face to him, and frowned. 'I'm tired, my darling, that's all,' he said, tracing a finger along her jawline.

Tired! How could a man be tired on his wedding night? she thought.

'It's not that I don't want to make love. It's just—'

'I understand,' she said. 'We've got the rest of our lives together . . .'

They lay there silently, holding hands, watching shadows moving on the ceiling. She watched his chest rising and falling in a steady rhythm. She then circled his waist with her arms, slid her toes between his thighs. He gently finger-combed her hair, fanned it out onto the pillow, planted a firm kiss on top of her head.

'Oh, Angel, my sweet girl,' he murmured. 'I do love you,' as shadows moved across the room, and Evie's eyelids felt heavy and she drifted off into sleep.

Forty-Nine

She awoke with a start, not knowing where she was, sat bolt upright and gasped.

'Evie,' whispered Lawrence. He was in his shirt; there was a tray with toast and a steaming cup of tea at the end of the bed that room service had provided.

'Need to get back to Terry,' said Evie, yawning.

'He'll be fine with Beryl's sister. Take your time.'

She buttered the toast and drank the tea.

'I feel like a princess,' she said.

'It's what you deserve, dear,' he replied. 'I'm only sorry we have to leave here so early. As soon as this season is over, I'm taking you somewhere wonderful for our honeymoon. Paris, maybe. For a proper two-week uninterrupted holiday. I know a little hotel just off the Champs-Elysées.'

'Paris!' she gasped. And then her face fell. He hadn't even considered the baby. 'Paris would be lovely,' she added, deciding now was not the moment.

Fighting the urge to stay curled up in bed, she walked over to the window, opened it, came out onto the tiny balcony and breathed in. Immediately she felt her lungs prickle with the cement and dust. Lawrence went off into the bathroom. He had left his trousers in a crumpled heap on the floor beside their bed, and yesterday's creased shirt hanging over one arm of the chair. She picked up the shirt, smoothed it out lovingly as she folded it.

She could hear the tap running. Lawrence's voice spoke over the sound of gushing water. 'Sugar, I ordered us some poached eggs to have on the balcony. If the room service boy comes, give him a shilling. There are some coins in my wallet. It's on the tallboy.'

The wallet wasn't on the tallboy. She cast her eyes around. It was lying on top of a pile of clothes spilling out of his open carpet bag. But there were no coins in the wallet, only notes. Perhaps the coins had fallen out. She ran her hand over the bottom of the carpet bag, feeling deep in the creases of the lining. What was this? Not a shilling. But a small piece of cheap jewellery.

No. Surely it couldn't be? A bracelet. And then her heart began to race. *The* bracelet? The bracelet that Frankie had bought her and that she had given him a few weeks before he left for Canada? The one with the letters F and E hanging off it. Hidden in the bottom of Lawrence's bag? It didn't make sense. None of it made sense. She looked again at the bracelet – it felt almost as if it was burning a hole in the palm of her hand. Panic rose to her throat, and a sharp knot of pain was tightening in her stomach. Folding away things that might worry or upset her, not letting people know what was going on in her head, usually came easy to Evie, but she would be sorely tested with this.

Fifty

Cooper's was filling up, but Edna had already reserved a table by the window. A couple of ladies in fur coats made their way past the tables and headed upstairs, where they would dine at tables with white linen napkins and silver service. Fronds from a plant on a stand behind her tickled her ear, and she moved her chair an inch closer to the table.

Evie took off her white gloves. She was wearing a pair of brown Cuban-heeled court shoes and a navy-blue woollen peplum dress.

'So go on, tell me all about it,' said Edna.

Evie spilled out in a rush of words about the flowers in the room, how the bed was like a cloud, how you could drown in the swirling carpets.

'Forget about the furniture and the flaming carpets, how was *it*? You know . . .' she asked. And then she winked. Evie felt herself blushing. She didn't really want to go into the details, especially not *those* details, or rather the lack of them.

'Grand,' she said.

'And how's married life? Still in heaven?'

Evie smiled. She knew handsome men were meant to make women's hearts ache, but perhaps not quite as early on in the marriage as this. But she didn't want to dwell on the fact that three more days had passed and Lawrence still hadn't been near her. So she told Edna about how Lawrence had been busier than ever, with one play in rehearsal and another in performance. 'Weekly rep doesn't take much notice of newlyweds,' she said.

'No, I expect not.'

'Still, Lawrence says he's taking me to Paris when this is over.'

'Paris! Ooh la la! You lucky girl . . . What's the matter?' Edna said. 'You don't seem very happy.'

Evie dropped her gaze to the table, moved her china cup around the saucer, and repositioned it.

'I am. But I'll have to find someone to look after Terry. Maybe Mabel can do it. If she's resting. That's what they call it when you're relying on the Labour Exchange . . . and her *men*, of course.'

'Oh, don't ask Mabel. What does she know about babies? Besides, I would try and see that one off if I were you,' Edna said.

'Why?' Evie asked, frowning.

'Nothing. Just . . . crying all over the place. Draping herself all over Lawrence. Kissing him. On the lips. And on his wedding day . . .'

'Lawrence says that's what actresses do.'

'I don't know. Always huddled in a corner.'

'They're practising their lines.'

Edna quirked an eyebrow. 'Is that what it's called? Those two are so close you couldn't get a knife between them,' she said.

'You don't think, you don't think? Lawrence and Mabel?' Evie cast her eyes to the floor. She paused as she tried to gather her thoughts, slowly unfurling in a ribbon of anxiety. Was that why he'd not come near her?

'What's wrong?' said Edna.

'Nothing. I . . . I . . . Lawrence . . .' She raised her head, looked at Edna desperately. 'I found this . . . do you think it's strange?'

'What is it?'

Evie took out the bracelet that she had been carrying around in her little velvet clasp purse for three days now. She laid it on the white tablecloth.

'Remember that charm bracelet Frankie gave me after the works outing in Southport? I found it in Lawrence's bag.'

Edna paled.

There was a long silence.

'What? Say something, Ed.' Edna's brows knitted together. 'Ed, you're panicking me. What is it?'

'Evie, I have to tell you something.'

'Is it about Mabel?'

'No. Forget Mabel. You're right. That's just actresses. It's about Frankie.'

'Frankie?'

'He's in Liverpool. I'm so sorry, love. I should have told you before. But I didn't want him to spoil things for you . . .'

'Oh, Edna!'

'I'm sorry . . .'

Evie shrugged. 'Probably for the best. Too late now . . .' And then she continued, 'Edna, I tried. I can't tell you how hard I tried. Letter after letter I wrote, after he left for Canada. But I didn't know where to send them.'

'I know. But you can't turn back the clock now, and it would be a bloody disaster if you tried to start to wind it up again. You've moved on now, and just because he hasn't, doesn't mean to say you should worry about him. Let's pray to God that he keeps away from you. Let's hope he doesn't pester Stanley.'

Evie sighed. She had long since stopped praying to God. In fact, if she really thought about it, she had given up praying to God, the saints or the Blessed Virgin on the day her mother had left. Her mind swam. She took a mouthful of her scone, but it tasted dry and sour in her mouth. She thought of Lawrence and decided that right now, she needed to be sensible.

Evie walked in through the front door of the factory. Waves of familiarity washed over her. It was strange to be back, her visit underscored by the sounds of pounding, rattling and clunking, the smell, the sweetness lacing the air so that when you licked your lips, they tasted of sugar. She knew all eyes would be on her. But she was married now – she had a piece of paper to prove it, and she was not going to be shamed by anyone.

The girls were sitting at their machines. It was time for the shift to end, but instead of jumping up from their workstations when the klaxon sounded, they sat and stared. There was a low murmur of voices as Evie passed down the aisle on her way to Stanley's office, a small room jutting out from the fourth floor with windows on three sides so that he could look down at the shop floor.

'Stanley,' she said. 'Frankie O'Hare. You seen him?'

'No.'

'Well, in case you do, tell him to stay away from me if he comes around asking where I am. Tell him I've left Liverpool. You hear?'

'Right y'are,' he replied, thinking marriage hadn't softened her – she was still as spirited and as mulish as the day he had first met her. 'Right y'are, Evie.'

Fifty-One

When Lawrence returned, he noticed the room was different to how he'd left it. The chair that was usually left snugly underneath the table was pulled out at an odd angle. There was a mark left on the table, a mug half filled with cold tea and a plate with a crust on it. He had told Evie about the mice in this place – they were so near to the docks here, they always had to have a broom at hand, and the merest sight of breadcrumbs would bring them running. They would boldly scurry out from holes in the skirting boards and gaps between the walls, stop in the middle of the room, right there on the rug and stare at the human beings who thought they owned this place.

He made his way to the tiny kitchen. No Evie. She must be sleeping, he thought. Which was odd again. She would usually wait up for him to come home from the theatre; he would kick his boots off and they would sit either side of the dying fire, where he would tell her stories of what had happened that night at the theatre. Of Mabel, and Mr Sausage Fingers. Of Gordon at the stage door, who had refused Mr Sausage Fingers entry to Mabel's dressing room, and the ensuing fight. Of the latest twist in the saga of Mabel's elusive movie role. Of the new director from London with his new-fangled ideas, who smoked Gauloises and insisted they all wore black tights and pranced around the stage each morning in their bare feet, wasting a good three hours of precious rehearsal time.

Instinctively, he knew something was wrong.

He found her upstairs. She had placed herself next to the window, so he had to walk around the side to meet her eyes.

'Come and sit with me, downstairs,' he said.

Fiddling with the cheap bracelet, she curled her fingers around it and felt it blazing in her hand. Lawrence brought her a plate of bread and cheese and one for himself, but when they sat at the table, she didn't feel like eating. She absentmindedly prodded at the food, then pushed the plate away.

'Can you explain this to me?' she said, suddenly and with a tremor in her voice. She put the piece of jewellery on the table, straightening and re-straightening it. 'Edna has told me everything. Frankie's back in Liverpool. Where did you get it?'

Lawrence frowned. After a pause where he raked his hand through his hair, he answered with a troubled sigh: 'A chap gave it to me. He came to the stage door.'

'And you didn't think to tell me?'

'Why would I?'

Evie paused. 'The stage-door Johnnie was Frankie. Did you know that? Tell me the truth.'

He struggled to find the words. 'Yep. I suppose I did. Eventually. Game's up, Angel. But I thought . . .

I thought if you found out that this chap was in town, you might leave me. That's why I hid the bracelet at the bottom of my bag.'

'Well, you didn't hide it very well.'

'With the excitement of the wedding. I forgot it was there.'

She reached out a hand, placed it flat against his cheek. 'Oh, Lawrence, I'm not going to leave you. I'm your wife. I just wish you had told me.'

'Do you love him?' he asked.

'Of course not,' she answered, quickly.

He took her hand. 'Evie, if you want to see this chap . . . if you have feelings for him . . .'

Feeling the muscles in her top lip begin to quiver, she flinched, hoping to give herself a moment to recover.

'No,' she said.

She was shocked at the merest suggestion. Her first thought was that she would never do anything that might complicate Terry's life, now that she finally could see a future for them.

Later, as she and Lawrence got ready for bed, she lifted Terry from the cot and buried him into the curves of her body. His eyelids fluttered and he sighed contentedly. His thumb found its way into his mouth. So what if Frankie was running around Liverpool proclaiming his love for her? This wasn't about her; this was about Terry. This was about her child's happiness. And to turn her back on Lawrence, that would be madness. He had offered her a warm bed and his love. He was generous and nurturing. She had found someone who wanted to marry her and make her a respectable woman. What did Frankie O'Hare have to offer? A few laughs, a shared history, a song or two. He would be leaving soon.

She felt Lawrence move towards her as she began to undress, stood by the fireplace with her bare back exposed. 'Evie? Are you angry with me?'

'No . . . No . . .' she stuttered. 'I just . . .' She felt her brow beading with sweat, battled feelings of anger and hurt. 'It's just that I still think you should have told me about Frankie. You and Edna.'

'I wanted to. I nearly did. Then the moment passed, and then that moment stretched into days and we were getting married – and you and I, well, we were still getting to know each other. Still are. I didn't know how you'd react. You might have flown off the handle. Don't forget, I'm used to women like Mabel. She would have—'

'Maybe that,' she said, 'is the problem, Lawrence. We don't know each other. You and Mabel are so tight, so . . .' Her words ran out and she made a gesture, interlocking her fingers.

And when he said: 'Mabel? What are you talking about?' she immediately regretted it.

'Edna said—'

'Mabel?'

She thought how quickly and strangely the conversation had turned from Frankie to Mabel. Suddenly this had become about something else entirely. But maybe Mabel was a useful vessel into which Evie could pour all her hurt over the bracelet incident.

'Lovey. My life will be spent with actresses floating

about looking for attention, jealous minxes. You're going to have to get used to that. I fell in love with you because you were different. A different type of girl to Mabel and all the others. But if it turns out you're all the same . . .'

'I'm sorry,' she said. She rubbed her temples. Was she really just looking for something to argue about?

'I love you,' she said suddenly.

'I love you too,' he said.

Though what he wanted to say was something altogether different. He wanted to say that this was the first time he had heard her say those words – but he was an actor and he was in the business of truth, and he knew when someone was going through the motions. When you're in the business of faking it, you can recognize it a mile off. The fact that it was his beloved Evie just made it all the harder to bear.

Fifty-Two

Dear Frankie,

I have heard from Edna that you are in Liverpool. I suspect you have learned I am married. Please, don't try and find me. My husband is a good man. He's not the obvious person for me, but he loves me. He has given me a home and respectability. In my bleakest hour, I would never have imagined someone could save me from myself like he has done.

I know it was my fault that I destroyed what we had because of my stupid jealousy and stubborn nature. I wish I could turn back time, but the fact is, I can't. I'm determined to make this marriage work. I wish you every good luck for your future and for your happiness.

Yours,
Evie

Lawrence dropped the blotting pad from the candle-light. The impression that the pen had made on the pad was clear – one of these new ballpoints everyone was buying that magically didn't need a bottle of ink. The soft nib of a fountain pen might have allowed him to live in oblivion, but not this.

'Oh, my Angel,' he murmured sadly.

Terry had seemed to be up all night, chewing on his teething ring and sticking his fist in his mouth. A strong wind had been prowling about the streets, upturning dustbins and pulling at roof tiles. Evie found Lawrence sitting at the table, breakfasting on Player's No. 6, when she came in to light the fire. There were rings under his eyes, and his hair was greasy. His greying five o'clock shadow looked more like a beard. As she waited for the embers to catch light, she wandered around picking things up, putting them away in drawers, taking them out again.

With Terry wedged on her hip, sucking on a rattle that he really shouldn't have been putting anywhere near his mouth, trying to calm him and handing him his bottle of sugared water, at the same time she filled the kettle from the sink in the corner of the room. Finding it impossible, she put him down, but within minutes he was crawling determinedly towards the door. A moment later and he would have gone out onto the landing and probably tumbled down the three flights of stairs, if she hadn't hooked a hand under his romper suit and pulled him back from certain disaster.

'I've been up all night, thinking,' Lawrence said as he laced his shoes. 'You should see Frankie. Tell him about the child. It's the least you should do.'

She looked at him in shock. 'I don't want to.'

'There's no point in us making a life together, if you don't see him and tell him the truth about the baby.'

'Why?' she said, alarmed.

'Do it, Angel. Do it for me. For us. Honesty is the only way forward. Better to face the consequences now than in twenty years' time. Lies have a bad habit of turning everything sour.'

She thought of her mother, and how the lies about what had happened to her had taken hold and ruined so many lives. Lawrence was right about being honest. He was right about so many things.

Fifty-Three

For the next two days, Evie devoted herself to doing things around the flat. The hinges were coming off the door, and she asked Lawrence to get a piece of wood and put it across the door frame so Terry wouldn't fall down the stairs.

'Me?' he replied. 'With these hands? I'll have you know someone once said these hands would be my fortune. They match my face.'

She wasn't sure if he was joking. 'You have a day off and you're not working until tonight. Maybe today we could go to the wood merchant's and get a piece of wood.'

'Sweetie, just because I'm not working until tonight doesn't mean to say I'm not working up here in the day,' he said, pointing at his head. 'I'm *preparing*. Might look like I'm lounging on the sofa, but I'm not. Anyway, if you want a door fixing, you should have married an odd-job man. I'm afraid I'm useless with a hammer,' he said.

She thought about how different he was to other men she knew, what her father might think of this, how he would consider it unmanly. Lawrence had told her about not fighting in the war, how his flat feet had been his saviour and that he would much rather play a soldier than risk his life actually being one – but just once, he had hinted that he felt ashamed because of it. In any case, wasn't real life what he had wanted from her, at least a semblance of it? Would he ever be ready to embrace it in all its scrappy, dirty, raggedy shapes and forms?

'And Angel, whilst we're on the subject of my job, please don't ever say "break a leg" to me again. Actors never say that to each other. And please God, don't ever say I'm "resting" when I'm out of work. Say I'm on the dole. That's another thing that puts my teeth on edge and sets you lot apart from us.'

You lot? She thought back to all the times she had said 'break a leg' to him. Up until now he hadn't seemed to mind. Not once. Pondering this, it came as a shock when he added casually, 'You arranged to meet Frankie yet?'

She blushed, stammered that she hadn't and had no intention of doing so.

He left early that evening. Evie watched from the window as he disappeared down the flinty road, then went to settle Terry into his cot.

The knock at the door half an hour later was loud and firm. Evie hurried back to the window. She could see a figure, but it blurred into a shapeless form behind the squiggles of rain running down the glass. Who on earth was it? She pulled back the curtain further and squinted into the street, shading her eyes against the glass. Down on the pavement, the figure moved back, looked up at the windows, then stepped towards the door and banged on the brass knocker. Evie tutted. No one answered the front door in these flats in a hurry and the last thing she wanted was whoever it was waking the whole house. Terry had only just fallen asleep. She took a shawl, wrapped it round her shoulders and went downstairs. She flung open the door, fully expecting to send off the person at the door with a few short, sharp words telling him that if it was Lawrence he wanted, Lawrence was working.

She looked at Frankie in shock, nearly dropped the oil lamp she was holding and fumbled when she tried to hold it close to her and away from him.

'Frankie! What are you doing here?'

'Come to find you.'

He had hardly changed; the same thick dark hair, the same strong body, the same blue eyes – perhaps the lines around them a little more defined, but that was only to be expected. He looked as wild as ever.

'You must leave. You must leave now.'

He wanted to hold her hand; he was feeling that if he didn't reach out and touch her, she might slip away forever. More than this, he wanted to tell her that she had blossomed into a beautiful young woman, lips fuller and redder, skin creamier, red hair burning bright and her long lashes and delicate brows framing her green eyes.

'My husband is about to arrive home . . .'

'Husband. I can't bear it, Evie. What have you done?' he said, his voice dropping to a low register. It was as if all the blood had drained out of his body. It felt like his legs had ceased to function as they buckled underneath him. A searing sensation painfully flashed through his brain like electricity. Cold pearls of sweat appeared on his brow.

'Go,' said Evie. She could feel herself shaking, and tears were filling her eyes. 'Go away,' she said.

The lights in the street flickered. There was the sound of a foghorn coming from somewhere far off.

'Evie, I tried. I wrote to you . . . It was difficult. You can't believe how far away Canada is. A week after I left here, when I came out on the deck of the ship and saw a polar bear on an iceberg, it hit me what a stupid thing I'd done. We left Toronto pretty quick. The people we knew there turned out to be an odd couple, so we went even further away to a place called Barry's Bay. Grasslands, wild rattlesnakes and mountains, no regular mail.'

Bewildered tears pricked Evie's eyes. Her heart ached. But what on earth did Frankie O'Hare think he had to offer her? Nothing. Compared to Lawrence, who had saved her and given her a respectable life, who had rescued her from the nuns and the shame, and the dreadful worry of always what was to happen next.

'Oh, Frankie,' she said, softening. 'I know now that it was just a stupid overreaction of mine to Carol, that day at the factory. But as soon as I came to my senses, you'd gone. I didn't know where you were. How was I to find you?'

The thought of Terry swirled around in her head. Should she tell him about the baby, like Lawrence had said? But wouldn't that ruin all their lives?

She tried to shut the door on him, but he put his foot in it to prevent her.

'Please, Evie.'

'Too late,' she said. One desperate thought after another ricocheted around in her head.

'And the child? You have a child,' he said. 'I brought him this,' he added, taking a small red toy racing car from his pocket. It was a pathetic gesture.

'He's not yours,' she said quickly.

He bit into his bottom lip to stop it trembling, dropped his hand, put the toy back into his pocket.

How did he even know about the baby? she wanted to ask. Had he found her da? Surely not. How would he know they were living in St Helen's? Had he been to the factory? Edna, she thought, darkly. It must be Edna.

She was silent for moment. She dropped her head.

'Frankie . . . I'm sorry. It really is too late.'

He stood there screwing up his wretched cloth cap, shifting from foot to foot.

'May I see him?'

'Why?'

'Because he's mine, isn't he?'

Evie looked at him, a frown denting her forehead. She puckered her lips. 'Who told you that?' she asked warily.

'Stanley Mulhearn.'

Her sharp intake of breath was audible. 'Stanley had no right to. I told him not to. Sorry. No. It's not your baby. Why ever did you think that? That's just the gossip . . .' Seeing the sad expression on his face, then seeing a single tear spill onto his cheek, it hurt her just to draw breath.

'This time, if I leave, I'll not come back. I have a ticket booked. So please, I'll ask you again, are you telling me the truth about the baby?'

She faltered. But then she repeated the words,

harshly, passionless – 'Not yours' – and drawing her shawl around her, shut the door. She made her way upstairs slowly, painfully, to check on Terry and to ponder on the dreadful lie she had just told.

When Lawrence got home, she had sat up all evening, nervously waiting for him. She could smell the drink on his breath.

'You're late,' she said.

'Late? I wasn't aware that there were rules in this house?'

'Sorry,' she said. She knew when to smooth things over, so she went and laid a hand on his shoulder.

'Don't say sorry. There's nothing to be sorry for. But Angel, I find that kind of petty thing so stifling. And feeling stifled leads to death.'

Suddenly she leapt up and sobbed into his arms.

'Oh, my darling, Angel. Don't cry. I should have told you I was going for a drink after the show.'

But when she said to him it wasn't that – that the reason she was crying was because Frankie had come to the house – he faltered. He stroked her head and kissed her, but all he could think of as she related the story of Frankie's appearance, Frankie's despair, was: *who* exactly was she crying for? Frankie? Or Terry? Or herself? Not him, he was sure of that.

'Hey, Angel. What's the matter?'

And yet still the sobs rose, like a wave, a huge wall of sadness that she couldn't stop.

And he knew then. He just knew.

Fifty-Four

The lights from the theatre illuminated the sheets of rain. Evie had fixed her hair, tucking the unruly strands under a blue velvet cloche hat, and worn her best dress. She paused, looked up at the posters outside. She still couldn't believe it. That handsome man, with Mabel in her sheer satin dress staring lovingly up at him, was her husband. Perhaps she should spend more time here and come to see his plays more often. Even though she still felt a little awkward, as if she would never belong in a place like this, she should perhaps try to understand his world a little. The matinee would just be finishing. She had in her pocket one of the pickle and corned beef cobbler sandwiches that he loved.

Gordon at the stage door barely looked up when he saw her come in. He nodded her through. 'He's taken the key to his room. You may as well go and wait in Mabel's dressing room. Spends more time there than his own.'

She felt her blood run cold. There it was again. That feeling. Perhaps she should turn back and go home.

Instead, she walked quickly on down the corridor. Mabel's dressing-room door was open. She stepped inside, rather than wait in the narrow corridor where

381

stagehands and dressers were scurrying past. The suffocating smell of greasepaint and face powder hit the back of her throat. She saw Mabel's wig and hairpins scattered over the dressing table. There were cards stuck round the illuminated mirror; some of the bulbs were working, most were not. She wondered if one of the cards was from Lawrence. Tentatively she moved forward, read a couple, put them back quickly, read a couple more. She recognized Lawrence's handwriting immediately. The card had a man in an air force uniform on the front. 'To my dearest Bug – Good luck. You will always be my Patricia and I will always be your Lyle. All love.' Her heart jolted. The play, she remembered Lawrence telling her, was about a love triangle.

Taking an inventory of the room, she looked about her. Lipsticks without their lids on, a pot of cold cream lying open, a single stocking draped over the top of the mirror. Evie sank into a battered, spindly red velvet chair. She could hear through the tannoy that they were coming to the end of the final act. The sound of laughter, ripples of it coming over the speaker, a tinny, unpleasant sound that was clear enough for her to hear Lawrence's voice, arch, an exaggerated RP accent. Then Mabel giggling and lisping, and the audience laughing again.

Evie looked at herself in the mirror. The blonde wig sat on a polystyrene mannequin's head. Tentatively she reached out, took off the wig, wedged it onto the top of her head, and looked at her reflection. A blonde flibbertigibbet. Flighty, a bit of fun. Was she just too serious? But then again, so many serious things had happened in her life. She heard the applause building, and then the sound of seats flapping up as the audience rose to their feet to give even more rapturous clapping. Suddenly, coming here seemed like a ridiculous idea. She pulled off the wig. What am I doing here? she asked herself. She shouldn't have turned up unannounced. She could hear footsteps coming down the corridor, and froze. The door was pushed open heavily from the outside.

'Remind Mabel to put her smalls in there . . . I'll come round and collect them after this evening's performance,' said a girl, shoving a laundry basket into Evie's hands. Friday night was washing night.

When Mabel walked into the room a moment later, flushed and happy, she looked shocked to see Evie sitting there. 'What are you doing here?' she said, as she plonked herself down, took a large scoop of cold cream and smeared it onto her face. 'Who's looking after Terry?'

'My friend Linda,' Evie said. 'Where's Lawrence?'

'He'll be along in a minute. How are you, sweetie?' said Mabel.

'I brought a sarnie,' replied Evie.

'A sarnie?' asked a puzzled Mabel. 'Here, unzip me,' she said, turning her back to Evie and placing her hands on her hips.

Evie tentatively pulled down the zipper, fumbling slightly. The dress dropped to the ground in a waterfall of ivory satin. Mabel stepped out of it and stood there unembarrassed in her stockings, suspenders and camisole.

'How are you, dear?'

383

'I'm fine.'

'Married life suiting you?' Mabel twisted away, began rubbing the congealing cold cream into her skin.

Evie nodded.

'You seem a little unsure. You can tell me, sweetie.'

But Evie was losing confidence, her sense of purpose evaporating. The sandwich seemed like a stupid idea. Tears welled up in her eyes unexpectedly, and she dropped her head.

Mabel glanced away, picked up a lipstick, reapplied her lips, blotted them on a tissue, and then slicked her tongue over her white gapped teeth. 'Lolly will be here in a minute . . .'

Lolly. She hated it that Mabel had a pet name for him. She also hated it that Lawrence sometimes called Mabel 'Bug' – because of her bug eyes, he said, but she hated it nonetheless.

'Sit down. Stop fiddling with your hair like that.'

'I have to go,' said Evie, suddenly. 'Tell Lawrence I left him his cobbler sandwich.'

The sickly yellow lights around the mirror, and Mabel's ghastly cold-creamed face, seemed strangely ugly. 'Will do,' she said, using an eyelash curler.

Evie scurried off.

By the time Lawrence arrived at Mabel's dressing room, Evie had gone.

'Your Evie was here. She brought you a *sarnie.* Thick as a doorstopper, it is. She told me it was called a cobbler,' laughed Mabel.

Lawrence, with a cigarette dangling from his lips and his braces looping about his thighs, his white shirt unbuttoned to his chest, the dickie bow hanging undone about his neck, waved the smoke away with his hand.

Mabel's blonde hair, tied up in a chignon, uncoiled itself as if on a spring as she undid the ribbon she was wearing, and she let it hang loose about her shoulders. When she shook it out a tinkling cascade of pins fell onto the table. She got up, still in her stockings, walked across the room and took a blue tea dress off a hanger.

'Can you zip me up, darling?'

Lawrence put the cigarette in his mouth, did as she asked him. Then he stopped.

'Mabel,' he said seriously, 'I need to ask you a favour.'

Fifty-Five

An hour later, at half past five, Evie sat by the fire, sewing. Terry was sleeping. She opened a window to let the air in. Walking from room to room, not knowing quite what to do as she filled in time, she began to pick up stray socks. There was an ashtray of Lawrence's to be emptied, a glass of whiskey half drunk.

The knock at the front door was firm and loud. She froze. Not Frankie again? Moving to the window and squinting from behind the curtains, she looked out to see a woman. Mabel? It was Mabel. What on earth was she doing here?

Mabel caught sight of her in the window and called up, 'Can I come in, Evie?'

Evie nodded. She found the key. 'It's the top floor. It's stiff. You have to—'

'I know,' said Mabel, flatly. 'I just need the key.'

Evie threw it down, heard the tinkling sound of metal on the pavement. She waited for the front door to slam, the creak of the stairs as Mabel ascended.

'What is it?' asked Evie from the landing as Mabel appeared around the bend in the staircase. Her blonde curls were framed in the fur-lined hood of a midnight-blue velvet cape, tied at the neck with a ribbon. It looked like a costume, not something a normal person would wear. 'Haven't you got another performance this evening?'

'Yes. But I have an hour or so before curtain up. Can I come in, dear?'

Evie nodded.

'Well, this place has changed since I was last here,' Mabel said, sweeping into the room. She cast her eyes around, pointed at the painted frieze of daisies on one of the wooden panels above the window. 'That's a nice touch. Did you do that?'

Evie nodded, embarrassed. It seemed childish, ridiculous. 'We're hoping to move soon,' she said. 'I'm hoping the council might help us.'

'Really?' said Mabel. 'Can't imagine Lawrence living in one of those funny little boxes in the sticks, or those high-rise flats in the sky.' Mabel frowned. 'Can I sit down?'

Evie nodded, gestured her to the kitchen table. 'What are you doing here, Mabel?' she asked.

Mabel sighed. 'I've been thinking about what you said earlier. And the fact is . . . I wasn't entirely truthful with you. And I'm worried. I know you think I'm just a floozy, not a serious kind of person at all, but if I can't be honest with you now, well, it's a matter of life or death for your future with Lolly. And I couldn't live with myself if the whole thing were to fall apart.'

Evie paled. There it was again: Lolly. She loathed it. 'What do you mean, my future with Lawrence?' she asked.

'Sweetie, what I'm about to tell you might upset you.' Mabel paused.

'What, Mabel?' Evie felt her heart pounding.

'I'll come straight out with it. I have a confession to make. I'm afraid Lawrence hasn't been entirely straight with you. The fact is, what you must understand is that theatre people, well . . . with theatre people, a different set of rules apply. I had hoped Lolly had changed when he met you. He so much wanted to. But then, people so rarely do.'

'Mabel, you're frightening me.'

'There's nothing to be frightened of. I'm just putting you in the picture. Oh dear, where to start?' she said glibly.

'Why not at the beginning?' said Evie.

'Very well. First of all, though . . .' she said, and then paused. 'It only happened a few times.'

Evie felt sick.

'Whilst we were on tour. It can be ever so lonely, you can't possibly imagine, holed up in some dreadful digs in Crewe or Croydon, so far away from where you'd hoped you'd be – Hollywood or the West End, that's a laugh. Here you are in Stoke-on-Trent, mice in the dressing room, bad-tempered landladies, bored and disappointed, and sometimes you need a little comfort. The fact is, your Lawrence fell into my bed and before we knew it, there we were. Probably playing out some kind of drama in our heads. Trying to forget who we were for a brief moment. Desperate, maybe, and it was over before it started. It meant nothing. I know he was telling you he loved you and all that, but to be fair, you weren't actually married then.'

How can you be so glib? Evie wanted to scream.

This is my life, in ruins, yet again. 'Why are you telling me?' she asked. 'If it meant nothing?'

'Because I think you ought to know. I think you ought to know what you're getting into. Hey. Oh darling, don't cry, you mustn't cry. It wasn't serious. Just a fling. It's not like we have plans to run off together. What a disaster that would be, hopeless. We'd spend the whole time fighting for the mirror.'

Evie fought back the tears, which were coming in hot, silent stabs.

'What, dear?' asked Mabel.

Evie visibly shuddered, folded into herself like a wounded bird. Mabel sighed, reached out and squeezed her white hand. 'Evie, you wanted the truth. I'll say it again. It meant nothing. Honestly, nothing. We actors get carried away with ourselves sometimes. The drama of the situation.'

Evie could feel herself shaking, the blood rushing up to her cheeks. What was she saying? She felt disgusted. Disgusted with this place, disgusted with Lawrence; all his talk of truth and honesty and the noble behaviour that came with his way of life. It was all a fantasy, nothing was real here. The whole thing was laughable. Had he reduced everything to this? This sordid confession, made all the more grotesque by the sickly yellow glow of the oil lamp, the creeping damp on the wall, the balding velvet chaise longue and overflowing ashtrays. His protestations of love had turned into something horrible, something unimaginably hollow.

'Lawrence always says that being a good actor is all about being truthful. And once you know how to fake being truthful, you'll be a *great* actor. Bear that in mind. I'd hate for it to happen again. But he does love you, Evie. I'm sure he's not faking that. So buck up.'

Evie's bottom lip trembled.

'Come on, Evie, stop it now. Stop snivelling. No one said marriage was going to be easy, ducky,' said Mabel. 'And how dull, if it was. You know people can have sex just for fun, Evie. It's not the end of the world.'

'Don't patronize me,' Evie said under her breath. Her sadness was turning to anger. She didn't want to ask any more questions about the affair. That was just pain added to more pain.

'Lighten up. And if it does happen another time with someone else, so what? You've not seen much of life, have you, dear? That's all I'm saying.'

Evie's eyes flashed black. 'I've seen more of life than you ever will!' she snapped back, hard and angry.

'Steady on, darling,' said Mabel, taken aback by her forcefulness.

Evie was shaking. 'My mother left us, and I had to bring up a family when I was thirteen – I had a child when I was seventeen, *on my own*. I fought to keep that child, and believe me, it wasn't easy when at every turn people wanted to take him away from me. I've known such poverty it would make you faint. I have seen awful, *awful* things. Children abandoned because they're the wrong colour, or who are not quite as they should be, left to lives of despair with heartless people who couldn't care a jot about them. Desperate women in back streets. Fallen girls having their babies torn out of their arms to be near enough sold off, because of the fear of scandal, just because the useless fathers have buggered off and left them. I've had to wade through riptides of shame that drag you off your feet every time you try to walk down the street. So don't tell me I don't know about the world! You have no bloody idea, Mabel, whatever your bloody stupid made-up name is!'

Suddenly she was aware of someone standing at the door. Oh God, that ridiculous white scarf tied around his neck. Who wore stupid clothes like that in Liverpool? She wanted to cry.

'What's all this about?' Lawrence asked, shaking dust off his coat as he took it off and came into the room. He shot Mabel a look.

Evie felt her ribcage heave, felt that with each new word she uttered, both their lives were about to change irrevocably.

'Lawrence, I think I ought to leave . . .' Mabel said, getting up out of the chair with a flourish. Lawrence looked at her in shock. Then back at Evie, whose face was ashen.

'It's me who should leave,' said Evie. 'I can't believe I've been so idiotic!' she muttered, gathering up her coat and scarf in a bundle. Lawrence's eyes widened.

'Good God, Mabel! What have you said?'

'Just trying to be honest with the girl. Put her in the picture, so to speak.'

He paled. 'Oh no, Mabel. You haven't told her, have you? I told you not to! I told you what it would do to her! Why would you do something like that?

You swore that you wouldn't say a word,' he said, horrified. He gestured dramatically back at Evie. 'You owe that poor, innocent girl a bloody apology!' he cried. His voice sounded sharp, his eyes looked cold, his nostrils flared. He seemed distant and strange – and stone-cold sober, so there wasn't even drink as an excuse. This was a side of Lawrence that Evie had never seen, and it chilled her to the bone.

'*Me!* I didn't want any part of this, honey!' said Mabel.

'Neither did I. But if you hadn't told her, we wouldn't be having this conversation. Evie would never have known. You've ruined everything . . .'

Evie reeled, swallowed air and choked. Lawrence, you adulterer, you vain, stupid, adulterous liar, she thought. But when she spoke, her voice was steely and controlled. 'Please be quiet. You'll wake Terry from his nap.'

Mabel put up her hood over her quivering curls. 'I thought I was doing the right thing. It's discouraging to think how many people are shocked by honesty, and how few by deceit . . .' she said as she swept out of the room.

Evie's mind looped wildly. Her head was swimming, and her limbs felt hollow. Was this really how people behaved? To think this brief affair – if that's what it was – that it meant nothing to either of them, a mere distraction, was almost worse. She felt sick to the stomach. She had never imagined for a moment that it would be Lawrence who would lose heart in their marriage, and embarrassment made her drop her head into her hands. 'It's over, Lawrence. I don't want you to come back here tonight after the show. I want you to take your things and stay at the theatre. I'll move out when I've found somewhere . . .'

'Where will you go?'

'Doesn't matter.'

'You're not going back to those nuns? I feel such a heel. Do you hate me?'

'Oh, stop it, Lawrence. Stop making those stupid faces. You might need to live your life on drama, but we don't all have to buy a ticket for the flipping performance. Now go. It's six o'clock. Less than an hour until curtain up. The show must go on. Isn't that what *you lot* say?'

Fifty-Six

After hearing the whole sorry story emerge in tearful sniffs and sighs, Edna cleared out her back room, removed the clutter from the sofa and asked Evie why she had waited three days to tell her.

'I didn't know what to do,' said Evie.

'The sofa is always warm for you here. We'll make a cot for Terry, and then we'll decide. Go and get the rest of your things. I'll stay here with the baby. Gives me the chance for cuddles.'

Evie went back to Paradise Street, stuffed a bag and took a final look around the flat. Strange how shabby it looked in the daylight – and yet in the evening, by candlelight, how romantic and decadently lush this place was. Lawrence's beige mackintosh hung on a hook on the back of the door. It was like a cocoon that he had shed before becoming a butterfly and fluttering off to live the life he could never have done with her. She sighed and heaved her bag off the large dresser.

The following morning, nursing a mug of tea against her cheek, she sat in Edna's chair with glassy tears in her eyes.

'I have to find Frankie before he leaves,' she said, urgently.

'What if he already has?' said Edna, gently.

'He can't have. He can't. I have to tell him that I lied about Terry.'

Edna smoothed down her hair. 'I know, love. But do you have any idea where he is?'

'No,' she said, shaking her head. 'I wrote him a letter and wandered around knocking on the doors of a few boarding houses, but it was useless.'

Tears gathered in her eyes as Edna left the flat to go to work. Terry began to squirm. He looked up at her, his little face full of worry. 'Ssh. Mummy's fine. Mummy's fine,' she murmured. 'When we find your daddy, Mummy will be just fine.'

She tried Jacky first, Stanley, the factory, the Boot Inn, the Throttle's Nest. For three days she wheeled Terry up and down Church Street in the pram with the wonky wheel; the dock road, the Pier Head, Lime Street, until her feet ached and she had to stuff cardboard in her shoes, they were so full of holes. And every evening she went to bed a little more despondent than the last. Then one afternoon, Edna came hurtling through the door.

'Evie! I've had a brainwave! The passenger lists! Beryl knows a fellow at Cunard's. Shall we give it a try?'

But even that came to nothing. And so, exhausted with the effort of it all, she finally began to give up hope. This isn't fair to Terry, she thought, after another fruitless morning. To be dragging a child around Liverpool like this. She rolled up her sleeves, took Terry's cardigan off and went outside, where she sat him on her knee on the front step, letting the warm sunshine soothe his face.

On the opposite side of the street, a group of kids were playing with a ball in the end of an old stocking.

'One, two, three O'Grady, down the airy, four, five, six O'Grady . . .' they chanted, as a girl swung the ball around her body. Their voices were soft, rhythmic, lulling Evie into relaxation.

'Matthew, Mark, Luke and John, next door neighbour carry on, next door neighbour got the flu so I pass it on to you . . .'

A small boy separated from his friends. Evie could see that in his hands he had something, a toy, that he began pushing along the line of the gutter.

When he reached the step, her whole body jolted.

'Love, where did you get that car?' she asked the boy, leaping to her feet and tugging on his jumper.

'It's mine,' he said, hugging it to him.

'I know. I'm not going to take it from you.'

He regarded her quizzically. 'Fella give it me, missus. It's a racing car. He came knocking at your door but there weren't anyone in. He said I can have it. I'm not giving it back. He's gone all the way to Canada. Getting the boat this avvy. Said I can keep it forever.'

Her voice shook as she spoke. 'This afternoon? Canada? When? What did he look like?'

'Like me da.'

'What does your da look like? Oh, doesn't matter,' she said.

When Edna suddenly appeared around the corner, carrying a bag of kindling from Paddy's market, a panicked Evie shoved Terry into her arms. After a garbled explanation, she grabbed her coat.

'Look for the Blue Peter, Evie!' Edna cried. 'The blue flag the ships fly if they're about to sail!'

Running as fast as her legs could take her to the Pier Head and taking huge gulps of air, Evie finally arrived at Prince's Dock. The cobbled streets were slippery. This was the kind of slipperiness that pulled you off your feet without warning, so she trod carefully, but she still managed to stumble. The boat was moored up to the landing stage – RMS *Ascania*, it said on the side – still battered and bruised after the war, and painted gunmetal grey with a red funnel. There was the blue flag that Edna had said to look out for. As was the custom, there was also a small brass band gathering at the bottom of the gangplank, where families had congregated to wave off their loved ones.

'Eh la, you can't go past there!' shouted a man in a navy jacket with silver buttons, hooking his arm under Evie's elbow as she tried to dart under the metal chain that stopped people from going onto the landing stage.

Evie's heart was bursting out of her chest, slamming against her ribs. As she spoke, she desperately tried to calm herself down so that he would take her seriously. 'I have to find someone!' she cried. 'I have to find someone *right now*. Before the boat goes . . .' She looked past him desperately. The harbourmaster stood with a rope looped around his forearms; the funnel blasted out its foghorn.

And then she saw him, standing on the deck. Just his silhouette – the shape that she knew so well, every curve, the slope of the shoulders, the turn-out of his leg. The peak of his brown hair blowing in the wind.

'Frankie! *Frankie!*' she cried.

The figure turned. It wasn't him. Evie could feel her eyes burning in their sockets as, leaning against the rail, she watched the boat slowly slip away further into the mouth of the Mersey, where it met the swell of the tide and drifted off towards a pink horizon.

She walked back towards the esplanade, a small, hunched, desperate figure, hurrying along the quay. The evening sunshine was refusing to be shaken off. The Three Graces towered above her. Her legs grew tired. She would have to tell Edna that she had missed him. He had boarded the boat. She should have listened to her friend. What on earth was she going to do now?

'I'm sorry,' she said, as she felt another body bump up against her.

'Look where you're going Evie.'

Twisting her head against the gathering breeze that pasted her clothes to her body, she turned to see Frankie. She didn't know whether to laugh or cry. The relief of seeing him, being able to reach out and touch him, to know that he was still here in Liverpool and not slipping away down the Mersey on that boat, was immeasurable. She plunged into his arms and burst into tears. And then he was kissing her, every inch of her face, her cheeks, her eyes, her mouth.

'Don't speak,' he said in between kisses. 'Don't speak!'

'Oh, Frankie. I'm sorry.' The veins stood out lavender blue on her neck; her complexion was heightened with colour. 'It's all my fault!' She gestured wildly. 'The baby . . . of course it's your baby. *Our* child . . .'

A flock of seagulls swooped above them, wheeling, cawing and looping over the river. The wind, colder now coming off the Mersey, blew in their faces. It tore through their bodies and was as sharp as knives, but they barely felt it.

'I love you, Evie. The world is making another go of it after all it's been through, all this death and war. Can't we?'

'Oh Frankie . . .' she said. 'Yes, yes, *yes*.'

He held her at arm's length. 'God, Evie, you look even more beautiful than I remember.'

Evie blushed and shook her head.

He took off his jacket, put it round her shivering shoulders. She smiled at him, and it was a smile that came from a long way back: from her mother, from the times when they were children, from before the war, from the factory. Was it these experiences that would make them stronger together than apart? She felt such a sense of relief. The familiarity between them made her feel purposeful and secure. She understood him, and he understood her. They walked along the wide pavement.

He pushed a strand of hair behind her ear, and the smell of him consumed her as he wrapped her in his arms.

'And Lawrence Childs?'

'Lawrence?'

'What will he say?'

'Oh, you know, for a short time, I convinced myself it seemed possible. But it was never right. He wanted to save me – but I'm not sure I wanted to be saved. I think he felt he had to make up for the fact that he didn't fight in the war. It made him feel he was somehow not enough. Loving Terry and me somehow made him part of the real world. But he'll be all right. He'll find someone to love. He's a handsome man. Handsome men are never alone for more than two minutes.'

Frankie looked at her and smiled. The light was fading around them. 'Sometimes I think people don't believe ordinary folks like us can love. But by God, I'm going to prove the world wrong, Evie – you see if I don't. Will you marry me?'

She frowned. 'Oh, Frankie. One day at a time. I'm still married! But you know, there was a time when I would have said yes immediately. I would have been desperate for you to make me an honest woman. But if there's one thing Lawrence and Mabel have taught me, it's not to care what the world thinks. I won't marry you just yet. But that doesn't mean to say we can't be lovers.'

He blinked away tears.

'I'm not saying no forever. Just for now. For now, will you help me look after our boy? You need to meet your son . . .'

'Oh, Evie,' he said, clasping her tightly.

He offered to walk her back home. He talked animatedly about how he had a meeting with the shipping office about his idea for importing maple syrup. How they had already agreed to ship over a thousand bottles; how Lewis's grocery store wanted to buy the first shipment. That was why he was still here.

'I know people,' Evie said, firing up with excitement. 'When I was working for Tate's I got to know all the businesses in the city, the shops, Bunney's, Blackler's, TJ's, and restaurants – Cooper's, George Henry Lee's.'

'It will make us rich, Evie . . .'

She threw back her head and laughed. 'Who would have thought it would be sugar that might be our future?'

'You and me together, we'll be unstoppable. "Out of the strong came forth sweetness." That's what it says on the tin,' he said.

'Oh Frankie. I do love you. I always have. You know that, don't you?' she said, suddenly.

'Aye,' he replied. 'And my heart is yours forever.'

'Look at that,' she said, suddenly. 'A rainbow!' And, filled with a new hope that lifted both of their souls, they fell silent, enraptured with love and happiness and marvelling at the startling band of colours that spanned the Mersey sky.

Fifty-Seven

Lawrence sat in front of his dressing-room mirror. Mabel came up behind him, gently placed her hands on his shoulders and rested her chin on the crown of his silky head. The wreckage of the drama with Evie still hung in the air even though a week had passed, and their ghastly made-up pale reflections looking back at them underscored the mood.

'Still missing her?' she said.

Lawrence blinked, ran a thumb under each eye.

'Yes, dear.'

'Are you sure you did the right thing?'

'We gave the best performance of our lives.'

'As long as you have no regrets.'

'Sure, dear. It was the only way; but I can't say it doesn't hurt, knowing the one who you love doesn't love you.'

'You're a saint, Lawrence. Will you ever tell her none of it was true even though my performance was so brilliant I almost convinced myself!'

'Not whilst there's a chance she might think she's making a mistake leaving me. I'm missing Terry, for sure. But this way she can walk away with no regrets.'

'Perhaps that's true love. When you give up

someone because you want them to be happy. Because their happiness is worth more than yours.'

'Now steady on, Mabel. Not sure I want to be sainted just yet. Maybe it's just because I know she never loved me. Not really. Can't think why,' he added with a smile, looking at his sad reflection in the mirror and raising a chuckle in Mabel. 'I know how fickle us creatures can be. True, I will always love Evie, but she deserved someone better than me. And who knows – was I just in love with the idea of being in love?'

'One thing's for sure, you'll always *believe* she was the one for you. The one that got away . . .'

'She might have only held my hand for a short time, but she'll hold my heart forever.'

'Is that a line from a play, darling? Sounds like it is.'

He smiled. 'Probably, but I can't think which one.'

'The one where the handsome actor falls in love with a factory girl.'

He sighed.

'You know, I think you're rather enjoying the sweet pain of your grief. Just think, you can pour all that agony into every performance you give. Oscar-winning, I bet.'

'Oh, Mabel. What'll become of us shallow things?'

Mabel sighed. 'You're not shallow, sweetie. You've done something noble and kind.'

'Don't know if the world will see it that way . . .'

'They will. And in time, so will Evie.'

'I doubt it. The world has a pretty poor picture of us lot. And whatever world Evie was seeing in her dreams, I had no part of it. I don't know if I'll ever get over this.'

'You're still young,' Mabel said.

'Oh no, we actors age in dog years. I'm about two years from being washed up.'

She laughed. 'Come on, love. Fancy a drink to cheer us up? There comes a time in one's life when the only thing that can make it all better is champagne. The bar is still open . . . I need you to be my wingman. I dread Mr Sausage Fingers turning up. He's threatening to come back to Liverpool with a new film offer.' She smoothed a finger over his brow, kissed him gently on the lips. 'Sorry I can't love you, dear,' she added. She withdrew, stuffing a cigarette into a gold holder.

'Sorry I can't love you either. Not in that way. But if it's any consolation, I'm not sure I'll ever know how to love a woman.'

'Oh, sweetie, you've tried your best. Had a damn good go at it.'

'If darling Evie couldn't be my saviour, perhaps it's time to face up to who I am.'

'Maybe. Don't fret about it too much. We're in the business of pretending, and I'm happy to go through the motions of being your girl if you want.'

'And I'll love you tomorrow night as Patricia in the play, and you'll love me as Lyle. That's enough for now, Cheery Bubbles . . .'

The bar was filled with smoke. When they walked in, there was a ripple of applause.

'Bravo,' said a woman sitting on a high stool. 'Wonderful performances tonight. Rattigan at its very best.'

Mabel turned to Lawrence and squeezed his arm. 'Chin up, dearie . . . The show must go on. At least Doctor Theatre will keep giving us a dose of his medicine each night to mend our hearts, hey?'

Epilogue

The annulment was done and dusted in three months. Sister Mary Clotilda had arranged for Evie to be interviewed by a stern young woman who fortunately didn't think much of war dodgers like this Reginald Hardbottom, and readily sympathized with Evie. Edna, who to everyone's surprise had just got engaged to a quiet, softly spoken man who ran a bookie's in Allerton and did what he was told, had been a witness. She did her job enthusiastically, telling the woman scratching away at a piece of paper with a pen that Evie and Lawrence had been entirely unsuited, and the marriage had never been consummated. Fortunately, the list had been long that morning and the woman was just happy that this spouse, Mr Hardbottom, hadn't objected.

Once the papers came through, Evie, who had so far resisted Frankie's weekly proposals of marriage, began to talk about setting a date for the wedding. She and Terry were now living quietly in a small flat above the office where Frankie conducted his business with the port terminals that were bringing in more and more consignments of maple syrup each month.

406

Evie was arranging for batches to be delivered to restaurants and shops around the city. They were spending so much time together that getting married seemed like the natural thing to do.

'Kiss me, Evie,' said Frankie, sitting behind a mound of paperwork, invoices stuck on a metal spike.

'I will not,' she said. 'I've got that meeting at Bunney's about that repeat order . . .'

'Then marry me instead,' he said. 'Marry me tomorrow.'

She placed her hands on her hips, smiled. 'Don't be ridiculous, Frankie O'Hare. Weddings have to be arranged. They take time.' There was a moment's pause. She was about to say that it had taken weeks to arrange her wedding to Lawrence, but she didn't want to bring him up again. She had promised herself she wouldn't, after the last time.

She had found the scribbled note, shortly after clearing out the last of her things from Paradise Street. It was stuffed into an old envelope, under a pile of *Picture Post* magazines. She recognized Lawrence's handwriting straight away. Her hands trembled as she began to read it. At first, she thought it was a love letter, but then she realized it was something quite different: *So think of me as the director Mabel, do exactly as I say and get this into your feather-brained head. Some of the words are quotes from* Blithe Spirit, *thank you Mr Coward for that, but they probably won't be familiar to Evie. When you get to the part where you let it slip that we've been lovers, don't over-egg this bit, Mabel. Speak the words as naturally as you can. You've a tendency to be melodramatic. She's got to believe this is the truth even though it's not.*

The shock had rippled through Evie's body and mind. I should have known, she had thought. No doubt they had been word perfect.

'Don't you see, Frankie? He pretended he'd been unfaithful, but he wasn't at all. I found his speech. It was his way of letting me go. He was a good man at heart,' she'd said.

'A good man?' Frankie had replied, smarting. 'I still don't understand why you don't hate him for it.'

Evie wondered if it was even worth trying to explain. She had a feeling that if she saw Lawrence today, she would probably thank him. But Frankie was only human; so she'd said nothing and resolved never to speak his name again, and that had been the end of the matter. Evie leaned across the desk and took his chin in her hands. 'I'll kiss you at least,' she said.

Three weeks later, with the help of Edna and Beryl – whose dressmaking business was going from strength to strength, which meant she had moved out of her sister's and found the money to rent a small flat for herself and Kim – Evie and Frankie married one morning in April quietly in a registry office in Bootle, without much fuss.

'So how's married life? Two months in and still going strong?' asked Edna, smiling across the table at Cooper's tea rooms.

Evie smiled. 'Grand.'

'Thank goodness. I still can't get over how badly Lawrence treated you.'

Evie frowned. 'Edna, don't be too harsh on Lawrence. You see, he and Mabel . . . well, they made up their affair. It was all a pretence. But I realize now why they did it.'

'No! Why?'

Evie explained in halting sentences. 'So you see, I'm pretty sure they did. But I don't mind.'

'Really?'

'I don't mind about any of it. I wasn't even jealous at the time – just sad. I wouldn't change anything: not the time I had with Lawrence, not losing Frankie for that year, not even the month I had at St Sylvester's. There's been so much sadness along the way; but how do you know you're happy, if you don't know what it's like to be unhappy?'

'Listen to you! When did you get to be so wise, dear?' said Edna. 'You're still only nineteen.'

Evie smiled, patted her stomach. 'Can you share a secret?'

'Oh my. When's it due?'

'Next Christmas.'

'Waiter! Two Babychams, please!'

'Close your eyes,' said Frankie the following morning.

'Where are you taking me?'

She gasped when they stopped outside a house midway along a Georgian terrace, with delicate iron-mongery and elegant windows. It stood in the shadow of the Cathedral; Hope Street was the name of the road.

'If you stand in the top room, you can see the Mersey and the whole of the city stretching out below.'

'Oh, Frankie,' she said. 'Are we the luckiest two people alive?' She squinted through the beautiful stained-glass panels in the front door, decorated with a bell and a boat on cresting waves. She reflected for a second. From Paradise Street to Hope Street. Wasn't that something?

Two weeks later, Frankie scooped her up in his arms and carried her over the doorstep. The roses growing in the window boxes were in full bloom and a heady, musky scent followed them in, wafting through the house as Evie flung open doors and pulled out drawers.

'I have a plan. I want to fill this house with our babies, but there's so many rooms, Frankie. If things continue the way they are, and money is finally turning to profit . . . I want to take in other people's babies. Foster them. Just one or two at a time, whilst their mothers get back on their feet. Can we do that? Children who need a clean, warm bed, and food. Rest and respite. People aren't so quick to judge these days. They shouldn't have their babies taken away. These girls aren't wicked, they're just young. Business is doing well, isn't it?'

They were supplying all the fancy restaurants now. If you had a pancake in Liverpool, chances were Frankie's maple syrup would be poured on top of it.

He smiled. Looked around at the upturned packing cases, at rugs being rolled out, at Evie unwrapping candlesticks from newspaper amongst clouds of dust, he said: 'Whatever you want, dear.'

They settled in quickly. Early one morning, a dray

horse clip-clopped up the street with a delivery. Terry stirred, rubbing the sleep from his eyes and yawning. Evie leaned her head in close to him and kissed him lightly on the top of his head. Flinging open the curtains and looking around the sunny bedroom with its high Georgian ceiling, she thought it was miraculous how things had worked out for everyone. Edna had announced her engagement. Beryl was courting a fireman. Even Joan was making her very best effort to be civil, and Vic and the girls would often come from St Helen's to stay at the weekends. Everything was dandy.

But then, as she stepped out into the hallway, a letter plopped onto the mat.

Evie gasped. She recognized the handwriting immediately, even though it had been years since she'd last seen it.

> *Dear Evie,*
> *Sister Mary Clotilda has given me your new address. I am so sorry for everything. Since I left, I have been wracked with regret. Luigi Galinari had me under some kind of spell. And those four years your father was away during the war were so long, I began to think he would never come back. But now is not the time for excuses. Just apologies.*

Evie blinked away tears. She didn't want to read on. She put the letter down, picked it up, put it down again, paced the room. But it sat there, screaming out to be read. With a sigh, she picked it up again.

For so long now I have wanted to reach out to you, but for the life of me I haven't known how. Or, if I'm truthful, maybe I have been too scared to face up to what you might say. But I'm not well, Evie. And I'm coming back to Liverpool. Amazingly, your Aunt Renie has helped me out. She knows someone in Daisy Street with rooms. I expect nothing, but I just wanted you to know. In case I were to meet you, or you were to hear from someone else before me that I was back. Your father's new woman finally tracked me down, and I have decided I shall finally give her what she has been asking for for years now. A divorce. She chased me halfway across Ireland and I still said no, but I'm here to put that right now.

Evie let the letter fall into her lap.

A divorce! I always knew that's why we weren't invited to his wedding with Joan. But now it's confirmed. There wasn't one! Holy Joan is living in sin. Ha!

I hear you and Frankie O'Hare have a child. That's wonderful news. I will not come and see you unless you give me your blessing. But I'm begging you to give me a second chance. I'd like to see your brother and sisters too, if they're willing.
Your mother,
Josephine

Terry, wearing a yellow towelling playsuit, came hurtling through on a trike, his stubby little legs pedalling madly.

'Not in here!' Evie cried. 'Come on. Off you go!' And on her way to bustle him out, she scrunched up the letter and threw it right across the room and into the wastepaper basket.

'Good shot. Right where it belongs,' she said.

'Good shot, Mam!' echoed Terry.

The following morning, after it had rained for hours, the sun unexpectedly burst through the clouds. It reminded Evie of the day she had married Lawrence; and it also reminded her that life had a way of not turning out as you expected. No matter how bleak it seemed, there was always hope. And today the whole city of Liverpool was celebrating hope. The Prime Minister had declared that the Festival of Britain was going to renew and revive the city, with festivities and a carnival the like of which had never been seen before in Liverpool. A flotilla of small boats was going to sail up the mouth of the Mersey. There would be fireworks on barges on the river. Aeronautic displays. The cinemas were showing newly released films and the theatres had been advertising for months now plays with stars from London. Margot Fonteyn and Frederick Ashton, no less, were going to be performing in a ballet at the Empire Theatre. Evie thought of Mabel and Lawrence, and felt a prickle of joy at knowing she had experienced something of this exotic world.

She pored over the *Echo*. Such wonderful things.

Orchestras, brass bands, high diving at New Brighton, motorcycle racing, cricket matches, the dock workers' sports day that her father had signed up to do the tug-of-war in at Breck Park. Street parties. And the glorious torchlight procession through the council estates of the city, directed by the famous Tyrone Guthrie.

Frankie wandered in, his head in a sheaf of papers. Evie took them out of his hands. 'Not today, love. We're having a day off today. We're celebrating. Look at all these things we can do. Vic and the girls are coming over from St Helen's for the procession. We need to get torches.'

He stood behind her and gently placed his hand on her head as he read over her shoulder. 'Blimey. Ooh, and look,' he said. 'Can't miss that. Chipperfield's Circus. And the boxing at Sefton Park. Changing of the Guard! And Music Hall! *"I say, I say, I say, Me ma and da are in the iron and steel business. Me ma irons, and me da steals . . ."*'

'Very funny,' she said, grinning. 'And a bit too close to home, Frankie.'

He moved off, smiling to himself. Evie turned the page of the newspaper. And there it was: a photo of Lawrence that took up nearly half the page. RANK STAR AND HIS NEW WIFE RETURN TO LIVERPOOL FOR FESTIVAL OF BRITAIN CELEBRATIONS, shouted the headline. Evie scanned the page quickly. *Playhouse Theatre favourite Lawrence has signed for three movies, and Hollywood beckons for him and his wife.* Wife? That was quick, she thought, wondering who it was he had married. Frankie moved over to the sink and she closed the paper quickly, sliding it under the cushion of the chair.

'Mammy!' cried Terry, waddling in. 'Vic, Nell and Sylvie is here!'

Sylvie appeared, whirled around the kitchen, showing off her dress and the huge satin bow in her hair. Nelly had styled her curls in ringlets. Vic was in his best suit.

'Hey!' Vic shouted, when Nelly barged past him to get a look at the programme.

'Hay is horses, not for people!' said Evie, and everyone laughed as Vic neighed and Terry giggled.

Half an hour later, they walked down the street. A magnolia tree was in late flower. Each leaf, each pink bud, each white petal, seemed new and perfect. Frankie offered Evie his elbow so they could link arms. Beyond, in the distance, the river glittered and the cloudless sky was bluer than blue. There were flags and bunting, and Liverpool was finally beginning to look like a new city. A more prosperous, forward-looking city than the one that had been battered by the war. New buildings were everywhere now, new roads smelling of fresh tarmac, Blackler's and Lewis's open for business again; talk of a new cathedral, even a new tunnel. They began picking themselves up, dusting themselves down, and slowly everyone was getting used to starting again.

Frankie lifted Terry onto his shoulders and they all gasped as the ships sailed by adorned with flags, a jaunty procession that left them momentarily speechless.

'I forgot my torch,' said Nelly, her face crinkling up.
'Oh no, you didn't? You silly girl.'
'I don't want to miss the boats,' she said, tearfully.
'I'll go back and get it,' replied Evie.

She headed back up the hill. A woman with a tray of toffee apples was weaving through the crowds on the pavements outside the Empire Theatre. 'Free!' she said, throwing them into the air, and people surged forward. By instinct, Evie reached up her arm and caught one. As she bit into the delicious sweet-tasting apple, the sugar crackled. She wondered what the commotion was. To be giving out free apples was quite something. Pushing herself forward, she saw there was a red carpet rolled out on the pavement. The posters said that Margot Fonteyn was dancing in *Sleeping Beauty*, but she knew that already. Swept up behind more people jostling to get a look, she tried to push her way through. People were waiting behind a rope, excited, waving autograph books and pencils.

'Move, love. You're in my way. I can't see. Lawrence Childs is about to arrive.'

'I saw him in the West End in *While the Sun Shines* in London a month ago. Thrilling,' a woman said, jostling up against her.

Really? The play he had dragged around theatres in Southport and Crewe and Runcorn to empty houses? Now that he was about to be a film star, evidently it was the hottest ticket in town. Clearly the world was ready to fall in love with him up there on the screen – and, knowing Lawrence, he was ready to love the world back.

She watched as flashlights popped. And then the sea of people parted, a car drew up, and out stepped Lawrence. Evie gaped at him. He had the same floppy hair, a lick of it falling over his eyes, and he pushed it off his face in exactly the way she'd seen him doing so many times before. Perfect for Hollywood, she thought. Those cheekbones, that luminous skin, those searching eyes. And on his arm – Mabel! Of course, Mabel! Her dress falling away in cascades, a waterfall of luxurious cream satin.

'His wife is beautiful!' someone said. Mabel had jewels on her fingers, not cheap paste, Evie could tell that.

This was the man she had married. This man had been her *husband*. Laughter bubbled up inside her. It seemed unreal, a strange, insane, part of her life for a brief moment in time.

'Bloody beautiful, your missus, Lawrence!' someone said. How the crowd loved them.

Their smiles were professional: two happy newly-weds, ready to take on the world. They gave away nothing of the truth. Evie thought Mabel's teeth looked different – larger somehow, whiter – and then she let her fur stole slip from her shoulders, revealing too much flesh. 'Oops!' she said, and put her fingers to her lips. Everyone laughed. As Lawrence swept into the foyer, Mabel lingered and made her way down the line, signing autographs.

'Who should I sign it to?' said Mabel, head bent, as Evie offered her the Festival programme and a pencil.

'Evie.'

Mabel looked up in shock.

'Good God!' she gasped. 'Evie . . . I'm . . .' She was uncharacteristically lost for words. 'Evie, I . . . Are you . . . ?' She clutched her hand.

Evie smiled. 'Pregnant again. Yes. I'm fine. I'm married. I'm happy, Mabel. Please tell Lawrence. I hope you both are too . . . ?'

Mabel looked her in the eye, squeezed her hand tight. 'Aren't we lucky we've all been given a second chance at happiness?'

'We are.'

'I'm sorry. Lawrence never meant you any harm. Neither did I. There's something I should tell you—'

'No. Don't say anything. I know you and Lawrence were play-acting. It was all for the best.'

The crowd surged. 'Miss, here!' cried an impatient woman, next in line.

Mabel scribbled something on the paper, kissed Evie on the cheek and was hurried off to meet the next adoring fan.

Evie moved away and when she found a quiet corner of the street, she read the words on the programme.

To Evie. Our sweetest sugar girl. May you always be happy. Love, Mabel and Lawrence. P.S. We play our parts well, don't you think?

Walking off up the hill in the soft, pearly estuary light, she thought of Mabel and Lawrence exploring new continents. Touching her swelling belly, she decided that her own dreams would always be in this city.

And what better place to be? For the city that she

loved was on the brink of something new and wonderful. This city where it felt that each particle of dirt, each atom, each fleck of dust swirling in a shaft of light, was a little piece of her. She was forever *in* these streets, in the walls and in these paving stones under her feet. Seeing such life, such energy all around her, only made her feel more hopeful for what was to come. Evie O'Leary, she thought, raising her face to the sky, you're the sum of your rich experience. You are no longer your mother's mistakes.

When she got back to Hope Street, someone had left the wireless on. They were playing the King's speech again. She knew it by heart, they had listened to it so many times. 'We must have faith in our future . . .' said the halting voice of the King. 'All people may be lifted to greater happiness . . .'

All people, murmured Evie.

With the pink-and-gold hue of sunset flooding the room, she sat at the rosewood desk in the large bay window. She knew she had to find her little sister's torch, but there was plenty of time, and there was something she wanted to do whilst the house was quiet. She took out a piece of paper and a pen.

> *Dear Mam,*
> *I received your letter. I am here most days at five o'clock, though my husband is often working until late. Do let me know when you would like to visit.*
> *Much love,*
> *Your daughter,*
> *Angel*

She laid down the pen, stood and went upstairs to find the torch in the girls' room. She walked over to the window, drawn by the sound of a brass band playing somewhere in the distance. And then she saw the breathtaking spectacle of a river of fire already snaking its way down Mount Pleasant Hill. Voices were lifted in a rousing song. It took a moment for her to recognize it. Of course: 'Angel Voices Ever Singing'. For a moment she listened, hummed along and smiled to herself. Then, pushing her arms into the sleeves of her coat, she set off.

Frankie and the children would be waiting.

Acknowledgements

Thank you so much to Gillian Green for bringing me along with her to pastures new. Thank you also to my agent, Judith. Thank you to my Dad for telling me the story of the man who fell into the sugar every time we drove along Liverpool's dock road and went under the Tate & Lyle shute. I still don't know if he made it up.

Thank you to all the wonderful theatre people with whom I had such happy times working with over the years. This book is dedicated to them. Thank you to Peter as always, for reading and re-reading, and being so detailed when helping me to get the references in this book right for my actor characters. Also, to Louis and Joel, for remaining cheerful and resilient whilst I wrote this book in what was a difficult year for all of us, but for the young people in my life especially.

And finally, to my fellow convent girls from Liverpool for keeping me going with their humour, and whose spirit I have tried to capture in the pages of this book.